Hearts of Blue
L.H. Cosway

Copyright © 2015 L.H. Cosway.

All rights reserved.

Cover pictures taken from Shutterstock.com.

Cover design by RBA Designs.

Editing by Indie Author Services.

This is a work of fiction. Any resemblance to persons living or dead is purely coincidental. No part of this book may be used or reproduced in any manner whatsoever without written permission from the author.

"Stealing, of course, is a crime, and a very impolite thing to do. But like most impolite things, it is excusable under certain circumstances. Stealing is not excusable if, for instance, you are in a museum and you decide that a certain painting would look better in your house, and you simply grab the painting and take it there. But if you were very, very hungry, and you had no way of obtaining money, it might be excusable to grab the painting, take it to your house, and eat it."

- Lemony Snicket.

Prologue
London, 2000

The room was freezing, so cold you could see your breath mist in front of your face.

There was something about it that made everything feel wet. The electricity had been cut off several weeks ago, and with it the central heating. The old couch in the living room was damp to the touch; so too were all the blankets and pillows in the bedroom Lee shared with his three brothers. He climbed into bed and closed his eyes, tried to ignore the discomfort of damp bedding and just go to sleep, but it wouldn't work.

He'd never admit it to any of his friends, but he often cuddled tightly to his older brother, Stu, for warmth. Liam and Trevor shared the bed on the other side of their small room, while their cousin Sophie slept in his mum's old room. His aunt Jenny had abandoned her there months ago, right after Lee's mum passed away. She'd then gone on an extended holiday with her boyfriend; "messed up" didn't even begin to cover it. As far as social services were concerned, Jenny had moved in to take care of her late sister's children. In reality, she was off sunning herself in Magaluf, boozing it up to her heart's content and leaving all five kids with an envelope of money to survive on that had long since dried up.

There was a man who wore a suit and gold rings who'd started coming around more and more often, offering Lee a way to take care of his family. He'd seen him a few times about the estate. Once he'd been beating a man half to death because he couldn't pay back the money he owed him, and another time he'd been visiting a woman whose husband died, bringing her a hamper of food to feed her kids. It was difficult to reconcile the violent man with the one who helped the widow. How could someone be both kind and cruel?

Still, Lee wanted to trust him. He wanted what the man was offering to be real and not a con, because he saw his expensive suit and stylish car, and deep in his gut he coveted those things for himself. He was tired of suffering, tired of seeing his brothers live a life of poverty. He wanted to make sure his family was never cold or hungry again, and the man represented an opportunity to do that.

Stu coughed and turned on his side, his eyes open, clearly unable to sleep, either.

"I hate her," he said, drawing Lee from his thoughts.

"We all hate her," Lee replied. "What she did was selfish. She deserves to be hated."

"I'm not talking about Aunt Jenny. I'm talking about Mum. She was worse than Jenny. She never loved us. Mums are supposed to love their kids."

"She didn't even love herself," said Lee as he thought of her. "Junkies don't love anything but getting high." Both his mum and her sister had grown up in a house that was the worst kind of dysfunctional. It was no wonder they turned out how they did.

Stu let his head fall back and stared up at the ceiling. "I'll never do drugs. I'm swearing it now. If I ever try to touch a single pill, I want you to punch me in the face."

Lee chuckled quietly. "No problem, bruv."

"I'm serious," Stu insisted. "I'll even let you break my nose if it stops me from being such a stupid fucking fucker."

Stu's proclamations woke up their younger brothers. Liam, who was just nine and the youngest, whined, "You two are being loud."

"Our bad, little man. Go back to sleep. We'll be quieter," said Lee in a hushed voice.

"I'm hungry," said Trevor, sitting up and rubbing at his eyes.

Lee and Stu had been shoplifting food for weeks, but it was only going to be so long before they were caught. They couldn't keep doing it. They had to find an alternative. Again, the man in the suit invaded his thoughts.

"When is Aunt Jenny coming back?" Liam asked, too young to realise she was never coming back, not for them anyway.

"She's not," Stu gritted out abruptly. He didn't have Lee's sensitivity when it came to dealing with the younger boys. Liam's eyes started to shine right before he burst into tears, and Lee climbed from the bed, going to his side to comfort him. He threw his arm around his little brother's shoulders and brushed away his tears with his thumb.

"It's going to be all right. We don't need her," he promised him.

"How can you say that?" Trevor asked bitterly. "We have nothing. We're just a bunch of kids nobody gives a shit about."

"I give a shit," Lee threw back. "I give a shit about all of us. And I'm going to figure out a plan."

"A plan?" Liam piped up, sniffling.

"Yeah. I don't care what I have to do or who I have to step over — I'm going to make sure we never want for anything ever again. I'm sick of living like this." A silence elapsed as he felt all three boys stare at him. He broke the quiet when he asked finally, "Who's with me?"

Stu immediately reached over and placed his hand on top of Lee's. "I am."

"Me, too," said Trevor.

"And me," Liam agreed.

Lee made eye contact with each of his brothers, their pact sealed. Tomorrow he'd go see the man in the suit, and, with any luck, their lives would change.

He just hoped it would be for the better.

One
London, 2010

Karla

The first time I met Lee Cross, I was doing something as ordinary as shopping for groceries.

Standing casually outside a betting shop, he'd called on my best friend, Alexis, who he knew because she'd dated his brother. Time seemed to move in slow motion when his eyes landed on me, and I immediately felt flushed. Almost against my own will I found him attractive, from his tousled brown hair to his mischievous blue eyes, to the tattoos that peeked out from the ends of his shirt sleeves.

Long story short, he asked me out. I shut him down. He'd tried to lure me into saying yes by whispering in my ear.

"If you come, I'll make you come with my tongue, and I won't expect anything in return."

Can't say I wasn't tempted, but that was probably just my ten-month dry spell steering the wheel. I was a police constable. I took my job seriously. And I only had to take one look at Lee Cross to know that he didn't live on the same side of the law as I did. Plus, he was too young for me. Sure, it was only three years, but still.

The second time I met him, I was providing Alexis with some moral support, because she'd asked Lee a favour and he'd come over to our flat. He'd been cocky, lounging next to me on the couch and flirting. I had to keep reminding myself that he was off limits, especially when he flashed me that confident little grin of his. The one that said, *One word, and I'll fuck all that frustration right out of you, babe.* Real annoying, like. I'd never give him that word. I'd never let myself say yes to Lee Cross.

And the third time I met him, well, that brings us to the present, as I chased some hoodie down a back alley. Just seconds earlier I'd caught him attempting to rob a car parked outside a newsagents, and the second he saw me he scarpered. I worked out several times a week, but this fucker was too fast for me. Needless to say, I was relieved when I saw that the alley had a dead end. Too bad for him. There was nowhere to go, and my shift partner, Tony, would be rounding the corner any moment. My relief quickly deflated when the hoodie effortlessly jumped the ten-foot wall like it was nothing. What the hell? Just before he dropped down the other side, he turned and shot me a wink.

Cheeky. Little. Bastard.

I'd recognise those blue eyes anywhere, because his older brother possessed an identical pair. Trevor was the second-youngest member of the Cross family. He had a number of arrests to his name, all minor stuff, and he hadn't done any prison time. *Yet.* I was willing to bet that if he kept going the way he was going, he'd end up behind bars sooner or later.

A second went by before Tony came up beside me, hands on his hips as he tried to catch his breath.

"Did he just jump the wall?"

"Yep."

"Fucker."

"My sentiments exactly. Come on, I think I know where we can find him."

After my first two encounters with Lee, I'd done my homework. I knew he lived on a council estate in Hackney. I knew that he was twenty-five years old, and owned a garage with questionable operations just a couple minutes away from my nick called Cross Bros. And I knew that, just like his younger brother, Trevor, he hadn't done any time. But like I said, it was going to happen eventually.

Admittedly, I'd gone a little overboard looking into him, and I couldn't say why I was so interested. I guessed I just wanted to know what I was up against, since every time I ran into him, he seemed determined to win me over.

Tony and I returned to the patrol car, and I hopped in the driver's seat, my destination already in mind. My hands felt prickly and my heart thrummed at the idea of going to Lee's house on police business, but I'd caught his brother in the middle of committing a criminal act, and no way was I letting him off the hook.

"That's four I've counted so far," said Tony, resuming our often-played game of counting the trainers hanging from power lines. It was a sign to show that drugs were being sold in the area. Sadly, Tony and I always counted more trainers than we had time to deal with. Plus, it wasn't like we could use a pair of dangling sports shoes as a reason to go searching somebody's house. That's why the trainers worked so well. Everybody knew what they meant, when technically they didn't mean anything.

When we reached Lee's street, which consisted of two long rows of houses, I noticed that some were in okay condition, while others were either boarded up or falling apart. It was the kind of place you didn't want to get stuck walking through at night, or during the day, for that matter. Lee's house, number 52, was probably the best kept. It had triple glazing, and parked outside was a souped-up black Ford Focus RS with tinted windows in the back.

"How did you know to come here?" Tony asked, derisively eyeing the car in the same way I was. It was just too fucking typical.

"I recognised the guy. This is where he lives," I answered, gripping the steering wheel as I glanced out. We were exiting the car and making our way to the house when Tony said, "Dealt with him before, did you?"

I shrugged right before I lifted the knocker and banged three times on the door.

"Something like that."

The curtains twitched on the window of a house two doors down, and I saw a little old lady peek her head out. She seemed to startle when she caught me looking and quickly let the curtain fall back into place. I could hear the TV playing and voices talking inside Lee's. Then somebody walked down the hallway and opened the door. It was a small woman, probably in her early twenties, with a pixie face and short brown hair. I wondered if she was Lee's girlfriend. She was chewing gum as she cocked her head and gave me a blank stare.

"Yeah?"

"Good evening, miss. We're looking for Trevor Cross, want to ask him a few questions about his whereabouts earlier this evening. Is he in by any chance?"

The woman continued giving me her blank stare before rolling her eyes and turning to shout over her shoulder, "Lee! The old bill are at the door asking about Trev."

"I'm cooking dinner. Tell them he's not in," Lee called back, and I got a little fizzle in my stomach at the sound of his voice. It had been two, maybe three months since I'd last seen him. Needless to say, I wasn't too happy about my reaction. I knew he was telling the truth about dinner when a waft of garlic hit my nose. Whatever he was cooking, it smelled delicious.

She turned back to me, and I levelled her with a hard expression that made her swallow.

"Don't think they're gonna leave so easily, cuz." So she was his cousin?

"Fine, I'll be there in a minute," Lee snapped.

She gave me a pointed look that said, *Happy now?* before turning and strutting back inside the house. I glanced at Tony. He seemed bored. This sort of thing was business as usual for us; however, the fact that it involved Lee Cross meant I was far from bored. I adjusted my radio and ran my hands over the notebook tucked safely inside my shirt pocket before straightening out my tie. I was fidgeting, my agitation drumming itself up higher the longer Lee left us waiting.

I heard some shuffling, and then a little boy of about three or four years of age shyly poked his head around the door. He was adorable, and I was grinning like an idiot before I had the chance to school my expression.

"Hey, what's your name?" I asked, bending down a little to meet his eyes. The second I spoke, he dashed off. Sometimes kids got scared when they saw the uniform.

A second later Lee was walking down the hallway toward us, wiping his hands on a dish cloth. He wore jeans and a T-shirt, and I allowed myself a brief moment to take in the intricate tattoos that adorned his arms and the way his jeans hugged his trim waist before straightening my posture. Lee's eyebrows lifted when he saw me standing there. His expression didn't give much away, and his attention wandered briefly to Tony before returning to me. He seemed at ease. This was his territory, and I didn't like it. He had the upper hand, no question.

A slow, easy smile spread its way across his mouth as he eyed me. "I knew you'd come a-knocking sooner or later, Snap."

"There was a little boy," I blurted. No idea why I said it.

"That's Jonathan. He's my cousin Sophie's kid. They live here with us."

"Oh," I said, staring at him dumbly for a second before remembering why I was there. I cleared my throat. "Well, we're here on official business. I've just come from chasing your brother Trevor down an alley after I caught him trying to steal a Honda. If he's here, I'd like to speak with him."

Lee folded his arms. "Like I said, he's not in. But how do you know it was Trev? Lots of blokes out there who look like him, good-lookin' son of a gun that he is. I think you've got your wires crossed, babe."

"You're talking to a police constable, son. Show some respect," Tony said, bristling at Lee calling me "babe."

Lee looked at Tony, then at me, and smirked as he dipped his head forward and spoke low. "My apologies, *Karla*." The way he said my name gave me that fizzy feeling in my stomach again, but I didn't let it show. Up until now, he'd never called me by my actual name, always by the nickname he'd decided to give me: Snap, or the longer version, Gingersnap.

"That's Constable Sheehan to you," I said firmly.

Some recognition flared in his eyes as he ran a hand over his jaw. "Did you just say Sheehan?"

I narrowed my gaze at him. "That's right."

"*Fuck.*"

"Did I not just tell you to show some respect?" Tony cut in, disgruntled now.

Lee didn't even look at him this time. His attention was all on me. "Any relation to Superintendent Sheehan?"

I swallowed, my throat growing dry all of a sudden. He knew my dad. Fantastic. "That's none of your concern. Now, if you could assist us in locating your brother...."

"Oh, Christ, you are, aren't you? What is he, your uncle? Your old man? Please don't tell me you're married to the prick, because that'll just put me off my dinner."

His statement made me forget myself for just a second as I screwed up my face in disgust. "Eww, no. He's my father, you...." I caught myself right before I added the word "idiot" onto the end of my sentence.

"Shiiiit! Your dad? Bloody hell, Snap, now I just feel sorry for you."

He wasn't joking, either. There was genuine sympathy in his expression, but I plastered a stoic look on my face. Most everyone who knew my father knew he was a hard-arse, belligerent fucking bully of a man, but he excelled at his job. His personal life, not so much.

"I'm not discussing this with you. Call your brother and tell him to get down here. If he's innocent like you say he is, then he shouldn't mind us asking a few questions."

Lee didn't breathe a word; instead, he stared at me in a way that made my uniform feel too constricting, my stab vest too heavy. Slowly, he reached inside his jeans pocket and pulled out an iPhone. After tapping on the screen a few times, he lifted it to his ear, eyes on me as the call rang out. I was close enough to hear it go to voicemail.

"He's not answering."

"Amazing that," Tony deadpanned before gesturing to me. "Come on, we're not going to get anywhere with this one."

"Aw, not staying for dinner?" Lee teased, his mouth shaping back into a grin as he held his hands out. "And I went to all this trouble."

Tony was about to throw some barb back at him when his radio went off with a call from dispatch. He stepped away so he could answer it, thus leaving me alone with Lee, who leaned against the doorjamb and gave me a heated little look. "I have to say, I like you in uniform."

"Oh, shut it." I rolled my eyes. There was nothing attractive about my uniform. It was basically men's clothing on a woman.

"I'm not lying. How's about you come up to my room for a bit, and I'll show you how much I like it?" He paused, eyes flicking to the top of my head as he winked. "You can even leave your hat on."

Completely against my own will, I snickered a laugh, folding my arms across my chest. "No thanks, Tom Jones."

"I think you'll find it was Randy Newman who penned the tune. Tom Jones did the cover," Lee quipped.

I made a concerted effort to regain my professionalism and throw a bucket of cold water over his flirty banter. "When you see your brother, tell him to get himself down the nick to see me."

"Fucking hell, Snap, you really are Ross Sheehan's daughter. Growing up must have been shit for you."

The empathy in his voice caught me off guard. I swallowed but didn't say anything. Our gazes locked and held, something thick and unspoken passing between us. He took a step outside, past the threshold of his doorway and onto the street. I glanced down at the toes of my boots and back up again, a strand of hair falling from behind my ear. Lee's hand reached out, as though he were about to tuck it back in, but then he froze before he could touch me. Touching a constable could *technically* be considered assault. And *technically*, I could arrest him for that. Maybe that's why he stopped. Or maybe it was something else.

His eyes softened when he whispered, "If that cranky string of piss weren't with you right now, it'd be a whole other ball game."

I looked to Tony, who had just finished with his call. Lee turned and casually went back inside his house, closing the door softly behind him. Giving me a nod, Tony gestured for me to follow him back to the patrol car.

I was about to do just that when the door to the next house burst open and a little girl ran out. She was only about five or six years old, and somebody was shouting loudly at her to get back inside. I stared at her, from her unkempt brown hair to her blue eyes and ratty clothes. Her gaze was wide and full of fear. She returned my stare for just a second before she hurried to Lee's door and began knocking furiously. The door opened and Lee reappeared, the girl instantly rushing to his side and hugging his leg. He bent down and gently petted her hair.

"What is it, sweetheart?" he asked, and the girl whispered something in his ear. His expression hardened as he nodded and told her to go on inside the house. When his gaze landed on me, it was only for a second. He didn't say a word, just stood up and closed the door over again.

There was something about the scene that caused a deep part of my heart to ache. Uncared-for children were my one true sore spot, and there was a reason for that. Seeing the girl run to Lee like he was her golden saviour made me feel things I wasn't ready to explore. I heard somebody clomping their way down the stairs of the house the girl had fled right before a skinny woman with greasy hair and bags under eyes came out, yelling after her daughter.

"I swear to God, Billie, you better get your arse back in here before I give you something to cry about."

She stopped in her tracks once she saw me, her eyes narrowing in anger. "What the fuck do you want, pig?"

"Was that your daughter?" I asked, clenching my fist tight. I already hated her. It wasn't my job to hate people, but in this particular case I couldn't seem to help it. She stepped out of her house, like she was actually considering putting it up to me. Why did crackheads always think they could take you? They had one swing in them, tops, before their energy dried up. She was pointing her finger at me now.

"That's the problem with you lot, always sticking your oars in where they're not wanted."

I heard Tony getting back out of the car and making his way over to us.

"There a problem here, miss?" he asked the woman.

At the sight of my broad, six-foot-three colleague, the woman's bravery died a quick death as she shook her head. "Nah, no problem," she hurried to answer before going back inside her house and slamming the door.

Tony patted my shoulder. "Come on."

Once we were back in the car and buckled up, I let out a slow breath. "Sometimes I wish I was a bloke. Nobody's scared of a five-foot-six woman."

"Hey, I've seen you spar. You could take down half the men at the station before they've even had a chance to blink. Everybody should be scared of you," said Tony with a grin.

I shot him a small smile. It was true. I practiced eskrima twice a week, which kept me fit and well able to defend myself should the need arise. And in my line of work, the need usually arose.

"So, how do you know that one?" Tony went on, looking back at Lee's house while I put the car in gear.

"My flatmate used to go out with his brother. She learned her lesson." *And he makes me feel things*, my conscience added, *things I have no business feeling.*

Tony pursed his lips and looked out the window at the less-than-pleasing scenery. I thought where I lived was rough, but this place was pretty dire.

"I imagine she did," he said. "Families like that, Karla, they have trouble stamped all over them."

I hated that he was right. "Tell me about it," I sighed, and then we headed out to deal with a traffic accident on the A10.

***

When I finally clocked out that night, I had nothing on my mind other than a nice, long soak in the tub and maybe some Chinese takeaway. Unfortunately, my happy thoughts were interrupted by Detective Inspector Katherine Jennings. If a person could be the equivalent of getting shit on by seagulls, then it was DI Jennings. I bumped into her on my way out of the station, and I mean I literally bumped right into her. Damn Lee Cross with his cheeky handsome smiles and probing eyes taking up all my thoughts.

"Watch where you're going, Sheehan, for Christ's sake," she snapped.

Katherine had it in for me, *big time*. I knew it had something to do with an old feud between her and my dad. Apparently, he'd called her a no-account, dried-up old cunt during a particularly brutal argument when they'd been working on the same case together years ago, but if you asked me, there was more to it than that. Anyhow, thanks to my dear old dad, she now despised the very ground I walked on, and had done everything in her power to make my job difficult since the moment I started working under her.

"Sorry, ma'am, I'll watch where I'm going next time." My words were said plainly, with absolutely no sarcasm or sass, but Katherine had a knack for detecting aggression where there was none.

"Take that tone with me again, Constable, and I'll have you transferred to some shithole district in the back arse of nowhere before you even have time to go crying to Daddy."

Not once in my life had I ever gone "crying to Daddy," but I let her have the final word. It was the only way to keep from incurring more of her wrath. Nodding, I internalised my frustration and quietly turned on my heel, continuing on my way.

When I got home, I found Alexis lying face down on the couch while a soap opera played on the TV. I didn't know whether to laugh or worry. This moping behaviour had been a regular occurrence with her ever since the love of her life had disappeared off the face of the planet. Long story short, she'd had an affair with her boss, and he'd done a runner after beating the living daylights out of his own father, almost killing him.

Never let it be said that our lives were uneventful.

"Man, the couch must smell really good," I commented dryly as I came in and set the bag of Chinese takeout on the coffee table. "Can I get a whiff? I love a good couch-sniffing session."

"I'm not sniffing the couch," Alexis whined before sitting up and shooting me the stink-eye. "I was trying to convey my complete and utter sense of loneliness and despair. You know, like performance art, but shittier."

I laughed and gave her shoulder a small squeeze. Her heart had been through the ringer the past few months, so I could understand where she was coming from. "Seriously, though, how are you feeling?"

"Crap, like usual."

"I've always loved you for your honesty, you know that?" I got a hint of a smile out of her as her eyes wandered to the bag.

"And I've always loved you because you're the kind of class act who brings food home after a shift. Can I?"

"Have at it."

She picked up the bag and brought it over to the kitchen, finding plates and dishing out the chow mein. I kicked off my boots and went into my bedroom to change out of my uniform. When I returned Alexis was back on the couch, digging into her food while a plate had been set out for me.

"So, how was work?" she asked between mouthfuls.

"It was fine until I bumped into DI Jennings on my way home. I swear, she has this way of draining happiness out of me like nobody else." I made the decision not to tell Alexis about my run-in with Lee, and I wasn't quite sure why.

She held her fork in mid-air and let out a long sigh. "I'm telling you, Karla, you need to close tabs on this bitch. Otherwise, she's just going to keep on pushing until you snap, and then she'll have a real reason to fire you."

I stared at her. "Close tabs?"

She stared back at me. "You know, like on the computer."

I failed to suppress a chuckle. "I know what it means, Lexie. I've just never heard it used quite in that context before."

"Well, you've heard it now. You need to *shut her down*. You've never done anything to warrant her behaviour, and it gets on my tits that you're just sitting back and taking it. No friend of mine takes shit."

I chuckled some more. She narrowed her gaze. I sighed.

"Look, I get where you're coming from, but I just feel like my dad did something really horrible to her that nobody else knows about. I wouldn't put it past him. I mean, she's hardly a ray of sunshine with everyone else, but with me it's real hatred. You don't feel that level of vitriol toward someone without good reason."

"You should ask your dad about it. Get it all out in the open."

"Um, have you met my father lately? He's hardly the sharing kind."

Alexis shot me an understanding frown, and we finished our food in companionable silence. I was still thinking about Dad later on as I ran a bath and climbed in for a long soak. Both my parents were born and raised in North Belfast during the height of the Troubles. Let's just say, being a Protestant in Northern Ireland during the 1960s and '70s did not equal a harmonious existence. My dad worked for the PSNI up until the mid-eighties before being offered a job with the Metropolitan Police here in London. I was born about two years after the move, the only child of a couple where the power mechanics were greatly uneven.

My father was six foot four, lean and mean, with brown hair and blue eyes. My mother was five foot nothing, small and timid, with red hair and brown eyes. At five foot six, tough but sensitive, with red hair and blue eyes, I was an even mix of the both of them.

My mother was my father's doormat, and the sad thing was that she seemed quite happy to continue in that way. Never in my life could I remember a time when I wanted to be like her. And never in my life could I remember a time when I wanted to be like my dad. I know, funny that I say it, since I seemingly followed in his footsteps and joined the police. The thing is, I never joined the police to please him. I joined the police because I wanted to help people, but more importantly, I joined to prove him wrong.

As a kid I was a tomboy, idolising characters like Sarah Connor and Ellen Ripley, yet every day I'd have to sit around and listen to my dad say stuff like, *They shouldn't let women on the force, they're too weak-willed,* and, *What's the point of a female police officer? Strength-wise, she'll never be able to take down a man.*

At the same time I had to deal with his constant criticisms of both me and Mum, and somehow that transformed into a deep-seated need to do everything in my power to prove my worth. The only problem with that? Katherine Jennings hated my guts, and as long as she did, I was never going to make sergeant. Seven years on the force and I was still a lowly constable. Needless to say, Dad was over the fucking moon that I'd never managed to rise in rank. It proved *him* right.

Every time I went to dinner at my parents' house, I had to listen to him go on and on about how I should just quit my job and go do something less hazardous *for a woman*, like say, become a waitress or a florist. I swear, one of these days I wasn't going to hold back the tirade of venom that had been piling up inside me for years. One of these days I was going to let him have all of it.

Taking a deep breath and sinking into the bubbles, I tried to rid my thoughts of my father and think of something more relaxing. Somehow, Lee's face flashed in my mind, which got my blood up in a *very* different way. I couldn't win. Involuntarily, a tiny laugh escaped me as I thought of what my father would think if I brought Lee home with me for dinner some evening. And you know, it'd almost be worth it just to see the look on his face, to see that vein in his forehead throb, the one that looked like Vesuvius ready to erupt whenever something pissed him off.

Closing my eyes, I slid farther into the bath, dunking my head under the water as I remembered the first time I met Lee.

"*You got a boyfriend?*" *he asked, hands braced casually on the metal end of my shopping trolley. He had really intense eyes, and the way the muscles in his forearms flexed was a little bit mesmerising.*

"*That's none of your business,*" *I replied, trying to focus on the shelved packages in front of me.*

"*You act like you've got a boyfriend, or are all coppers this uptight?*"

A small laugh escaped me. "*Look, you're barking up the wrong tree and I've got groceries to shop for, so could you please leave me to it?*"

He leaned a fraction closer. "*How long have you known Alexis? She never mentioned you while she and Stu were together.*"

Cocking an eyebrow, I replied, "*Hmm, I wonder why that is? People don't generally mention the fact that they have friends in law enforcement to someone like you.*"

I instantly regretted how judgmental I sounded, but it was the truth. Lee had "dodgy" stamped all over him, from the tattoos to the wiser-than-he-pretends-to-be gleam in his eye. I'd met blokes like him before, usually while I was working. They'd have your wallet and phone from your pocket before you ever realised you were a few hundred quid lighter.

The curve to his lips was at odds with the hardness that suddenly marked his expression. "Someone like me?"

"Look, I'm sorry, I shouldn't have said that. I don't know you."

"Yeah, you don't."

"And I don't want to."

He let go of the trolley and came around to stand before me, whispering, "Now, we both know that's a lie." I looked up at him from beneath my lashes, sucking in a breath at his proximity. He smelled like cigarettes and cologne, and I suddenly realised I was enjoying his closeness. Standing back, I shot him a hard stare that told him not to push his luck. He didn't take the warning, and instead reached out to pull a strand of my hair between his fingers.

"I fucking love this hair. You're gorgeous. Let me take you out."

So, he was one of those men, the kind who had a thing for redheads. Before I had a chance to respond, I was saved by Alexis, who came up behind Lee and slapped him cheekily on the arse. God, I loved her. Sometimes it was great having a friend who knew exactly when you needed saving.

I rose out of the water, inhaling a deep breath, and tried to shake my thoughts of Lee. Thinking about a man I could never have was a waste of time. So, doing my best to clear my mind, I endeavoured to enjoy the rest of my bath, minus the inner ramblings.

Two

"Getting high off his own supply. Bloody typical," my workmate Steve tutted as he recounted the story of a dealer he'd busted the day before.

I wasn't too fond of Steve, mainly because he was fond enough of himself for the both of us, and his alpha-male braggadocio tended to rub me up the wrong way. It was a Saturday morning, and I was stationed with him, Tony, and another constable, Keira, outside Emirates Stadium, where a football match was to take place between Arsenal and Spurs.

We were mostly there for crowd control, but also because of the old rivalry between the teams that meant there was a small chance of trouble after the game. Football hooliganism was a real pet peeve of mine. These people would fight to the point of seriously injuring one another, all in aid of some perceived feud between sides. It was ridiculous.

"It couldn't have been very hard booking him, then, if he was high," I said in an effort to take Steve down a peg or two. I got my argumentative side from my dad. It was a flaw, sure, but at least I could own up to it.

My workmate eyed me, bristling at my comment. "He was on cocaine, Karla. Have you ever met a cokehead right after he's snorted a few lines? Fucking mental cases."

"She's met plenty," Tony put in calmly, and I could tell he was trying to pre-emptively defuse any bickering between Steve and me, ever the father of the group. "We all have. Saturday nights on the beat are hardly a cakewalk."

"True that," said Keira past a yawn. She'd had a late shift last night, and I could tell she was exhausted. I'd wanted to let her take the morning off, but the stadium was at full capacity, so we needed all hands on deck.

We were stationed close to the entrance, where the Arsenal fans were queuing up, a sea of red and white jerseys. I was on autopilot, scanning the crowds for any signs of disruption, when I caught sight of a familiar face. It had been over two weeks since I'd paid a visit to his house, and I really shouldn't have been feeling butterflies right then, but I couldn't seem to prevent them.

Lee Cross and his brother Stu were walking toward the stadium. Both of them were the sort of men who demanded attention, so it wasn't too much of a surprise that mine was drawn in their direction. Just behind them were their two other brothers, Liam and Trevor. Liam was the youngest, a baby-faced version of Lee. Trevor was the second youngest, and he was prettier than half the girls I knew. Stu, the one Alexis had dated, was the eldest, and he was handsome in a rough and rugged sort of way.

Before I could give it a second thought, my feet were on the move. I managed to bypass Lee and went straight for Trevor.

"Excuse me a moment, sir, but can I have a word?" I said, placing a hand out for him to stop. He paused mid-stride and eyed me closely, like he knew my face but couldn't quite pin down where he'd seen me before. The moment he took in my uniform, though, his gaze widened with recognition. Still, he didn't get spooked and instead flashed me a smile, standing back as Liam arched a brow at me.

"Of course, Constable, what can I do for ya?" said Trevor, his sparkly blue eyes dancing. Was this a game to him? Small hairs suddenly prickled at the back of my neck, like a spooky sixth sense. Glancing quickly behind me, I saw Lee standing mere feet away with Stu.

"Problem, Snap?"

I swallowed, my eyelids fluttering nervously. What the hell was wrong with me? I never got nervous like this when I was working. It was Lee. He had a weird effect on me. For some reason, I grew flushed at the same time my jaw tightened. His little nickname for me was really starting to get on my nerves. I ignored him and turned back to Trevor.

"Two weeks ago, on Friday the twenty-first, between five and five-thirty, can you remember your whereabouts?"

He scratched his jaw, like he actually had to think about it. I'd been in touch with the newsagents where the car he'd tried to steal was parked. I requested their surveillance tapes but, and I knew this wasn't a coincidence, the camera was angled in such a way that it hadn't caught him.

"It's hard to remember such a specific time, you get me?" said Trevor right before Stu stepped up, a hostile slant to his mouth.

"You were with me, bruv, down at the garage, remember?"

"Oh, right, yeah. That's where I was. At the garage." Trevor nodded.

I looked between the two of them, still incredibly aware of Lee at my back. He had this way of making me feel entirely seen, like he sensed just how uncomfortable I was under his watch. The thought made me even more determined not to let his brothers away with their blatant lie. I should have known that one of them would give Trevor an alibi, though.

"Is there anyone else who can corroborate this? Any other workers at the garage?"

"Of course there are. The place is closed for the weekend, but you be sure to pop over on Monday, and we'll get you speaking to some of the boys," said Lee, coming to stand next to me. I sucked in a small breath and tried to remain in control, which was hard to do, considering I was surrounded by Cross brothers amid a crowd of football supporters. I finally allowed my eyes to meet Lee's, and the way he was looking at me caused me to swallow thickly.

"Yeah, I'll, uh, I'll do that," I answered, a little befuddled, before looking back to Trevor and Stu. "You all enjoy the game."

I was stepping away when Stu called after me, "We will, and you tell Lexie I was asking for her."

Resisting the urge to roll my eyes, I gave him a quick nod. Stu was drop-dead gorgeous, but his attempts to win Alexis back were pointless. Her heart belonged to another. Lee's shoulder brushed mine as he turned to follow his brothers, and I couldn't for the life of me explain why, but I reached out to grab his wrist.

Steve, Tony, and Keira were just yards away, but the area was so crowded that they'd never be able to see I was touching him. He glanced down at my fingers before his eyes rose to my face, and he looked intrigued.

"Can I talk to you for a second?"

I breathed heavily when his thumb slid slowly along my palm before rubbing tenderly at the inside of my wrist. Withdrawing my hand like I'd just been burned, I saw his lips twitch in amusement.

"What is it, Snap?" he whispered.

"I, uh, I...." Jesus Christ, was I tongue-tied?

"Karla," said Lee, and he sounded concerned, "are you all right?"

I blushed, unable to help it, before summoning my resolve. "Yes, I'm fine. I'd just like to ask if you could quit with the nickname. It suggests a familiarity we don't have, and it undermines my position as a police constable. I have a feeling that's why you do it, and to be perfectly honest, it's patronising."

Sticking my chin out, I looked him dead in the eye, and his expression softened. "If that's how it comes across, then I'm sorry. But I don't call you Snap to patronise you — I do it because I like you."

Damn, why did I have to find his honesty so disarming? He looked like he wanted to touch me again, which made me feel the need to move swiftly on. I wasn't looking directly at him, but somewhere in the vicinity of his shoulder, when I continued, "Anyway, the other thing I wanted to talk to you about is Trevor. If he's lying — and I'm not stupid, Lee, he and Stu are clearly lying — then he could find himself in big trouble down the line. He seems like a good kid, but you need to teach him to be smart. And I'm not saying this to be cruel — it's just the truth — but a boy who looks like him in prison? That wouldn't end anywhere good."

I finally managed to meet his eyes, and when I did, I was shocked at what I found. For a second Lee looked guilty, his every feature filled with remorse before it was replaced with something that looked a lot like anger. He took a deep breath and ran a hand over his jaw.

"Are we done here?" he asked curtly.

Soberly, I nodded, and he turned and walked away. It was ridiculous that I felt bad about what I'd said, but it needed to be done. Somebody had to remind Lee of the reality of how his family was living, and exactly where it would lead.

When I went to rejoin the others, I noticed Steve looking in the direction Lee had gone.

"Were those the Cross boys you were talking to just now?" he asked curiously.

I glanced at him. "Uh-huh."

"What have they been up to this time?"

Tony stepped in to answer for me. "Karla and I had a run-in with one of them a couple weeks ago. Found him trying to nick a car. Never caught him, though."

Steve chuckled derisively. "Well, you wouldn't." He paused and eyed me. "You see the two younger ones? You'll never catch either of them. At least, not on foot. They're into all that free-running business. Little shits will be halfway down the side of a building before you've even stopped to catch your breath."

"Seriously?" said Tony.

My mind reeled as I remembered Trevor jumping a ten-foot wall like it was nothing. So it was definitely him. Tony and I shared a glance, like we were both thinking the same thing, and my determination returned. Maybe I *would* pay a visit to Lee's garage on Monday after all. It couldn't be that difficult to catch one of his employees out on a lie.

Don't get me wrong — I wasn't doing it because I wanted to put Trevor in a jail cell. I was doing it because I thought it might be enough of a scare to get him to start abiding by the law.

Once the crowds had dispersed and everybody was inside the stadium watching the match, Keira and I went to grab some coffees and sandwiches for an early lunch. After that there were a couple of incidents to handle while the game was on, mostly drunk and disorderly behaviour. Sport plus alcohol generally equalled a bunch of rowdy imbeciles.

The game finished 3-1 to Spurs, which meant there was going to be a whole lot of pissed-off Arsenal fans coming our way, including Lee and his brothers. We were controlling the flow in such a way that the fans of opposing teams didn't mix. Unfortunately, a group of Spurs supporters, not wanting to wait in line, managed to jump one of the barricades. Before we knew it, they'd mixed in with the Arsenal fans.

I'd experienced a number of riots in my time, but had never actually witnessed the moment that instigated it all. It was amazing how something so small could lead to such chaos. One guy wearing a Spurs jersey knocked into an Arsenal fan, heated words were exchanged, and before I knew it, punches were being thrown. I looked to my left and right, but Keira and Steve were too far off, and they wouldn't be able to get past the crowd on time. I'd have to deal with this myself.

My hand instinctively went to my baton; I wouldn't hesitate to use it should things get out of control. It was times like these that I really wished all UK police carried firearms. People generally backed off when you were pointing a gun at them. We had armed units, but the main workforce carried only an extendable baton, CS spray, and a Taser. I tried to use the spray and Taser only when absolutely necessary, and usually the sight of my baton was enough to keep most people in line.

The problem in this particular situation? Alcohol.

Both men were angry drunk, the worst kind, so I knew I was going to have a battle on my hands.

"Hey! That's enough, fellas," I called out as one man threw a left hook at the other guy's jaw. A crowd was starting to gather, gangs of people egging them on. Out came the baton, and an onlooker to my left blew a low whistle. This was where my martial arts training came in handy, because a baton was about the same length of an eskrima stick. It wasn't exactly ethical, but to a certain level you could adapt the skills.

"Both of you need to back off. This is your last warning," I shouted with authority. When neither of them heeded my advice, I started to approach. Somebody placed their hand on my shoulder, and I turned swiftly to find Tony standing there.

"Let me help," he said, and I nodded, allowing him to go ahead of me. Grabbing one guy's arm and twisting it behind his back, Tony managed to subdue him, while I went straight for the other man. Sliding my baton back in its holster, I pulled out my cuffs.

"Hands above your head," I ordered, making the mistake of touching his shoulder. He interpreted it as a sign of aggression, too drunk to realise I was a police officer, and swung around. Luckily, I managed to duck quickly and avoid a blow. Seeing he'd missed his mark, he threw another punch, but I was faster. Sidestepping the hit, I grabbed his other arm and locked it firmly behind his back.

"You fucking bitch," he slurred, struggling in my hold.

"Oi," Tony shouted, seeing him resist me. "Do as the constable tells you."

"Piss off!" the drunk spat as I slapped a pair of cuffs on him.

"Stop acting like a twat," a bystander put in. It didn't help matters.

The drunk man grew incensed and lunged for the bystander. I was momentarily distracted, and he slipped out of my hold. Still cuffed, he dove forward and head-butted the man, who threw his hands out in an effort to defend himself. A couple of people tried to break up the scuffle, but it only resulted in more fighting. Soon I was standing in the middle of a riot, and I couldn't see Tony anywhere. My heart rate picked up, my palms growing sweaty. How the hell had things escalated this quickly?

Bodies seemed to be everywhere, and before I could react, somebody ran right into me. I caught myself before I fell, reached for my baton, and ordered several rioters to cease and desist. The thing was, there was one of me and dozens of them, and they completely ignored my instructions. I approached two men, both in their mid-twenties, my baton out. I shouted a warning, but neither of them listened, so I gave one of them a measured blow to the shin. He immediately turned on me.

"Get down on the ground," I ordered at the same moment he grabbed for my baton. I levelled a kick to his abdomen and he bent over, knees hitting the tarmac. Just as I about to pull out my second pair of cuffs and arrest him, a glass bottle somebody had thrown came sailing through the air, hitting me right on the forehead.

"Shit," I swore, growing dizzy, and saw the man crawl forward to steal my baton once more. Before he could get away, somebody slammed their foot down on his wrist and I heard a voice threaten, "Drop the stick and fuck off."

Looking up, I saw Lee, but I was too busy trying to regain my composure to pay him much attention. A second later he was in front of me, his hands on my face. "Karla, are you okay?"

"I'm...I'm fine," I said as he settled an arm around my waist and pulled me forward.

"No, you're not. Come on, let me get you out of here. It's not safe."

The urge to protest almost bubbled out, but my head hurt too much to speak. Lee's body heat sank into me, warming my bones. He kept glancing at me in concern as he led me away from the rioting. Seconds later I was standing in a narrow doorway as he crowded me in. I allowed my weight to rest against the wall while he pulled a napkin from his pocket and began dabbing at the cut on my forehead.

He muttered angrily to himself, but I was too out of it to properly listen to what he was saying.

"Where's Tony?" I finally managed to ask in an unsteady voice.

Lee's hand paused. "Lanky bastard? Didn't see him."

I tried to push him out of the way. "I need to go back and help."

He stood firm, his hands bracing my shoulders. "You're hurt. You won't be any use. Now hold still and let me clean you up."

I took a deep breath and went quiet. This was probably the closest we'd ever been, and I found myself studying his face. He was concentrating on dabbing the blood from my forehead, so I had a chance to properly take him in. God, he was handsome. There was a hardness to his features, and I felt a strange need to smooth my fingers over the crease between his eyebrows. It seemed like he worried for me, which made those butterflies begin to flutter once again.

My eyes traced the lines of his strong jaw, angled cheekbones, and masculine lips. Then I looked up and found him watching me study him. Those lips I'd just been staring at now curved into a smile. His body moved forward, his heat surrounding me, and against my own will I trembled.

"Oh, Snap, what are we gonna do?" he whispered right into my ear, and I flushed the second his breath hit my skin. The way his weight pressed on me wasn't unpleasant.

The noise of people shouting and glass shattering rang out, but somehow Lee's presence seemed to mute everything. All I could hear were his breaths and mine. All I could smell was his soap and cologne. His fingers came to my neck, but my collar was too high for him to be able to access much skin. Still, the parts of me that he was touching were on fire.

"Do you feel dizzy or sick?" he asked, and I shook my head. I'd had a concussion enough times in the past to know I didn't have one then. Our gazes locked, and I wasn't quite sure how much time had passed when he asked another question.

"How did you know where I lived?"

"What?"

"The other week you came by my house. How did you know where I lived?"

I tried to think of the least embarrassing answer, because the truth was that I'd gone snooping. "All of your brothers have a record, Lee. Not to mention Stu served six months in Feltham as a young offender. Your address is in the system."

"Yeah, but you went looking, didn't you?" His smile returned.

"That's correct. I went looking right after I caught your brother trying to steal someone's car," I told him pointedly.

He quirked an eyebrow like he didn't believe me. "You're that quick, huh?"

My throat grew dry. "All it takes is a call to dispatch."

His chest rubbed off mine, and even through my stab vest I could feel it. "And how did you recognise Trevor? You'd never met him before."

Christ, was this an interrogation? "He has your eyes," I blurted without thinking.

This gave Lee pause, and a long silence fell between us, his gaze searching mine. "That's a whole lot of attention to pay to someone you don't want to know," he said finally, throwing my own words back at me, the ones I'd spoken the first time we met.

"Lee," I pleaded, desperately needing him to back off. "You're too young for me."

"Karla, I'm perfect for you," he countered, right before his mouth dipped in and his lips brushed lightly across mine. It was hardly anything, and yet, every nerve ending in my body came alive. Just as his mouth was about to descend on mine again, I dug my heel into his ankle. He grunted and reared away, leaving me enough space to get by him. Unfortunately, I didn't get very far. I'd barely taken three steps when Lee caught hold of my arm and pulled me to him, my back to his front.

"What you just did, not advisable," he breathed harshly.

There was no mistaking the threat in his voice, and a shiver ran through me. Gone was the playful flirtation, and I was reminded once more that this man was bad news.

"Take your hands off me right now or I'll arrest you," I ordered, my tone harsh.

Seconds passed, like he was deliberating over what to do. Then he released me, but not before delivering a final statement. "One day, Karla, you'll understand that me having my hands on you is never a bad thing."

My skin prickled. It took me a moment to absorb his words, but by the time I turned around, he was already gone.

***

Once I'd managed to regain my sanity after my encounter with Lee, I called in the troops. An hour later we had the rioting under control, a number of people were arrested, and the remainder were emptied from the stadium. The wound to my forehead was superficial, so, thanks to Lee's clean-up job, I was still able to finish my shift. It was difficult to comprehend the fact that he'd helped me, but I reminded myself it was all an act. He only wanted to bang a police woman so that he could brag about it to his mates afterward.

I was just leaving the locker room that evening when I heard somebody ask, "Shit, what happened to you?"

I winced slightly at the sound of my ex, Gavin's, voice. Usually, I went out of my way to avoid him, and in the ten months since we'd broken up, I'd managed to reduce the number of times we ran into one another to the barest minimum. Gavin worked for the armed unit, and his job tended to veer toward the more dangerous end of the spectrum, while my daily shifts were *usually* less hazardous. Today was not the usual.

"I was stationed at Emirates Stadium. I presume you heard about the rioting," I said, stepping past him and hoping he wouldn't try to prolong the conversation. In my mind, there were two categories of men who signed up for the police. You had the well-meaning, family kind, like Tony, who just wanted to make the streets a safer place for his daughters to grow up. Then you had the borderline sociopathic kind, like Steve, and, let's face it, my dad, who joined the force because it meant they got to wield power over people.

Gavin fell into the latter category. I'd broken up with him for two reasons. One, he'd been a controlling fuckwad, and two, I'd caught him shagging another woman – *on* my birthday, *in* the ladies' bathroom of the club where my party was being held. Nothing like a bit of adultery on your birthday to make you feel like truly celebrating – that was sarcasm, by the way.

In conclusion, Gavin was a dickhead, and I was better off without him.

"I did hear, but I didn't know you were there. Shit, that cut looks bad, Karla. Have you had it checked out?"

"It's fine. Now if you don't mind…." I lifted a brow and gestured for him to get out of the way, but he didn't move.

"Ah, come on, don't be like that," he said.

I rolled my eyes, shook my head, and walked around him. He wasn't even worth the effort of a hostile conversation. He called after me, so I threw my hand in the air and gave him the finger. His growl of irritation was infinitely satisfying. I'd just climbed into my car when my phone went off with a call from Alexis. I put it on speaker.

"Hey."

"Karla! I just saw the riot on the news. Are you all right?"

"I'm fine, nothing a glass of wine and a good night's sleep won't fix. I'm on my way home. Do you need anything?"

A pause. "Well, now that you mention it, you wouldn't mind popping by the McDonalds drive-through, would you? I have a hankering for chicken nuggets and a chocolate fudge sundae for dipping."

I resisted the urge to gag. "Bloody hell, that sounds disgusting. Are you pregnant?"

She snorted down the line. "Piss off. I'm not pregnant. I'm depressed. There's a difference."

"Fine. I'll get you McDonalds. Be home in twenty."

"Aww, you really love me, don't you?" she crooned.

I laughed. "Yeah, to my detriment sometimes."

Three

The next day at work, Tony pulled me into one of the briefing rooms, opened up a laptop, and hit "play" on a video. It was surveillance footage from an apartment building, showing the outside grounds. Nothing happened for a second, and then off to the left a man approached. He wore a dark hoodie and jeans, his face shielded by a black balaclava as he reached up and grabbed hold of a window ledge on the bottom floor. Swinging himself up, he balanced himself perfectly on the narrow space, his movements swift and graceful like a stuntman or an acrobat.

"What is this?" I asked, glancing at Tony.

"Just keep watching," he urged me, his lips curving into a smile.

My eyes returned to the video, where the masked man grabbed onto the next ledge and swung his body up the same as before. The footage cut to a camera higher up, showing he'd climbed something like ten floors, only to land on a thin brick outcropping that ran around the middle of the building.

"Somebody watched too much Spiderman as a kid," I said cynically, though really, I was impressed, *very* impressed. No average person could pull off something like this without some extreme amount of skill. The pit of my stomach began to tingle with a little rush of excitement to see what would happen next.

The footage cut again to another camera, showing the man stop at a window and push it open with ease before slipping inside the building. Tony fast-forwarded a couple minutes and the man was back, emerging through the same window. However, this time the rucksack he wore appeared distinctly fuller than it had previously. He began moving along the ledge the same as before, only now he didn't climb between the windows.

For some reason, my eyes fixed on the line of his shoulders, the way he moved his body, and some strange sense of familiarity hit me. I couldn't quite pin down what it was, so I concentrated back on what was happening.

The video cut to yet another camera, where a scaffold was set up on one side of the old building. The man began swinging from bar to bar, his movements more panther than monkey. When he got as low as the top of a nearby street lamp, he leapt through the air, caught onto the lamp, and swung deftly to the ground, like a fireman going down a pole. The camera was angled just right to catch him running off into the night, and then he was gone.

"The boys down in evidence had this footage put together after somebody dropped off a rucksack full of jewellery and a note tipping us off about one of the units in that building," said Tony. "We paid a visit, and it turns out there was a cash-for-gold scam being run out of the same flat our guy broke into. They target older people, usually those who live alone and don't have anyone to tell them it's a scam. They put leaflets through their letterboxes saying if they send their old gold to a P.O. box in the city, it'll be valued, and a cheque for the same amount will be sent back to them."

I nodded. "Yeah, I heard about that one."

Tony sighed. "Obviously, weeks go by, and the cheque never comes. Bunch of scumbags, taking advantage of the elderly like that."

"So this bloke stole the jewellery back?"

"That's about the size of it."

I had to admit, I was sort of fascinated. "Forget Spiderman, maybe he thinks he's Robin Hood. Perhaps his granny got scammed, and he was pissed and decided to dole out some vigilante justice," I joked.

"Whatever way you want to spin it, you've got admire his gumption. Though I don't condone the method, at least there's a few less people out there being taken for mugs."

"Yeah," I said, staring at the frozen screen of the laptop and again trying to shake off that odd sense of familiarity. "At least there's that."

***

Confession time: I had a crush on my eskrima instructor.

His name was Felix, and he came from the Philippines. He was also in his forties and married with three kids, but hey, it wasn't like I ever planned on doing anything about it. I was simply happy to admire him from afar. He was short, but he had a perfect body, muscles draped in smooth tanned skin.

The truth was, I had a thing for small, handsome men. Give me James McEvoy, Elijah Wood, Daniel Radcliffe, hell, even the guy who played E from *Entourage*, and I was giggling like a schoolgirl. I think this derived from my deep-seated resentment of my father, who was the opposite of a small, handsome man. Therefore, they represented a comfortable ideal, something non-threatening and safe.

Lee Cross was neither small nor extremely tall, but somewhere in the middle. He was unclassifiable. Huh.

I sat on the mat beside my good friend Reya, stretching and staring at Felix as he stood by the doorway, chatting with a guy who was interested in joining the class. For some reason, there was an abundance of new members today. We practiced twice weekly at my gym, which was handy because it meant I could go for a swim afterward to cool down, or spend some time in the sauna.

"You're staring again," said Reya, nudging me with her shoulder.

I chuckled sheepishly and pulled myself out of my Felix-induced trance. "Sorry. But look at the man. He's perfect."

She laughed. "You're such a weirdo sometimes."

Reya and I had met under somewhat unusual circumstances. I'd been out one night at a jazz bar with Alexis, and Reya had been on stage, singing and playing piano. She performed under the stage name Queenie, and was perhaps the shyest singer-songwriter I'd ever come across. All through her act she never once opened her eyes, but her lyrics had hit me square in the gut. They were just so brutally honest, full of pain and heartache, and I couldn't understand how a girl so young could have experienced that amount of hurt. It was clear that she'd been a victim of some kind, so I'd determined to approach her after the show.

When I did, I told her how much her music had affected me, invited her for drinks with me and Alexis, and the rest is history. Somewhere along the way, I suggested that she learn how to defend herself, and now she was a full-fledged member of the class. I went to see her play gigs whenever I got the chance, but she still never opened her eyes. I guess you could call it a work in progress.

After a few minutes, Felix came and gave a little talk to all the new members, and we finally got started. When we were done I was a hot, sweaty mess. Apparently, another gym nearby had gone into receivership, which accounted for all the new members. Reya and I were making our way toward the showers when I heard a familiar voice shout, "Come on, Smithy, you've got more in you than that!"

Glancing to my right, I got a shock to see Lee Cross and a couple of other guys sparring in the boxing ring. Fuck my life. I couldn't seem to get away from him. Only yesterday I'd seen him at the football match, and now he was attending my gym. Some higher being was seriously trying to test my willpower. It was too ridiculous for words.

So ridiculous that my feet were suddenly glued to the spot as I watched him throw a punch. He wore protective gear, of course, but he had no top on.

I repeat: Lee Cross was just yards away from me, wearing no top.

My skin prickled with awareness as I watched the way he moved. Right off the bat I could tell he was no amateur, from the way he threw his punches to the way he angled his body.

His skin shone with a thin layer of sweat, making the movement of his muscles so much more captivating. His dark eyebrows furrowed as he concentrated, and when he finally took the other guy down, I felt a quiver between my thighs.

God, I was so embarrassed by myself sometimes it wasn't funny. My female hormones had me acting like a complete stereotype, and I hated how just the sight of Lee exerting his dominance over another man could reduce me to a tingling mess.

"Karla, are you coming or what?" Reya called impatiently.

As soon as he heard my name, Lee's head turned, and I found myself caught in his stare. He lifted a bottle of water to his mouth and took a long gulp. All the while his eyes never left mine. At once my skin felt too hot and too cold.

He lowered the bottle and wiped his mouth, and the spot between my legs continued to ache with a need I refused to acknowledge. Turning sharply, I went and followed Reya to the ladies changing rooms, stripped off, and stepped under the hot spray of the shower.

The way Lee had looked at me, like he already knew me intimately, was stuck in my head, replaying in a loop. It mixed with my memories of the day before, when his lips had brushed over mine and my frustration reached uncontrollable levels. I really wanted to do something about my arousal, but I didn't. I wasn't going to let my attraction to Lee make me act out of character, because I certainly wasn't the kind of woman who got herself off in a communal shower room at the gym. That was just yuck.

Taking a second to gather my nerve, I got out, dried off, and turned to find Reya studying me curiously.

"So, who was the guy in the boxing ring?"

I frowned at her. "Who?"

"Um, the guy whose body you couldn't take your eyes off. You were looking at him the same way you look at Felix, but with more *hunger*." Reya was real big on the hand gestures and dramatics, ever the artiste. So yeah, she was shy until she got to know you, and then she never shut up talking. She was also highly perceptive. It was kind of annoying sometimes.

"Oh, fuck off."

She laughed. "I'm being serious. I don't know what the story is between you and this bloke, but even I could sense the chemistry. It was so delicious I could almost mould it with my hands," she enthused, continuing with the gestures.

"Go write a song about it, then," I deadpanned, and she scowled at me.

"Don't start putting up the aggressive front. You're not in cop mode now, and I'm not a perp. I'm your friend. You can talk to me."

Her expression showed she was a tiny bit hurt that I wasn't opening up to her, especially since she'd opened up to me about her past. It made me want to give her something, so I said in a low voice, "Look, this is all I'm telling you. He's got a record. He's seemingly into me. And I'm not touching that shit with a ten-foot bargepole."

"Why do people always say that?" Reya asked irritably. "Do you normally go around touching things with bargepoles? It makes no sense."

"Yes, it does. Bargepoles are notorious long."

"Well, anyway, I think it's stupid. Besides, do we even use bargepoles anymore? I don't think so, not since like, the Middle Ages when armies wanted to storm a castle or something."

I laughed loudly, because seriously, she cracked me up. "That's not a bargepole, you numpty, that's a battering ram. A bargepole is quite literally a pole used to propel a barge. It's all in the name."

She narrowed her gaze at me. "Oh, my God, I just enabled you in changing the subject, didn't I? You're a sneaky little bitch."

I grinned.

We were rounding the reception area and making our way toward the exit when I caught sight of Lee again and my grin faltered. There was no avoiding him, because he was standing right by the door with a couple of the guys he'd been training with. I glanced at him quickly, relieved to find he hadn't seen me yet. Then, just as Reya and I were about to leave, he stepped forward and opened the door for us.

"Ladies," he said, and smiled.

Reya gave him a shy little nod of acknowledgement and stepped past.

"Constable, how's the head?" asked Lee, eyes flicking briefly to the small bandage covering my wound.

"It's healing," I answered, and frowned. It had been irritating me that I'd never gotten the chance to thank him, even if his help had all been an act. "Thanks, by the way. For yesterday."

His expression softened. "No thanks needed."

I glanced around. "I've never seen you here before."

Lee nodded. "Murphy's closed down, so we all had to find a new place to train."

"Hmmm."

"Hmmm," he mimicked, a grin shaping his lips as he leaned down, his hand braced against the door above my head. "Miss Sheehan, do you think I'm stalking you?"

Involuntarily, I snorted, and subsequently flushed with embarrassment. Staring at the floor, I muttered, "My ego's not that big."

I felt his breath whisper across my skin when he replied, "It's a good thing mine is." His wink told me he wasn't talking about his ego.

Feeling the need to flee, I quickly stepped by him and outside to join Reya. All the while, I got the sense he was watching me leave. I gave her a lift to the tube station and then set off for my parents' house. Yeah, I still visited, but it was mostly out of duty to my mum. I was patiently waiting for the day when she stood up to my dad and finally left his sorry arse for good. That would be the same day that elephants sprouted purple wings and scientists declared the world wasn't round but flat. So, never.

Pulling up outside their house, I grimaced at the sight of the small front garden with its pristinely trimmed rosebushes and perfect little patch of grass. It was contrived, just like everything else about my family. Perfect on the surface, broken beneath.

Using my key to go in the front door, I could hear my dad talking loudly. The Northern Irish accent was a distinctive one, and it had this way of always sounding threatening, even when the speaker was merely commenting on the weather. He was on the phone, and from the gist I got of the conversation, it was a work call.

"We need to pin down McGregor sooner rather than later. He's a snake — always when we think we have him, he manages to dodge the final bullet."

Shop talk on a Sunday afternoon. Lovely.

I bypassed the lounge, where my dad was having his phone call, and headed straight for the kitchen. Mum was standing by the cooker when I came in, pulling her roast out of the oven.

"He's not in the best mood today, love," she whispered quietly, not even bothering to greet me. "It's probably advisable not to try and rile him."

"It's nice to see you too, Mum," I said, annoyed, and went to pour myself a glass of water. "And I never *try* to rile him. He riles himself. By the way, why the hell are we whispering?"

"Because I told you, your father's in a terrible mood. The case he spent the last few months working on has fallen flat." She paused, eyes moving to my bandage as she reached up to touch my forehead. "What happened here?"

"Hazard of the job," I answered flippantly, and refocused on what she'd said about Dad. "What case was he working on?"

Dad sometimes liked to decompress by telling Mum about his work. He thought it was safe, because even if she wanted to tell someone, she didn't really have anyone to tell. He'd seen to it a long time ago that she didn't have any friends. Sometimes, though, if she was stressed, I could trick her into talking.

"Some bigwig called McGregor. Your father's been trying to get him for years," said Mum, waving away my questions. "Will you go and set the table, please?"

I wanted to ask more, but I knew she'd clam up if I did. So I went and set the table just like she'd asked, and a couple of minutes later we were sitting down to eat. Dad came in, shoving his phone in his pocket, and shot me a frown. That was about as much of a greeting as I ever got from him. We ate for several minutes without conversation, and, in spite of Mum's warning not to rile him, I couldn't seem to help it.

"Hey, do you know I was at Emirates Stadium yesterday?" I said, eyeing Dad and pointing to my forehead. "Not that I expect you to express concern over the fact I'm sporting a bandage or anything."

Letting his knife and fork clatter onto his plate, he grunted, "I'm sure you'll survive."

"Yeah, I'm sure I will," I answered. It wasn't so much what I said but the way I said it that caused his brow to furrow.

"Something like that would never have happened if you were working in an appropriate field."

"An appropriate field like what? Becoming a housewife?" I replied derisively. "Not going to happen."

"Yes, well, maybe that's for the better," said Dad cuttingly as he casually tucked back into his food. "I'd pity the man who took you for a wife."

"Not all men are like you. Some want a woman who can think for herself," I threw back.

Dad let out a dark chuckle, going directly for the lowest of blows. "Is that why you're still single?" What he said didn't hurt my feelings. My feelings were battle hardened, and we'd had this conversation a hundred times before.

"He's right, Karla. You really should think about settling down," Mum put in, oblivious as always. "You're twenty-eight now. It's a pity you're not putting your looks to good use." Was she serious? I swear, sometimes I thought she might be worse than Dad. The way they both spoke was practically medieval.

I sat back and let out a long sigh, while a mischievous idea entered my mind. "Now that you mention it, I am seeing someone, actually," I lied.

"Oh." Mum perked up. "How long has this been going on?"

"It's fairly recent."

"Well, both your father and I would love to meet him."

"Maybe I'll bring him home sometime."

"That would be lovely. I could make my special recipe cottage pie."

I resisted the urge to snicker a laugh. I was never going to do it, but it still pleased me no end to imagine bringing Lee Cross home to meet my parents. Dad narrowed his gaze at me suspiciously, like he knew I was up to something, and it satisfied me to know I'd ruffled his feathers.

***

The next day I was on shift with Steve, which meant I had to drown out most of the conversation to keep from shooting myself in the face. I mean, I really didn't want to hear about the birds he shagged over the weekend, or how he beat his previous lifting record at the gym. I only started listening again when I heard the name "Cross" come out of his mouth.

"What was that?" I asked, pretending like I'd been concentrating on driving.

"We need to go visit the Cross brothers' garage. Tony mentioned something about interviewing some of the employees."

"Yeah, I was, uh, going to go after lunch."

"Well, let's get it out of the way now while things are quiet."

My pulse thrummed at the prospect of seeing Lee yet again. After not running into him for months, his presence in my life was starting to become a daily occurrence. A couple of minutes later we pulled up outside the garage; it had a blue and white sign over the entrance that read "Cross Bros." I found it curious that it wasn't "Cross & Sons," because these sorts of businesses were usually handed down from parents. Given that Lee was only twenty-five, he was quite young to own his own business. Then again, if my suspicions were correct, the place wasn't all that it seemed.

A youngish guy wearing coveralls was standing outside, having a smoke. The second he saw the patrol car, he stubbed out the butt and hurried inside. We were just approaching the entrance when Stu stepped out, his T-shirt stained with motor oil.

"All right, Karla?" he said, eyeing Steve as he wiped his hands on a dirty rag.

"We're here to interview your employees about Trevor," I said, and Stu gestured for us to head inside.

"Yeah, I remember. Lee's in the office. He said you can use the room for your interviews."

"You go on ahead," Steve told me, a sudden look of interest on his face. "I'm just going to take a look around."

I glanced at him, unsure what he was playing at, but made my way to the office nonetheless. Knocking on the door first, I heard Lee call for me to enter. When I did, I found the room to be small, with a tidy row of filing cabinets along one wall and a desk pushed up against the window. He was on the phone, the short sleeves of his T-shirt rolled up to reveal the full length of his arms. His hair was ruffled and looked like he'd just stepped out of bed, but maybe that was intentional.

I cleared my throat and he glanced up, looking like he'd expected me. Had that guy run in to warn everyone that the police were outside? Lee quickly ended his phone call and stood.

"Um, Stu mentioned you said we could use your office?" I began, uncertain.

"Of course, come on in and take a seat," he said, shooting me a warm expression. Why did he always have to be so…welcoming? It made it difficult to be cool with him when he acted like that.

"This shouldn't take long. Standing is fine."

Lee stared at me a moment, still smiling, then ran a hand over his jaw. "Fine, we'll play it your way. I'll send the boys in to speak with you one by one."

"Thank you."

He left, and I took a moment to scan the room. Nothing immediately jumped out to me that screamed illegal, but then again, it wouldn't. Criminals didn't generally run around advertising what they were. At least, the clever ones didn't.

A minute or two later the first guy came in, and I quickly asked a couple of questions. There was still no sign of Steve, and I had to wonder what he was up to. Unfortunately, when I'd finished speaking with everyone, all of their stories checked out. Steve still hadn't shown, so I left the office to go find him.

When I stepped into the main area of the garage, things looked the same as before, just a bunch of young men working on cars. But then I saw Lee, Stu, and Steve having what looked like a heated argument close to the entrance.

"Get the fuck out of here before I do something I regret," I heard Lee threaten as I approached. He looked seriously pissed off, as did Stu.

"Hey, what's going on?" I asked with concern, and all three men turned to face me.

"We're leaving," said Steve, before turning and stalking out the door.

Lee eyed me. "Can I talk to you for a minute?"

I nodded and followed him back into his office. His posture was tense, and when I shut the door behind me, he looked ready to break something.

"Lee?" I said in a quiet voice, sensing that anything louder might set him off.

He turned, and his expression was furious as he pointed to the door. "You see your partner out there? He's bent as fuck."

"Excuse me?" I replied in surprise.

"Something wrong with your hearing, Snap? I said your little buddy is a dirty fucking copper, and I swear to God, if he ever shows his face around here again, I'll break it for him."

Tentatively, I took a step forward. "Calm down for just a second and tell me what happened."

Lee took a few deep breaths before steadily settling his gaze on me. "The prick came in, started looking around, then went up to Stu and tried shaking him down. He said that if we set him up with two grand every month, he wouldn't report what he found on our premises."

"What did he find?" I asked, my tone serious. The news that Steve was dirty didn't exactly surprise me. I'd always known there was something off about him. However, the fact that he might have found evidence of illegal activity inside the garage put me on alert.

"He didn't find anything. Nothing that belonged to us, anyway. He claimed there was a bag of coke hidden under some tiles in the bathroom, but it's bullshit. None of the boys do drugs, and if they did, I wouldn't allow them on the premises."

What he said sparked a memory of Steve bragging to me, Tony, and Keira about a coke dealer he'd busted last week. I wouldn't put it past him to keep some of the drugs he seized to use in a situation just like this.

"He planted it," I said as it all fell into place.

A look of surprise crossed Lee's features. "You believe me?"

I glanced up at him. "Yes, actually, funnily enough, I do."

"Well," he said, looking at me differently now. "I'm not giving that fucker two grand. He can go and swing for it."

"You don't have to give him anything. I'll deal with him."

His expression grew serious. "I don't want you getting caught up in this. More than likely, the bloke has a whole network of scams going on. The way he spoke, he didn't strike me as a first-timer."

I took a moment to absorb that, trying to come up with a plan on how to deal with him. It went without saying that there was no love lost between me and Steve, and if I tried to get in the way of whatever little corrupt network he had running, he wouldn't hesitate to mess with me and my career. Hell, I wouldn't put it past him to try to blackmail me in exactly the same way he'd tried to blackmail Lee.

I flicked my eyes up to meet his, firming my lips. "Leave it to me. I'll think of something."

"Karla," Lee murmured tenderly as he came to stand directly in front of me. "Don't get involved. I don't need your good deeds. And anyway, your boy doesn't realise who he's fucking with. The next time he shows his face, I'll make sure he gets the message."

It took me a moment to comprehend what he was saying, mainly because of the way he called me by my name, but also because of how his smell was infiltrating my senses this close. Finally, his meaning sank in, and I frowned.

"Who *is* he fucking with?"

Lee didn't answer, and instead he took a step forward, forcing me to back up if I didn't want us to collide. The problem with this meant my back hit the wall a moment later.

"You're so pretty, Snap," he said, voice low, as he dropped his face to my hair and breathed in.

I wasn't wearing a hat, and my hair was tied up in a bun. My entire body trembled when he wrapped his arms around my waist, inhaled deeply, and pulled me into a hug. This was a distraction, I knew it, and yet, I let him distract me. I wanted to be distracted, and I was just glad that the blinds in his office had been pulled.

Standing in his embrace for at least a minute with silence all around us, I was unable to move. I liked having Lee close, loved the warmth of him and how he could make feel so...surrounded. Despite all the warning signs, my attraction only grew stronger. There was just something about him that called to me.

"Lee."

His mouth moved against my hair. "What is it, Karla?"

"Why are you hugging me?"

"You looked like you needed to be held." His response was low, and the affectionate undertone had me swallowing deeply. At long last I summoned the willpower to break the hug. His arms fell away from me easily, my stomach churning with confusion. What the hell was I doing?

I stared at the floor when I spoke. "I have to go."

Heading for the door, I paused when he said gently, "Hey, I needed it, too."

I didn't turn around, but instead practically ran from the office. Moments later I was strapping myself into the patrol car where Steve had been waiting. My heart hammered at Lee's words, feelings beginning to stew deep in my belly. He was playing me, he had to be. Blokes like him weren't romantic. They fucked you and then they left you.

"What took you so long?" Steve asked, eyes narrowed on me with suspicion.

Remembering Lee's warning for me not to get involved, I lied, "I just had a few more questions I needed to ask."

A silence elapsed.

"And?" Steve prompted.

"And, uh, all of their stories checked out. Sorry."

"Huh. They must have been ready for us, then."

"Yeah," I said. "Must have been."

Four

About a week passed, and I didn't see Lee at all. For a while it felt like he was everywhere, and then he was nowhere. And I'll admit that every time I went to the gym, I kept my eyes peeled, eager for a glimpse of him.

Yeah, it was just as pathetic as it sounded.

I was driving home late one evening when I passed by a newly constructed office building. It was built in such a way that there were lots of steep stairways and criss-crossed walls surrounding it. The building, however, wasn't what caught my interest, as I pulled to the side of the road and peeked out the window. There was a group of young men there; all of them looked to be in their late teens or early twenties, and all of them were pulling off some pretty impressive stunts. It was only when I took a closer look that I recognised Trevor Cross.

He was a little bit mesmerising. It was sort of like watching somebody play a video game, where the avatar could effortlessly jump and leap from building to building without injuring themselves. Trevor ran along the edge of a high wall, then leapt several feet through the air to land on the next one.

My eyes caught on another figure, and my breath hitched involuntarily when I saw it was Lee. He wore jeans, a long sleeved T-shirt, and a peaked cap that shielded most of his face. My heart pounded at the sight of him, and my pores began tingling as something electric pulsed inside me. I could watch him from the comfort of my car without him ever knowing I was there.

His shirt fell forward, revealing his stomach, as he balanced his entire body on his hands. He was on the edge of one of the high-up walkways. I saw several of the guys cheer when he dropped one arm, letting it hover in the air as he held his entire weight on one hand. He maintained the hold for several seconds before lowering his hand back down, bracing himself, and then launching into a backflip before making a perfect landing on the ground.

Whoa.

The way he moved was skilful, and I remembered Steve talking about how the brothers were into free running. But he only mentioned the younger ones. Perhaps Lee was more discreet about the things he could do, like Willy Wonka pretending he needed a stick to help him walk.

The official name for the sport was parkour, and it killed me to see how talented he was, while at the same time knowing he was using that talent to lie and steal.

It was with a hopeless sigh that I restarted the engine and pulled away. Tired after my shift, I went home and fell asleep almost instantly. I had two days off, and I planned on making the most of them. I knew I'd overslept when I woke to daylight streaming through my window and scrambled for my phone to check the time. Ten-thirty. I only became aware that somebody was sitting at the end of my bed when I sat up and saw Alexis slumped over, staring at something she was holding in her hands.

"Lexie, what's wrong?" I asked in a scratchy voice.

She didn't answer, and all I heard was a sniffle. She'd been crying a lot since King disappeared, so this wasn't anything too unusual. Sometimes she liked to hide her pain behind humour and sarcasm, but I knew she was hurting badly on the inside.

I got up and went to her, sitting down and throwing my arm around her shoulders. She leaned into me, taking the comfort I offered without a word. It was only when I looked down to see the pregnancy test she was holding that I gasped. The little window showed two red lines, and I didn't need to be a genius to know what they meant.

"You're pregnant?" I said, my voice airy with disbelief. Just the other week I'd joked about it, but that's all it had been, a joke. I never actually thought it was true. And, by the looks of it, neither had Alexis. This was a massive shock for her. King had been missing for a while, which meant she had to be at least three or four months gone, and I knew she hadn't been with anyone else since him.

Her smile was sad. "There was me thinking it was a cake shelf I was sporting," she said, hand going to her belly, hiding her feelings with humour like always.

I swallowed, trying not to let my own personal feelings affect me right then. When I was a teenager, I'd been in a very bad car accident. My dad had been behind the wheel, my mum in the passenger seat, and I was in the back. Long story short, I'd been injured far worse than my parents, and the damage meant I'd never be able to have kids. It was why I got so angry when I saw people neglecting their own children, but I'd come to terms with the fact a long time ago. Still, a strange, phantom-like pain always passed through me whenever I was reminded of it. Alexis knew all about my accident, but I didn't think she knew quite how much it hurt me, knowing I'd never have a child of my own.

"It's King's, isn't it?" I finally asked, pushing my own feelings aside.

She nodded and stared at her feet.

"Have you had any luck finding him? Any clues as to where he might be?"

"Nothing," she croaked. "It's like he never even existed." And then the tears began to flow. I sat with her for a long while, just hugging her and letting her cry. Finally I managed to get her to her own room, where she climbed into bed and went to sleep. She'd been up all night, wracked with worry.

I spent the day tidying the flat and hanging out. I even baked a batch of brownies, thinking they might cheer Alexis up. Unfortunately, she was acting completely out of character when she woke and barely even gave the brownies a second glance. Normally, she was the sort of girl to take life's challenges in stride, so it was disconcerting to see her like this.

I was watching television that evening when she suddenly sat down beside me and asked, "Can we go out tonight?"

"Out where?"

"Anywhere. I need to get away from these four walls before I go insane. We could go to a bar and I could watch you drink. It'll be fun." The look on her face told me she was desperately trying to convince herself of that. I didn't want to upset her, though, so I nodded.

"Sure, just let me grab a quick shower and we'll head out."

An hour later we were in a cab, headed for the bar where Alexis used to work before she changed career paths. At the moment she was in between jobs, but she did some modelling every once in a while to pay the bills. I was guessing she might have to take a break from that once she started to show.

I wasn't sure why she wanted to go visit her old workplace. Well, I wasn't until we walked inside and I saw Stu standing by the pool table. How had I not predicted this? I could only see the back of the person he was playing with, but I knew instantly that it was Lee. He wore jeans and a Fred Perry T-shirt with the collar turned up, the uniform of cocky little fuckers everywhere.

"What are you up to?" I asked, narrowing my gaze at my friend. She just shook her head and walked over to the bar, ordering a glass of wine and a Coke. I was guessing the wine was for me. I hadn't really dressed up, but I suddenly became more aware of my appearance. I'd left my hair down, and was wearing a pair of khaki green trousers with a tight black wrap top and boots.

Even when Alexis had worked here, I'd never really visited. Truth be told, it was a bit of a dive. It was Stu's local, though, so it had to be Lee's, too. It was also where Alexis and Stu had originally met.

"I hope this isn't what I think it is," I said as she slid the glass of wine my way and led me over to sit at a booth.

The look she gave me was miserable, and she ran her hands through her hair before replying, "I'm lonely, Karla. And yes, I know I'm probably going to regret this in the morning, but just let me regret it, okay? Tonight of all nights I just need somebody to make me feel good."

Her answer shut me right up, and a pang of sympathy hit me square in the gut. I'd never lost someone I loved like Alexis had lost King, so I had no business judging her. Instead, I sat quietly and drank my wine. A couple of minutes later, Stu spotted Alexis and sidled up to our booth.

"Lex, what brings you around these parts?" he asked, eyes dark with interest as he slid in next to her.

I thought I heard her mutter "desperation" under her breath before she looked up and mustered a smile for him. "Just having a quiet drink."

"Mind if I join you?" he practically purred.

"Uh, you already have," I commented dryly.

Stu shot me a wide grin, unfazed by my comment as he gave me his full attention. "This is a dangerous place for the likes of you, Karla. Taking a walk on the wild side, are we?"

"What, are cops not allowed into dive bars now?" I asked smartly.

Stu shook his head and answered, "That's not what I'm talking about," just as I felt a warm body take the empty spot beside me in the booth. My every muscle grew tense.

"Clarky," said Lee, nodding to Alexis. She gave him a similar head nod in return.

"Snap," he went on, his mouth a lot closer to my ear than it needed to be.

"Lee," I said, shifting away and meeting his eyes.

There was a moment of silence, the two brothers grinning, while Alexis and I frowned. I thought that maybe we both felt the same way right then. On one level we wanted to be there, and on another we really didn't.

"So, what's everybody drinking?" Lee asked.

"Coke," said Alexis, lifting her empty glass.

"I'll have another beer," Stu put in.

I stayed quiet. No way was I letting him buy me a drink. No effing way.

"Snap?"

"I'm good."

"*Babe.*"

My brow furrowed, and I simply shook my head at him to let him know that the whole "babe" thing wasn't happening. His grin widened, like he enjoyed the challenge. Instead of asking me again, he simply leaned in, picked up my glass, and took a sip.

He winced when he tasted it. "One glass of vinegar coming right up."

"Hey, it's not her fault this bar serves shit wine. Go have a word with Keith and tell him to get some better stuff in," Alexis complained. I was guessing Keith was the landlord.

"I'll get right on that," Lee replied sarcastically before heading over to the bar.

I rubbed at my eyelids, frustrated. This certainly wasn't how I planned on spending my night off, but I couldn't abandon Alexis in her time of need. Looking across the table, I saw that Stu was already moving in on her, his arm resting casually along the top of the booth. He bent down and whispered something in her ear. She nodded and said something in reply, but I couldn't hear over the bar music. It didn't take long for her to warm up to him, and then they were full-on flirting with one another.

I couldn't have been more uncomfortable if I'd tried.

Oh, no, wait. I spoke too soon.

Lee returned with the drinks, placing a fresh glass in front of me. I glanced at it, no intention of drinking any. Alexis and Stu were deep in conversation, so I might as well have been sitting alone with Lee. It was too awkward for words. Well, it was on my end. Lee didn't look like he had an awkward bone in his body.

"Relax," he murmured. "You look like you're afraid I might jump you or something."

"I'm not afraid of you," I said defensively.

"Would you like to tell that to your clenched fist?"

I glanced down, and, sure enough, my hand was tightly clenched into a fist. I was all kinds of worked up. Loosening my fingers, I looked back at him and said curtly, "I'm here for Alexis, that's all."

"And there I thought you were after the pleasure of my company," he deadpanned before lifting his pint. "Look, I get it. I'm a scumbag, not fit to lick your boots, etcetera, etcetera."

Something about the way he spoke made me feel bad. My expression softened when I replied, "That's not what...look, I'm sorry, can we start over?"

Lee nodded. "Already forgotten. So, what's up with Clarky? The last time I checked, she was shacked up with that fancy-pants rich bloke."

"She was. He's gone. She's been trying to find him for months but hasn't had any luck. Today has kind of been a rough day for her."

Understanding showed in Lee's expression. "So, what you're saying is, she's here to use my brother for sex?"

I grimaced. "It sounds horrible when you put it like that."

Lee chuckled. "Stu will have her any way he can get her. Don't worry about it. He has a talent for keeping his emotions out of his sex life."

"Oh?" I said, curious.

Lee looked away and drank some more of his beer. "Yeah, some of us don't have that skill."

When his eyes returned to mine they were fierce, and it took a conscious effort for me to breathe normally. I really wished I wasn't so attracted to him. That way I wouldn't feel so weak right then. Involuntarily, I crossed one leg over the other, which caused Lee's attention to wander to my thighs. He stared for a good ten seconds, taking his time.

"How often do you work out?" he asked almost absently.

"A couple times a week. Why?"

He lifted his head. "Don't take this the wrong way, but you've got a killer fucking body, and I'm saying that from a purely athletic standpoint. I admire your dedication."

"Um, thanks," I said, swallowing awkwardly.

"We should train together sometime."

"I don't box." Nor was I particularly interested in jumping off buildings for fun, but I didn't say that, because then I'd have to fess up about spying on him.

"But you fight. I can tell by the way you carry yourself."

I grew self-conscious again, feeling shy and wondering how he could tell that. "I practice eskrima, but no, I don't think us training together would be a good idea."

"Yeah, you're right. All those hormones and sweat flying around, who knows what might happen." He looked away, smiling into his pint glass.

"You just can't help being a tease, can you?"

He turned back to me and shook his head. "Not with you, babe."

"Oh, my God, okay. We need to get this straight, no more babes, no more Snaps. My name is Karla. Be a normal human being and use it."

He opened his mouth, ready to reply, when Stu cut in. "Bruv, I'm taking Lexie back to ours. You coming or staying put?"

"He's coming," said Alexis. "He needs to keep Karla company while you…keep me company." She burst out laughing, and it was the first time I'd seen her properly laugh in a while, even if it was at the ridiculousness of the situation. Stu gave her a sexy smile, and I was just relieved that her mind was off her problems for a change.

"Sure, we'll come," said Lee, standing while Stu ushered Alexis out of the booth. I remained in place, unsure what do to. I didn't want to go to their house, but I didn't want to abandon my friend, either. Though technically, she was the one abandoning me.

When I looked up, Lee was standing there, his hand outstretched. There was something about his eyes right then that made me reach out instinctively and take it. As soon as my palm slipped into his, I felt electricity shoot through me. It was strangely exhilarating to do something as ordinary as hold his hand. He pulled me up and I let go, blushing furiously. Taking his hand had been all instinct. My brain hadn't even had a say in the matter.

By the time we got outside, Stu and Alexis had already flagged down a cab. They both climbed in the back, and Stu pulled her onto his lap, not wasting any time as he kissed her hard right on the mouth. She didn't stop him. Lee held the door open for me to slide in next, and he hopped in last. He told the driver his address, and then we were off.

Needless to say, it was possibly the most uncomfortable cab ride of my life. Lee and I sat across from Stu and Alexis, who had progressed to full-on snogging. The radio hadn't been turned on, and the driver wasn't feeling chatty.

The only sounds were kissing sounds.

Well, that and heavy breathing. I stared at my lap, sensing Lee's eyes on me, but I refused to look at him. It would only make things worse. But damn, his stare must have had magnetic qualities, because eventually I couldn't help lifting my gaze. His eyes had settled on my lips, and whatever dirty thoughts he was having were written all over his face. I sucked in a deep breath and wished my heart wasn't beating so erratically. I swore he could see my pulse hammering in my neck.

His attention flickered between my eyes and my lips when he spoke. "Hungry?"

I blinked, afraid for a second that he might have read my thoughts. "What?"

His lips curved as he repeated his question. "Are you hungry? I could cook for you when we get to our place. I give good food."

"Is that supposed to be a euphemism?"

He shook his head, laughed, and answered simply, "Nah."

I cleared my throat and shifted in my seat. "Well, what do you make?"

"Anything. What's your craving?"

I turned and stared out the window, because all this talk of food was strangely sexy. "I have no idea."

Lee leaned over to nudge me with his shoulder. "Guess I'll just have to surprise you, then."

Thankfully, it wasn't long before we reached the house, and we all got out while Lee paid the driver. Alexis and Stu were already inside and climbing the stairs by the time I hesitantly stepped in the front door. Lee came in behind me, bumping me with his chest and forcing me to move farther down the hallway. Stepping back, I waited for him to lead the way into the kitchen. The place was clean and tidy, which was the last thing I expected, given that four brothers lived there. Then I remembered their cousin, Sophie, and her little boy. Perhaps she did the cleaning.

Passing by the living room, I saw a gigantic flat-screen TV on the wall and a designer leather couch. The kitchen was sleek and new, at odds with the age of the house. I guessed the place was built around the '50s or '60s, one of those old red brick council jobs. Usually, these builds were a two up, two down affair, but I knew there had to be more rooms, given that six people lived there. Sure enough, a hallway led off from the kitchen to an extension out the back. I was willing to bet the loft had been converted, too.

All in all, it was fairly obvious that the brothers had a decent amount of money coming in, though you'd never think it from the outside. Lee eyeballed me for a second, shrewd as a fox, and I knew he could tell I was taking everything in and coming to one conclusion. Unless his garage was doing a booming business, his money had to have come from elsewhere. This was why I couldn't understand him inviting me over. Either he was allowing his attraction to cloud his judgement, or he was up to something.

I sat down on a stool and he turned away, opening the fridge to check what food he had in.

"It must get hectic, living with so many people under one roof," I said, attempting to make polite conversation. After all, I wasn't going to be a bitch to the man in his own home.

"I'm used to hectic, Sn...I mean, Karla," said Lee, pulling ingredients from the fridge. "Me and my brothers have been living here since we were kids. Back then there were four of us in one room, though we've had the place updated a little since." He paused and pointed to the extension. "Sophie and Jonathan share the downstairs bedroom. Stu has his own room upstairs, Trevor and Liam share, and I'm in the attic."

"So your parents don't live here?"

"You like spaghetti?" he asked, perhaps to change the subject. "I make my own sauce from scratch."

I nodded. "Sounds good."

A moment of silence elapsed, and I wasn't expecting him to answer my question about his parents, so I got a surprise when he did.

"Mum died when I was fourteen. Overdose. Dad left when we were little, but he still comes around every so often. Waste of fucking space."

I sucked in a breath. "I'm sorry to hear that. Who took care of all of you after your mother passed?"

Lee cocked an eyebrow like I was being nosy, which I was. "Took care of ourselves. My aunt, Sophie's mum, fooled social services into believing she was moving in to care for us. What she really did was dump Soph here, then fucked off to live with her junkie boyfriend while getting a nice little government payment every month."

He was chopping tomatoes, onions, and garlic as he spoke, throwing them all into a blender.

"But if she took the money, how did you survive?"

He paused, looked me dead in the eye, and asked low, "How do you *think* we survived?"

I stared back at him, and in spite of what he was inferring, sympathy churned in my gut. I didn't know how to respond. He pointed his knife at me for a second, which was a little jarring.

"Everybody's always so quick to judge, but we're all born into our own patch. Some patches are worse than others, and yeah, most of the time you get a choice on what way to live. Trouble is, sometimes the choice is between bad and worse. I had two choices, and if I had picked the one I didn't, my brothers would've been split up and shipped off to a bunch of shitty care homes, where they'd-a been turned into victims. Instead, I chose the other option and turned them into survivors."

I stared at Lee, but he didn't meet my gaze, concentrating on the food instead. It made me uncomfortable to see things from his perspective. I'd always looked on the world from the viewpoint of a cop. Somebody who stopped people from taking what didn't belong to them. The problem was, some people had nothing, and their only option was to take.

There were so many things I wanted to say. Like, why didn't Stu get a job to support them? He must have been at least sixteen at the time. Yeah, the best he could've done was minimum wage, but at least it was honest. Then again, I doubt that kind of money would support a house of five growing kids. Plus, Stu wasn't exactly the sharpest tool in the shed. I could imagine him looking to Lee, who seemed a lot savvier, for guidance, and who obviously saw a more lucrative path.

"What I'm saying," Lee went on, "is that we all have our reasons." A loaded silence fell, and I grew self-conscious as he studied me. "So, what's yours?"

My brow furrowed. "I don't get you."

"Somewhere along the way you decided to become a copper. What was your reason?" he asked, seeming genuinely interested.

I rubbed my palms on my thighs. "It's a little more complicated than that."

"Your old man?"

"What about him?"

"Did he push you?"

I laughed, resting my elbows on the counter, surprisingly engrossed by watching Lee cut vegetables. He had those fancy knife skills, like the chefs on TV. "No, actually. The exact opposite. He doesn't think women are fit to be police."

Understanding lit up his eyes as he grinned. "Ah, so you did it to piss him off. I knew there was a reason I liked you."

My smile began to fade. "That's only a part of it. I want to help people, too. A lot more than I want to stick it to my father."

Lee's eyes flickered between mine, his expression contemplative. "Yeah, I can see that." A silence fell between us, and for the tiniest second I felt like we truly saw one another. All the flaws and all the good bits. The moment was broken when he continued, "Anyway, look, I'm not judging you for the thing with your old man. In fact, this means we have something in common. My dad's a prick, too."

"How do you know him?" I asked before clarifying. "My dad, I mean."

"Now, there's a story. Just let me get the spaghetti boiling first." His reply intrigued me, and I waited as he put some dried spaghetti in a pot. Once he was done, he went back to the fridge, pulling out a can of beer and a bottle of white wine. He held it up to me. "This is Sophie's. It's got to be better than the shit you were drinking at the bar."

I shrugged and he poured me a glass before popping the seal on his can. Taking a stool and resting his elbows on the counter, his posture almost matching mine, he recounted his story.

"So, I'd just turned eighteen and I was at my mate's house party. Some weed was being passed around, the usual. All of a sudden, the lights went out and somebody starting banging down the door. A neighbour must have called the police to come and break things up, and your dad was heading the team. Turns out the dealer at the party had been on their radar for a while, and your old man was dead set on booking him. Usually, I'd have been out the back window before you can say zip-a-dee-fuckin-doo-da, but I was shitfaced drunk. Before I knew it, your dad was slapping a pair of cuffs on me and hauling me off for a night in a jail cell.

"'Is that a truncheon in your pocket, or are you just pleased to see me?'" I'd joked. Your old man didn't take too kindly to that. Bastard twisted my wrist, nearly fucking broke it, and gave me a warning. '"One more word out of you and I'll have you up for drugs charges."'

"'Fuck you, I don't have anything on me.'"

"'You have whatever I say you have.'"

"Even though I was drunk, I knew to shut my mouth after that. Liam and Trev were still only young at the time, and I couldn't afford to get sent away, even for a couple of months. I've had a few other run-ins with him over the years, and he's a mean motherfucker. So yeah, my condolences and all that."

I narrowed my gaze at him and shook my head. I didn't doubt that my dad had said those things, but I was uncomfortable having Lee know what he was like, because that meant he also knew that my childhood wasn't a walk in the park.

"I...I don't know what to say. I'm sorry he did that," I replied at length.

Lee levelled me with his eyes. "Yeah, well, I think the fact that you're sticking it to him is the fucking business, Snap."

He was back to calling me Snap again, but I just shook my head. It was a losing battle trying to get him to stop. Returning to the cooker, he poured his sauce into a pan, stirring it every so often. He made quick work of draining the spaghetti, and before I knew it, there was a plate in front on me. It smelled absolutely mouth-watering, so I could only imagine how it was going to taste.

"Um, thanks," I said, glancing at him as I lifted the fork. I wanted to mouth a silent "wow" to myself when I finally tasted it. It was by far the best thing I'd eaten in a long time, and it was only spaghetti. I could just imagine what he might do with a more adventurous recipe.

"Well," said Lee, "what's the verdict?"

"Amazing," I blurted before I could censor myself, and he grinned wide. "I mean, not that I'm the best judge. My work doesn't leave a lot of room for fancy cooking. More often than not, I just end up grabbing something from the local takeaway on my way home."

Lee's grin didn't falter, but his eyes did flick to the ceiling for a second.

For the past couple of minutes, I'd been trying to ignore the subtle banging coming from upstairs, but it was gradually getting louder. I glanced at Lee and he smirked, and then I laughed and he laughed, too. We shared a moment of eye contact before I shook my head.

"So, your brother is, uh, kind of vigorous." I frowned at myself. Why the hell hadn't I brought up a different topic? Like, say, one that didn't involve discussing the fact that his brother and my best friend were having a roaring good time right above our heads.

"Vigour runs in the family," said Lee.

I sputtered a laugh. "That was smooth."

He flashed his teeth at me when he smiled. "You know it."

The banging from upstairs petered out, and my heart gave a thud of relief. I continued eating my food, because honestly, it was too good to ignore. I was also downing the wine like nobody's business, and when my glass was empty, Lee refilled it. I wasn't a big drinker, so, needless to say, the three glasses I'd had were hitting me hard. I was tipsy, and being tipsy in the presence of Lee Cross was dangerous territory.

"So, you like to cook?" I said to break up the silence.

"Yup."

"I hope you don't mind me saying, but it's kind of a strange thing for a twenty-five-year-old guy to enjoy."

Lee let out a breath. "Yeah, well, when you can remember a time when you couldn't afford food, you tend to make the most of it when you can."

His answer took me off guard. Damn, coming to his house had been a really bad idea. More and more I was empathising with him, and I didn't like it. I mean, nobody likes being forced to admit they might have been a tiny bit wrong in their first impressions.

I finished eating my spaghetti, hoping it might soak up some of the alcohol. I knew Lee was watching me the entire time, but I refused to acknowledge his attention. Instead, I kept my eyes levelled in the vicinity of his right ear and told him about some innocuous story I'd seen on the news earlier that day. Lee seemed amused as ever, and if I was looking at his face, I was sure I'd encounter a knowing smile.

Taking our empty plates, he carried them over to the sink, then turned back to me. "You want to go sit in the living room for a while? I'm sure Alexis will be down soon."

"Okay," I replied, and followed him to the next room.

Beside the TV was an iPod dock. Lee switched it on and scrolled through his playlists while I took a seat on the couch. If there was one thing men did better than women, it was pick out sofas. They went for the most comfortable option, while women generally went for what looked good. Not unexpectedly, I sank into the plush leather with relish. A moment later Lee approached, and even though there was lots of space, he decided to sit right next to me.

My gaze wandered to his arm, which rested along the back of the couch, and I swallowed, my body tensing.

"So, how long have you lived with Alexis?" Lee asked, his attention focused on me, and my skin prickled with awareness. He was way too close for comfort, and I could tell he was the kind of bloke who looked at a person and saw everything.

"A couple of years, but we've known each other since we were kids," I answered. "We grew up on the same street."

Lee's eyebrows rose. "Really? Do your folks still live there?"

I narrowed my gaze, wondering why he cared where my parents lived. Was he cosying up to me to get information about my dad? "No. They moved to a nicer area a few years ago after Dad was promoted," I answered, intentionally leaving out where exactly they'd moved to. If Lee noticed this, he didn't comment on it.

"And did you start cop training right after you finished school?"

"Uh-huh. Why all the questions?"

He gave me a small smile. "I'm just trying to get to know you, no ulterior motives, I promise. If you don't want to talk about you, we can talk about me. Or we could just sit in silence."

God, he was such a smart-arse.

I shook my head. "Let's talk about you. When did you leave school?"

"Around the same time Mum passed. Didn't have time for schooling after that. Stu stopped going around that time, too. I kept Liam and Trev in until they turned eighteen, though."

I had to admit, I was surprised by that, and it obviously showed on my face, because Lee went on, "I live for my family, Snap. I'd do anything for them."

"So much so that you had them join the family business instead of sending them to Uni?"

Now he frowned. "I gave them a choice. Working at the garage was the one they picked."

"You know, I saw Trevor free-running the other day. He's really talented." I left out the part that I'd seen him, too, because I knew it'd please him to discover I'd been spying.

"I know what he's capable of. Your point?"

"He could be doing other things."

"Fixing cars is hardly gutter work," said Lee, and strangely, the more hostile he grew, the closer he got to me. I was growing incensed, too, as I dug my fingers into my palms. We were talking about Trevor, but maybe deep down I was really talking about him. Because he was just as talented, channelling all his energy in the wrong direction.

"I think we both know that fixing cars isn't all you and your brothers do."

Lee eyes turned fierce, and I got a fright at the intensity in them. "Nah, we don't know that. In fact, you don't know anything."

"I know enough."

Lee dragged his hand through his hair and surprised me when he rose swiftly from the couch, pacing back and forth. "Don't come into my fucking house and judge me."

I shot him a look like he was on crazy pills. "Um, if you recall, I never asked to come here. You invited me."

"And you could give me a little respect by leaving your cop hat at the door."

"I'm not wearing my cop hat. I'm just being myself," I retorted, standing to face him. "You see, you think you like me, but you don't. Not really. This is me, and look at you — you hate it."

I had to tilt my head back to meet his gaze. His chest was rising and falling with his temper, and all of a sudden my skin felt too tight. Electricity pulsed between us like a living, breathing thing. Tingles radiated down my spine, his laboured breaths somehow reminding me of sex. I found myself staring at his lips, and he caught me looking. The tension between us grew thicker. He circled me like I was prey, and when he spoke, he was practically growling. I felt it right in the pit of my stomach.

"I don't hate anything about you, Karla."

The words had barely left his mouth when he reached out and grabbed me by the neck to pull me forward. He bent down and rested his forehead on mine, our breaths mingling.

Only a second passed before his lips sought my lips, gently at first, a light nip of exploration. I whimpered, and the sound did something to him, because a second later he crushed his mouth to mine and I trembled under his assault.

A pleasured noise rose from my throat. I felt crazed. My hands gripped his neck, feeling the corded muscles and warm skin. His tongue dipped inside, slick and wet. A second later he lifted me up, fitting my thighs around his waist and carrying me to the couch. He sat with me astride him, his hands wandering from my neck, down my shoulders and hips until he reached my thighs.

I felt so fevered right then that I barely had time to think, to step outside the moment and see the gigantic mistake I was making. As soon as Lee's hands wandered around to palm my arse, I was gone, lost to sensation. I felt owned, claimed by his hands and mouth. He pulled back slightly, drawing my lower lip between his teeth and biting down hard. I fisted his T-shirt, muttering a feverish "please" into his mouth before we were kissing again. He broke away just long enough to whisper back, "Tell me what you need, baby."

He squeezed my arse, and I jumped in fright when one finger slid between my cheeks, teasing me over the fabric of my pants. It felt shockingly good, forbidden, which was enough to jolt me out of my moment of weakness. I swore and climbed off him, then strode to the other side of the room. I was panting, and I knew my face must have been as red as a stop sign. Lifting a finger, I pointed between him, me, and the couch.

"This never happened."

Lee smirked, his lips slightly redder than before. I felt a deep sense of embarrassment at how hungrily I'd attacked his mouth. I knew he'd been the one to initiate things, but I'd been a more than willing participant.

"Which part, babe?"

"Every part. And stop 'babe-ing' me. I'm not your babe."

"A second ago you felt like you were," Lee murmured darkly before moving across the room. My back hit the wall when his chest met my chest. Then his mouth was at my ear. "You wanted it," he whispered.

I was staring at the hardwood floor, my fluster getting the better of me when I replied shyly, "I just don't get how *that's* your first port of call."

His eyes searched mine for a second, his brows furrowing, and then he burst out laughing. His hands cupped my cheeks before he pulled me into a hug. "God, you're cute."

In spite of myself, I sank into his hold. He took a deep breath, like he was smelling me, and there was something about it that made my stomach do a flip-flop. The whole situation was just ridiculous. And I was drunk. Yes, that's why I was bringing up anal play like a flippin' weirdo. Levelling my hands on his chest, I pushed him back and stepped away to put some distance between us.

"Look, you can quit the nice-guy act. It's fooling no one."

He regarded me tenderly. The affection in his voice was making me feel things I didn't want to feel. "There's no act."

"You, me...us, it would never work, you know that, right?"

"Not sure I agree."

"Yeah, well, you're not the one with a reputation to uphold."

"Oh, really? What do you think my boys would say if they knew I was sleeping with a cop?"

I cocked my head and put a hand on my hip. "I don't know, Lee. According to you, they wouldn't have a reason to say anything."

He stared at me for a long hard moment, not speaking, the stoniness in his eyes giving me chills. I felt like our conversation had come full circle, rounding back to the argument we'd been having before he kissed me. Thankfully, the tension was broken when the door opened and Alexis stepped inside. Her hair was wild and her makeup smudged. In fact, she was still putting her clothes back to rights and looked like she was fleeing the scene of a crime.

"Lee, can you give us a lift home?" she asked in a rush.

He shot her a perplexed expression. "Sure."

I frowned and shook my head at him. "Don't put yourself out. We'll get a cab."

"We don't have time to call for a cab. We need to leave now," Alexis insisted.

"Why?"

I didn't have to wait for an answer, because Stu stormed into the room.

"Where the hell do you think you're going?" he demanded.

He wasn't wearing a top, and the fly of his jeans was still open, which meant I was copping *quite* the eyeful. Stu was ripped, and honestly, I totally got why Alexis sought him out for company. I mean, if you were going to have meaningless sex, you might as well do it right. I tried to keep my eyes fixed at twelve o'clock, rather than veering toward six. Okay, so maybe I took a quick peek at five. Oh, who was I kidding? My gaze was headed straight for six, and I didn't even feel guilty about it.

Hello.

Aaand, back to the matter at hand. Judging from the angry look on Stu's face, I thought that maybe he wasn't as great at keeping his emotions out of his sex life as Lee said he was.

"I told you this was just sex," Alexis muttered, her slumped posture showing me she was disappointed in herself.

"But why? That prick left you, Lex. I'm here. I want you. Give us another chance."

Oh, wow. I never thought I'd see the day that Stu Cross showed his emotional side.

"You don't get it," she replied, turning away. Stu reached out and grabbed her shoulder.

"What don't I get?"

"Hey, don't be rough with her like that, she's...." I stopped myself right before I finished the sentence. It didn't matter anyway, because a second later Alexis let the cat out of the bag.

"I'm knocked up, okay? And before you ask, no, the baby isn't yours. Now will you just let me leave?"

Stu stared at her, frozen in place. Alexis turned and walked out the door. Lee shot his brother a stern look that told him not to follow her. Then he touched his hand softly to my lower back and led me out of the house. A minute later, both Alexis and I were in the back seat of his car as he drove us home. It was quiet until Lee announced sarcastically.

"Well, Clarky, that's some stunt you just pulled. You should be real proud of yourself."

"Don't talk to her like that," I warned him.

His eyes caught mine in the overhead mirror, and I was the first to turn away. I couldn't look at him right then, not when I could still taste him in my mouth, still feel his hands on my body. What had happened lingered between us, heavy and unspoken.

"No, Karla. He's right. What I just did to Stu was shitty. And I'm not proud of myself, not at all."

"I'll tell him you said that," Lee responded, looking slightly appeased.

"I thought you said that Stu was emotionally uninvolved when it comes to women," I said. "He didn't seem that way tonight."

Alexis pulled a face. "Oh, my God, Lee, you corny bastard. I didn't know you were dealing in clichés now."

He suppressed a smirk. "What? It's the truth, though he's always had a soft spot for you. Maybe you'll be the one he finally decides to turn over a new leaf for."

"Yeah, because I'm such a special snowflake. That shit only happens in rom-coms, and my shit stinks the same as everybody else's."

"Ugh, you had to go and make it gross," I complained.

"Hey, you'd better get used to it. I'm going to be a single mother, and I've decided you'll be godmother. That means lots and lots of nappy changes."

Even though we were joking around, what she said made me emotional, and my voice got a little scratchy. "You want me to be godmother, seriously?"

"Who the hell else would I ask?! Of course I do."

I reached over and grabbed her hand, forgetting for a second that Lee was in the car with us. "You know that means a lot to me, right? I'll never take it for granted."

We shared a meaningful look, and I squeezed her hand before letting go. The car fell silent, and when I looked up, I found Lee watching me again. I swallowed and glanced away, staring intently out the window. A few minutes later, we'd reached my and Lexie's building. She got out first and hurried toward the door entry system. I hovered, looking back to Lee. There was something about his expression that made me think he wanted to say something, but he didn't. Instead, he shot me a sober nod and restarted the engine.

"See you around, Snap," he said right before he pulled away from the kerb.

I stood on the path, watching his black car disappear into the black night and worrying about how my life was changing, all because he was in it.

Five

"Oi, Burrows, where'd ya get the shiner?" Tony called after Steve, who'd just stepped inside the break room. Steve flicked his attention to Tony, a face like thunder and a black eye to boot.

"Your missus wanted to try something a little different in the sack," he sneered, and Tony bristled. My workmate wasn't an easy man to rile, but what Steve had said got his back up. He went silent, and believe me, since he was normally a happy, chatty sort of bloke, Tony was at his scariest when he was quiet. Steve gave him a snide look before going to sit on the other side of the room from us.

"Don't listen to her — she's just crabby because she got into another catfight. Handbags at dawn, it was," I said, grinning at my friend. "She needs to learn how to act like a lady."

Tony let out a loud laugh, and Steve scowled. He kept quiet, though, which was out of character. Normally, the man had a mouth on him that Niagara Falls couldn't shut up. This niggled at me, because if Steve had gotten into a fight on the job, he'd be bragging about it with endless talk of "you should see the other guy." The fact he was keeping schtum was worrying, and it reminded me of Lee's threats when we'd visited the garage. Maybe Steve tried to pay another visit, and Lee had made good on his promise.

Hmmm.

Tony and I had just finished eating, so we packed up our stuff and left Steve to sit out the rest of his break alone.

"Have you ever suspected he might be up to something dodgy?" I asked my friend once we were out of earshot.

Tony shot me a cynical look. "Is the sky blue?"

I sighed. "He needs to be dealt with."

"You're telling me. As soon I have even the slightest bit of evidence, I'm turning him in."

I nodded, wondering how long it'd take Steve to slip up. A little while later, we were on the beat, walking down the high street, when I caught sight of a disturbance outside a greasy spoon.

"I'm not letting you spend time with Jonathan until you clean up your act!" a woman yelled, levelling her hands on some tall guy's chest and pushing him away from her. A kid stood in the doorway to the café, his thumb in his mouth and tears running down his face. I'd only seen her once before, so it took me a second to recognise Lee's cousin, Sophie. The guy she was arguing with was about her age. He was tall and thin, and, if I was being honest, sort of slimy-looking. I was guessing from the nature of the argument that he was her son's father.

"Is everything all right here?" I asked, stepping up to them as Tony went and bent down in front of the boy. He spoke to him quietly, asking if he'd been hurt.

Sophie turned to see who was interrupting and frowned when she saw me. "You again."

I nodded. "Is this man bothering you?"

It took her a second to answer, as she glanced between me and the man. "Yes, he is bothering me. I want him to go."

As soon as the words left her mouth, I turned to the guy and gestured down the street. "Sir, I'll have to ask you to leave now. You're upsetting this young woman."

"That's only because she's trying to keep my kid from me," he spat.

"Yeah, and can you blame me when this is the kind of attitude I have to deal with?"

"Maybe if you'd quit being such a fucking bitch, I wouldn't have an attitude."

Tony stood and shot the man a hostile look.

He bristled, his posture stiffening, before he backed away a few steps. "This is bullshit. I'm outta here," he said, and skulked off.

A moment passed before Sophie glanced up at me, her cheeks red with embarrassment. "Thanks for that. I promise I don't normally go around having domestics out on the street, but David showed up unannounced and tried to take Jonathan." She turned back to her son, who hurried to her side and buried his face behind her leg. For some reason, my eyes went to her left wrist, where she was tugging her sleeve down as far as it would go. A small bruise peeked out, and I knew she was trying to hide it.

I stepped closer and lowered my voice, speaking softly as I asked, "Has he ever tried to hurt you?"

She stared at me, unshed tears shining in her eyes, and I knew the answer was yes. She didn't say anything, and a moment later she sucked in a deep breath. "We should get going."

I stepped in front of her, blocking her exit. "I can help you, you know. All you have to do is file a report. We can have a barring order put in place so that he can't approach you or your son."

She shook her head. "No, I don't want to do that. Come on, honey, let's go." She took hold of Jonathan's hand and walked away. I let out a breath, my eyes meeting Tony's. We both knew there wasn't much we could do if she wasn't willing to cooperate.

For the rest of the day, my encounter with Sophie was stuck in my head. I wondered if Lee had any idea what was going on between her and this David character. I couldn't imagine he did, judging by how fiercely he told me he'd do anything for his family. I doubted David would've gotten within ten feet of Sophie if Lee had known.

I was so preoccupied by these thoughts that I almost forgot I'd organised a girls night for Alexis. I'd invited Reya over, and Alexis' friend, Bradley, who was an honorary girl. We were going to watch chick flicks, order pizza, and, well, try to make her feel better about being pregnant. She thought she was alone, but she really wasn't. I planned to be by her side through all of it, but I was worried about her falling deeper into depression. It wouldn't be good for her or the baby.

Everyone was already at the flat when I arrived, so I said some quick hellos and went to take a shower. I always liked to wash after a shift; it was almost a compulsion. Somehow the water felt like it cleaned away all the crap I'd seen that day, leaving me fresh and new.

Alexis was scribbling down a list of everyone's pizza orders when I came out, my hair in a towel and wearing a pair of clean pyjamas.

"Can I have a meat-lover's pizza, chicken tenders, potato wedges, and some coleslaw?" said Reya. "Oh, and a diet Coke."

I couldn't help teasing her. "Yeah, because that'll undo all the damage."

"Hey! I actually prefer diet," she argued, and Bradley chuckled.

"Can't get enough of that sexy chemical taste, huh?"

I laughed and leaned forward to give him a high-five.

"You two, stop ganging up on little Reya," Alexis butted in, throwing her a sympathetic look. "Don't mind them. They're a pair of bullies."

I found it funny how Alexis called Reya little, since she was more woman than us two put together. I guessed we considered her little because she was six or seven years younger than all of us. I didn't know her exact heritage, but I thought I remembered her telling me once that her parents were Spanish, which was where she must've gotten her dark looks from. She was actually quite statuesque, with skin the colour of honey and curves that went on forever. I mean, Alexis did plus-size modelling, but she had nothing on Reya.

Once the food was ordered, Bradley hit play on the DVD. We were watching a movie called *He's Just Not That Into You*. Needless to say, I hadn't been a part of the selection process. The title was so fucking condescending it kind of made me want to hurt someone. Thankfully, it didn't take long for our food to arrive, distracting me from my daydreams of grievous bodily harm.

It was later on, while Bradley and Reya were chatting in the living room, that I managed to corner Alexis in the kitchen. I knew she was going to give me endless amount of stick for this, but I had to put my pride aside for a minute. I just didn't have it in me to ignore the fact that Lee's cousin was being hounded by her ex. If he'd been violent with her in the past, then I had to do something to prevent it from happening again.

"Do you have Lee's number?" I asked quietly as I washed dishes and she dried.

She gave me a shrewd look. "Maybe I do. And why, pray tell, are you looking for it?"

"It's complicated. But I assure you, I have no romantic designs on him whatsoever, if that's what you're thinking."

"I dunno, you'd make a good cougar." She smirked. "They'd call you 'racy red'."

"Shut your face," I whisper-hissed, trying not to laugh. "I'm way too young to be a cougar. And he's way too old to be my boy toy. If I was going to go down that route, the guy would have to be in his, like, late teens or something." Good grief, I was rambling.

Alexis full-on chuckled. "Ooooh, I didn't know you were into the barely legal scene, Constable."

I grew impatient. "Do you have his number or not?"

She sighed. "Yes, I have it. And just so you know, if you were thinking of hitting that, I'd be in no position to judge, especially after the shit I pulled with Stu the other night. *However*, being in your line of work, it's probably not the best idea." Her brows rose meaningfully on the none-too-subtle hint.

"It's a good thing I have no intentions of hitting anything," I said, drying my hands and returning to the living area.

"Well, you've got to hit something every once in a while," she called after me.

I turned back around long enough to give her an Italian chin flick that said something along the lines of, "piss off."

***

For the next couple of days, Lee's number burned a hole in my pocket. Alexis had given it to me and I'd programmed it into my phone, but I was hesitant to call him. Depending on the person you were talking to, a phone call could be kind of intimate, and I knew for a fact it'd be that way with Lee. He had this way of making me feel strange and tingly, and I couldn't deny he had a sexy voice. It was all deep and rough around the edges.

Anyhow, I was working the late shift, or the early morning one, depending on how you wanted to look at it. Keira and I were driving through town, keeping an eye on things. Sometimes it felt like I could wax lyrical about Camden at 2 a.m. on a Saturday. Litter covered the streets, blowing back and forth like waves in the ocean. People fell over drunk, scrambling for a connection they weren't brave enough to seek sober.

Okay, so maybe not so lyrical.

The radio went off with a request from dispatch for us to go check out a violent disturbance outside a nightclub just a few minutes away. Keira hit the sirens, and within seconds we were on our way. When we got there, we found three men involved in a scuffle, two of whom were beating the crap out of the third. He lay on the ground, crouched in the foetal position as the other two laid into him. I didn't hesitate to pull out my Taser, and the threat of incapacitation was enough to get them to back off. Before long, we had the attackers cuffed and sitting in the back seat of the patrol car, ready to take down to the station, while the bloke they'd beaten was being carted off in an ambulance.

I was exhausted beyond belief by the time I got home, dropping my keys on the coffee table and flopping down onto the couch. I could hear Alexis snoring lightly in her room as I closed my eyes and let out a weary sigh. I wanted to go to bed, but Lee's number was still calling to me. I couldn't sleep soundly until I'd let him know that his cousin might be in trouble.

Dialling his number, I waited tensely for him to pick up. It rang for so long that I began to wonder if he was going to answer. Then, just as I was about to hit "end," his voice filled my ear, tired and sexy.

"Whoever this is, it better be important that you're calling me at...." He paused, and I thought he must have been checking the time. "Five-ten on a Saturday morning."

I cleared my throat. "Hi, uh, this is Karla. Alexis gave me your number."

"Snap?" Lee asked, sounding surprised.

"Yes, I'm, eh, sorry for calling you so early. I wasn't thinking. The late shift does weird things to my brain."

There was a smile in his voice when he responded low, "You can call me whenever. Excuse the tone, thought you were Liam or Trevor looking for a lift home or something."

"A lift home at five in the morning?"

"The young'uns like to party hard."

I laughed involuntarily. "Oh, and what are you now, an old dog?"

"I've definitely got some city miles going on."

I laughed, *again*. Man, he was charming even when he'd been woken up at an ungodly hour. "Pfft, you have zero city miles, and we both know it," I blurted before I had a chance to think it through.

"Oh, yeah? You been checking out my miles?" he asked flirtatiously, and I heard the sound of sheets rustling. That reminded me he was more than likely in bed. I did not need to be visualising *that*.

I bet he sleeps naked, the dirty side of my mind mused, causing a tiny shiver to trickle down my spine.

"*Anyway*, I called you for a reason."

He sounded amused. "My apologies. Go ahead."

More rustling of sheets. God grief, what was he doing over there?

"Could you stop moving around for a second? The noise is distracting me."

Lee let out a deep, raspy chuckle, and I swear it did me in. I found myself reaching for my shirt collar and undoing several buttons, feeling hotter by the second.

"Mm-hmm, easily distracted, are we?" His voice was pure sex, and I just knew that he was bare-arse nekkid. Nobody spoke like that when they were clothed.

I swallowed and tried to summon a steady tone. "Quit it with that voice."

"What voice?"

"The *distracting* one," I practically shouted and heard a gap in Alexis' snore. It started up again a second later, and I exhaled heavily. For a second there, I thought I'd woken her up. Lee chuckled down the line, and the sound of it was so delicious that I felt it in my long-neglected lady parts.

"Again, I apologise. Now go on — tell me what's on your mind, baby."

I let the "baby" slide, because honestly, we'd be on the phone all night (or morning) if I didn't get on with it. "Okay, so, the other day while I was working, I bumped into your cousin, Sophie. She had her little boy with her and his dad was there. They were arguing. I wouldn't normally stick my nose in like this, but I think he's been hitting her. When I asked if she wanted to report it, she brushed me off. I just thought you should know."

Lee went deathly quiet on the other end of the line, and I could almost sense the anger radiating off him. A long moment passed before he spoke. "This was David, yeah? Tall skinny prick, hair like he dipped it in a deep fat fryer?"

"That's the one."

"They split up months ago. Sophie never mentioned he was back on the scene."

"Well, from what I saw, he is."

Lee let out a slow breath. "Thanks for the heads-up. I'll make sure he stays away from her."

"Good," I said, and a silence fell. I should have hung up then, but something prevented me. I didn't want to end the call, because as much as I hated to admit it, I was a tiny bit addicted to interacting with him.

"Is that all you wanted to say?" Lee asked, his voice quiet, almost a whisper. I could imagine him inside me, talking to me like that, like I was the centre of his world.

"Um, yes. I mean, no." I paused for a second before continuing, "Do you remember Steve? The guy who came with me to your garage the other week?"

"Hard to forget a prick like that."

"Mm-hmm, you wouldn't happen to know anything about the black eye he's been sporting?"

"Nope."

"Oh, well, I just thought I'd ask."

Lee moved again, like he was trying to get into a comfortable position.

"You sound tired," he commented.

"I am. I told you I was working tonight. Well, last night and this morning."

"So what'll you do today, just sleep and hang out?"

"Pretty much. Maybe head to the gym later."

"I could come over and cook for you. A working woman should have a man to take care of her needs."

I could just imagine his cheeky grin. And honestly, that sounded good, too good. I had to laugh at his brazenness. "Never took you for a feminist."

"Oh, but I am. In fact, I think they should bring in a new law that says all women should receive several orgasms a week. I'd be more than happy to support that," he said, and against my own will, I chuckled.

"I'm sure you would be."

"Yep. Hey, did you know they had these doctors back in the day who women visited to be treated for hysteria? The doctor literally jilled them off to relieve the tension, then sent them home happy as clams. Excuse the pun. Saw that shit on a documentary."

I laughed loudly, unable to help it. "You're crazy."

"God's honest truth. Google it if you don't believe me. So, you gonna let me come over?" Lee purred.

"I don't think so."

"Aw, but I was going to bring my baked cheesecake. You haven't lived until you've tried my baked cheesecake."

I had to admit, I found it hilarious to imagine Lee baking, tattooed ne'er-do-well that he was. I shouldn't have indulged him, but I couldn't seem to help it. "What flavour cheesecake?"

His voice dipped low. "Whatever flavour gets you to say yes."

"You're such a flirt."

He chuckled, and I got up from the couch, heading for my bedroom. "I'd better go. It's been a long night."

"Don't go yet."

I was yawning as I replied, "I have to. Otherwise, I'll fall asleep while we're talking."

"I don't mind. Stay on the line."

I closed the door to my room. "Okay, well, I'm going to put you on speaker for a minute because I have to change out of my uniform."

I heard him groan just as I hit "speaker" and placed the phone on my bedside dresser. "Forget talking on the phone. I should come over."

I laughed. "Nice try."

"No joke. I can be there in fifteen minutes, maybe less."

"You're incorrigible."

"Oh, that's fightin' talk. Where'd you learn those fancy words, Constable?"

"Lee, you're flirting again. Quit it or I'll hang up."

"Okay, no need for drastic measures. I'll behave."

A quiet fell as I pulled off my shirt and tie, then unbuckled my belt.

"So, are you naked yet?"

I huffed a breath. "I thought you just said you were going to behave."

"I will, but at least give me something. I'm trying to visualise here."

A second later my trousers were off, and I threw all my clothes in the laundry basket. I was too tired for my usual shower, so I just put on an old T-shirt and climbed into bed. "Sorry to burst your bubble, but nothing even remotely sexy is happening over here. I've been working for the past ten hours, and I stink. Go put that in your spank bank."

Lee groaned again. "You can't say 'spank bank,' Snap. It'll give me ideas."

"Don't you dare," I warned him.

His laugh was devilish. "For all you know, I could've been rubbing one out this whole time."

"For all you know, so could I," I countered.

"Fucking hell. Okay, you win that round." He swore and moved away from the phone for a second. I thought I heard him scratching his stubble while muttering "Jesus Christ" under his breath.

I tried my best to change the subject. "So, have you got any plans for the day?"

"Other than coming over to yours?" he asked confidently. When I left him in stony silence, he added, "Kidding, kidding. No big plans. It's a friend of mine's birthday tonight, so I'll have to show my face."

"Oh, well, I hope you have a good time," I said sleepily as I snuggled into my pillow and we were both quiet for a minute. I could hear him breathing on the other end of the line, so I knew he was still there.

"You nearly gone?" Lee asked softly. For a moment it felt like he was there beside me, whispering in my ear.

"Almost," I answered past another yawn.

"Bet you look a picture right now," he murmured.

"Mm-hmm," I mumbled, closing my eyes.

"Go to sleep, beautiful," he said, his voice a caress.

Seconds later, I was dead to the world.

Six

"Guess how many bras I'm wearing?" Reya asked as she jogged alongside me on the treadmill.

I sputtered a laugh. "Um, I'm hoping the answer to that is one."

She shook her head. "Nope, I've got three of these bad boys on right now. Otherwise, the girls'd be flopping around like an elephant on a trampoline."

I laughed harder, feeling breathless. "Oh, my God, stop! You're putting me off my stride."

"I'm being serious. I bet you've never even had to double up, whereas I'm here tripled up and could probably do with a fourth. I curse you, Karla Sheehan, you and your perfectly manageable boobs."

The guy on the treadmill next to Reya's cocked his head, clearly listening in to our conversation. I couldn't blame him.

"You know what?" she went on. "I'm thinking of getting a reduction. I want a pair of Claire Danes–style bee stings. She can probably go around free as a bird day in and day out without so much as a back twinge."

The guy listening almost tripped over his own feet, and I sort of felt bad for him. Reya was always very chatty when she was around me because I made her feel comfortable. The problem with that was that it often meant she didn't think to censor herself.

"Why don't you just get a sports bra, you big freak?" I asked when I finally managed to stop laughing.

"Because I'm broke, but also because sports bras are bullshit. They might give you support, but they barely cover the nips. I don't want to be going around flashing my headlights at everyone."

"You have to shut up. Seriously, you're giving me a stitch," I complained, laughing so hard I had to reach for the buttons to slow down my machine.

I'd slept until midday and then Reya had called, asking if I wanted to go to the gym for a workout. Since I felt unusually refreshed after being lulled to sleep by Lee, I agreed. Now, here we were. And yeah, I was refusing to think about the fact that Lee Cross's voice had sent me into the best night's sleep I'd had in forever.

"I'm going over to the rowing machine. Come find me when you're done," I said, stepping off the treadmill and heading to the other side of the gym. I'd been rowing for a couple of minutes when out of the corner of my eye I saw someone take the machine next to mine. I didn't pay them too much attention, and focused on the music streaming from my MP3. For some reason, I preferred listening to metal when I was working out, and James Hetfield was currently growling in my ears.

It was only when I started to slow down that I sensed a familiar presence, intense and all-consuming. I slowed to a stop, pulling out my earbuds. A second later I turned to see who had my instincts on alert, and there he was.

Lee glanced over at me, wearing workout clothes and a towel draped around his shoulders. I wiped the sweat from my brow and narrowed my gaze at him. After a millisecond of eye contact, I stood, making my way to the water fountain. I knew for a fact that this wasn't a coincidence. Last night on the phone I distinctly remembered telling him I might go to the gym today.

He followed heavy on my heels, dipping his head and asking, "Sleep well last night, Constable?"

I bent over the fountain, took a drink, then straightened. "Well enough."

The T-shirt he wore wasn't exactly tight, but his perspiration had caused parts of it to stick to his chest. I tried not to look and failed. Lee took the opportunity to stretch his arms up over his head, causing his T-shirt to rise and reveal several inches of toned stomach. I knew he'd done it on purpose, but still, I couldn't stop staring. That was when my gaze wandered to his right hand, where the knuckles had been bandaged.

"What happened there?"

Lee glanced down, then back up to me. "David happened," he answered casually. "Let's just say, he won't be bothering Sophie anymore."

"You fought him?"

"Had to. No other way of getting through to blokes like him. Words don't work, but fists sure do."

I didn't know how to feel about that, because if David had really been violent with Sophie, a tiny little pixie of a woman, then he deserved some sort of punishment. I just wasn't sure that punishment was a beating.

"You should have reported him."

"So your lot could give him a slap on the wrist and then he'd be back hassling Sophie within the month. No, thanks. I told you I'd do anything for my family. Sometimes that means doing things that fall into a…grey category."

I eyed him closely, a frown shaping my lips. The thing about Lee was that I never quite knew whether or not I agreed with him, and it was disconcerting. I didn't get too much time to contemplate this further, as he distracted me by nodding over to the boxing ring. "Fancy sparring with me?"

I shook my head and tried to keep a neutral expression. "No, thanks."

"Worried I'll show you up?" he asked, a challenge gleaming in his eyes as they wandered over me intently. I felt like he was chronicling every tiny detail, from the way my workout pants clung to my thighs to the sheen of sweat glistening on my neck.

I laughed, trying not to let his attention affect me. "No, actually, the opposite. I wouldn't want the whole gym seeing you get taken down by a girl."

Lee stepped closer, so close I could smell him, soap and sweat and man. He bent his head to reply, "Hmm, I sense a wager coming on."

Our gazes locked, and it was the first time that I noticed we had almost the exact same eye colour, except his were the tiniest shade lighter. A moment of insanity must have struck me, because there was something about his challenge that I couldn't back away from. I was riled, and I wanted to show Lee Cross that boxing was bollocks when put up against a real martial art.

"What do I get if I win?" I asked, levelling him with a hard stare.

His smile was slow and sexy. "What do you want?"

"Hmm, let me think. How about for you to steer clear of this gym when I'm around."

His mouth was inches from mine as he replied, "But there's no fun in staying away."

"Sometimes fun isn't worth it."

"Sometimes it is."

I groaned. He really wasn't going to let up. "We're done here."

He grabbed my arm as I turned to walk away. "Okay, fine. If you win, I'll keep my distance, but if I win, you've got to let me come around to yours tomorrow and cook you dinner."

I stared at him, incredulous. "You want to cook me dinner?"

Lee nodded firmly and held his hand out to me.

I grew flustered. Why did his end of the deal have to sound so...so romantic? A small part of me kind of wanted to lose, and that part began with a "V."

After a moment of indecision, I finally shook with him. A couple of minutes later, we were both in the ring. I couldn't use my eskrima sticks, because then it wouldn't be a fair fight. It didn't matter, though; I had a number of empty-hand techniques I could use on him. I got in position, and Lee stood less than two feet away, knees bent slightly, fists up.

"Just so you know, I'm not gonna actually hit you. This isn't about hurting one another, it's about submission. First person to achieve a takedown wins," he said.

I sputtered a laugh, circling him. "It's not a real fight unless you hit me."

"Yeah, well, I don't want a real fight with you. Play fighting is sexier," he said, flashing his teeth and swinging. I moved quickly, dodging the would-be strike. He swung again, and I coiled my hand around his arm, pushed his other hand out of the way, and locked his arm behind his back. He dropped his body and pressed his foot down on my ankle. I released him. He backed away a few feet.

"That was slick."

I just smirked in response before asking, "So, we never really set the rules. Is kicking allowed?"

"Sure," said Lee, and before I could react his leg shot out, making light contact with my upper thigh.

I shook my head at him. "Dirty move."

"Hey, we just agreed to kicking."

"Yeah," I grinned. "We did." Making sure I had enough space, I launched into a wheel kick. My foot got him right in the lower abdomen, and he drew back, winded.

"Hey, ease up, Mr Miyagi."

"Mr Miyagi does karate." I feigned offence. "Don't insult me."

Lee chuckled at my response and I went for him again, but this time he was quicker, and he caught my foot before it could descend. I lost my balance and fell to the floor, hard.

"Ah, would you look at that. Miyagi got taken down," Lee teased, and I scowled at him, reaching around to rub the base of my spine.

"Thought you said you weren't going to hit me." I winced, pretending I was in real pain.

Lee's smile fell and he hurried forward, holding out his hand to help me up. "Shit, did I hurt you?"

"I'll survive," I said, placing my fingers in his, but instead of letting him pull me up, I dragged him down, making short work of wrapping my legs around his shoulders and capturing his head in a lock. Grappling was kind of my forte, and I actually had a little experience with ground fighting. I squeezed my thigh muscles around his neck, and even though I knew he had to be hurting right then, he laughed.

"Is this what heaven feels like?" His chest rose and fell as he fought for breath.

I smiled wide, a little breathless myself from the effort it took to keep him down. "Pretty much."

He struggled, moving his body and testing me, trying to find a way out of the lock.

"This is a good look for you, Snap."

"I agree. I also think I just won."

"Not yet."

"Aw, that's cute. You actually think you're getting out of this, don't you?"

In a shameless move, he turned his head to the side by the tiniest fraction and nuzzled his nose into my inner thigh. Electricity shot right between my legs, the shock enough to make me loosen my hold for a millisecond as he grabbed me and flipped me on my back. Before I knew it, he had my wrists captured in his hands as he straddled my waist.

"Well, what do you know," he purred. "I managed to get out of it after all."

I tried to kick my legs, but his body was pure muscle, and with the way he was holding me, I might as well have been weighed down by steel.

"That was another dirty move," I complained, breathing heavily.

"Sorry, but you can't complain about dirty moves when you use them yourself. I tried giving you a helping hand and you exploited my kindness." He tutted, shaking his head at me smugly.

I had no intention of giving in. "You do realise there are a number of much more efficient ways you could be restraining me right now, yet you pick the sexiest option."

"Yep, I'm well aware of that."

I grunted irritably, uncomfortably aware of the strength of his thighs locked around mine and the way our bodies were so conveniently aligned. Flicking my eyes up to his, I was sure he saw my frustration. There was a softness in his gaze, and I exhaled a breath when he loosened his grip and lowered his body so his entire weight rested on top of me.

His pecs were hard planes, his abdomen a firm press against my stomach.

"What are you doing?" I whispered, conscious of every breath he took. The noise of other gym users and trashy workout music streaming from the overhead monitors was a distant reality. There were any number of ways that I could have gained the upper hand right then, but it didn't feel like we were sparring anymore, and I couldn't have moved a muscle even if I tried.

"You're so fucking sexy," Lee whispered back, his nose dipping to the spot below my ear.

"You need to get off me. Somebody might see," I said, desperate.

"I love that about you," Lee continued to whisper, still nuzzling me.

"What?"

"How you act all tough, but as soon as I touch you, you melt and go all shy. It's gorgeous."

I was momentarily glad that this wasn't a cop gym, and that none of my coworkers had a membership here. I could just imagine the crap I'd have to deal with if anyone I knew saw me in my current clinch.

"You need to get off me now." I repeated my plea, trying to make my voice hard and failing. There was way too much air in it.

"If you want me to get off you, I will," said Lee, moving his hips slightly. I felt something firm press into me and knew he was hard. This was so many levels of wrong, I didn't even know where to begin. "Do you want me to?"

I closed my eyes for a second and tried to breathe. I'd never felt so weak, and we both knew I didn't want him off me, not even a tiny bit. What I wanted was for us to be magically transported somewhere private where he could show me exactly what he planned on doing with the stiff length in his pants.

When I didn't reply, Lee continued talking. "I can't get your taste out of my mouth."

The smallest whimper escaped me, and I felt myself grow wet at his words. I wanted so many things right then. In the end I opened my eyes, and I was sure he recognised the defeat in my expression.

"You win."

I hated to admit it, but the way he smiled in response was beautiful. "Does this mean I get to come over tomorrow?"

All I could do was nod reluctantly. Maybe Alexis would feel like doing me a favour and sticking around the flat while Lee was there, like a buffer. She'd hate it, but hey, it wasn't like I hadn't done favours for her in the past.

"Okay, so…." Lee's voice dipped as his eyes travelled over my heaving chest. "I guess the only thing left for you to do is kiss the victor."

That did it. I couldn't take any more as I twisted my wrists out of his hold and used my hip bone to break the tenseness in his thighs. Within seconds I was out from under him, walking to the other side of the ring and searching for my towel. Once I found it, I dabbed my brow and slipped out between the ropes.

"Hey, Karla," Lee called after me. I turned and waited for him to say something. "I know you could have done that any time." He stopped, not saying any more because he didn't have to. We both knew what he was inferring. I could have gotten out from under him, but I didn't because I liked having him on me, and that was the scariest part of all.

***

Chicken noodles were my dreamboat. I tended to get crazy hungry when I was on a shift, so the sight of Tony walking into the station with a bag of Chinese takeaway was like music to my ears, or, I dunno, a beautiful artwork to my eyes.

I was manning the front desk and decided to eat while I worked because the station was a madhouse. Halfway through my dinner, and having dealt with a number of drunks, one prostitute, and a woman who'd had her handbag stolen on the tube, I had a call come in about an illegal rave going on in a warehouse down in Brixton. They needed extra backup because there were hundreds of people there, a lot thought to be underage, and apparently some dodgy drugs were being passed around. It was with a forlorn sigh that I said goodbye to my noodles and hopped in the patrol car with Tony.

"Okay, here's one for ya," he began, and I knew I was going to be hit with a brain teaser. Tony and I had a thing for trying to figure them out together. When you worked with someone day in and day out, you came up with ways to pass the time. "If it were two hours long, it'd be half as long until midnight as it would be if it were an hour later. What time is it now?"

I glanced at him, screwing my mouth up in concentration as I repeated the question to myself over and over. The problem was, the more I repeated it, the less sense it made. In the end I just gave up. "Ugh, I've got nothing. I'll have to think about it some other time. Hey, so what's the deal with these drugs at the warehouse?"

"Little white pills," said Tony. "Been going around for the last few months and a couple of kids have OD'd.

They're saying it's E, but it's not normal E. Tests done in the lab say there's all sorts in there."

I shook my head and looked out the window, my gut churning with anger and worry. Teenagers seemed to be willing to put anything into their bodies without a care to the fact that it could kill them. I noticed lights flashing behind us and turned to see an ARV following. My ex, Gavin, was more than likely inside. Fantastic.

"Is that really necessary?" I asked, flicking my eyes to Tony and then back to the van behind us.

"Our informant says the rave is being organised by Tommy McGregor. He's serious business and his people will likely be tooled up."

"Oh, yay. So they're sending us in to get shot at?"

"You're in a delightful mood today. And no, the armed unit will go in first. We'll be outside to clean up after."

As though reiterating his words, the van overtook us. The name of the gangster running the rave kept ringing in my head until I remembered where I'd heard of him before. This was the same guy my dad had been trying to put away, the one he hadn't been able to pin down. Since Dad tended to work on the more hard-core cases, I was guessing this bloke really was serious business, like Tony said.

Rolling down my window and letting the cold night air waft into the car, I heard thumping music echoing in the distance. We were close. Tony followed the van and turned into a fairly dilapidated area. Lights flashed glaringly from the windows of the warehouse, and I recognised Swedish House Mafia blaring from the building so loudly it was almost deafening.

"Never mind the drugs and the underage drinking — this place looks like it's ready to collapse," I said.

"Bloody disaster waiting to happen," Tony agreed unhappily.

He had two teenage daughters, and these were the sorts of places he tried his best to keep them away from. A number of other police vehicles had already arrived, and I noticed a stream of people, all dressed in club clothes, running out a back exit of the building. The girls wore tiny dresses and skirts that barely covered their backsides, while the guys were decked out in jeans and muscle Ts. Some of them were even going topless, with luminous bands around their arms and necks.

"Hey, turn here and see if we can catch a few of them on their way out," I said, and Tony swung the car around sharply. They were like ants scattering in all directions. Catching sight of two girls, I noticed they were pulling along a third and seemed to be crying out for help. The girl they were helping looked completely out of it, her head lolling to one side and her hair hanging across her face. I hopped out before telling Tony to go park and that I'd catch up to him.

"What's wrong with your friend?" I asked in an authoritative voice as I ran up to the girls and shone a flashlight on them.

"She...she took something. I don't know what, but she passed out a few minutes ago," one of them answered, on the verge of tears. I felt a maternal sort of worry for them, because they couldn't have been any older than sixteen or seventeen.

"Both of you go stand over by the wall while I check her out," I ordered them.

"You're not going to call our parents, are you?"

"Your friend might need to be hospitalised, and you're worried about your parents finding out? You should be glad you're not in her boat."

They looked guilty and upset, but they did as I said. I knew they weren't a bad sort, just misguided. A lot of girls would have abandoned their friend and run for the hills. I took hold of her and checked her vital signs. She was in a bad way. Settling her against my hip, I then led the girls to the front of the building, where a bunch of people had been rounded up. The paramedics were already on the scene, and I handed the girl off to them.

"Her friends said she took something. More than likely it's those new pills that are going around," I told the medic before I was called away.

"Sheehan, see if you can get that music turned off. It's giving me a migraine," a sergeant ordered me, and I hurried inside the building to see if I could cut the electrics somehow. It was dark inside, and there were still a number of members of the armed unit running around. I hadn't heard any gunfire, which was a good sign. Maybe this would all be taken care of peacefully. I could understand the sergeant's annoyance with the music, because it was even worse inside, and combined with the dim lighting, was a little disorienting.

I saw some wiring running along the skirting boards and followed it up two floors, hoping it'd lead me to a power source. I was on the third floor when I sensed movement to my right. Turning, I saw three blokes, one of them heavyset, running down the stairs. They must have been on the top floor and were trying to get outside without bumping into any police.

"Stop right there," I shouted, but it was likely they couldn't hear me over the music. And even if they could hear me, I doubt they'd have stopped. I chased after them, my booted feet pounding down the stairs. The two slim guys were fast, but I managed to catch up with the bigger one. We collided, and in his struggle to get away, I had to pin him to the ground, making quick work of cuffing him as I recited his rights. He swore loudly, and one of the guys he'd been with stopped running and turned around.

Time moved in slow motion when I looked up and saw Lee Cross's blue eyes staring back at me.

Seven

A number of emotions hit me all at once, first shock, then disappointment, followed by the third, anger. I was pissed that he was there, because somewhere in the back of my mind I'd been holding out hope that maybe he wasn't a bad guy, that maybe he didn't consort with criminals. But hope was often futile, and mine certainly was.

This was a place for underage kids looking to party and criminals looking for a place to do business. Since Lee wasn't an underage kid, I had to assume he was the latter. My anger rapidly transformed into determination as I stood and walked toward him, leaving the big guy cuffed on the ground. I half expected Lee to turn and run, but he didn't. He stood in place. Perhaps he was just as shocked to see me there as I was to see him, or maybe he didn't think I'd actually arrest him. Well, he was dead wrong on that account.

Somebody must have found out how to cut the music, because it went off suddenly and a stark quiet fell.

"Turn around," I barked.

"Karla," Lee began, but I cut him off.

"I said, turn around."

He must have seen something in my eyes that told him I wasn't playing games, because his jaw firmed and he turned. I began searching him, my hands moving carefully down his body to check for drugs or weapons.

"You're under arrest. You have the right to remain silent. Anything you say or do can and will be used...."

"Snap, wait, will you listen to me for a second?"

I closed my eyes, took a deep breath, and shook my head.

"Stay quiet," I clipped out, and continued telling him his rights. He didn't have anything on him other than a wallet, a set of car keys, a packet of cigarettes, and a lighter. I pulled out my second pair of cuffs. When I looked down, I found that my hands were shaking, and I knew Lee must have felt it, too. A moment elapsed as I tried to gather some calm. My head was swimming, and the noodles I'd eaten earlier were gurgling around in my stomach, waiting for a chance to resurface.

Why did it have to be him? I could've handled arresting Lucifer himself, but not Lee.

For the second time in a matter of minutes, time stood still. I stared at his broad, muscular back and quietly gasped when he captured my shaking fingers in his. Everything slowed down, the air around me growing electric and tense. Lee's thumb slid soothingly down the centre of my palm, and I shivered.

"Relax," he whispered, and a string deep in my heart pulled tight. I swallowed, tried to steady my breathing, and abruptly shoved his fingers off mine. He made me feel so much, *too* much, and it was an intimidating task to assert my dominance over a man I desired. A man who was strong and virile, ever the alpha in any environment.

Finally, I snapped the cuffs closed and stepped away, my pulse pounding in my ears. Lee stood in place as I went and helped the other guy to stand, but I could feel his eyes on me the entire time. His friend must have been about two hundred and fifty pounds, so I was surprised he'd managed to run as fast as he did before I caught him.

As I led the two of them out of the building and lined them up next to the others who'd been arrested, I felt my throat grow dry with nerves. DI Jennings was there, barking orders at people, and for a second I had a nightmarish vision of Lee telling her he knew me, that I'd been to his house and that we'd kissed. None of these things were crimes, of course, but, knowing Jennings, she'd find some way to use it against me.

Nerves coiled tight in my belly.

Lee didn't breathe a word, though. No, he wore a blank expression, hands behind his back, a stoic figure as he stood at the end of the line. I was just about to go and find Tony when Jennings spotted me, lips pinching tightly in my presence.

"Don't move a muscle, Sheehan. I want you to help keep an eye on this group. Make sure none of them think to do a runner."

"They don't strike me as the type to sacrifice a thumb to get the cuffs off, Inspector," a familiar voice butted in. It was Gavin. This night just kept getting better and better. He held his gun at chest level, his dark hair cropped short to his skull.

"I just gave the constable an order, Matthews, so shut that hole you call a trap and do something productive," Jennings snapped at him, and I sort of wished we were friends for a second so I could high-five her. Unfortunately, we weren't, and a second later she was gone, off shouting orders to somebody else like the little Hitler that she was.

"Karla," said Gavin, giving me a quick sweep up and down. "How've you been?"

I was overwhelmingly aware of Lee standing mere feet away, closely watching the exchange. "I was great until I clapped eyes on you," I replied grumpily, and thought I saw the edges of Lee's lips curve in smirk.

"Bloody hell, you on the rag or something?" said Gavin, annoyed.

I narrowed my eyes to slits and shook my head. "Just piss off, yeah?"

A couple members of his unit showed up then, alongside a few constables, including Steve. Christ, what was this, the flipping wankers' convention or something?

A woman who'd been arrested and who was wearing an indecently short sequined dress shivered, holding her arms around herself.

"Would you look at this," one of the armed police said, eyeing the woman lasciviously. "Didn't think to bring a coat, did ya, darlin'?"

She scowled at him and he laughed, as did the others. I made eye contact with Lee for a second, and yeah, he was still watching me. His stare was intense. I would have killed to know what he was thinking. His attention flicked to the men, and there was such loathing in his expression that it caught me off guard. He really didn't like them, not at all. I guess it surprised me because they were cops, but so was I, yet he'd never acted like he hated me. Not once.

"If she brought a coat, she wouldn't be able to show off those legs, now, would she?" somebody else butted in. Surprise, surprise, it was Steve.

"Or those tits. What are you, love, a D-cup?" said another. The woman looked like she was mentally decapitating each and every one of them, and I couldn't blame her.

"Oi, you lot," I called out. "Put your dicks away and go do your jobs."

"Aw, don't be jealous, Karla," said Gavin. "You know I'll give you a good seeing-to if you ask nicely."

The men laughed, and out of the corner of my eye I saw Lee bristle, his shoulders tensing and his mouth drawing into a tight line.

"Pity I never had a taste for cocktail sausages," I threw back, and Gavin's smile fell instantly, while his buddies let out "ooohs" of amusement. If I wasn't mistaken, Lee's chest shook with restrained laughter, and it felt good to get one over on my ex.

Noticing the woman shiver once more, I turned and went over to the ambulance, nabbing a spare blanket for her. When I returned, I draped it around her shoulders, and she shot me a look of thanks.

"If they start in on you again, you let me know, okay?" I said, eyeing her meaningfully. Just because she was at this party didn't mean she deserved to be berated like that. I sensed Lee watching the exchange, and glanced at him just in time to see Steve recognise who he was. An evil grin graced my coworker's mouth as he nudged the guy beside him before slinking to the end of the line. I was too far away to hear what they said to him, but Lee looked about ready to blow a gasket.

A moment later DI Jennings was back, instructing us to lead those under arrest to police vehicles, where they were to be transported to back to the station. More than likely, most of them had a night in the cells to look forward to. They'd all been searched, so it was just a matter of paperwork now.

I found myself at the end of the line, right behind Lee. Steve and his friend had cleared off, but for some reason my protective instincts were kicking in. I wanted to stick by Lee to make sure Steve couldn't get another ego trip out of him.

When we cleared the side of the building, I was vaguely aware of a small gap between two outer walls. Everything happened in rapid succession after that. One minute Lee was walking along in front of me, hands cuffed behind his back, and the next he was turning, using his broad shoulder to back me in between the walls. Since we were at the end of the line, nobody else was there to see what he'd done.

I struggled to get by him, but he leaned his entire weight on me, pinning me to the bricks. His scent invaded my senses and my whole body trembled.

"You have two seconds to let me go or I'm going to start screaming," I threatened him, my heart rate picking up.

"Don't shout. Just listen to me. You have to uncuff me, Karla," Lee said, his voice soft and pleading. There was a desperation in his eyes.

"Why the hell would I do that? Do you know how much trouble I could find myself in?"

Lee's breath hit my cheeks as he looked at the ground, his posture slumping. "I know. And I'm sorry for asking, but I can't spend a night in the bin. *Believe me.*" His blue eyes flickered between mine, pleading with me to do it. I stared back at him, quite literally stuck between a rock and a hard place. Yes, he'd been at the rave. Yes, he was likely involved in some shady dealings. But he hadn't had anything on him. Letting him go wouldn't be the worst thing in the world, would it?

Swallowing, I asked, "What were you doing here tonight? Because seriously, Lee, from where I'm standing, it doesn't look good."

He nodded, some relief shaping his features. "Yes, I know. It looks shitty, and it is shitty. I know this place has no licence, and I know alcohol and drugs were being sold to underage kids, but I was here for my friend. You remember when we spoke on the phone? I told you I was going to my mate's birthday party. That's why I was here. His party was inside."

"In that case, you might want to be a bit pickier when choosing your friends in future. But why is it so important that I let you go? This is hardly a first for you."

Lee swore under his breath and levelled me with a serious look. "The black eye your boy Steve had? I lied. It was me who gave it to him. I don't have time to explain right now, but the fucker had it coming. And believe me, if you don't let me go, sometime tonight that prick is going to round up his buddies and come find me. Let's just say, I'll be lucky if I'm not in a hospital bed come the morning."

As I listened to him speak, it all sank into place. Since Steve was dirty, I well believed he'd put a beating on Lee once he had him locked up. It was difficult to think straight, but in that moment, I knew what I had to do. I had to let Lee go.

"Okay," I said breathlessly. "Okay, turn around."

"Thank you," Lee whispered gratefully, letting his mouth drop to my forehead as he placed a soft kiss on my temple. The contact made me shiver. Unfortunately, just as I was about to pull out the keys to his cuffs, I heard Jennings' voice shouting loudly, "Where's Constable Sheehan? She was here only a moment ago."

"Shit," I cursed, and swiftly twirled Lee back around, grabbing his arm and pushing him forward.

Jennings was just rounding the corner when we stepped out.

"Sorry, ma'am, this one almost got away from me," I said breathlessly, while internally I was freaking out. How on earth was I going to get Lee out of spending the night at the station now?

"See that it doesn't happen again," she snapped before walking with us back to the patrol cars. Lee was silent as I opened the door, placed my hand on top of his head and gently guided him inside. Tony, who was sitting in the driver's seat, studied Lee through his overhead mirror, his brow furrowing. I walked around and got in the passenger seat, and then we were off.

"Isn't that the bloke whose house we visited a few weeks back?" he asked me curiously.

"Yep," I replied, a brick sinking in my gut.

"Huh."

"You know, I'm right here. You don't have to talk about me like I'm in another room," Lee put in, the comment reflective of his usual cheeky personality. It was the tightness around his eyes that told me he wasn't as relaxed as he was letting on.

"Shut it," said Tony, eyeing Lee again with a stern expression.

Lee slumped back in his seat, and silence filled the car. All the way back to the station, I was tense and frazzled, especially since Lee wouldn't take his eyes off me the whole time. They asked a question: *Are you going to help me out of this?*

The problem was, now that Tony had recognised him, there was no letting him go. If Lee just so happened to disappear, Tony would come looking in my direction for answers. Since I was on shift for the rest of the night, I determined to keep an eye on Lee and make sure Steve didn't get him alone.

A couple of minutes later we reached the station, but it was almost three hours before we'd finishing booking everyone. Lee was taken to the cells with a number of other young men, and just as he was being escorted off, I shot him a look of apology. There was really nothing I could do for him, not here at the station where there so many watchful eyes.

I was back on the front desk again when I saw a call come in about a home invasion, so I asked Steve to go check it out. He didn't look too happy to be sent away, but he didn't seem suspicious, either. He had no idea that I knew Lee in any capacity other than an official one. Once he was gone, I felt like I could relax, and lost myself in paperwork. By the time my shift came to an end, I was ready to spend the day in bed.

However, as I was making my way outside, rummaging in my bag for my car keys, I spotted Lee and Stu leaving through the opposite door. Stu must have come to collect him, and other than appearing a little tired, Lee didn't seem any different than usual. Steve hadn't gotten to him, thank God.

"Hey," I said, a small bit awkward. "Everything okay?"

Stu wore a hostile expression while Lee glanced at me and replied shortly, "Fine and dandy."

It was only when he spoke that I heard the strain in his voice, which alerted me to the fact he was walking more stiffly than usual. He stood up straight but held his hand to his stomach as though he was in pain. They were both walking away when I hurried to catch up with them.

"Lee, hold on. Are you sure you're all right?"

He turned slowly and stared me down, a moment passing between us as my gaze flickered over his face. There were no visible signs that he'd been hurt, but that didn't mean he hadn't.

"We need to get going, bruv," said Stu, hands braced on the roof of his car.

"Are you driving home?" Lee asked, and I nodded.

"Follow us, then, and I'll buy you breakfast."

With that he turned and carefully lowered his body into the car. I stood there for a second while Stu's car hovered just outside the station, as though waiting for me to get a move on. Sucking down a deep breath, I hurried to follow them, and a couple of minutes later we were parking along the street outside a small, rundown café.

Stu went in ahead of Lee, who waited for me to catch up. Despite the fact that he was clearly in pain, he held the door open for me. I stepped by him, murmuring, "You don't need to do that."

He only stared at me, and we walked to where a waitress was seating Stu at a table by the window. I was momentarily grateful for the fact that I'd changed out of my uniform and into civilian clothes before leaving the station, because if anyone here knew the Cross brothers, I was sure they'd find it odd to see them eating breakfast with a cop.

The brothers chatted while I sat next to Lee, quiet. I didn't know how to bring up the questions I wanted to ask him, mainly because of how guilty I felt. Not only had I arrested him, but because of that he'd taken a beating. Unease twisted in my stomach. The waitress returned and took our orders. I asked for coffee and a croissant, while Lee and Stu ordered two full English breakfasts. Silence fell over the table as the brothers eyed me and I grew uncomfortable.

Unable to think of anything to say, I suddenly remembered Tony's brain teaser from the night before. "Hey, are either of you good with puzzles? There's this one I've been trying to figure out. It goes like this: If it were two hours long, it'd be half as long until midnight as it would be if it were an hour later. What time is it now?"

I thought I saw Lee's lips form something close to a smile at my rambling. Then, without missing a beat, Stu answered, "Nine p.m."

I frowned and looked at him. "Oh, have you heard that one before?"

He shook his head. "Nope."

"Then how did you come up with your answer?"

"Sixty minutes in an hour. X = 60. Midnight minus 180 minutes = 9 p.m."

I stared at him wide-eyed, trying to figure out his equation and coming up empty. When I glanced at Lee, he was grinning. Stu got up from the table.

"I'm going to take a slash."

I sat back, folding my arms. "Well, that was unexpected."

"Stu's got dyslexia, but numbers are his thing. I have him do all the accounts at the garage."

"Seriously? Imagine what he could do if he hadn't left school so early."

"Yup."

I was still contemplating Stu's unforeseen show of intelligence when Lee began coughing fitfully. He winced as he held onto his stomach.

"Tell me what happened," I said quietly, moving closer and touching him softly on the arm.

"Prick got to me around four this morning and brought two of his pals. Did a number on my ribs."

I gasped and found myself scrambling for the hem of his T-shirt, pulling it up and finding two large, dark bruises along one side of his ribcage. "Lee! You need to go to the hospital."

I was touching him then, frantically running my fingers along his injuries. He let out a gruff breath as he closed his eyes.

"Not that I don't enjoy you fussing over me, but I've had broken ribs before, and these aren't broken. It looks worse than it feels."

"It doesn't look like it feels very good."

"I'll heal."

I couldn't have been frowning any harder if I tried. "He can't get away with this. As soon as I clock in for work tomorrow, I'm going to my sergeant and filing a report."

Lee turned his body, and my hands fell from his bruised ribs. "Karla," he murmured. "No." There was a finality to the word that brooked no argument. I argued anyway.

"I'm doing this, Lee. Steve Burrows is a disgrace to the uniform he wears, and he won't be wearing it much longer if I have my way." Christ, I might even go to my dad about it.

"It was payback," said Lee. "And, like the saying goes, she's a bitch. I've had far worse beatings in my time. I'm not having you involved in this. Burrows will get his, never doubt that." His hand slid along my shoulder before grasping my neck. I closed my eyes for a second, savouring his touch before I shifted away.

"So, why did you give him the black eye?"

"Huh?"

"Last night you told me you lied, that it was you who hit him but you had a reason. What was the reason?"

Lee huffed out a breath. "He came around again looking for money. I sent him on his way, just like I said I would."

I didn't like that, didn't like how seemingly easily violence came to him.

"You hit David, too, to warn him away from Sophie. How long do you think using your fists as a solution is going to last, Lee?"

"If someone hurts my family, I hurt them back. If somebody threatens me with blackmail, I hurt them, too." Lee shrugged. "I'm not saying I like it, but if you live in a war zone, you don't survive with peace and love."

"And what about when you get hurt? You're hurt now, and you don't seem to care."

"Every method has its flaws."

I stared at him sadly, thinking of the life he'd lived and how it had hardened him. Stu returned to the table then, and a second later the waitress was there with our food. I took my time stirring sugar into my coffee while the brothers dug into their breakfasts.

"These eggs are bullshit," said Lee. "Have they ever heard of seasoning?"

I couldn't help but smile, for a moment forgetting my worries. It was sort of cute how much of a foodie he was.

"It's a greasy spoon," said Stu, mouth full of bacon. "What do you want?" It sounded more like "whaddayawant."

"Some cracked black pepper wouldn't go amiss. Maybe a pinch of sea salt," Lee replied, goading his brother on.

Stu shook his head and continued shovelling down bacon as he flipped Lee off. I wasn't too sure if Stu liked me much, but in a strange way I enjoyed watching the two of them interact as siblings. Feeling my phone buzz in my pocket, I pulled it out and found a text message from Tony, informing me that the girl I'd handed off to the paramedics last night had to have her stomach pumped, but she was doing well now. Her parents had been called to the hospital.

I shot off a quick message thanking him for letting me know and glanced up to find Lee watching me. He raised an eyebrow.

"Everything okay?"

"Yeah," I answered, brow furrowing. "Uh, do you mind if I ask a question you might not like to answer?"

"Hit me."

I cleared my throat. "Well, there's this new ecstasy drug all the kids are taking. I helped a girl last night who'd been in a really bad way. You wouldn't happen to know who's distributing it, would you?"

Stu whistled low, shaking his head. "You have some balls asking that, Karla."

Lee shot him a silencing look and turned back to me. "Sorry, but I can't help you there."

I knew instantly that he was lying. "So what you really mean is, you know but you're not going to tell me."

"I'm not your PI, and I'll never be a snitch. So, like I said, I can't help you."

I narrowed my gaze at him. "Are *you* involved?"

Stu slammed down his coffee cup. "Fuck me, Constable. You need to stop asking questions."

Lee seemed offended. "I told you how Mum died. She was a heroin junkie nearly all her life. Liam was born addicted, and it's a miracle he survived." He paused to look me dead in the eye. "I'll never be involved in the drugs trade. Never. There's your answer."

I went quiet then, feeling guilty for assuming things about him. Unfortunately, being suspicious and asking lots of questions was second nature to me in my line of work. I finished the rest of my croissant in silence. At some point Stu's phone rang, and he went outside to take the call.

"So," said Lee once we were alone. "Now it's my turn to ask some questions. What's the story between you and the mouthy fuck with the gun?"

He was asking about Gavin. I should have expected it. "Not much of a story. We used to go out. He cheated on me, so I dumped him. End of."

"Has he been trying to get back with you?"

I laughed. "No, and even if he was, it'd be a wasted effort. People get one chance with me."

Lee smiled. "Bit of an ice queen, are we?"

"Not really. I just know that past behaviour is typically an indicator of future behaviour. Dr Phil taught me that."

"You and Phil are tight, huh?" Lee joked. "I knew you were a cool broad."

I narrowed my gaze at him, making an effort not to smile and failing. "Make a note — women don't generally like being referred to as 'broads,' cool or otherwise."

He shifted his body closer, and I noticed his slight wince, reminding me he was still in pain. "Oh, they don't?"

His face was only inches away from mine, and I couldn't help staring at his mouth. He had really nice lips; they weren't too full, but they had a good masculine shape. He also had a strong jaw, and his skin was flawless even though he clearly hadn't gotten a wink of sleep.

I let out a small yawn, and somehow Lee managed to move even closer. "Tired?"

I nodded. "You must be, too."

"I'm exhausted. You should come back to mine and sleep with me."

Inhaling sharply at his words and what they inferred, I shot him a wry expression. "Nice try."

"I'm being serious, and I do mean *sleep*."

I just laughed. He was such a chancer.

"Come on, Snap, don't leave me sitting here feeling all rejected."

Shaking my head, I asked quietly, "Lee, why do you like me?" The question had seriously been niggling at me ever since last night. There was clearly no love lost between Lee and law enforcement. In fact, judging by the deathly stares he'd been giving Steve and company, I'd even go so far as to say he hated cops. Therefore, I was genuinely puzzled as to why he was so keen on me.

He reached forward and took a strand of my hair between his fingers. His eyes stayed fixed on it as he answered, "Honestly, I'm still trying to figure that one out."

What he said intrigued me. "What do you mean?"

He let out a breath and continued to toy with my hair. "When we first met, Alexis told me you were old bill, and, like a greedy little fuck, I wanted what I couldn't have. Now, Jesus, Karla, I don't even know. I just...I see you do things, and it kind of obsesses me. Like how you stuck up for that woman last night, or how you want to help me with Steve even though I can take care of myself. I understand it, and at the same time I don't. Because I help people like you help people, but only if they're family, only if they mean something. I don't know why you'd do it for a stranger, someone who'd never do the same for you. When I stand up for my brothers, it's to protect them and me, but when you stand up for any random person on the street, you're putting yourself at risk with no payback. So I guess when I look at you, I see a little piece of myself, but braver. That's why I like you."

His answer surprised me the hell out of me, and I felt the need to help him understand my motivations. "It's not so hard to comprehend when you think about it. Have you ever read the newspaper and seen some horrible story about a kid who's been hurt or killed? Or about innocent people being victimised, and just feel so angry you could burst?"

Lee studied me. "Yeah, once or twice."

"Well, that's how I feel all the time. Maybe there's something wrong with me, but ever since I was a kid, I always worried about people being hurt in the world. It was probably because of my dad's job and being aware of all the awful things that happen. So I don't really see it like I'm putting myself out there and getting nothing in return. I see it like I'm fighting against all the bad people, all the killers and rapists and paedophiles. They're just one big giant wall of badness that I want to disassemble piece by piece. Knowing I do that every day lets me sleep soundly at night."

Our gazes locked, the both of us silent as we shared a bizarre moment of understanding in a rundown East End café. After what I'd said, he was looking at me like I was the sexiest woman alive, and I wasn't sure I understood his reaction. Maybe my hero complex was a turn-on.

"You're kind of incredible," Lee whispered, his breath on my ear as he bent his head to speak. "You should come back to mine. We'll go to bed. I'll even let you keep your clothes on. I'll hold you tight, and we'll fall asleep." He stopped a moment to see if he was convincing me, before continuing in a lower voice. It hit me right in the pit of my stomach. "Then we'll wake up a little while later. You'll be wet, I'll be hard. I'll peel off your clothes and slip into you so easily, like I was always supposed to be there. Afterward I'll cook, and we'll eat dinner in bed. By the time you're full, you'll want me in you again."

I was barely breathing once he finished talking, and my thighs were clenched so tight I was in danger of pulling a muscle. I wanted what he had described so badly it was almost a physical pain to say no.

"I can't go back with you, Lee," I whispered. "I'm sorry."

He frowned at my reply, and I realised his hand had moved as he spoke and was now gripping my upper thigh. I shifted away from his touch just as Stu returned from his phone call, glancing between the two of us.

"All done?"

"Yeah," said Lee, wiping his hands on a napkin. "We're done. You can go wait in the car."

Stu nodded and went back out the door. Lee nudged me with his hip, needing me to stand so he could get out. I rose and so did he, brushing past me as he walked up to the counter, pulling his wallet from his back pocket. When he was done paying, I moved to his side, catching him by the elbow and looking up at him.

"If I wasn't me and you weren't you, I'd go home with you in heartbeat. You know that, right?" I told him quietly.

For a second he glanced away, then bent his head to reply, his voice husky, "It's because you're you and I'm me that we want each other, Karla. And I wouldn't have it any other way." Before I could stop him his mouth dipped to mine, and he laid a soft, lingering kiss on my lips. His tongue slipped inside for just a moment, like a promise. Without another word he turned to walk away, and I stood there, my heart trying to beat its way right out of my chest.

"Thanks for breakfast," I whispered, but he was already gone.

Eight

Two days passed. Forty-eight hours, and about ninety percent of those I spent with Lee on my mind. I was worried about him, especially after seeing the state Steve had left him in. I wanted to know how he was doing, but I was wary of texting, afraid it might give him the wrong impression...or the right one. Anyhow, I was single-mindedly determined to deny myself what I wanted. I was a grown woman, and I could resist my desire to sleep with someone I knew was no good for me.

Right?

It was six o'clock, and I'd just gotten home from a shift when my resistance gave way. My need to touch base with him was almost physical in its urgency, so, pulling my phone from my pocket, I tapped out a quick message.

Karla: How are you feeling?

I'd popped a ready meal in the oven for dinner when my phone pinged with a response.

Lee: Like crap...you should come over and kiss me all better ;-)

I scoffed at his reply.

Karla: You never stop.

Lee: Not with you.

Barely a second went by before he sent another message, and laughter bubbled out of me. In truth, I nearly snorted.

Lee: I want your big hard truncheon, Constable, all sleek and girthy.

Karla: We don't carry truncheons any more. They're called batons.

Lee: You're so good at sexting. I think I just came.

I really did snort then. He could be such a sarcastic little shit at times.

Karla: Can you be serious for a second? I want to know if you're okay. Did you go see a doctor?

Lee: No doctor. Liam fixed me up. Kid's got some mad skills with a medi-kit.

Karla: So you're feeling better, then?

Lee: If I say yes, does that mean you're not coming over?

Karla: I was never coming over.

Lee: Remember our bet? I still owe you dinner.

Karla: As tempting as that sounds, I don't think it's wise.

Lee: How you wound me.

And that was how things progressed between us for the next two weeks. No phone calls, no in person meet-ups, just text messages at random, any time of the day or night. It felt safe, comfortable. If I couldn't have him in real life, then at least I could have his texts.

Lee: What you up to, Snap?

Karla: Just getting ready for work. I'm on nights again. FML. You?

Lee: Watching Anthony Worrall-Thompson bake lemon cakes and trying to figure out the recipe.

Karla: I'm sorry. I didn't realise I was texting my grandmother.

Lee: Hahaha! We both know you want my lemon cakes.

Karla: Is that your trick? You lure women into bed with baked goods?

Lee: Pretty much. My milkshakes bring all the girls to the yard, too.

Karla: I'm just glad you didn't say boys.

Lee: Hey, if I wanted the boys I could get the boys.

I laughed.

Karla: Shut up.

Lee: Don't be jealous. If you wanted the girls, I bet you could get the girls.

Karla: I don't want the girls.

Lee: Too bad. There's got to be some serious amount of licence lickers in your line of work.

Karla: That's a stereotype.

Lee: What about the sour-faced old bird who was at the warehouse the other week? Now there's a high wall built to hold back water if I ever saw one.

Oh, my God, was he talking about DI Jennings? It took me a second to get what he was saying and then I burst out laughing, both at his wording and how he described her. She *was* sour-faced, always looking like she'd just tasted something rotten.

Karla: She's my superior, and I have no clue about her sexual orientation. I've got to go to work now. Talk later.

Lee: Later, Snap.

The next day I got a message with a picture attached. It showed Lee making a kissy duck face into the camera, the gym in the background. I chuckled when I saw it before reading the text below.

Lee: Workin on my selfie skills. What ya think?

Karla: I think it's disturbing.

Lee: Whaaa? Where am I going wrong?

Karla: Try to look less like an aquatic bird.

Lee: Okay, how's this?

He'd attached another picture, this time with him grin/smirking, his T-shirt plastered to him with sweat. God, he looked good, and had obviously been working out. Without thinking, I saved the picture to my phone, trying not to delve too deeply into why.

Karla: Better.
Lee: Your turn :-D
Karla: Fat chance.
Lee: Oh, go on. I miss your face.

I paused, my finger on the screen as his words sunk in. My tummy fizzled with a bubbly sensation. In a way, I'd have liked to send him a picture in return, but it was dodgy territory. Texting him at all was dodgy territory, but I needed it. It was the least form of communication we could have, and I wasn't ready to give it up yet. Unable to deal with his sweet statement, I tried to change the subject.

Karla: Why are you texting me at the gym? Get back to working out, lazy bones.
Lee: Just finished sparring with a few of the boys. Not the same as doing it with you, of course ;-)

I ignored the innuendo, even though it made me flush slightly.

Karla: You know, I never asked. Do you box professionally?
Lee: Nah, just to keep fit. I'm a lover not a fighter.
Karla: Haha. Do you do any other sports?

I asked because I wanted him to tell me about the parkour. Having seen him in action, I could tell he'd clearly spent a lot of time honing his technique, but he never mentioned it in conversation. It was almost like he didn't want people to know how good he was.

Lee: This and that. Gotta go shower now. Talk later.

Huh. I couldn't tell if he was being evasive or if he really just had to shower. Either way, I obviously wasn't going to get what I wanted.

Karla: Okay. Talk later.

***

"Me, Ingrid, and Gina are going out tonight," said Reya as we left the gym on a Saturday afternoon. "You should come. Let your hair down."

Ingrid and Gina were her friends from the Royal Academy of Music, where Reya was doing her degree. I mostly tended to spend time with her away from her usual social circle, because they were all a little too young for me. Reya was different. We connected on a level that transcended age, but her friends? They spent a lot of time talking about celebrities or the latest Facebook scandal, and I didn't have the patience for that shite.

"I don't know. I was planning on a marathon of *Heroes* with Alexis."

"You can do that anytime! And Alexis should come, too. It'll be fun."

I knew for a fact that my best friend wouldn't want to go out. One, because she was still mourning after King, and two, because she was pregnant and couldn't drink. Every time I tried to have a glass of wine around her, she'd put on this sad puppy face, making me feel guilty that she couldn't enjoy one, too.

"Okay, let me think about it," I said, and Reya threw her arm around my shoulders, smiling widely. She knew she'd won.

Later that evening, I changed into a black bodycon dress and heels. I left my hair down with a slight curl, and I'd gone a little heavier on the makeup than usual. If I knew Reya and her friends, I was betting I'd get dragged to either a hipster music bar or a rock club, and I wanted to look the part.

We were having some crazy weather of late, heavy rain and random thunderstorms, which meant the electricity kept cutting out. I'd been halfway through styling my hair when the flat went dark and I heard Alexis swear loudly from her bedroom.

"Bloody hell! Now I'm going to miss the end of *Coronation Street,*" she moaned, and I tried not to laugh.

"You can catch the repeat when they show the Omnibus," I called to her.

"This *was* the Omnibus!" she shouted back. "Now I'll never know what happens."

A second later, the lights came back on and Alexis let out a hoot of triumph. I shook my head and finished doing my hair. Once I was ready, I called a cab so I could go meet Reya & Co. I was sitting in the back seat when my phone lit up with a message.

Lee: Could you see the lightning at your place?
Karla: No, I missed it :-(
Lee: It was HUGE.
I chuckled.
Karla: Oh, really? Tell me more.
Lee: Dirty girl.
Karla: Can't talk now. I'm on my way out.
Lee: Anywhere fancy?
Karla: Just meeting a friend at a club called The Evil Beetle. Don't ask.
Lee: I know the place. Didn't take you for a Goth.
Karla: It wasn't my choice. My friend's a music student. Pretentious muso clubs come with the territory.
Lee: Ah, got ya. Have a fun night. Xxx.

Karla: You too :-)

I stared at his last message, frowning. After two weeks of correspondence, this was the first time he'd sent me kisses. They made my throat feel weird and scratchy, and the fact of the matter was, I missed him. I wanted to see him in person, because although I enjoyed talking to him through texts, it was no substitute for how he made me feel in person. How his eyes followed my every movement and how his closeness gave me tingles.

Thankfully, I didn't have too much time to ponder this further, as the taxi stopped outside the club. I paid the driver, got out, and walked down the line, searching for Reya. I found her about midway down, wearing a purple hippy dress under a long navy coat. Her friend Ingrid was blonde and wore *a lot* of eye-liner, while her other friend, Gina, had a pixie haircut and wore a number of studded belts around the waist of her skinny jeans. I felt slightly overdressed, but I wasn't too bothered about it.

The four of us made small talk until we reached the door and were immediately let through by the bouncer. Heavy rock music blared as a DJ with blue dreads spun the decks. I went straight to the bar, ordering in a round of drinks for everyone. I wasn't exactly flash with the cash, but since I was with three starving students, I decided to be generous.

Not surprisingly, Gina and Ingrid nodded eagerly when I asked them if they wanted a drink. We found a table in a dark corner where it was just about impossible to carry out a conversation, but we gave it a go anyway. At this rate, I was going to have tinnitus by morning.

An hour or so went by, during which I'd had three more drinks. We were currently on the dance floor, dancing to Guns n Roses' "Night Train." Reya grabbed my hands and swayed with me to the music, while her friends screamed the lyrics, knowing every word. It was as my eyes travelled over the sea of heads surrounding me that I thought I recognised a familiar one. The guy disappeared, and I shook it off.

Lee wouldn't come here, would he?

There was a brief second of quiet between one song and the next when I felt my phone buzz in my pocket.

Lee: You're a good dancer.

I gasped as I read it, swiftly typing a response.

Karla: Where are you?

My heart pounded, and my skin grew clammy with nerves as I contemplated the idea that he was here. There was something about the fact that we'd been communicating but hadn't actually seen each other for weeks that heightened my anticipation. I felt surrounded, too hot, and my fingers shook as I waited for him to reply. The screen of my phone remained dark, and I felt Reya nudge me. Glancing up, I saw her frowning as she sent me a look that asked, *What's wrong?*

Shaking my head to let her know I was fine, I slid my phone back in my pocket and tried to focus on dancing again. It was no use, though, and I found myself frantically scanning the club. After a minute I spotted him over by the bar. He was with some other guy, knocking back shots. The guy turned, and I recognised Trevor, the second-youngest Cross brother. His pretty blue eyes flashed in the darkness as he smiled at something Lee said, showing off a pair of handsome dimples.

I guessed Trevor to be about two years younger than Lee, which put him at around twenty-three. He had a very laid-back, sort of skater-boy style, and every girl who passed him by gave him a second glance. Lee had the same good looks, but despite the grin that was perennially plastered across his face, there was something harder about him, something a little bit more intimidating and unapproachable.

Almost as though he sensed me watching him, his eyes flashed to mine and held me captive. I shot him a look of irritation and pulled out my phone.

Karla: I hope you didn't come here for me.

From across the club, I saw him looking down at his screen, reading my text before his fingers began tapping. A second later he glanced in my direction and grinned. My phone lit up in my hand.

Lee: I have no idea what you're talking about.

Ugh, he was such a smart-arse. My attention was drawn away from my phone when Reya nudged me again. Cupping her hands around her mouth, she shouted in my ear, "I just saw the guy from our gym. Did you invite him here?"

I shook my head in response.

"Who's that with him?"

"His brother," I answered, adopting her hands-around-the-mouth approach. I wasn't sure why people did that when trying to be heard over music, because it didn't seem to make much of a difference.

We continued dancing, but now I was noticing Reya's eyes return to Trevor, clearly checking him out. I wasn't surprised. He was too pretty not to look at. Lee's back was turned from the bar, his elbows resting along the counter as he drank a bottle of beer. My hips swayed to the music and he took a swig, wiping his mouth with the back of his hand.

The music changed from rock to a more techno song. There was something about the rhythmic beat, combined with Lee's attention, that got my blood pumping. Crazy lust built within me, and I had to turn away before I did something stupid. My pores tingled with barely restrained energy, and I was suddenly aware of how tight my dress was, how it moulded itself to my form.

Losing myself in the music, I danced. Strobe lights flashed, stark white, red, and blue, causing my vision to blur and the movement of the people around me to seem choppy and staccato. Reya and the girls had caught the attention of a group of guys, but I stayed just outside their circle, trying my hardest to forget Lee's presence.

He shouldn't have been there.

This was going to end in disaster.

We lived in two different worlds.

And yet....

No. This couldn't happen. We weren't supposed to see each other. It was supposed to be only texts, nothing as close as this. The fact that I wasn't in uniform added an extra tension. I was well aware that I wore my profession like a shield with him, something to keep his advances at bay. But the fact of the matter was, it scared me how much I wanted him, how needy he made me feel. With just one touch, he could lure me into jeopardising years of hard work and dedication.

I heard a shout above the music right before it cut off and the club went dark. My heart pounded. The weather must have been picking up again, resulting in another power outage. I wondered if there was a generator and how long it'd take to kick in. Now that I was unable to see a thing, the voices that surrounded me were almost louder than the music had been. People were either complaining about the blackout or yelling like maniacs, excited by the fact that we'd been plunged into darkness.

Within seconds everybody had their phones out, using the dim light from the screens to find their way. I looked around for Reya, but it was still too dark to see. All of a sudden my skin prickled with awareness, like my body sensed him. Strong arms slid around my middle and pulled me into an even stronger body. He didn't have to say a word for me to know it was him, because I'd memorised his touch, his smell. His mouth went to my exposed neck, licking just below my earlobe.

"Snap," Lee whispered.

I shivered at the sound of his voice. There was something about the darkness, about the fact that no one could see us that made me feel reckless. I turned in his hold, threw my arms around his neck, and rose up on my toes. Tentatively, I drew his lower lip into my mouth and he pulled me close, capturing my lips with his fiercely. His hands travelled from my waist, all the way up my spine, before sinking into my hair. When his tongue dipped inside and fluttered along mine, I moaned, the sound of it reverberating up my throat.

Lee pulled my body so tightly to his that I could feel the sharp outline of his erection in his jeans. It nudged into my stomach, filling me with a deep, all-consuming lust.

Right in that moment, I wanted him, and I didn't want to think about the repercussions. There, in the dark of the blacked-out nightclub, we waged a war with our tongues and lips. It was almost like I was fighting him with how hard I kissed him. He drew away, breathless, and pressed his mouth to my forehead as he laced his fingers with mine.

"Come with me," he purred, tugging on my hand.

Helpless to do anything else, I followed.

I wasn't sure where Lee was taking me, but before long we'd left the main area of the club and entered someplace quieter. Lee had his phone out, holding it up with the screen illuminated to try to light the way. I had a vague idea of being in a hallway before Lee pulled a door open, swiftly dragging me inside. The door closed with a quiet *snick,* and then he was on me, backing me into a wall as his hands sank into my hair again, his crotch pushing against me with need.

"I want you."

My breath caught at the roughness in his voice.

His fingers trailed down my body and found the hem of my dress, frantically pushing it up so he could gain more access. Effortlessly, he lifted and held me, my legs wrapping around his waist. His mouth was everywhere, tasting every inch of me, from my chin to my jawline to my neck.

"You smell amazing," he growled as his hands gripped my thigh muscles. "And fuck, you're fit."

"Touch me," I begged him, my underwear exposed now that my dress had been pulled up around my hips. All that separated us was two layers of fabric, his hard cock in his jeans creating a delicious source of friction. I fumbled for his belt as he held me, attacking my lips with the most mind-melting kiss I'd ever experienced.

"What do you want, beautiful?" Lee asked in a husky whisper as I pulled his belt buckle free, unsnapped his jeans, and slid my hand inside. His entire body shuddered when my palm met his cock, and I savoured the hot, silky feel of it against my skin. I moved slowly up and down, pleasantly surprised by his size.

"I want this," I said, nipping at his lips with my teeth and squeezing him in my palm.

"You're killing me," he growled into my mouth, turning us and carrying me across the space. A second later my bottom hit a hard surface, and Lee's hand slipped beneath my underwear. He hissed out a breath when his fingers found me wet and I trembled against him. No one had ever touched me like Lee touched me, like he wanted to consume me. The combination of skill, passion, and need drove me crazy, and when he plunged two fingers inside, I almost lost my mind.

My mouth fell to his shoulder, biting down hard to keep from making too much noise. This was a packed-out nightclub, and though I had no clue what room we were in, I knew somebody could come in at any moment.

"That's it, baby, hurt me if you need to," Lee breathed, his voice gruff, moving his fingers in and out as I grasped his cock. His tongue plunged inside my mouth, and I wasn't sure how much time had passed. It could have been a minute. It could have been an hour. All I knew was that I didn't want this to end, didn't want him to ever stop kissing me.

Finding my clit with his thumb, he began rubbing slow circles, and I felt my abdomen draw tight. The need to come made my vision blur with lights and stars that weren't there.

"God, I missed you," Lee whispered. "I missed your voice."

There was something about how he said it, like he truly meant it, that made my heart clench. I couldn't deny it any longer — I had feelings for him, and those feelings both terrified and excited me.

"Please," I begged, my voice a breathy whisper. I needed him right then, needed him to fill every inch of me and own me like his eyes always promised he would.

Lee swore profusely as his fingers left me to pull my underwear off. He bent down to run his mouth along my inner thigh, the bit of scruff on his jaw creating a pleasurable scrape. Rising, he fumbled in his pocket, pulling out a condom as I shoved down his jeans, unable to wait any longer.

His tongue slid along the shell of my ear when he leaned in close, his voice low and gravelly. "Do you want it *hard*, Constable? Or *slow*?"

His emphasis on the words made me melt, my entire my body trembling at his question. For a second, I was too embarrassed to answer.

"Please," I moaned again, my hands slipping under his shirt to feel his hard abs beneath. They trailed down his stomach, and I savoured the way his muscles jumped at my touch.

"Tell me," he insisted, teeth nipping at my earlobe. Tingles skittered from the skin below my ear and all down my spine.

I looked at him then, blue eyes meeting blue eyes in the dark, and an understanding passed between us. Lee let out a low, pleased growl as his mouth found my lips again. "Okay, Snap. I'll give it to you hard."

As he tore open the condom packet, the sounds of our laboured breathing filled the small room. A second later, he positioned his cock against me, his hips rocking gently back and forth. I felt like I'd die if he didn't slip inside me soon.

As I let out a frustrated moan, Lee leaned close so his mouth was on my ear again. "You belong to me," he growled, and butterflies fluttered in my stomach. "Say it."

"Just shut up and fuck me," I begged him.

He groaned when he shoved into me in one swift, hard motion, but withdrew quickly and ordered again. "Say it."

"I can't," I whimpered.

"You can," he insisted, plunging into me once more but pulling out again too soon.

Unable to stand the torture any longer, I surrendered softly. "I belong to you."

His eyes gleamed with victory, like he'd just won something. And then he fucked me so hard I forgot my own name. His hips jutted back and forth with exquisite precision, and I let my face fall to his neck. I loved the sounds he made, how he grunted as he pounded me. My fingers dug into his shoulder muscles so harshly I was going to end up leaving marks. He felt amazing, so good I could feel myself clenching around him, like I might come from the inside.

"Fuck," Lee swore, feeling it, too. "You really like me, don't you?" he said, his voice laced with arousal.

I refused to look at him, burying my face deeper into his neck as he buried himself deeper inside me. His fingers pulled at my chin, bringing my face up so that I'd look at him. It was right then that the lights flickered back on, and I saw his face clearly, saw the possession and need in his eyes.

Our gazes locked, and I couldn't look away. I was mesmerised by him. The way his eyes captured mine made me feel like I was his entire world. His hands came up to cup my cheeks, and I felt my muscles clench again, an orgasm building until I came on his dick.

"Jesus," Lee groaned, his eyes fluttering closed as he savoured it.

It wasn't long before he came, too, and I watched, fascinated by the how he looked, so overtaken by pleasure. His body dropped onto mine and his arms wrapped around me, pulling my torso tight to his. I felt his mouth at my neck, planting kisses all the way down to my collarbone.

Finally taking a second to look around, I found we were in a small, unused office. There was an old filing cabinet by the door, and I was sitting on what used to be somebody's desk. I'd never had sex in a public place before, and the unsettling fact that I'd just broken the law sank in.

The scariest part was that I didn't even feel bad. I couldn't, not with Lee's smell surrounding me and his mouth worshipping my skin with tender kisses. His hand reached for my chest, briefly cupping my breast before slipping inside and palming it fully. His thumb flicked over the tight nipple.

"God, your tits are perfect, and I haven't even had a chance to taste them yet." He groaned as though in pain, his mouth dipping lower to suck on my cleavage.

"We can't stay here," I protested.

"The fuck we can't."

Closing my eyes, I moaned when he pushed the cup of my bra down and closed his mouth around my nipple. I looked down and he stared up at me, the heat in his gaze telling me he wasn't done by a long shot.

Unfortunately, the rest of the world had other ideas, and my phone began buzzing loudly in my bag where I'd dropped it over by the door. Lee's teeth pressed down around my nipple, the pain agonisingly sweet.

"Ignore it," he ordered.

"I can't. My friend Reya will be wondering where I am."

"Karla," said Lee, his mouth leaving my breast as he rose to look me dead in the eye. "I've wanted you for months, haven't been with a single person since the day I met you. No way are we done here."

Startled by his admission, I drew back, my hands braced on his chest. "You...what?"

"You fucking heard me. Now, come here," he murmured in a sexy voice, but I was already getting up from the table, putting my dress back to rights and trying to find my underwear. I looked around the room before turning back to Lee. His mouth formed a smirk when my eyes trailed to his pocket, where he'd stuffed my black lacy thong.

I held my hand out. "Give me that."

He shot me a challenging stare. "Come and get it."

I pouted in frustration. "You can't just say stuff like that and expect me not to freak out."

He stepped forward, and I stepped back. "Stuff like what?"

"That you haven't been with anyone since you met me. What does that even mean?"

He ducked his head, levelling his eyes on me as he answered simply, "It means you left an impression."

"That's...that's ridiculous."

"Is it? Have *you* been with anyone?"

I folded my arms over my chest, causing Lee's attention to wander to my cleavage. "That's different. I haven't been in a relationship, and I don't do one-night stands."

"Well, that's good to hear, because I plan on making *this*" — he paused and motioned between the two of us — "a regular thing."

I gaped at him. "That's *not* going to happen, not unless you also plan on changing your entire way of life, because I won't conduct a relationship with a criminal."

I was well aware of what a hypocrite I was being, but I couldn't seem to help it. The wiring in my brain just fizzled out whenever I was around him, causing me to do things I never would normally.

"Ouch, hit me where it hurts, why don't ya?" Lee chuckled, and my temper rose.

"This is all just a big joke to you, isn't it? Just a bloody game to occupy your time."

"No one's playing games. I like you a whole hell of a lot, Karla. I've told you that already, so stop trying to convince yourself otherwise."

All the air left me when he moved forward, backing me into the door and cupping my face in his hands, his gaze reverent. "Give me a chance, and I'll prove to you that everything you think you see is blurred by perception."

His lips met mine, soft and tender, and after a moment of resistance, I kissed him back. My hands fisted in his black T-shirt. The sweet way his mouth worshipped mine hit me even harder than having him inside me. With a sharp breath he broke away and drew me into a hug. We stood there, holding one another but not saying a word. When my phone started buzzing again, I knew I had to go find Reya.

Lee bent down to place one last kiss on my lips before pulling my thong from his pocket and bending to help me back into it. He smoothed down my dress, then ran his hands through my hair. Lastly, he swiped a thumb under both my eyes to fix my makeup.

"All better," he whispered, and my heart thrummed. I knew we'd just had sex in a musty old office, but that was probably the sweetest thing a man had ever done for me.

Unable to form words, I nodded, and Lee laced his fingers through mine, opening the door and leading me outside. He stayed with me as we searched the club for Reya, finally finding her outside in the smoking area. Ingrid and Gina were nowhere to be seen, and I got a surprise to see her sitting with Trevor, deep in conversation.

"Reya," I called out to grab her attention.

She turned to me, and I was uncomfortably aware of how her gaze lowered to my hand, which Lee was still holding. She cocked an eyebrow, and I dropped his hand instantly. I didn't turn to see his face, but I knew how quickly I'd let go must have bothered him.

"Uh, hey," I said, stepping over and casting a hesitant glance in Trevor's direction.

"Where were you?" Reya asked, the knowing slant to her mouth telling me she already had her suspicions.

"Have Ingrid and Gina gone home?" I asked, ignoring her question because I didn't know how to answer it. Lee was unnervingly quiet beside me, and I could feel his eyes practically scorching a hole in my head.

"They went back to a party with those guys from earlier. I stayed to wait for you, and that's how I bumped into Trevor here."

My brow furrowed. "Oh, do you two know each other?" Sitting there, they seemed way too comfortable for two people who'd just met.

"Nah, never laid on eyes on her before," Trevor cut in with a charming smile before glancing back to Reya. "Which, quite frankly, is a travesty."

She narrowed her gaze at him, but she wasn't doing a very good job of restraining her smile. Trevor grinned wider, like he knew he had her in the palm of his hand, despite her acting unimpressed.

"Well," I said, clearing my throat, "we should get going. Do you want to share a cab?"

At this I felt Lee's hand press into my lower back. "I'll drive you."

I glanced at him. "I don't think so. You've been drinking."

"I had one shot and half a beer. I'll be fine," he insisted.

"He's not lying. I've seen him drink a whole bottle of tequila and still score a perfect bullseye on the dart board," said Trevor.

Lee patted his chest. "Strong constitution."

"Let him drive us," said Reya shyly. "I don't want to pay for a taxi."

I thought it was more that she didn't want to say goodbye to Trevor yet, but I didn't call her out on it. Giving in, I sighed and said, "Fine."

A moment later, Lee was wrapping his arm around my middle and leading me from the club, while Reya and Trevor followed behind. I bristled at his show of possession, my body growing rigid.

"Ashamed of me, Snap?" Lee whispered in my ear, and I looked up. The way his eyebrows dipped down made me feel terribly guilty for my behaviour.

"I'm not ashamed. It's just complicated. You know that. If anyone I work with saw me here with you, it'd create a whole host of problems."

There was understanding in his eyes before he bent to whisper in my ear, "Let me drop your friend home and then take you back to mine. I need to be inside you again."

I shivered at his words, but I knew I couldn't say yes. Having sex with him had been even more intense than I'd imagined. Going home with him was too close, and I knew that if I spent the night in his bed, I'd end up falling for him.

"I can't," I said, my throat constricting.

His thumb rubbed back and forth over my hip. "Don't make me beg."

"I have a, uh, a thing early tomorrow morning," I said, my brain scrambling for an excuse but coming up empty. There were too few plausible commitments that took place early on a Sunday morning.

Lee didn't say anything as we walked around the corner to where he'd left his car. I spotted it right away, but frowned when his arm around my waist tightened. That was when I noticed the guy standing there. He was all alone, wearing a black hoodie and dark jeans. A peaked cap shielded his face from view, but somehow I felt his eyes fall on me with interest.

"You all right there, mate?" Lee called, his voice hard. Everything in him was coiled tight as he scanned the figure standing on the footpath.

"Just passing through," the man answered, twisting his head to take a leisurely look at Lee's car before he turned and walked away. Lee was frowning, and Trevor seemed just as tightly wound. They shared a moment of silent communication.

"Who was that?" I asked, a feeling of unease coming over me, and I wasn't quite sure why.

Lee wore a faraway expression as he answered, "Someone trying to send a message."

"What does that mean?"

Shaking himself out of it, he blinked before replying, "Nothing, Karla. Come on, let's get you home."

I knew instinctively that there was something he wasn't telling me, but I allowed him to lead me into the car anyway.

Nine

Lee spent several minutes checking out his car before finally starting the engine. He seemed distant, his mind elsewhere as his fists white-knuckled the steering wheel and he drove in the direction of Reya's house. She lived with a couple of other students and was always complaining about how messy and rude they were. I didn't envy her.

Glancing through the overhead mirror, I saw Trevor with his arm resting along the back of the car seat while he asked Reya questions and she gave him tentative answers, trying not to blush at his attention. I was jolted out of watching them when I felt a warm hand grasp my knee, and looked to the side to see Lee's eyes flickering from the road to the hem of my dress. His thumb grazed the inside of my thigh, and I was suddenly remembering our time in the office room, how good it felt to have him inside me, invading every one of my senses.

God, I wanted to go back to his place so badly. Being with him tonight hadn't quelled my hunger at all. On the contrary, it only grew stronger.

A few minutes later, we were stopping outside Reya's. Trevor got out and walked her to her door. When he returned, he let his head fall back, grinning like the cat that got the cream.

"Okay, this is probably verging on TMI, but that is *the* finest rack I've ever seen."

Lee chuckled at his brother, and I twisted around in my seat to eye him. "That's my friend you're talking about, and she's more than just a pair of tits, so show some respect."

"Oh, calm your knickers. My intentions are pure – purely sexual."

I narrowed my gaze at him as Lee warned, "That's enough, Trev."

The younger brother flopped back in his seat, muttering, "Your girlfriend needs to chill out."

"I'm not his girlfriend," I protested at the same time Trevor's gaze wandered to Lee's hand firmly grasping my thigh. He shot me a cynical look that said it all. *Sure you're not.*

A second later, his phone beeped and he pulled it out to read the message. I turned back around in my seat.

"Hey, where are we, bruv?" Trevor asked.

"Just coming up to Bethnal Green."

"Pull up here and let me out. Got a few things to take care of."

Lee stared at Trevor through the mirror, and they shared a moment of that weird silent communication again. Without questioning him, Lee stopped the car and his brother hopped out. When we were back on the road, I shot him a curious look.

"Where's he off to?"

"Fuck if I know."

"It's almost two o'clock in the morning."

"And Trevor's a big boy. He can take care of himself."

Now that we were alone in the car, Lee's hand moved farther up my thigh. My skin prickled with goose bumps and I closed my eyes for a second, trying to summon the ability to think straight. When I opened them again, the engine was off, and I looked up to see we were parked outside my building.

"Come here," Lee said, his voice a low command.

"I'd better get inside."

"Not yet," he argued, and grabbed my hand.

He lifted my body deftly until I was sitting astride him in the driver's seat, his fingers trailing up and down the outside of my thighs. I heaved a shuddering a breath. He stared up at me with his mouth hanging slightly open. Looking like that, he was more or less impossible to resist. The adoration in his eyes made my chest feel too tight, and when he began to harden against me, I was done for.

It was late, and there was nobody around. Still, I shouldn't have been considering having sex with Lee Cross in the front seat of his car where anyone could see.

"I can't do this," I said, shaking my head.

Reaching forward, Lee gripped the back of my neck and pulled my mouth to his for a quick, hard kiss. "Break the rules, Karla. Just this once," he said breathlessly as his hands trailed down my body to palm my arse.

I whimpered when he squeezed, pulling me tight to his erection. Before I could protest further, he slid my underwear to the side and plunged two fingers inside me.

"Wet," he hissed, and I melted against him, my face falling to the crook of his neck.

"Look at me. I need your eyes," Lee said, and I pulled back, watching while he coaxed me to orgasm. He continued fingering me, and when his thumb moved over my clit, I moaned. "That's it — give me those eyes. You're so beautiful."

His chest rose and fell as he watched me, his gaze glittering in the dark. The intensity in his expression made me flush, my breaths and sighs filling the small confines of the car. I bent down and kissed him. When I slid my tongue inside his mouth, I was rewarded with a deep, masculine groan, and the next time he circled my clit, I came with an unexpected ferocity right on his hand.

It took me a long time to recover, but Lee just held me, one hand running soothingly up and down my spine.

"Come on, I'll walk you up to your flat," he said, finally breaking the quiet.

I was uncomfortably aware of the fact that he was still hard. Moving my hand to his crotch, I rubbed and whispered, "Do you need something?"

Lee groaned but grabbed my hand, stopping my movement. "As much as it pains me to say this, I'll be okay."

Staring at him, I watched his Adam's apple as it bobbed in his throat, and I knew it really had taken a lot for him to say no. I wondered why all of a sudden he wanted the night to be over. Dark shadows flickered in his expression, and I knew he had other things on his mind. Things that hadn't been there earlier tonight. It was the guy who'd been standing outside his car; something about the whole encounter had been just downright off.

My voice was quiet when I asked, "Do you have a lot of enemies, Lee?"

He turned back to me, his face intense as he answered, "It comes with the territory, Karla."

***

It didn't take me long to fall asleep that night, but the next morning when I woke up, everything came crashing down on me like a tonne of bricks. I couldn't believe what I'd done, couldn't believe I'd given in so easily. I may not have been the strongest woman in the world, but I'd always prided myself on living my life by a firm set of principles. Then Lee came along and threw a bomb on my rules, reducing them to a pile of meaningless rubble.

Now I wasn't sure I had it in me to resist him, but really, it was all my fault. I never should have started texting him so regularly. It had allowed me to get to know him, but, more importantly, it had allowed him to get under my skin.

Seeing him in the club last night after interacting with him remotely for so long had felt drugging; I'd been completely under his spell.

Anyhow, at least I had the day off and could take some time getting my head around everything. Alexis and I went grocery shopping, and then we caught a movie and got gelato on the way home. If my best friend hadn't been so wrapped up in her own problems, I was sure she would have noticed there was something wrong with me. I'd deliberately left my phone off all day, telling myself it was because I wanted to go unplugged for a while. The truth was, I was afraid of Lee calling, and even more afraid of the fact that I wouldn't be able to resist answering.

Remembering the man standing beside his car the night before, I knew I had to stop this before I got in too deep. He had enemies, and if any of them discovered Lee was conducting a relationship with a cop, it wouldn't end pretty for either one of us.

Several days passed and I was back to work, finding a strange sort of relief in keeping busy. Tony and I were sent on call after call, from burglaries to street muggings to road accidents. We'd just pulled up outside a high-end clothing boutique, where a young woman was being held after a shop assistant caught her trying to steal some lingerie.

"You want to take this one?" Tony asked, shifting uncomfortably in the passenger seat.

"Hey, I took the lead on the last call, and I need a break. You should go in. Fair's fair."

He frowned. "Fine. I'll be back in a few."

Getting out, he slammed the car door, disgruntled, and made his way inside the boutique. Picturing him having to question the woman on the nature of the items she'd stolen made me grin, and I realised it had been my first proper smile in days. My phone chimed in my pocket and I pulled it out, finding a message from Alexis asking if I could grab milk on my way home.

I'd received a number of calls and messages from Lee, but nothing in the last two days. After I'd consistently ignored him, perhaps he'd given up. A guy like Lee didn't need to pine after any woman; I was sure there were harems just waiting for a chance to keep his bed warm. All of a sudden, my grin faltered and I found myself frowning. I rubbed my thumb across the screen, scrolling through the texts he'd sent and feeling forlorn. I wanted him, but this was for the best. As I'd said, nothing good could come of us being together.

It was just as I was sliding the phone back in my pocket that I heard the car door open and Tony climbed inside.

"That was quick," I said, lifting my head. When I saw who'd entered the car, all thought fled my mind. It wasn't Tony. It was Lee. How the hell had he found me here?

I swallowed thickly, a bunch of gobbledygook coming out of my mouth, "You…ah…what the…huh?"

Lee didn't smile at my fluster, but instead he stared forward, his lips set in a firm line as he slammed the door closed. He didn't say a word as I gaped at him, and when the silence became too much, I finally managed to ask, "What are you doing here?"

His eyes slid to the side. "You've been ignoring my calls, so I had to get creative."

"Uh-huh, and how did you know where I was? Just happened to be in the neighbourhood, did you?"

One eyebrow rose sardonically. "Nah, I had to bust out the old police scanner."

I sputtered a laugh but went silent when he shot me a serious look. "You're not joking."

"Nope."

I sat up straighter. "Well, be that as it may, you need to go. Tony will be back any minute, and if he sees you here, it won't take him long to put two and two together."

Lee bristled, working his jaw. "Do I look like I give a fuck?"

His question angered me as I twisted in my seat to glare at him. "Well you should give a fuck! If you have any feelings for me at all, you'd care whether or not I lost my job."

His expression softened, and he seemed remorseful for his flippancy. "It's not like they can fire you for having a sex life, Karla."

"Maybe not. But my superior has it in for me, and if she ever caught wind that I was seeing someone with a record, she'd use it against me. Not to mention she'd probably start looking into you and your business," I said, pausing to eye him meaningfully. "Is that what you want? Do you want police sniffing around your garage, Lee?"

"They could sniff all they wanted. They wouldn't find anything."

"Right, because it's all above board."

His expression sharpened. "Not what I said, Snap."

A leaden silence fell between us. I wanted to tell him to leave, that he was committing an offence by the simple act of coming inside a police vehicle without permission. At the same time I didn't want him to go. I'd missed him. And every night my dreams had been full of his voice and heated looks, how it felt to finally be with him.

"Why does your boss have it in for you?" he asked, breaking the quiet.

I turned my head to see he wore a fierce look, and for some reason it made me thaw slightly. Letting out a slow breath, I answered, "She and my dad have had some feud going on since like, forever. So, even though I was barely out of nappies when it happened, she hates me just as much as she hates him."

Lee's brows drew together. "What did he do to her?"

"Beats me. Everyone says they had an argument and he'd called her some pretty horrible names, but that's hardly the sort of thing you carry around for decades."

"I dunno, your old man's quite the fucker. He's pretty much universally hated by everyone I know. And to be honest, with the amount of big players he's put away, I'm surprised he's still breathing after all these years." He paused and slid his eyes to mine, picking up a pen that had been resting on the dash and flicking it between his fingers. "Though as they say, the devil can wait for his own."

I stared at him, conflicting emotions warring within me. At once I wanted to agree, because he was sort of right about Dad. But then again, this was my own father we were talking about, the only one I was ever going to have, and the insinuation that he was going to hell pissed me off. Any of the warmth I might have felt toward Lee vanished as I told him sternly, "You need to leave now. Otherwise, I'll have no other choice but to arrest you."

"Any excuse to slap a pair of cuffs on me, eh? If I didn't know any better, I'd say you were something of a fledgling dominatrix," Lee joked before leaning in close to whisper, "But we both know that's not true." A pause. "Fucking beautiful sight to see you give yourself to me like that, Karla."

I swallowed thickly and closed my eyes, memories of the nightclub flooding my mind. They were so visceral I could almost feel his fingertips digging into my hips, taste his tongue as it invaded my mouth. Suddenly I was too hot, unable to find enough air. I desperately wanted to undo some buttons on my shirt, but I wouldn't give Lee the satisfaction of knowing he was getting to me.

"I can't do this. It needs to end before it begins."

Moving closer, he closed his hand over my knee, his voice deadly serious. "This started a long time ago."

Before I could react, he reached out and grabbed my chin, turning my face to his and laying a quick, butterfly-inducing kiss on my lips. After only a second of hesitation, I pushed him off me.

"Get out," I told him, breathless.

"So this is how it's gonna be, then?"

"There isn't any other way," I replied.

Without another word, he opened the car door and slid out. Only a minute later, Tony returned. He opened the door and guided a handcuffed brunette into the back before coming around the front and dropping into the seat Lee had just vacated. I sent him a tight-lipped smile, noticing he seemed a little perplexed.

"Everything okay?" I asked, nervous tension coiling inside me. Had he seen Lee?

"I just don't get it."

"Don't get what?"

"Why someone would risk being arrested for the sake of a piece of string to stick between their arse cheeks."

The woman in the back seat scowled furiously while I burst into laughter, a small part in relief that he hadn't spotted Lee.

"People are bonkers."

"Tell me about it."

***

The next few days on the job were fairly quiet, and Tony and I were practically chomping at the bit for some action. It wasn't like I wanted anything dangerous to happen, but when your day consisted of dealing with minor incidents and paperwork, you needed something to break up the monotony.

I was about to get my wish.

We were sitting in the patrol car, having a quick coffee break, when a call came in about a Gran Coupe that had just been reported stolen. Apparently, it was headed in our direction, and when the vehicle went sailing by seconds later, I immediately hit the sirens and started the engine.

As soon as the assailant saw us following he increased his speed. I'd been driving since I was seventeen, and, not to brag, but learning how to drive in London gains you a lot more skill than learning to drive in other places. I could park in the smallest space known to man, but more importantly, I could manoeuvre my way through narrow streets and cobbled alleyways at high speed like nobody's business.

"I think we need some music," said Tony as I yanked on the gear stick a little too hard.

"Don't even think about it," I told him, unable to stop the smile from spreading across my face.

He smiled right back. "But it's tradition. You can't break with tradition."

"Fine, put it on and shut up. I'm trying to drive here."

Tony tapped a few buttons on his iPod, and seconds later the opening chords to "Thunderstruck" by AC/DC came blasting through the speakers. Don't laugh. The very first time we were in a high-speed chase, this song had come on the radio, and it had been so appropriately badass that we'd made a tradition out of putting it on when chasing down a stolen vehicle ever since.

It also had a strange way of helping me concentrate, kind of like how surgeons listened to "Stayin' Alive" during operations. I pressed harder on the gas pedal.

Whoever was behind the wheel of the BMW had some mad skills, though, and even I had a hard time keeping up when they made a sharp left turn. If the music wasn't so loud, I was sure I'd hear tires squealing. I almost lost control of the wheel, but Tony launched himself forward in time to grab it. Before long we were on the motorway, and I swore loudly, because it was going to be harder to catch him now. Or her.

The assailant dipped dangerously in and out between vehicles, causing several drivers to swerve, almost leading to an accident. It was moments like these that I wondered if we should continue chasing him, because if he kept up the dangerous driving, people were going to get seriously injured, or worse, killed.

Tony was on the radio, reporting our location and proximity to the stolen car, while I tried my best to get closer. I saw the vehicles up ahead start to slow, traffic building up. The BMW pulled left to drive in the empty bus lane, and I followed suit. Unfortunately for him, about half a mile ahead there were a number of buses using the lane, and what with the traffic on the other side, he had nowhere else to go.

I had to brake suddenly when the BMW screeched to a halt and the driver's-side door flew open. A man exited, and Tony was already out of the patrol car, running after him as I spoke into my radio.

"The perp is now on foot. Male, about 5 feet, 9 inches, wearing jeans and a black hoodie, white trainers. PC Pollard is in pursuit."

Slamming the door closed behind me, I went after Tony. Thirty or forty yards ahead of me, he chased down the thief, who had jumped over the metal railings separating the road from the area beyond. I was out of breath as I ran, my legs pumping to catch up with them. Tony closed in on him, kicking his foot out to trip him up, and the guy went flying face first into the grass. As I reached them, I heard him swear and try to get back up, but Tony grabbed his arm to stop him as he ordered, "Hands above your head, now!"

The thief began raising his hands as Tony quickly pulled out his cuffs, locking his wrists together and lowering them behind his back. Next he instructed him to turn around, and that was when I came face to face with Liam Cross.

Ten

Liam was just twenty years old. I found this out when I accessed his file back at the station so I could fill in my incident report. He was looking at a court date within the next few weeks, and most likely prison time. The scary thing was, I didn't know how to feel about that. Stealing cars was like a job to him, and, growing up in his family, he saw it as a means to an end. Steal so you can put food on the table, or don't, and go hungry.

Lee and his brothers weren't little kids anymore; they could get out of this racket and make an honest living for themselves if they really wanted to. The problem was, I had no idea how deep in they were, who they had ties to, and if those people would ever let them get out.

I was still sitting at my desk, filling out the report, when Lee strode confidently into the station, all tousled hair and cocky swagger. He wore jeans and a white T-shirt with oil stains down the front, a work shirt tied around his waist. Clearly, he'd just come from the garage. Probably been working on a ringer, I thought to myself disgruntledly.

After that first glance, I refused to look at him again, staring intently at the papers in front of me and listening just as intently to his voice as he spoke. It quickly became apparent that he was there to post bail for Liam. The constable he spoke to scurried off, and Lee stood by the reception. I allowed myself one more glance at him and found him leaning back against the wall, his eyes scanning the space before they found me. I looked away again.

Jumping when my phone buzzed in my pocket, I dropped my pen and pulled it out.

Lee: You arrested my brother?

Oh, he had some nerve. I shouldn't have responded, but I couldn't seem to help myself.

Karla: I didn't arrest him. Tony did.

Lee: But you were there.

A second went by, and my anger flared. He was acting like I should have, what? Convinced Tony to let Liam go with a gypsy's warning and a slap on the wrist?

Lee: Not gonna come over and say hello?

Okay, that did it. Without thinking, I pushed up from my chair and strode across the room. I'd inherited my temper from my dad, and sometimes I just didn't have the strength to hold it back. Lee smirked when he saw me coming, but there was a hardness behind it. I cursed myself for giving him a reaction. I should have just continued ignoring him.

Checking to make sure nobody was watching, I grabbed his hand, yanking him around the corner and into an empty corridor.

"You've got some cheek," I hissed.

Lee held his arms out as he asked sardonically, "What? No hug? No kiss?"

I slapped down one of his arms. "Quit being a smart-arse. Your little brother could go to prison. He could do a seven-year stretch, and he's just a kid." My throat constricted with worry. I didn't even know Liam, but he looked so much like a younger version of Lee. Maybe that was why the idea of him doing time stressed me out so much.

Lee's eyes flickered between mine, his mouth firm as he studied me. It obviously surprised him to realise that I actually cared about what happened to his family. He took a step forward so that there was barely an inch between us.

"You think I don't know that?" he gritted out, voice low.

"I had no idea it was him in that car. I was doing my job. So don't you dare try to lay the blame on me."

Lee scowled. "When did I ever lay blame?"

"Your text."

"I asked you a question. I never blamed you. Liam's actions are his own, but I practically raised that kid. I'm allowed to be angry."

"I never said you weren't, but it's your own fault for leading him down this path in the first place, so don't go directing your anger at me. It could have been any number of officers chasing him. He still would have been caught."

Lee shook his head and turned away for a second. His shoulders rose and fell sharply, like he was trying to gain some composure. Finally, he swiped a hand down his face and turned back to me, one eyebrow arched, "Were you behind the wheel?"

I bristled. "I don't see how that has anything to do with it."

"Liam's driving is second to none. No ordinary cop would have caught him." He paused, some sort of interest lighting his eyes. "You must have some skills, Snap, chasing down a Gran Coupe in a Vauxhall Corsa." He actually seemed impressed.

"Yeah, maybe I should pack it all in and come work for you, huh?" I deadpanned, cynicism lacing my every word.

We locked eyes for a long moment, a silent battle of wills. He didn't like me insinuating he was a thief. Few people enjoyed the sight of their true reflection.

"Be real careful about what you say next, Karla," he warned me.

"Or what? Will you have some thugs come and rough me up? That's generally how it works with people like you, right?"

He neared me again, and my back hit the wall. His voice was low and measured when he spoke. "You have no clue what you're talking about. And, just so we're clear, I would never hurt you, *never*. If any man tried to lay his hands on you, I'd make sure that was the last thing he did."

I stared at him, not sure how to feel. I'd been all geared up for a fight, and then he went and said something that was so protective, but equally so wrong. It took me a long time to reply, and when I did, my tone was a good deal softer.

"I know what I'm talking about."

"No, you don't," he said, snapping his fingers over the material of my shirt. "When you put this uniform on every morning, you see a woman working to make the streets a safer place. To you, the law works to keep good people from hurting bad people, but ever since I was a kid, I knew that wasn't true. The police were just a bunch of pricks in black and white threads and a stupid fucking hat, trying to stop me from feeding my family."

His words hit deep, and I was just about to say something, anything, when I heard footsteps approaching. Immediately, I turned and walked back to my desk, picking up my pen and pretending like our conversation never happened. Lee went back to the reception area to wait for Liam, and all the while his words rang in my ears.

To you, the law works to keep good people from hurting bad people, but ever since I was a kid, I knew that wasn't true.

***

I was almost finished my shift and on my way back from a house call later that day when Keira texted asking if I'd pick up some drinks and sandwiches for the station. Making the mistake of stopping at a shop in a rough neighbourhood, I went in, threw a few things in my basket, checked out, and left to find a gang of young men waiting for me.

I counted them all, five in total, and clenched my fingers tighter around the plastic bag I was carrying.

"Your lot aren't welcome round 'ere," one of them called over, and I kept walking. I was outnumbered, so there was no point in responding. I didn't think they'd get physical, since I wasn't trying to stop them from doing anything, but then one of them stood in front of me, sucking on a smoke and exhaling right into my face.

"Good-looking for a copper, though. Hey, red, why don't you stick around and have some fun with us?"

"Look, lads, there doesn't need to be a problem here, so if you could quit the side show, I'll be on my way."

I knew instantly that my tone didn't sit well with the ringleader, as he flicked the butt of his smoke to ground and shot me a dirty look. He had tattoos on his neck and face, and, by the look of them, they'd been done in prison. This bloke obviously had some sort of chip on his shoulder about law enforcement.

"Side show?" he said, and glanced back to his boys. "This stupid bitch has a mouth on her."

He took a step closer. Quickly shifting my shopping bag into my other hand, I pulled out my Taser and held it at arm's length.

"Back off now," I ordered him, and he stared at me cockily, like he wasn't scared. Lifting his T-shirt, he revealed a gun tucked inside the waistband of his pants.

"You're not the only one who's packing, cunt," he spat, but I stood firm.

"Do you really want to pull a gun on an officer right out in the open? I'm pointing this Taser *directly* at you, so who do you think is going to be quicker?"

"Come on, she's not worth it," one of his mates said. A few seconds passed before he threw a few more ugly words at me and slunk off. Letting out a slow breath, I returned to the car, dropped my shopping bag in the back seat, and pulled out my phone to call the station. I made a report on the incident, described what the guy with the gun had looked like, and then hung up.

By the time I arrived home that evening I was exhausted, but I'd still managed to pick up some groceries for dinner – in a better neighbourhood this time. Turning my key in the lock, I heard Alexis chuckle, and stepped inside to find she had company. Needless to say, I wasn't too happy when I found out her company was Lee.

"What are you doing here?" I asked irritably, too tired to even pretend to be polite.

"I'm here to visit Alexis, see how she's doing with the baby and everything."

"Lee's offered to drive me to the hospital if I ever need to go when you're working," Alexis put in, eyeing me curiously. She had no idea about the stuff that'd been going on between me and man sitting across from her these last few weeks.

"How kind," I muttered, throwing the groceries in the kitchen before shutting myself inside my bedroom. I leaned back against the door and let out a long, weary sigh, really needing this day to be over. A knock sounded above my head, and I startled when Lee called, "I unpacked your stuff, Snap. Why don't you go relax for half an hour, and I'll get dinner started?"

Was he shitting me? And God, I just remembered that there was a packet of tampons in with the groceries. Wonderful. Not wanting to alert Alexis to any weirdness, I replied in an even tone, "That's quite all right. I can make my own dinner."

"Let him make it," Alexis called. "No offence, but Lee's a better cook than you."

"That's lovely."

"You know it's the truth!"

I grabbed a change of clothes and swung the door open. Lee, who'd been leaning his hand against the wood, fell forward slightly, and I suppressed a smirk.

"Fine, you can cook. I'm going to take a shower."

And with that I strode to the bathroom, affecting a casual demeanour and not giving either one of them a second glance.

"I put your tampons in the top cabinet if you're looking for them," Lee called after me, a smile in his voice.

Cringing, I resisted the urge to respond, my skin prickling as I undressed, knowing he was in the next room. I spent longer than necessary washing myself, not wanting to go back out into the apartment and wonder why exactly Lee was there. I knew for a fact that he hadn't come just to be all chivalrous and offer Alexis help while she was pregnant. No, he was there for me, and I hated how I couldn't seem to escape him, not even in my own home.

I spent time putting on body lotion and braiding my wet hair into a plait. I'd put on the T-shirt and shorts I usually wore to bed, but couldn't go braless like I normally did. Lee was standing in the kitchen when I came out, and the place smelled great. He'd taken the ingredients I'd bought and turned them into a chicken stir fry.

We made brief eye contact as I passed him by, his gaze dipping to my face, then dropping and lingering on my bare legs. I huffed a breath and went into my bedroom, dumping my clothes in the laundry basket before coming back out. Alexis sat by the TV, flicking through the channels, and I came to sit beside her.

"Oh, Tony called, by the way. He's been trying to get a hold of you, but your phone was off. He sounded worried."

"Yeah, my battery died. I had a run-in with a few thugs earlier. He must have heard about it and wanted to check if I was okay."

I didn't even realise Lee had been listening until he asked in a tight voice, "What did they look like?"

I turned to him for a second, finding his eyebrows drawn together. He looked pissed. I waved him away. "It's fine. I've already made a report about it."

"What did they look like, Karla?" He repeated his question, this time more firmly. I noticed he was holding a chopping knife.

Alexis motioned for me to tell him, like I had no reason not to, so I finally said, "Tall guy, shaved head, neck tattoo of some sort of bird. An eagle, I think. He was the main one who put it up to me. I didn't get a proper look at the others."

"When you say 'put it up,' what exactly do you mean?"

"He was just running his mouth, calling me a bitch. He had a gun, though."

Lee kept nodding, taking it all in, but I could see the cogs in his head turning. He went back to cooking dinner and I turned to the TV, trying to concentrate on the show Alexis had put on. Unfortunately, I couldn't seem to focus, and I kept wondering why Lee wanted to know what the guy looked like so badly. Did he plan on doing something about it? I remembered his words at the station earlier.

I would never hurt you, never. *If any man tried to lay his hands on you, I'd make sure that was the last thing he did.*

This guy hadn't exactly put his hands on me, but I had no doubt that he would have if I hadn't been so quick to pull out my Taser. A few minutes later dinner was ready, and Lee served us each a huge plate of stir fry. I was too hungry not to dig in right away, and he seemed pleased by my eagerness. He shot me a grin from where he sat on the armchair, and I rolled my eyes.

"Oh, my God, Lee, this is amazing!" Alexis enthused. "Jamie Oliver in da house."

He shot her a wink. "I'm more of a Gordon Ramsey type."

"Oh, yeah, I can definitely see that. You in the kitchen, swearing your head off at the staff because you can't bear to send out second-rate risotto to paying customers."

Lee chuckled. "That's the plan."

"No, seriously, you should chuck in all this car business and open up your own restaurant. I'm not joking."

Shaking his head, Lee settled his attention on the television. I noticed he hadn't made anything for himself, which left me feeling sort of guilty, but perhaps he'd already eaten. Once Alexis was finished, she declared she was going to bed. She seemed a little too quick to announce it, and I wondered if she'd sensed something between me and Lee and wanted to give us privacy to talk.

A few beats of silence passed before I asked, "How's Liam doing?"

"He's angry. We all are."

I didn't know how to respond to that. I mean, Tony, one of my closest friends, had arrested him, so if Lee was angry, then I didn't really understand why he was here in my flat, acting like everything was normal.

"If he can cut a deal, maybe he can avoid a stretch," I said finally.

"Already thought of that," Lee replied, his voice tight.

"And?"

"And it probably won't come to it. I've got a good solicitor."

My curiosity piqued. "And who would that be?"

His eyes sharpened. "William Dunning."

I blinked at him, my mouth agape. "You do realise how much that tells me about you, right?"

Lee shrugged, but his expression was fierce. He wouldn't make any apologies for who he was.

Dunning was a snake, and he represented some of the most powerful individuals in London. If he had Lee on his books, it meant that the man sitting before me was far more dangerous than I'd thought. I was suddenly anxious about having him in my home. Was he being monitored by the NCA? They tended to keep an eye on all the big players, but being so low in rank, I wouldn't know anything about it.

Somebody could be watching him right at that very moment. Since I lived in a huge tower block, they wouldn't know which flat he was in unless they followed him inside. But still, this was way too close for comfort.

Lee seemed to read my thoughts clear as day on my face. "Relax. Nobody knows I'm here."

"Why *are* you here?"

He frowned. "I needed to talk to you about something."

I motioned with my hand. "Then talk."

Letting out a long breath, he rubbed at his short-cropped hair and levelled me with his eyes. "You remember the bloke from outside the nightclub?"

"The creep standing beside your car? Yes."

"Well, let's just say, his boss and my boss have been having something of a disagreement of late. Long story short, things aren't safe, and this guy thinks you're my girlfriend. He's threatened to…do things."

My body tensed. "Things? What kind of things?"

Lee shook his head. "Nah, not going there with you, Snap."

A sick feeling crept into my stomach. "Does he know who I am?"

"He knows what you look like, that's all. But I have a plan to set him straight. In the meantime, I'm having Trevor watch you when you're off duty, just to be on the safe side."

"Nobody's watching me. I can take care of myself. And anyway, I'm not even your girlfriend, but if this guy so much as tries to lay a hand on me, I'll arrest him."

Lee shook his head. "That's not how this works, Karla."

"There is no 'this,'" I snapped. "If you'd just left me alone in the first place, then none of this would be happening."

Lee leaned forward so that his elbows rested on his knees. All of a sudden, I saw how exhausted he was. "Can you not fight me on this just once? Fuck, I know I should have left you alone. I tried, believe me, but I couldn't do it. Now our situation is what it is, so can you just stop being a cop for a second and let me protect you?"

I stared at him, unsure of what to say, or if I should even say anything at all. This entire situation was spiralling out of control, and we'd only been together once.

"Look, I know today must have been awful for you, and to tell you the truth, I hate that I helped catch Liam. But even more, I hate the fact that he was stealing in the first place. And yes, I understand your life's been tough and you've had to make hard decisions, but we have to make new decisions every day. Maybe tomorrow you can make the right one."

Lee's tired eyes rose to meet mine. "The right one?"

"Yes, like deciding to get out of this business you're in and go legit."

He let out a joyless laugh. "Because it's that simple."

"I can help you."

His gaze dropped to his hands, and his voice was quiet when he said, "There's no help for me."

A long silence fell between us, and he lifted his head to stare at me again. Shivers trickled along my collarbone, a heavy tension filling the air.

"I don't understand why you don't hate me right now," I whispered.

Lee looked at me, his crystal-clear blue eyes full of sincerity. "Neither do I."

What he said jolted me, because it meant he understood that he should hate my guts, and the idea of him hating me made my stomach twist with nausea. Though I didn't want to admit it, I felt sick at the thought of losing the affection he so obviously felt for me.

It was messed up.

After a minute he stood, turned, and walked to the front door. "See you around, Karla," he said before he opened the door and left the flat. Barely a second went by before

Alexis' bedroom door burst open, and my best friend stood before me, an open-mouthed look on her face.

"I bloody well knew it!" she exclaimed, marching around the sofa and coming to plonk down beside me. "I want to know everything, you secretive little tramp, and start from the beginning."

Eleven

For the next three days, I worked. Every once in a while I found myself looking around, trying to spot Trevor, but I never saw him. Perhaps Lee had decided to respect my wishes and not have his brother follow me. Or perhaps he was just good at hiding.

The night Lee visited our flat, I'd given in and told Alexis everything. She'd warned me off from the very start, and I had every intention of heeding her advice, but my heart, or maybe it was my vagina, had other ideas. In the end, she didn't berate me for my choices. After all, if anyone could understand what I was going through, it was Alexis. She'd had an affair with her boss, which in a way was just as illicit as what had been going on with me and Lee.

When I clocked out of my shift on Saturday evening, I'd almost forgotten about all the nasty business and threats to my safety. I had the entire weekend off, and I planned on making the most of it, starting with going to see Reya perform at a small music venue in Soho. Since I worked such unpredictable hours, I rarely got the chance to see her play, so it was a real treat for me.

I decided to catch the Tube into the city so that I could have a few drinks, and wore a dark blue pencil dress with a long royal blue coat and heels. It wasn't often that I dressed up in a proper girly fashion, so when I did, I put in the effort. I blow-dried and straightened my hair, so it looked shiny and sleek, and wore a small bit of makeup.

I was just walking out of my building when a head suddenly dropped down from above, giving me the fright of my life. Holding my hand to my heart, I stared up at

Trevor, who was hanging by his legs from an overhead bar like a goddamn monkey.

"What the hell?" I said, willing my pulse to slow down.

Trevor swung his body around and dropped to the ground, shooting me a wide, toothy grin.

"Sorry about that, Constable. I forget sometimes that people aren't used to my ways."

"Your ways?"

"I like to get around in an unconventional fashion."

"Uh-huh, and what are you doing here?"

"Watching out for your safety," he replied. "Though if you ask me, I'm not sure you deserve it, what with how you had a hand in fucking up my little brother's life."

Oh, for crying out loud. I was in no mood for this conversation. "Your brother fucked up his own life. I just happened to be the one to catch him doing it."

"Potato, potaaato."

"I'm serious, Trevor. I was doing my job."

Stepping past him, I tugged my coat tighter to defend against the cold and walked in the direction of the tube station. Trevor followed heavy on my heels.

"You know, that sounds a lot like something Hitler would say," he commented.

I rolled my eyes. "I appreciate a well-placed Hitler card as much as the next person, but in this case, you're completely off the mark."

Trevor gestured a Nazi salute and I narrowed my gaze, beginning to think that of all the Cross brothers, this was the eccentric one. He wore a pair of pale ripped jeans, chains hanging from the pockets, steel-toe cap boots, and a baggy grey T-shirt that read "Oh. Okay." under a red tartan bomber jacket. His build was slightly wiry, and his short dark brown hair was messy.

We walked side by side for a few minutes, begrudgingly on my part, before arriving at the Tube station. I swiped my Oyster card while Trevor proceeded to jump the barriers and continue toward the escalators like he hadn't a care. I looked around, irritated to find there were no attendants about.

"Hey, you can't just…." I called before stopping mid-stride, my mouth agape as I watched him jump atop the escalators and effortlessly slide down the middle. Several people watched in surprise the same as me, while one man shouted after him angrily, saying he was going to break his neck. I boarded the moving steps and looked down to see Trevor waiting for me at the end, casually leaning against a wall as he checked his phone. He slid it in his pocket when I finally reached the platform.

"So, where to?" he asked, like everything was perfectly normal.

"You…I…eh…." I mumbled, trying to get my head around what he'd just done. "Are you crazy?"

He held up his thumb and pointer finger. "Just a *little* bit."

"You need to go back up now and pay for your fare," I said, trying to sound stern.

Trevor shook his head. "Nah, don't fancy it."

I was about to protest further when he grabbed my arm and propelled me forward just as a train reached the platform. Before I knew it, he'd shoved me on board and was ushering me into a seat. I yanked my arm out of his hold and glared at him.

"You're going to get us both killed."

He let out a long sigh, sounding like a bored teenager as he replied, "You need to loosen up." He paused as he cocked a curious brow. "What is it that Lee sees in you anyway?"

What he said got my back up as I stood, walking away from him and down the centre of the aisle. I went through the doors separating the carriages and entered the next one. It had fewer passengers than the last, and I sat down in an empty seat, folding my arms across my chest. A second later, Trevor plonked down beside me, and I scowled hard.

"It'll take a lot more than storming off in a huff to get rid of me, Constable," he teased, a grin on his face.

"I'm not in a huff."

"You are," he said, pointing his finger into my shoulder. "You're all in a tizzy because I wondered what Lee sees in you, but you didn't wait to let me finish. I think it's the hair. He's always had a thing for gingers, though his last girlfriend, Tammy, had a dye job, that weird plum colour."

His mention of an ex-girlfriend caught my interest, and I slid my gaze to him.

Trevor's grin widened. "Oh, now she's curious."

"Shut up."

He nudged me. "All ya gotta do is ask, Constable. They don't call me 'old blabbermouth' for nothing."

I gave him a tiny smile. There was something about Trevor that was so playful and child-like that I couldn't seem to help being charmed by him, even if he had just broken several laws in the space of about three minutes. I was off duty, after all.

"So, tell me, then," I urged him.

"What do you want to know?"

"How long have they been broken up?"

"About six months. Lee called it quits when she started asking for too much stuff, wanted him to buy her a house, a new car. I mean, the brazen-faced cheek of it!" he exclaimed, and I laughed. "Seriously, though, Tammy wasn't too bright, didn't realise that the minute you start flashing the cash, people begin to take notice." Trevor eyed me meaningfully, and I didn't need him to explain further. My gut twisted as I was given yet more evidence of Lee and his family's criminality. "Anyway, Lee's been all 'wham, bam, thank you, ma'am' ever since. Well, until you came on the scene, that is."

"I'm not sure you should be telling me this."

"What you gonna do, arrest me?" he asked jokingly, though there was a bite to his words. He still hadn't forgiven me for Liam, not by a long shot.

"Believe it or not, I only want what's best for you and your brothers, and though it goes completely against everything I stand for, I care a great deal for Lee, more than I should."

Trevor eyed me, a quiet descending between us. I turned my head and stared out the window at all the blackness whizzing by.

The silence was only broken when Trevor asked cheekily, "So, does this mean I can start calling you sis?"

I shook my head at him, unable to hold back a chuckle. "Piss off."

At the next stop we got off, chatting on the walk to the venue where Reya was performing, and, surprisingly, Trevor bought me a drink when we got there. It was a couple of minutes before she was supposed to be on stage, and my unlikely companion was on his phone again. It was starting to irritate me.

"Who are you texting so furiously?" I asked.

Trevor chuckled. "I've never heard texting described as furious before. Do my fingers look angry or something?"

"Answer the question."

"It's Lee. He wanted to know where we are."

"Oh?"

"He also told me he'd break my balls if I try coming on to you. I told him you weren't my type."

"My disappointment is palpable," I deadpanned.

Trevor held his phone up to snap a picture. "Say cheese."

"What are you doing?"

"Lee asked for a pic," he answered simply, focusing on his phone. "He says he likes your dress. Wants to know what you're all dolled up for."

"Tell him it's because I'm meeting a man," I replied sassily.

Trevor widened his gaze but continued tapping on his phone. "If you say so."

I sipped on my drink and waited for Lee's response. Trevor chuckled. "He says he almost forgot you two had a booty call set for tonight, but he appreciates your effort."

"That's a lie."

"*Sure.*"

"It is," I exclaimed. "Anything that went on between me and your brother is over."

"Well, alrighty, then. So, what's on tonight? Anything good?"

"Reya's performing. Remember my friend you met at the nightclub?"

"Chesty Laroo? No shit."

"If you call her that to her face, I'll punch you in the testicles."

Trevor threw his hands in the air. "Hey, ease up. Though it might surprise you to discover, she's not my type, either. I just said all that stuff about her the other night to piss you off."

"Are you gay?"

"Nooooo."

"Well, you seemed to like her at the club."

"That's because I'm a shameless flirt," he said, batting his long lashes. I had to admit, they were pretty enviable. "I can't help it. Don't get me wrong, I'd give her a go for a night, but I'm not sure I'd be a returning customer, if you get me."

"You're disgusting."

"I'm just honest. People can't handle honesty these days. But anyway, I was talking to her because I have a gig I think she'll be good for."

"What kind of gig?"

"A 'none of your *bidniz*' kind of gig."

I levelled him with a deathly stare. "Whatever you're up to, don't you dare even think about involving my friend. Reya's had a rough enough time of it already."

"Oh, yeah, what happened to her?"

Lifting my martini glass, I threw his own line back at him. "None of your *bidniz*."

Trevor laughed loud enough that the women sitting on the other side of us turned their heads. When they saw who the source of the laughter was, they took their time checking him out. Trevor shot them a wink and a suave little, "Ladies."

Turning back, he eyed me up and down, a secretive grin shaping his lips. "Okay, I think I get it now."

"Get what?"

"Why my brother has such a hard-on for you. You've got a smart mouth. It's kinda sexy."

"Oh, shut up," I said, just as the house lights dimmed down and a brunette stepped onto the stage to announce Reya's performance. She had a quite a good following these days, so the bar was packed to the rafters.

A minute later my friend took to the stage, dressed all in black: black dress, black tights, black shoes. Her hair was styled in vintage waves, and her makeup was golden-era Hollywood. She looked striking without showing an inch of skin, and I noticed Trevor's attention was glued to her. He sipped on his pint as Reya's hands met her piano keys and she played the opening chords to her song. Mouth close to the microphone, she breathed in and out, creating a sound effect as though she was gasping for air. Her style was so realistically unique, and the very reason why I'd been drawn to her from the first time I saw her perform.

When she sang her voice was clear, her accent slipping through and making the lyrics sound more honest. She had the attention of every person in the room, and I noticed that Trevor was uncharacteristically silent. I thought I heard him mutter something under his breath, but I didn't quite catch what he said.

All too soon her set was over, and the crowd roared their applause. She gave a little bow and walked off the stage, disappearing behind a red velvet curtain. I knocked back the end of what was my third martini, or was it my fourth? Anyway, I finished it and nudged Trevor with my elbow.

"I'm going backstage to see Reya. You coming?"

He nodded and followed me. A minute or two later, we found her packing up her stuff up into a small duffle bag. Sometimes she brought her keyboard to gigs, but since the venue had its own piano, she'd played that instead. It meant she didn't have a whole bunch of equipment to carry home.

Rising, she hitched the bag up on her shoulder before she saw us. I hurried forward, pulling her into a hug and telling her how great the show was. She held her hand up to me, displaying a bandage on her middle finger.

"I almost had to cancel. Cut myself trying to get the crappy window in my bedroom open. It's killing me now, but at least I got to play."

"Well, you'd never notice."

"Bit of WD40 should do the trick," Trevor put in randomly, and Reya's eyes wandered to him. She seemed perplexed as to why he was there, but she didn't question it.

"Pardon?"

"For the window," Trevor explained. "If it keeps sticking."

"Oh, I'll keep that in mind," she said, an awkward silence elapsing.

Trevor stood with his hands clasped behind his back, studying her. "Why don't you open your eyes when you sing?" he blurted, something like disappointment in his voice.

"I...." Reya began. "I don't know," she lied before turning back to me and changing the subject. "Did you see how many people were here tonight? Crazy talk. It's a relief I'll be able to pay this month's rent now."

"I know," I exclaimed. "I'm so proud of you."

Reya beamed before a guy approaching us caught her attention. "Speaking of which. That's the club manager. I'd better go and collect my pay."

I motioned for her to go and a minute later she was back, frowning as she slotted an envelope into her bag.

"Hey, what's wrong?" I asked in concern.

She shrugged, not meeting my eyes, and I knew she was upset about something. "The bastard low-balled me.

When I booked this gig, they said I'd get to keep forty percent of the ticket sales, and now he's claiming we agreed on twenty. Since I never signed any official contract, there's nothing I can do. God, I'm such an idiot sometimes."

"Are you serious?" I said angrily. "He can't do that. I'm going to have a word."

Reya grabbed my hand. "No, don't. If I kick up a fuss, they won't let me play here again, and I need the money." We shared a moment of eye contact, and a second went by before we simultaneously realised that Trevor wasn't standing next to us anymore. Scanning the room, I found he'd approached the club manager, and appeared to be having a serious talk with him.

"Oh, my God, what's he doing?" Reya hissed, her grip on my hand tightening.

"I don't know," I said, pulling out of her grasp before she left a permanent mark.

The club manager gestured wildly with his hands while Trevor spoke over him, his stance confident. The manager frowned and rubbed his chin. Trevor said something else, and then the manager seemed to motion for him to calm down. A moment later he pulled some money from his pocket, counted out the notes and shoved them into Trevor's hand. Lee's brother turned and sauntered back to us, holding the money out to Reya.

"There ya go," he said.

"What's this?" she asked.

"The twenty percent he owed you."

"How did you...." she began, but Trevor cut her off.

"Nobody puts baby in the corner," he said, as though that explained everything. Reya stared at him, flustered, clearly no idea what to say.

"That doesn't even make any sense," I told him.

"Course it does. Now come on, I believe you two lovely ladies owe me a drink."

Yep, definitely the eccentric one, I thought to myself as we let him lead us back to the bar.

***

I woke up the next morning with the mother and father of a hangover. I'd stayed out longer than I planned to, letting Trevor convince me into going to nightclub after nightclub. The three of us drank and danced, and then drank some more. I literally lost count of how much alcohol I'd consumed, and that never happened. Every time Trevor looked at his phone, I got a little tingle down my spine, knowing he was texting Lee. It was disconcerting that just being around someone who had contact with him got me excited.

Though honestly? There was very little about my relationship with Lee that wasn't disconcerting. Or, well, my non-relationship, as seemed to be the case now.

Alexis gave me a smug grin as I trudged my way to the bathroom. She sat by the kitchen counter, eating a bowl of cereal, and looking pleased with herself now that she wasn't the only one who wanted to vomit their guts up first thing in the morning. Though at least she had a valid reason.

Instead of taking a shower, I ran a bath, pouring in extra bubbles before sinking into the soothing water. The honey and almond scent made me feel a little less like death warmed over. When I finally got out and dressed myself, I decided the first order of call was to go shopping for hangover food. It was after one o'clock when I left the flat to walk to the nearest shop.

Unlike last night, this time I spotted Trevor before he spotted me. He was hanging from the same metal bar, half his body suspended in mid-air.

"How's the head, Constable?" he called when he finally saw me.

"Thumping. Why are you here?"

"I'm on guard duty again. No rest for the wicked."

"Well, I'm just going to the shop. Then I plan on spending the rest of the day in bed, so you can head home," I said, continuing on my way as Trevor dropped to the ground, shoving his hands in his pockets and walking alongside me.

"Lee wanted me to invite you over to ours. When I told him about our escapades last night, he said you must be hung over as fuck, and in need of a good feeding. He's cooking a roast."

"I'm not going to your house," I said, my statement final.

"Why not? It's free food, plus you'll get to swoon over my brother and be all, *Oh, Lee, take me upstairs and handcuff me to your bedpost. I want you to take me prisoner this time,*" Trevor teased, pitching his voice higher. I smacked him on the arm and told him to shut up.

"I do *not* sound like that," I huffed, and he chuckled.

"I know you don't, you've got a bit of a husky rasp going on. Very sex-ay. But seriously, you've got to come. Lee said he wants to update you on everything that's been happening. I mean, he'll probably end up crying tears of sorrow into the gravy pot if you don't show."

I gave him a narrow-eyed look. "You're really weird, do you know that?"

"Oh, give it up, we both know you're charmed."

"I'm far from charmed."

"Then why have we already walked by the shop, huh? You've decided to come over and you don't even realise it yet."

"Why can't Lee just call me on the phone and 'update me'?"

"Maybe because that's the unsexy option. Or maybe because the phone lines are being tapped." He widened his eyes in mock terror.

I frowned, knowing I was never going to win with him. "But won't it be a bit awkward? Liam's got to hate me, and Stu's never exactly been my biggest fan."

"Lee's already had a word with them. They'll be on their best behaviour."

I eyed him for a minute, unsure whether he was telling the truth. Unfortunately, I couldn't deny that I really wanted to find out what was going on. Maybe my hung-over brain wasn't functioning properly, because after a minute I finally gave in and told Trevor I'd go with him.

When we got to Lee's street, I glanced up and down, checking to see if there were any suspicious-looking vehicles around. As it happened, there were only a few cars, and all of them were empty. Besides, being such a shrewd customer, I thought that if Lee was being monitored, he'd know about it.

Christ, what the hell was I doing? I really shouldn't have been there. The old woman I'd noticed peeking out her window at me before was standing by her doorstep two houses down, a sweeping brush in her hand as she swept dust from her hallway out onto the street.

"Hello, Trevor," she said with a warm smile, at the same time eyeing me somewhat suspiciously. Did she recognise me out of my uniform?

"Afternoon, Mrs Spencer," Trevor replied, "You're looking fetching this fine Sunday."

The woman chuckled and shook her head, waving him off. God, he really was a shameless flirt. I swear, if there was a cat in front of him, he'd find some way to chat it up.

Stepping inside the house, Trevor led me into the living room, where Sophie was sitting on the floor, playing with her son and another little girl. It took me a moment to recognise her as the next door neighbour's kid, the one I'd seen the first time I came here.

"Isn't that the girl from next door?" I asked curiously. I remembered how she'd run to Lee, like he was a safe place away from her nutjob of a mother, and how it had warmed my heart.

Trevor's expression sobered as he nodded, while Sophie explained, "This is Billie. I'm taking care of her because her mum's gone AWOL. She was in the house alone for two days before I found her. Some people don't deserve to have kids." She sounded angry, and I couldn't blame her. I remembered Lee telling me how Sophie's mother had abandoned her in a similar fashion when she was only little. Looking back at the girl, I saw that she was wearing clean clothes and her hair was braided into a French plait. It seemed like she was being well looked after, but I still wanted to suggest they call social services.

"Sophie's determined to foster her," Trevor told me quietly. "Lee's not sure the social will give her the green light, though."

I nodded, looking back to Lee's cousin and completely getting it. Even though she was young, there were some women who were just born to be mothers, and seeing how Sophie interacted with Billie and her son was evidence of that.

"So, you're with Lee now? Can't say I saw that coming," said Sophie, breaking me from my thoughts. Her expression gave nothing away, and I really couldn't tell how she felt about me.

"Oh, no, we're not...." I began, but she waved me off.

"Don't bother. I get it. I just hope you both know what you're doing," she said, her face serious.

And that was the problem, wasn't it? I wasn't sure either one of us had a clue what we were setting ourselves up for, or where this would lead. Ever since I'd first met Lee, a feeling of recklessness had formulated in my gut, and it had only grown bigger and bigger each time I saw him. A part of me didn't want to live by all the rules and procedures anymore; it wanted them to scatter in the wind.

Trevor turned to go into the kitchen, and I followed him. Stu was sitting at the table, typing on a laptop, while Lee stood by the cooker, checking on the food.

"What the fuck's she doing here?" somebody asked angrily, and my attention went across the room to Liam, who was leaning against the wall with his arms folded. I shot Trevor an annoyed glance. Clearly he'd been lying when he said Lee had told his brothers I was coming.

"Yeah, I second that," Stu piped in, his eyes narrowed to slits.

The two of them regarded me with open hostility, causing my stomach to twist with discomfort. The notion that I shouldn't have been there echoed in my head once more. Lee wiped his hands on a dishcloth and levelled each of his brothers with a sharp look. "The two of you, shut it. She's here because I say so."

Both Liam and Stu bristled at the authority in his voice, but they didn't argue. I barely had a chance to blink when Lee came toward me, his stride purposeful.

"Karla," he breathed, and the way he said my name made me shiver. He slid his fingers between mine and pulled me back out into the hallway for privacy.

"They're right — I should leave," I said before he could get a word in.

His hands went to my face, palms cupping my cheeks as his eyes flickered over my features. "You look tired," he murmured, his voice low and tender. The gravelly tone had a strangely arousing effect on me, and I suddenly felt too warm. I was also overly aware of how much I'd missed him. All of him.

Trying to summon some reserve, I took his hands and lowered them from my face before stepping back a bit. Clearing my throat, I said, "Trevor said you had an update for me."

Lee frowned and closed the distance I'd put between us. "Still all business, eh?"

"I don't see how I should be any other way."

We stared at one another in silence, so much want between us I could almost taste it on my tongue. Unable to resist, my gaze lowered to his lips. I missed how they felt on me, missed how his eyes could devour me from the inside out. Schooling my expression, I knew Lee could see just how much of a hard time I was having being this close to him. He took a deep breath and stepped away.

"All right. Let's do this your way, then. The update is that everything's been settled. Nobody's gunning for you anymore. It was mostly a precaution anyway, because they didn't even know your name."

Air rushed out of me all at once. "That's good news."

Lee eyed me speculatively. "Yeah, it is. So, are you staying for dinner, or are you gonna run off now that you've gotten what you wanted?"

"You could have just called me, you know."

"I know," Lee said, looking me up and down before whispering, "but then I wouldn't get to see you." He breathed in deep, moving closer, and I shivered slightly. "You smell incredible. What is that?"

"Uh, honey and almond," I answered, blinking. His proximity was causing me to flounder a little.

"Stay, Karla, eat. I want to spend time with you. And I promise I won't touch you unless you ask me for it," he told me huskily.

I should have tucked tail and fled right then, but I didn't. No, I was my own worst enemy, because I didn't have the willpower to say no to him. Finally, I nodded shyly and was rewarded with the handsomest of smiles. He took my hand in his again and led me back into the kitchen.

Twelve

I couldn't remember how long it had been since I sat at a table and ate a proper family-style dinner. Sure, I visited Mum and Dad's every once in a while, but that was different. There was no warmth between us. The Cross brothers did Sunday dinner the way it was supposed to be done. People passed bowls of food around, they spoke over each other, they laughed, but more importantly, it was clear that they all genuinely enjoyed one another's company. Well, aside from the fact that Stu and Liam refused to acknowledge my presence.

Still, it wasn't a chore like it was when I went to visit my parents. And really, it made me uncomfortable to think how much more functional this family of thieves was compared to the strict, law-abiding household I'd grown up in.

Sitting between Lee and Trevor, I tried to focus on my food rather than the fact that Lee's thigh was pressed up against mine, the weight of it sending butterflies flittering around in my stomach with wild abandon. As soon as he'd taken the seat beside me, he positioned his legs so we were touching. He was already breaking the promise he'd made in the hallway, but I didn't care. In fact, I savoured the contact.

For some reason, I couldn't take my eyes off Sophie where she sat at the end of the table, helping her son with his dinner. More so than ever I felt sort of…empty, knowing I'd never get to experience that maternal bond, or care for a child who belonged to me.

"You okay, Snap?" Lee asked, his eyes wandering from Sophie and then back to me. He'd obviously caught me looking.

I scooped some potatoes up onto my fork and nodded, before shovelling them in my mouth so that I wouldn't have to speak. Unlike Trevor, who seemed to have decided we were buddies now, Liam and Stu continued to ignore me.

When everyone was finished eating, Lee went over and took a plate covered in tin foil out of the oven.

"Liam, go bring this down to Mrs Spencer, would you?" he said.

Liam nodded and got up, taking the plate from him and heading out. He'd set aside dinner for the old lady? My heart really didn't know how to deal with that information, because it made him far more appealing than he had any business being.

I tried to help Lee wash up, but he told me to sit and relax. Next, dessert was served, which consisted of a delicious jelly trifle. I was stuffed by the time I was done, and Sophie invited me into the living room to sit with Jonathan and Billie while the boys cleaned up. Standing by the door, I felt unsure of myself, but then looked down and found Billie staring up at me, a doll in her hand.

"Do you want to play with Sally?" she asked, presenting the doll.

"Uh, sure," I replied, taking it while she led me into the room.

I sat next to Sophie while Billie informed Jonathan they were going to play a game of tea party. I almost laughed when Jonathan screwed up his face in displeasure.

"Trevor said you want to foster her," I said quietly.

Sophie let out a long sigh. "I suppose you're going to tell me it's a bad idea, that I'm too young."

"Not at all. I think it's a very honourable thing to do. In fact, I can send you some information if you'd like. It'd help you figure out where to get started."

She glanced at me in surprise. "Really?"

"Sure."

Her lip quivered slightly as she shot me a look of thanks and looked back to Billie. "She reminds me so much of myself when I was little, you know. I just hate the idea of her going through what I went through. If I can give her a safe place like Lee gave me a safe place, then I'll do everything I can to make it happen."

Lee gave her a safe place, and God, he was only a kid himself. The thought made my heart squeeze yet again. A silence passed between us before Sophie turned to me. "He's a good person, deep down. We all are."

Unsure of what to say, I took her hand and gave it a squeeze before finally replying, "I know you are."

After a while, I excused myself to go use the bathroom. Once there, I splashed some water on my face to freshen up, still feeling kind of crappy after last night's indulgence. When I returned, I found Lee had come in from the kitchen. He had Billie on his lap as he unravelled the French plait from her hair. I was struck speechless by the sight of him being so affectionate and caring with a child who wasn't even related to him, and a feeling of warmth spread across my chest.

"There, all done," he said before Billie turned and gave him a hug.

"Thanks, Lee. Sophie always plaits my hair way too tight," she told him, rubbing her head.

"Hey! I heard that!" Sophie exclaimed, feigning annoyance.

Lee chuckled, his eyes finding mine, and he saw how I was hovering. "Come in, Snap."

Stepping inside, I went to sit on the couch, but Lee grabbed my wrist and swung me around, pulling me down to sit next to him on the love seat. The heat of his body pressed all along the side of mine, and I felt a sudden bout of nervousness. It was doubled when Sophie gave Lee a knowing smile and announced she was taking Billie and Jonathan for a walk.

Lee picked up the remote, flicking through the stations. "You want to watch a movie?" he asked, his attention fixed to the screen. Peering at his profile, I took in the smooth sweep of his nose, the angular curve of his lips.

"Okay," I replied, my voice unexpectedly soft.

It snagged Lee's attention, and his gaze flicked to mine, catching me studying him. I looked away quickly, fighting a blush.

Without looking, I knew he was smirking. "You looked hot last night in your blue dress."

"Thanks."

"Pity I didn't get to see it."

"You saw a picture."

He let out a slow breath. "Not the same thing."

My attention returned to the screen as Lee selected a movie to watch. I settled into the seat, and he draped his arm along the back. I could feel his heat on my neck then, and there was something relaxing about it. He smelled of a fresh citrus cologne and fabric softener. I wanted to rest my head on his shoulder, but I wasn't brave enough. The house seemed quiet, and I wondered if his brothers had gone out somewhere.

As the movie progressed, I found my eyes drifting shut. Somewhere along the way, Lee's arm dropped down and was now tucked around me, holding me close. I felt warm and safe, so much so that I fell asleep. I only woke up when I felt Lee's nose nuzzling into my temple. The closing credits were rolling down the screen.

"I should get going," I said past a yawn.

Lee didn't respond, but instead his mouth dropped slowly to my neck, where he pressed his lips against my skin. A quiet breath escaped me, and his arm pulled my body close. His lips continued to travel from my neck to my jaw, and then finally to the edge of my mouth. When he kissed me, I trembled. It was slow at first, just a gentle press of his mouth before his tongue sneaked out to taste me. There was something about the slowness of his movements that felt drugging. His hands circled my waist, then lifted me so I was straddling him. The kiss intensified as our bodies moved, seeking friction. We stayed like that for a while, and by the time we came up for air, we were both breathless.

"Stay with me tonight," Lee murmured, his voice a sexy rumble.

I leaned back down to kiss him again, grinding myself off his erection, and his eyes flickered shut. His tongue dipped into my mouth while his hands roamed my bottom.

"Fuck," he swore. "Let me take you upstairs — otherwise, I'm gonna embarrass myself."

I felt a blush coming on again when I got his meaning, and allowed him to pull me up from the seat. Lee laced his fingers with mine and led me up two flights of stairs to the attic. His room must have been the biggest in the house. It had a king-sized bed, a flat-screen TV on the wall, a large wardrobe, and an en-suite bathroom. I let go of his hand and walked around, taking it all in. There were two windows, but instead of looking out, they looked up. The way I could see the stars was sort of romantic.

Lee approached me from behind, his arms sliding around my waist, pulling my arse flush with his cock. His mouth returned to my neck, and I swear my entire body turned to liquid.

"You can see the stars from here," I whispered.

"I'll make you see stars, Karla," he promised before pulling me over to his bed. He was unexpectedly tender when he laid me down. It was at odds with the predatory look he gave me as he climbed onto the mattress, his hands going to the waist of my jeans and unbuttoning the fly.

"What are you doing?" I asked, breathless.

When he glanced up his eyes were dark, and I shuddered, recognizing his intention. Seconds later my jeans were gone, and I was left in my T-shirt and boy shorts.

"Hmm, these are sexy," Lee said, humming. "But they need to go."

He pulled them off with practiced hands. Nerves coiled in the pit of my stomach when I was bared to him, suddenly aware of the fact that he hadn't even turned the lights off. This was so much different from being with him in the darkness of the nightclub. Here in his bedroom, he was going to be able to see *everything*. I clammed up, and he seemed to sense it.

"Don't do that," he whispered. "You're beautiful."

His eyes wandered between my legs, gently parting my thighs so he could see all of me. Letting out a low expletive, he rose long enough to rid himself of his clothes. I stared open-mouthed at his body, at the taut muscles and smooth skin. His cock was unmistakably hard, and when he fisted it, pumping up and down, a fire sparked within me. I was so wet for him I ached.

"You see what you do to me," he asked, voice gruff.

Biting my lip, I nodded.

"Let your hair down, babe."

I reached up, pulling out my clip and letting my hair fall around my shoulders. Lee's eyes blazed, eating up every inch of me. A second later, he was climbing back onto the bed, positioning his face between my thighs. A quiet gasp escaped me when his head dipped forward and his tongue flicked experimentally over my clit. I moaned, and a low growl emanated from deep in his chest. I squirmed a little, but his hands went to my thighs, holding me down. His stubble scraped deliciously along my skin when he pressed his mouth over all of me.

"Lee," I cried out, my hands fisting his blankets as my body bucked forward.

"Watch me," he said, his voice low and commanding.

His tongue flicked out and licked a line all the way up to my clit. One finger entered me, and I felt myself spasm around him. He moved it slowly in and out, intense pleasure shattering through me. When his tongue began circling my clit with determination, my eyes fell closed, unable to handle the intensity.

One of Lee's hands went to the hem of my T-shirt. "Take this off," he grunted between licks.

When I pulled it up over my head and threw it to the floor, his eyes moved over my breasts as though mapping every inch of them. Aware that there were people downstairs, I tried not to make too much noise, but it was difficult. Lee clearly knew what he was doing and he took his time, dragging it out, trying to make me beg. It didn't take long for me to give him what he wanted.

"Please," I mewled.

His hands circled my waist, fingers digging wantonly into the flesh of my hips. He groaned when our eyes met, and I watched his tongue as it moved on me. The sight was unnervingly erotic, and within seconds I came with thundering shudders right on his mouth. He continued licking me, drawing out every ounce of my pleasure. I was still revelling in a post-orgasmic haze when his heat left me, and I was vaguely aware of him opening a drawer.

A moment later he was back, rolling a condom down his impressive length as he knelt at the end of the bed. His head was tilted to one side as he murmured, "Fucking beautiful."

"I need you," I whispered, breathless.

Now that I'd come down from the high he'd just given me, I was desperate to have him inside. His eyes traced my body, stopping momentarily on the scar on my stomach. It was old, barely visible, really, but in that moment I was hyperaware of the imperfection. Lee didn't ask me where I'd gotten it, and instead continued to soak in the sight of my naked body like it was his favourite work of art.

Bracing his hands above my shoulders, he leant his head down to lick at my nipples. I moaned when he sucked one into his mouth and then the other, swirling his tongue around the needy flesh.

"You're all soft and ready for me," he said, his voice the sexiest thing I'd ever heard. "I can't wait to feel you, Karla."

My breathing began to quicken again when he lifted my thighs around his hips. He held me up, staring at me fiercely, and some sharp emotion cut through my chest. A second later he plunged into me hard, causing electricity to crackle all over my body. Our eyes stayed connected, and I felt like I could see right to the core of him in that moment. There was no wall up, no mask or pretence. All I saw was him, and it was beautiful.

He moved in me slowly, and I closed my eyes so I could savour the lazy drag against my nerve endings.

"Open your eyes," he whispered, pressing a soft kiss to my lips.

I did as he said, struck speechless by the emotions washing through the clear blue depths of his irises. Right then, I knew that this thing between us was real to him, that he felt things for me far stronger than simple lust. It was jarring, but at the same time it gave me clarity on my own feelings, and how I felt more than fleeting attraction for him, too.

He never sped up his movements, but instead continued to rock back and forth in an even pace. He was learning me, feeling me, making love to me. The sound of our breathing and the quiet slap of our bodies as they connected filled the room. I moaned when he reached down and pressed a finger to the bundle of nerves between my legs.

His forehead shone with a thin layer of sweat, the muscles of his abdomen tensing with every thrust of this hips. I loved the definition in his arms as he held his body above mine.

His movements became a little more frenzied when he leaned down and pressed his forehead to mine. "Come on my dick," he urged, his voice strained.

I clenched my thighs around him tight, feeling the sensation build in my core. He grunted when he began fucking me in hard, measured thrusts, and pleasure shattered though my body. Rubbing faster at my clit, he captured my lips in his and plunged his tongue against mine. I felt completely possessed, like he was everywhere all at once; his taste in my mouth, his noises in my ears, his cock doing wonderful things to my insides. Everything in me coiled tight, the onslaught that was Lee reaching his pinnacle, and I came for the second time that night. Only now it was so much more, because I felt him coming, too, filling me as his breathing grew choppy and his movements began to slow.

"Jesus," he said, his forehead resting on mine again.

Our hearts seemed to beat in time, our breaths matching as he held me to him so tight I didn't think he was ever going to let go.

"You make me feel so fucking alive," Lee said fervently, his words muffled by my skin. "Made for me."

I wrapped my arms around his neck and held him close, a strange fear clutching at my heart. A silence fell between us until Lee flipped us over, wrapping his arms around me and spooning me from behind.

"You're being awfully quiet," he whispered in my ear, and there was a touch of uncertainty in his words, like he was worried I was going to run on him.

I lifted his hand and intertwined our fingers. "I'm just frightened, Lee. The way I feel about you, it's intense. It scares me."

His arm tightened around me, pulling my body closer to his. "I feel it, too, the intensity. It shouldn't scare you."

For some reason, my eyes grew watery, and I couldn't understand why I was being so emotional. Maybe it was the way he spoke. Here, alone with me in his bed, his voice was different. There was no cocky bravado or teasing. He was just open, real, and it made it difficult to keep a handle on my feelings.

A single tear rolled down my cheek, and I was glad I wasn't facing him right then. He'd probably think I was a complete head case, crying after sex. It was just that being with him made everything else in my life a lie, and yet, the idea of being without him made everything seem empty and grey. So I was trapped in the lie. In fact, I'd walked right into it willingly with both eyes open.

I pressed my cheek into the pillow to dry away the tears and turned in his arms. Needing the comfort, I buried my face in his neck and felt a breath whoosh out of him.

"Karla?" said Lee, his tone questioning.

I spoke into his skin. "I just really, *really* like you. I like the things you do to me, and I don't want to lose them."

Feeling his jaw move, I thought he might be smiling. "If it's any consolation, I really like the things I do to you, too. Actually, I fucking love them. And you won't lose me, so long as you make the choice to be with me."

I lifted my head to meet his eyes. "But it's impossible. We can never have a normal relationship. Other than Alexis and Reya, there isn't a single person in my life I could tell about you, no one who wouldn't condemn me for it."

"It's simple, then — don't tell them."

"So what do we do, sneak around?"

"If that's what it takes."

My lips turned downward. "How would that even work?"

"We'd figure it out. I'm very inventive," he replied, waggling his eyebrows.

I laughed softly, and he caught my lips in his for a quick kiss. "For tonight, let's not worry about it. Tomorrow's a new day."

Lee pulled me back down into the pillows and I closed my eyes, snuggling into his chest this time. His hand stroked soothingly up and down my spine, and before I knew it, I was out cold.

I woke some time in the middle of the night, hearing voices. The room was dark, but a thin sliver of light trickled in from outside. Blinking my eyes open, I saw Lee standing with the door slightly ajar, wearing only his boxer briefs. Stu was outside, and he didn't look happy. I immediately closed my eyes, feigning sleep.

"I'm sorry, bruv, but you're losing it. All that cop pussy's blurring your vision."

"Oi, eyes on me. You try looking in my room again, and I swear I'll deck you," Lee warned him.

Crap. I suddenly realised that my legs and a good deal of my left breast were exposed. I must have kicked the blankets off in my sleep. My skin prickled with the need to cover up, but if I moved, they'd know I was listening.

"How do you know she's not snitching on us to her bosses?" Stu asked, his voice gruff.

"Because she doesn't know anything. Besides, other than what happened with Liam, we haven't caught an inch of heat lately. What's between me and Karla is between us. It's got nothing to do with her job or this family."

"It has everything to do with them. Christ, Lee, how can it not?"

Abruptly, I didn't want to hear any more, because if he said something incriminating right then, it'd put me in a bad position. I'd have to decide whether or not to report it, and I didn't want to report anything. I just wanted to forget about my job for a while and enjoy being with Lee for however long it might last. Letting out what I hoped sounded like a sleepy sigh, I shifted in place. Both brothers went silent before Stu said, "I'm going. Just think about it, Lee. You're supposed to be the smart one."

With that the door clicked shut, and I felt the bed dip as Lee climbed back in beside me. He didn't ask if I was awake, just draped an arm around me and pressed a kiss to the back of my head. Before long I heard his breathing even out, and I knew he'd fallen back asleep. I struggled with the decision on whether or not to leave, but his warmth felt too good, and in spite of the fact that Stu had spoken a lot of sense, I was far too comfortable in Lee's bed to go anywhere.

***

The next time I woke up, the bed was empty again. Somehow though, I sensed that I wasn't alone. Rolling onto my side, I rubbed at my eyes and blinked a few times. Lee was sitting in an armchair in the corner of the room. He was topless, his hair wet and a towel tucked about his waist. He must have taken a shower. His chin rested on his fist as he studied me, his expression pensive, and I wondered what he was thinking about.

"How long have you been sitting there?" I asked, holding the duvet to my chest as I sat up.

Lee cocked an eyebrow at my attempt to cover myself, obviously because he'd seen everything there was to see last night. "Not too long."

Our eyes locked, and I felt goose bumps rise on my skin. His gaze was possessive, knowing, and memories of what we'd done the night before flittered through my mind. I could still smell him on me, and it made my thighs quiver in want. Several quiet moments passed.

"Where'd you get the scar, Snap?" Lee asked, his curiosity evident on his face.

My heart gave a sharp thud of both pain and surprise. Surprise that he cared enough to ask, and pain because of what it represented. I hugged the duvet tighter around myself.

"When I was a kid, I was in a car accident with my parents. The impact came from the side and there were glass fragments embedded in my abdomen. I had some internal injuries, so I had to stay in hospital for a couple of weeks. God, it was boring," I said, trying to offset my discomfort.

Lee sucked in a sharp breath, his expression sympathetic. "Karla."

I waved him off. "It was a long time ago."

"Well, I always say that a scar's better than being dead."

"Uh-huh."

Lee frowned. "Is there something else you're not telling me?"

The tenderness in his voice made my throat tighten. I hadn't planned on telling him anything, but the truth just came spilling out of me anyway as I blurted, "My internal injuries were bad. I can't have children."

In the quiet of the room, the sentence sounded shockingly stark. Lee didn't speak for a second, and I stared at my hands. Before I knew it, the bed dipped and warm, muscular arms wrapped around me from behind. Lee pulled me into his embrace, and there was something about the gesture that made me feel worse and better at the same time.

"Did you always want kids?" he asked in a whisper, his mouth resting at my temple.

"Not always. But once something is taken away from you, you tend to want it more. I know I can live a full life without children, but it's like my heart gets all horrible and heavy when I think about the fact that I…that I can't."

"You could adopt," Lee suggested, his hand lowering to my thigh and stroking.

I let out a joyless laugh. "It's not the same."

He heaved a breath. "No, I suppose not."

A long quiet elapsed, Lee's chin resting on my shoulder, his breath warming the side of my neck. I couldn't remember a time when I'd been held like this, skin to skin, feeling cut open and exposed, yet sewn up and healed all at once.

Lee's voice was low and solemn when he said, "We're stronger in the places that we've been broken."

His words hit me square in the gut, the sentiment causing my eyes to grow a little wet, and I wondered who he was quoting from.

"Who said that?" I whispered.

"Hemingway."

A soft, surprised laugh escaped me, even though my eyes were still watery. "You read Hemingway?"

I felt him move his head in a shake. "There used to be this tunnel near where an old friend of mine lived. Lots of graffiti on the walls. I remember walking home one night and seeing this mural in crazy vibrant colours with that quote as the centrepiece. You ever read words and they just make sense to you? I had one of those moments."

"Yeah, the truth of them just kind of…resonates," I said.

Lee caught my chin between his fingers, turning my face so he could look me straight in the eye. I'd never seen his expression so sincere. "The strongest part of you is the broken one, and having kids isn't the only way you can become a parent, Karla. The way you protect people makes you a mother to the world."

His statement struck the centre of my heart and I clung to it, feeling a renewed sense of meaning about myself. I'd never thought of it that way before. Seriously, I had to change the subject, because otherwise I was seriously going to start bawling. The warmth of his hand felt soothing, and I was suddenly curious about him. "You'll probably have a dozen kids running around one day. I can definitely see that for you. You practically raised your own brothers, after all."

He was silent for longer than I expected, and he seemed thoughtful. Maybe it was the insinuation that his future would be with someone else, filled with someone else's children. The idea pained me more than it should have. His breath warmed my cheeks as he mustered a reply. "Nah, maybe raising my brothers was enough for one lifetime. And let's remember, I didn't exactly do a bang-up job."

"You did your best. You were only a kid yourself."

"I was ruthless, but that's only because I had to be."

I snuggled further into his arms and placed a hand on his cheek. "You know, I might end up regretting telling you this someday, but if I'd been in your position, I'd probably have made the exact same choices."

Lee's nostrils flared, and his gaze intensified at my words. They were the truth. I could sit on my high horse, spouting moral virtues, but I knew that if I'd been born into Lee's situation, I would have done whatever it took to survive. Perhaps we were more similar than I cared to admit.

Dipping his head, he caught my lips in a kiss and pulled me on top of him. Both his hands stroked my thighs as he stared up at me, his eyes hooded.

"I like you," he murmured.

"I like you, too."

"You shouldn't be so cynical about what we could be, you know."

I crinkled my brow. "What's that supposed to mean?"

"It means I know what you were playing at just now, talking about me having kids, like the idea of you being in my future is such an impossibility."

"Lee," I said, air whooshing out of me when his thumbs dug into my muscles, massaging out the kinks. "My dad would disown me if he knew I was with you."

"So what? You don't even like the man."

"I know that, but he's my father. Besides, he's a product of his environment. My parents grew up at a time when you couldn't walk down the street without worrying if a bomb was going to go off. That kind of thing hardens people."

"Hmm." Lee grinned.

"Don't 'hmm' me, you cheeky little shit. And what's the grin for?"

"It's for the fact that you're gonna forget all this serious talk in a minute when I fuck you."

"Oh, really?"

"Really. So hard it'll rewire that brain of yours, so afterward, when you think about the future, all you can see is me in it."

Reaching up, he palmed both my breasts, then bent forward and captured one of my nipples in his mouth. The action rendered me incapable of doing anything but surrendering. And when he flipped me over and pulled me onto all fours, he made good on his promise, because it might have been morning, but I really did see stars.

Thirteen

I was laughing so hard I had to bend over and hold my stomach, so hard that tears were rolling down my cheeks. Tony and I were sitting in the break room eating lunch and trying not to wet ourselves as Keira did an impression of DI Jennings.

"Constable, tuck your shirt in and straighten your tie. You look like the vagrant lovechild of Keith Richards and Worzel Gummidge."

"Stop!" I begged, trying to calm my laughter. "I haven't heard anyone use Worzel Gummidge as a reference since I was five years old."

"That's because you never bloody listen, do you, Sheehan? Cotton wool in the ears," Keira clipped, not dropping the act.

I swiped a thumb under my eyes, finally calming down, and glanced up. The smile immediately fled my features, because standing in the doorway was none other than Jennings herself. Keira had her back turned, continuing with her impression. Jennings' face was indecipherable, and I went completely silent, waiting for her to stride into the room and put Keira in her place. But she didn't do that. Instead, she cast me a quick, uncomfortable glance, turned on her heel, and left without a word.

I wanted to tell Keira that she'd been caught, but I knew it'd only make her worry. If Jennings planned on reprimanding her, it was going to happen whether I told her or not. Packing away the end of my lunch, I felt a strange urge to go after Jennings. Even if she did relish making my job difficult, I couldn't help but feel bad. I wanted to apologise for Keira, and for myself for laughing.

Leaving the break room and hurrying down the corridor, I made my way to her office, knocking gently on the door before stepping inside. What I saw when I entered made me wish I'd waited for her to call me in, because Jennings was sitting at her desk, dabbing tears from her eyes with a handkerchief. Her gaze widened when she took me in, and several moments of the most uncomfortable silence I'd ever felt fell between us. The woman had feelings. This thought unsettled me.

"I, uh, I'm sorry, ma'am. Excuse me," I said, and turned to leave.

"Don't you dare," said Jennings. "You just had the gall to burst into my office unannounced, so now you can stay and say your piece. I presume you have some sort of speech to make?"

"That's not why I…."

"Then why *did* you?" Jennings snapped, and I startled a little.

"I don't really know. I just wanted to apologise, I suppose, for what Keira was doing, and for laughing. Mostly for the laughing. You don't deserve that kind of behaviour, and it's unprofessional on our part."

Well, maybe she did deserve it just a little, but I wasn't going to say that to her face.

"Unprofessional behaviour from you is no great surprise, Sheehan. Christ, look at your father."

I gave her a funny look. "My dad might not be the most pleasant man in the world, but he's hardly unprofessional."

Jennings only snorted and dabbed once more at her eyes before tossing her hankie aside. I narrowed my gaze. "What's the deal with you two anyway?"

She glanced up in surprise. "Pardon?"

"You hate my dad like he murdered your grandmother or something. Why?"

Jennings straightened in her seat. "You have no business asking such questions. Now get back to work."

"No, I want to know. I've never done anything to you, yet you treat me like I'm a piece of dirt on the end of your boot. I deserve to be told the reason."

A silence fell, and Jennings eyed me shrewdly. "How's your mother these days?"

Her question seemed a little random, but I answered anyway. "Um, she's fine."

"I'll bet she is," Jennings muttered, and I wasn't sure why, but there was something in her tone that I found curious. It was jealousy with a hint of resentment.... Oh, *hell no*. Suddenly, everything fell into place, and to be honest, it made me feel a little queasy.

"Oh, my God," I whispered, gaping at her in disbelief. "No way."

"What are you prattling about?"

"You and my dad."

Jennings frowned. "Me and your dad, what? Bloody hell, finish you sentences, Sheehan, you're not a toddler."

"You and my dad had a thing, didn't you? Wait, don't answer that. I don't want to know."

She stared, her blue eyes cutting into me like a knife, and all at once I knew it was true. My dad had an affair with Jennings. I felt like I'd just stepped over the threshold and into the twilight zone.

"Your father is a spineless coward," said Jennings, her voice sober. "He is the worst decision I've ever made."

"Spineless?" My brow furrowed.

"Spineless," Jennings repeated. "Do you know that I was once beaten so badly by the members of an organised crime ring your father and I were investigating that I almost lost my life? Thugs broke into my home and attacked me, and when your father showed up and ran them off, he refused to give evidence or identify my attackers, because it would result in people discovering that we were conducting an affair. He allowed those men to walk free in order to save his reputation and keep his marriage intact."

My gut churned again, this time for a very different reason. I wanted to think she was lying, but she had no reason to, and her story didn't sound made up. In fact, the longer I contemplated it, the more it sounded *exactly* like something my dad would do.

"Go on, tell me I'm lying," said Jennings, folding her arms across her chest defensively.

"I believe you," I whispered, and her eyes flared in shock. A moment passed between us, and I didn't know what to say. In the end, I went with a simple, "I'm sorry that happened to you. And I'm sorry my dad is spineless coward."

Because he was. And even though Jennings was no ray of sunshine, no woman deserved to be treated like he'd treated her. She lifted her chin, and we shared a moment of eye contact. Finally, she nodded her acceptance of my apology, and I turned and left her office.

***

By the time I got home from work that evening, I felt emotionally drained. I couldn't stop thinking about Jennings and my dad, could barely get my head around it, really. He'd cheated on my mum with her, and then did something so abhorrent as to abandon her when she needed him most. At long last, her treatment of me all these years made sense. Hell, if I was Jennings, I'd hate me, too.

The flat was empty when I went inside, and I remembered that Alexis had an afternoon modelling job to go to. Dropping my keys on the coffee table, I pushed open the door to my bedroom and got a fright to see a man sitting at the end of my bed. Jumping back, my hand went to my baton, which, since I was still in full uniform, was resting in its holster. It took a second for my pulse to slow down.

"You almost gave me a heart attack," I breathed. "How did you get in here?"

Lee's eyes traced over me tenderly. "Alexis let me in about a half an hour ago." He paused and ran a hand over his short-cropped hair, seeming a little out of sorts. "I've been thinking about you all day. Last night my bed felt empty without you in it."

I could tell he was perplexed by his feelings, and truthfully, after our emotional conversation the previous night, I felt the same. His words made something inside me soften, and I let him pull me over to sit next to him on the bed. I'd left his house yesterday afternoon, after a night (and a morning) of life-altering sex, the kind of sex that made you realise you were being shafted with all the sex you'd had before it.

"I've had a strange day," I said as he gently pulled the pins from my hair and ran his fingers through its length. "A really strange day, actually."

His hands stilled for a second. "Strange how?"

"You remember my boss I was telling you about?"

Lee nodded. "The one who has it in you for you, yeah."

"Well, we had something of a heart-to-heart, or as close to a heart-to-heart as we could have. I know why she hates me now. She and my dad had an affair years ago, and it ended badly."

Lee's hands resumed their movement, this time massaging the back of my neck as he made a thoughtful face. "Didn't see that one coming."

"Me neither. Like I said, weird day."

His breath met my skin as he asked, "You want me to make it less weird?"

His voice was pure sex. I shivered, closed my eyes, and silently nodded as his fingers went to my shirt to undo the buttons. I sat back and allowed him to undress me, never once opening my eyes. When his lips brushed lightly over mine, my mouth fell open. I could almost sense his grin when his tongue slid along my lower lip and then dipped inside. My head tilted back, and I moaned when his lips travelled along my jaw and to the crook of my neck, where he began planting kisses that got me instantly wet.

He was already learning what I liked.

Somewhere between now and the night we'd spent together, I'd made the unconscious decision to let this happen, to let myself have Lee in whatever way I could. Maybe it was because of the sweet things he'd said, the way he understood me better than anyone else. Or maybe it was all down to the rush of being with him when I knew I shouldn't. I convinced myself that if no one ever found out, nothing bad could come of it.

I wore only my black bra and matching knickers when Lee pushed me to the top of my bed. He climbed over me, still fully clothed, eyes roaming my face as he spread my hair across the pillow, a halo of red. My chest rose and fell with my breathing, and my breasts rubbed against the fabric of his top, desperately needing him to remove my bra.

Instead, he took both of my hands in his and raised them above my head, then bent his mouth to mine and kissed me so fiercely I felt it all the way down to my toes.

He settled his weight between my legs and began to move his hips gently back and forth, his hardness meeting my softness. I gasped into his mouth right before something cold met my wrists and I heard a recognisable click.

Abruptly, I dragged my mouth from his and tried to lower my hands, only to find he'd handcuffed me to the bedpost. My heart pounded rapidly, my adrenaline kicking in.

"Lee!" I hissed. "Did you take those from my uniform?"

He smirked, still on top of me, and pressed his erection between my legs once more. "Spur-of-the-moment decision, couldn't help myself," he murmured, kissing me again. "Just go with it."

"Give me the key, now," I demanded between kisses, trying not to melt under his assault.

"Hush, you'll like this," he assured me, chuckling huskily as his mouth descended. He lifted my body slightly to unsnap my bra, and then he was caressing my breasts, running his lips tantalisingly over the peaks of my nipples and making me squirm in place. I wanted to protest more, tell him I'd kick his arse if he didn't release me within the next three seconds, but I couldn't, because the truth was that Lee was right. I did like it. In fact, I liked it a little too much. Especially when he sucked my breast into his mouth and his hand slipped inside my underwear, his fingers finding me instantly.

He groaned, his tongue flicking around my nipple, and broke away long enough to growl, "So wet."

It was both agonising and tantalising not being able to touch him. All I could do was lie there and let him do what he wanted to me. My pores tightened in anticipation.

"Take something off," I pleaded, frustrated that he still hadn't removed a single article of clothing.

He chuckled, and his mouth left me when he rose to pull his T-shirt off over his head. I allowed my eyes to trace the contours of his body, enjoying how his hips tapered at the waist of his jeans. His gaze trailed over me as his hands lowered to undo his fly, pulling a condom from his pocket before shoving off his jeans. With his mouth he tore the wrapper, then threw it onto the bed as he positioned his head between my legs.

"You," he began, kissing my inner thigh, "are the sexiest woman I've ever seen."

My back arched against the mattress when he pressed his lips to my folds, his tongue peeking out and giving a soft lick. His eyes were on my breasts, which were pushed high into the air with my position as he licked. I pulled my hands against the cuffs, my wrists knocking into the bed frame in my effort to struggle free.

"You've got to — " I gasped, stopping mid-sentence when he slid his tongue down and then inside me. "God, you've got to make me come."

He chuckled, not coming up for air, and continued to eat me out until I was just on the cusp of orgasm. Then his mouth left me, and I huffed out a breath of dissatisfaction. Grabbing the condom from where he'd thrown it on the bed, he rose up to his knees and rolled it down his stiff length. Barely a second later, he was thrusting inside me hard and fast, his hands circling my waist, eyes roaming my body as I lay there completely at his mercy.

He fucked me with abandon, his hips jutting in and out in a frenzy of lust. My vision grew hazy, and I could barely find my voice to speak.

"Mine," Lee grunted, his fingertips digging into my flesh. "This is mine."

"Yes," I breathed, my voice more air than sound as his eyes shone with a fierce victory.

"God, look at you. You're so beautiful when you let go, Karla."

"I need to touch you," I whimpered.

Lee smiled a beautifully handsome smile. "Not yet."

"Lee," I moaned needily. "*Please*."

His eyes captured mine as his movements sped up. After having his mouth on me, I was so ready to shatter, and every thrust of cock felt incredible. The keys must have been left in the cuffs, because he reached up and released them, taking one hand and lowering it between our bodies. "Don't touch me, touch yourself. I want to see you," Lee said, bringing my fingers to my clit as he continued to move. Coaxing me to draw lazy circles over my flesh, his eyes blazed with arousal. The knowledge that touching myself did that to him was a huge turn-on.

"Fuck," Lee swore, watching me, his gaze wandering from my fingers and up to my face. I felt my own wetness coat my hand, and the sensation of having his cock inside me while I brought myself to orgasm was unbelievable. I shook around him, moaning loudly when I came. Lee kissed me, swallowing my sounds as he sought his own release. His tongue swept across mine, over and over, until I felt his movements slow down. I opened my eyes, watching him come, his brows drawn together tight. He looked so masculine, so perfect. His body dropped to mine, his arms going around me and pulling me close.

When we fell asleep, he was still inside me.

Fourteen

The next day when I took my lunch break, I decided to visit a nearby deli to grab a sandwich. When I'd woken up that morning, Lee was gone, a note on my bedside dresser from him saying he'd be back that night. My heart did a flip-flop, knowing that at the end of the day I'd get to see him again, get to lose myself in his body. It was a new sensation for me, because I'd never felt like this during any of my previous relationships, had never craved a man in a way that made me feel quite so…crazed.

My mind kept wandering as I replayed his words when we had sex, or remembered his smell or the feel of him. I was basically walking around in a continuous state of arousal, and it felt a little bit obscene.

Almost as though my thoughts had summoned him, I glanced across the street from the deli, and there he was. Lee stood speaking with two other men I recognised from his garage, which was just around the corner. I was in uniform, so I knew approaching him wasn't an option, especially so close to the station. Not being discovered was key to this secret relationship we were conducting.

I chanced one last quick glance in his direction, and it was right at that moment that he looked up and saw me. His eyes flared, and I looked away swiftly. Hurrying inside the deli, I busied myself placing an order and tried to encourage my heart rate to slow down.

My skin prickled and I felt myself flush, suddenly recognising what was wrong with me. I was excited. Just knowing he was close sent my pulse racing. It was so wrong. When I emerged he was gone, and a sudden bout of disappointment hit me. Pulling my phone from my pocket,

I was doubly disappointed to find he hadn't sent me any messages or tried to call.

Continuing on my way back to the station, I let my thoughts wander to the day ahead and the paperwork I had to complete, when suddenly I was pulled around a corner and into an alleyway. The brown paper bag I was carrying fell to the ground as Lee crushed his mouth to mine in a kiss that sent adrenaline flooding my system. His arms pulled me in, but my uniform had too many layers and I couldn't get quite close enough.

His hands came up to slid inside my shirt collar, gently cupping my neck as his tongue made me dizzy. When we finally broke apart, I was practically gasping for air, my cheeks heating and my chest rising and falling rapidly.

"I woke up this morning still inside you," Lee whispered, his words making my tummy flutter. "Have you any idea how hard it was for me to leave?"

As he pressed his forehead to mine, his minty breath washed across my cheeks. He never broke eye contact when he moved one hand from my neck up to my lips, his thumb slipping inside my mouth. I moaned quietly, my head tilting back as I flicked my tongue over it and he slid it all the way in.

"Tonight," said Lee, still whispering, "I'm gonna get you down on your knees and slide my hard cock into this pretty little mouth." His shockingly dirty words turned me on, and I gasped quietly. He hummed low in his throat, his eyes fixed on his thumb as I felt the press of his erection against my hip. A second later his phone started ringing, and he growled in irritation.

"Fuck," he swore, lowering his hand.

"I should be getting back to work," I said, glancing around for my dropped lunch. It sat on the ground, relatively undamaged. I picked it up and straightened myself out. Lee grabbed my wrist, pulling me back to him and laying another intense kiss on me.

"Later," he promised when he broke away, breathless. I nodded, trying to calm my nerves, and then he was gone. Swallowing harshly, I waited a few seconds before walking around the corner and heading back in the direction of the station. I'd only made it a few steps when I saw another uniform coming my way. I almost stumbled over my own feet as Steve walked toward me, a smug gleam in his eye. For a moment I wondered if he'd seen something, but then again, he always looked smug. There didn't necessarily have to be a reason.

"Ah, picked up some lunch for me, did you, Karla? How kind," he said, and I narrowed my gaze.

"Funny."

Steve studied me, his thin eyebrows drawing together. "What's got your knickers in a twist?"

Something about his close attention caused me to grow a little flustered as I answered harshly, "Nothing." It was a mistake, because if I'd been acting normally I would have thrown some barb back at him. Now he looked suspicious. His gaze wandered over my shoulder, but I knew Lee was long gone. There was no way he could've seen anything. At least, I hoped there wasn't.

"You're acting strange," he said with a thoughtful expression.

"Time of the month," I threw back casually, regaining some of my composure. Steve screwed up his mouth in distaste while I strode past him and continued back to the station, all the while my heart pounded in my ears. That call was far too close for comfort.

I needed to be more careful.

***

My phone woke me early the next morning, and I rolled over to check who was calling. I frowned when I saw Tony's number, knowing he'd never phone at this hour unless it was something important. My shift didn't begin until midday, and I'd planned on allowing myself a few extra hours' sleep.

Lee's warm body surrounded mine, his breathing deep as he slept. He'd come over late last night after Alexis had gone to bed, and we'd been up until the early hours, hardly able to keep our hands off one another. I thought it was funny that he'd waited until Alexis was asleep, because my friend was far too savvy not to know something was going on. Plus, it wasn't like I hadn't already told her everything, unbeknownst to Lee, of course. My bed smelled like him, and memories of the previous night flooded my senses.

I sat on the edge of the mattress, staring up at him as he towered over me, his eyes dark with hunger.

"Take it out," he murmured quietly, his throat bobbing as he swallowed. I reached forward, undoing the buckle of his belt and pulling down the zipper on his jeans. His erection was already outlined sharply against the fabric, and when I slid my hand inside and caressed him, he was harder than I'd ever felt.

"Put your mouth on me," he urged, his voice strained.

I bent forward and pressed my lips to the side of his cock, then licked up the length of him. The masculine growl that emanated from deep in his chest made my thighs quiver as I lowered my mouth over his head. His hands fisted in my hair, the grip tight with an edge of pain that felt exhilarating. I began to move up and down in a leisurely rhythm. My eyes were closed, but when I opened them and looked up, I'd never seen such raw, animalistic need.

"Hello," I said, my voice groggy as I answered the call, trying to clear my mind of thoughts of the night before. Lee's body shifted slightly, but I couldn't tell if the ringing had woken him or if he was still asleep.

"Karla, is there any chance you could come in early?" Tony asked, an urgency in his voice. "We've had some information about that garage you and Steve visited a couple weeks ago, the one owned by the Cross brothers."

As soon as the words left his mouth, my body grew still, my thumb instinctively going to the button on the side of my phone and lowering the volume.

"Information?" I practically whispered.

"Apparently, it's being used as a base to chop and store stolen cars until they're ready to be shipped overseas. We've gotten a search warrant issued, but we need all hands on deck. I thought that since you've already been inside and know the layout of the place, you'd like to be on the team."

Even though I was lying down, I felt like I might pass out. My pulse thrummed as I tried to figure out how to proceed. I still couldn't tell whether or not Lee was awake, but if he was, could he hear what had just been said? Should I warn him that his garage was about to be searched? My gut sank as a horrible feeling took over. I was torn, didn't know which side I was supposed to be on anymore.

"Okay, thanks for calling. I'll be in as soon as I can," I said, trying to keep my voice even.

"See you in a bit," said Tony before hanging up, completely oblivious to the moral dilemma he'd just put me in.

Placing the phone back on my nightstand with shaky fingers, I felt my throat begin to tighten. Lee's breathing was deep and even, so I thought he must have still been sleeping. Turning in his arms, I gripped his shoulder and gently shook him. He made a disgruntled noise at being woken, and it took him a few moments to open his eyes. I stared at him, the decision I had to make twisting me up inside.

"Snap," he said, his blue eyes sharpening as he took me in. I let out a shuddering breath, and Lee's expression sobered. He must've sensed something was up, but he didn't comment on it. Instead, he asked, "What time is it?"

"Just after seven," I answered.

"I'd better get going. I've got a meeting with a supplier at nine."

Leaning forward, he placed a quick kiss on my lips before hopping out of bed. His swiftness caught me off guard, and I began to wonder if he'd been faking sleep, if he'd been listening to my entire conversation with Tony. It hit me suddenly that I'd been about to tell him everything, and it completely sobered me. I'd been about to warn a criminal that his business was going to be searched, and I'd barely even had to think twice about it. What the hell was happening to me? Being with Lee was changing everything, and I was one-hundred-percent sure I didn't like it.

He dressed like normal, and there was nothing in his demeanour that made me think he was anxious to leave. He acted just like any man who had a meeting to get to; hurried, but not overly so. Maybe I was overreacting. Maybe he hadn't heard the call. I sat up in bed, watching him dress, and when he was done he came toward me, kissing me one last time. Again, it was on the tip of my tongue to warn him, but I couldn't seem to find my voice. Lee hovered for a second, his eyes flickering between mine, almost like he was waiting for me to say something, but that couldn't be right.

As soon as he was gone, I got up, showered, and dressed, all within the space of half an hour. I had just enough time to grab a large coffee from Starbucks on my way to the station in lieu of a breakfast. When I arrived, I found DI Jennings in the briefing room, heading the search team. Steve had a list of the cars suspected of being stored at the garage, including all of the makes, models, and vehicle identification numbers.

All of a sudden, everything felt a little too real, and though I hadn't yet eaten a thing, I was struck by a wave of nausea. Tony drove and I sat in the passenger seat, with Keira in the back as we made the short journey to the garage. Keira prattled on about the fight she'd been having with her boyfriend, but I barely registered what she was saying. On the outside I might have seemed calm, but on the inside I was panicking.

Why hadn't I warned Lee?

Yes, he was guilty, and I'd always believed that guilty people deserved to be punished. But now that I had very real feelings for a guilty person, the lines were starting to blur. I pulled my phone from my pocket, on the cusp of typing out a message, but it was too late, and what on earth would I say to him anyway? It wasn't like you could flush a stolen car down the toilet or hide it under a rug.

A minute later Tony pulled up outside the garage, joining a number of other police vehicles. Jennings was standing by the entrance, her mouth moving as she barked orders at the assembled officers. Tony, Keira, and I got out and joined the others right before Jennings turned and banged three times on the door. My heart hammered as I waited, hoping like hell that it wasn't Lee who answered. In the end, it was Stu who appeared, and Jennings immediately announced herself and her intention to search the premises.

"No chance," said Stu, standing tall and crossing his arms over his chest. "This is private property." I was suddenly aware of his size, his broad shoulders and muscular arms, and how scary he appeared when facing down Jennings, who was half his size but just as fierce. She took her time pulling out the search warrant before smugly waving it in his face. Stu scowled at her for a long moment, but eventually stood back and let her pass.

Jennings turned and motioned for the search team to enter. I was one of the last to go inside, and when Stu saw me he shook his head, letting out a hard laugh as he shot me a look of pure disdain.

"Oh, this is fucking priceless," he said, not a hint of humour in his voice. I was thankful nobody else was paying attention to him.

I was about to follow the others when Jennings stopped me in my tracks. "Sheehan, stay here and make sure no members of the public try to enter."

I nodded at the instruction and went to stand by the door. The search team was noisy, barrelling through the garage, pulling open cabinets and toolboxes in search of anything even remotely suspect. Jennings knocked loudly on Lee's office door, and I went utterly still when I heard him saying something to her, the irritation clear in his voice.

Stu stood just a couple of feet away, leaning against the wall with his arms folded as he continued to eye me.

"I warned Lee about you, and now look. Knew you were going to be nothing but trouble for us."

"This hasn't got anything to do with me," I said quietly, fervently, unable to prevent the hitch in my voice.

Stu rolled his eyes. "Likely fucking story."

"I'm not lying!" I whisper-hissed, glancing around to make sure nobody was listening. "I care about your brother a lot."

"Not enough to warn him about all this, though," Stu responded, motioning to the search team currently rifling through the place.

"I never planned for any of this to happen, and if I could rewind the clock, I would. I'd try to make a better decision, but you should know that all of this would have happened whether or not Lee and I became involved."

He didn't say anything, just continued to stare me down, and I was surprised I managed to stand my ground. Stu was nothing if not intimidating, especially when he was angry. Eventually he turned and walked in the direction of Lee's office. I heard the two brothers talking and grew nervous, wondering if Stu was telling him that I was there. I expected Lee to come and find me at any moment, but it never happened. Over an hour passed, and I had to turn away a number of customers who stopped by. Clearly, there was a legitimate side to the business; I just didn't know what percentage it was compared to the non-legitimate side.

My stomach was rumbling loudly, a reminder that I hadn't eaten yet today, when Tony came over. There was a crease in his brow as he stared down at the clipboard he held, listing the stolen vehicles.

"I don't understand," he said, confused, and I perked up suddenly. "Not a single one of these motors matches the ones on this list."

I let out a breath, whether in relief or surprise, I couldn't say. "Do you think somebody gave Jennings bad information?"

"Either that, or someone tipped them off that we were coming," said Tony, his gaze drifting around the room, and all of a sudden I *knew*. There was no suspicion in his voice, only a statement of fact, and yet my stomach twisted like he'd just pointed an accusatory finger right at me.

"Has Jennings been told?"

Tony nodded. "I just informed her. She's on the warpath. Probably best to steer clear of her today."

"I hear that," I muttered, rubbing my fingers over my tired eyes.

It wasn't bad information. Tony had hit the nail on the head. They'd known we were coming, and it was all down to me. This morning had gone from bad to worse. First I felt guilty for not warning Lee about the search, and now I was fuming that he'd pretended to be asleep while he'd quite clearly been listening to a private phone call. Whatever way you wanted to spin it, he'd taken advantage of our personal relationship and jeopardised my job in the process. But really, I was even angrier at myself, because I'd jeopardised it too just by being with him. I was also dumb enough to think I could trust him.

Whatever happened to the woman who'd said she'd never let herself say yes to Lee Cross?

She forgot to use her brain, that's what. The more minutes that passed, the angrier I became. At some point I saw Jennings stride out of the garage, a face like thunder, and several members of the search team left with her. Only a few remained, and I took the opportunity to go and find Lee. He was standing in a back corridor of the building, one side of which led to a break room and the other to a bathroom. He had his back to me as he and Stu spoke in hushed tones. Looking behind me to make sure none of my colleagues were nearby, I grabbed Lee's arm and yanked him inside the bathroom before he could react.

"Hey!" Stu yelled as I slammed the door shut and flicked over the lock.

"What the fuck?" Lee swore, his expression furious.

I took a step toward him. "Don't look at me like that. I know what you did."

He cocked an eyebrow and splayed his arms out. "Oh, yeah, and what's that?"

"You took advantage of me, that's what. You weren't asleep this morning when Tony called, were you? You bloody well heard everything."

Lee didn't answer, just stared at me stonily. I let out a crazed laugh and placed my hands on my hips as I peered up at the ceiling. "God, how could I have been so stupid?" Suddenly, hurt began to mix in with my anger, a sharp pang shooting through my chest. "You and your brothers have probably been laughing at me all this time, laughing at the dumb cop who couldn't see through your act."

"You're wrong," Lee said firmly.

"Oh, yeah? Explain it, then."

His expression softened by the tiniest fraction as he stepped closer. "I can't do this right now, Karla. I'll come over to yours later and we'll talk, okay?"

His response made my temper flare as I pressed both hands to his chest and pushed him back. "You'll do no such thing. I don't want to see you after this, not ever. You're just a little boy playing around with fire, only I'm the one who got burned."

Before I could pull away, Lee caught my wrists, yanking my body to his as he glared down at me. "I was never a boy, not in this life. Even when I was a kid, I didn't feel like one, so don't give me that. And do you know how much I was willing you to say something this morning? *Anything*. But you didn't breathe a word. Not one fucking word. I should've known you didn't really give a shit about me after what happened with Liam. But no, I didn't listen to my gut, I just let my cock lead me, thinking you were perfect. That makes me the stupid one, not you."

His words cut me deep and I pulled at his grip, but he held me too tightly and I couldn't break free. "Don't you dare try turning this around."

"Why not?" he asked, his warm breath hitting my cheeks. "Yes, I listened to your phone call, but you were going to let me walk out of your flat completely oblivious to the fact that I was about to be fucked over. You know this isn't the life I'd choose if there'd been another option, yet you were going to let me go to *prison*, Karla. Let that sink in for a minute. It killed me when you didn't say anything, and I waited. I gave you every opportunity."

The hurt in his eyes was plain as day, and the wind went right out of my sails. "I wanted to tell you," I whispered. "But I just...I just couldn't."

"Of course you couldn't, because you care more about being a cop and saving all the people you perceive as innocent than you'll ever care about me. You'll never see that the world isn't all black and white." Anger and anguish mixed in his voice as it cracked around the edges, catching. "Sometimes the innocent ones are guilty only because the world didn't give them a chance to stay innocent. Maybe I'm the one you should think about saving."

Right in that moment my gut sank. His anger was too sad to be angry at in return, and for a second all I saw was a hurt little boy. When I spoke, I kept my voice gentle. "I've tried talking to you about going clean, but you won't hear a word of it."

His mouth twisted as he gestured around us. "Because I'm in too fucking deep, I told you that!"

"I can help you. There are things we can look into, procedures."

Lee laughed harshly, shaking his head, "God, look at you, still a fucking cop. Always a fucking cop. Can you just be on my side for one bloody second?"

Any tenderness in my voice vanished, and my expression hardened. "I was a cop long before I met you, Lee, and I've barely even scratched the surface of knowing who you are, so how can you expect loyalty when it hasn't been earned?"

He bent his head to look me directly in the eye, his lips mere centimetres from mine. "Don't pretend like you can't feel what's between us." He paused, his voice dropping low. "I've been deep inside you, Karla. I know who you are and you know who I am. You're just too scared to admit it."

I shook my head, refusing to listen to him rationalise so irrationally. "Lee, we need to be smart. This thing we're doing is going to destroy us. Look what's happened already. I love being with you, but all this" — I peered at him despairingly — "it's not worth it."

He shook his head. "You don't believe that."

"I do. I believe it. I'm not going to tell you how to live your life, but so long as it stays the same, we can't be together. I'm sorry."

I took a step back and he let me go. Tears prickled at my eyes, but I refused to let them fall, not wanting to look weak. Lee's features turned hard, his eyes thin slices of blue. We stared at each other for a long time, until the tension in the small room became unbearable.

"I have to go," I said, turning on my heel and unlocking the door. Stepping out into the hallway, I found it was empty, the garage quiet now that most of the search team had left. Lee didn't call for me to stay or come after me, and as I walked away from him, I brought my fingers to my cheeks, wiping away the tears.

Fifteen

Back at the station that afternoon, it was a rare occasion that I saw my dad. My emotions were still a little off kilter after what had happened with Lee, so I wasn't sure I was fit to deal with my father. Luckily, he was there in a professional capacity, to debrief the team after the failed search. Not surprisingly, Jennings was nowhere to be seen, and I had to admit I was slightly disappointed. There was some weird part of me that wanted to see them interact, perhaps do something to prove that Jennings had been lying about their affair.

I sat at the back of the room in between Tony and Keira, listening to him talk about how the search was connected to a much larger case, the one he'd been working on to take down Tommy McGregor.

I could barely breathe as he clicked through a series of projected images, all displaying pictures and evidence on the powerful crime lord. It was suspected that the Cross garage was one of his main sources of high-end stolen vehicles, and they had pictures of all the brothers. My heart stuttered when a surveillance shot of Lee came on the screen. He was crossing the street, his phone held to his ear as he took a drag out of a cigarette. Tiny pinpricks tickled at my palms, and my mouth felt dry as a bone.

They'd misjudged the setup, though, suspecting that Stu was heading the operation since he was the eldest. Everything fell into place. Lee's boss was McGregor; that was why he'd been at the warehouse the night of the rave.

"Unfortunately for the investigation," my dad went on sourly, "information was leaked that the garage was to be searched today, which as you all know, resulted in the place being cleaner than a priest on Sunday."

Little did he know, the source of that leak was me. I'd never felt more conflicted in my entire seven years on the job. When Dad finished up the debriefing, I stood on shaky legs and made my way to the front of the room, where he was talking seriously with one of the sergeants. I waited until they were done before approaching him.

"Dad," I said, and his eyes came to me.

"Constable," he replied formally, refusing to use my actual name. We never really spoke to one another at work, but it still hardened me inside that he couldn't even bring himself to acknowledge that I was his daughter in front of colleagues. It was perplexing that I'd approached him at all, but for some reason I had the sudden urge to talk to him.

"Do you have time for a quick cup of tea?" I asked.

For a brief moment he looked disgruntled, put out by the idea of actually spending some small amount of his precious time with me. A few moments went by before he finally nodded, glancing at his watch. "Yes, but not long."

"There's a café across the street," I suggested and got another nod.

We walked in silence out of the station and over the road, not speaking until the waitress had brought us our beverages. Dad studied me curiously, and a little impatiently, waiting for me to speak.

"I spoke to DI Jennings the other day. She told me some stuff," I began, and Dad's posture stiffened.

"That woman has no business telling you anything," he practically grunted.

"I'll take that as confirmation that what she told me is true, then, shall I?"

He turned away, staring out the window as he brought his teacup to his mouth and took a sip. I clasped my hands together, my stomach in knots.

"I can't believe you'd do that to Mum," I said, breaking the silence. "She's never been anything but loyal to you, more loyal than you deserve."

"It was a long time ago, Karla. I've put it behind me," he answered, dismissive.

"Well, Jennings certainly hasn't. Have you any idea what it's like for me working with her? She literally goes out of her way to fuck with me every single day."

Dad bristled at my use of language, but he didn't reprimand me for it. "Katherine's always been volatile," he said, and if I wasn't mistaken, there was a note of affection in his voice. Was he shitting me? I'd never heard him sound like that before, not even with Mum.

"You let the men who beat her go free," I said, and the vein in his neck began to throb.

"Don't try to act like you understand any of it, Karla. You were only a child when it happened."

"I understand that you could have easily given a witness statement describing the men who broke into her home, but you refused." What I really wanted to say was left unspoken, but I could see he knew what I was thinking. It was a cowardly act.

"Do you think I don't regret what I did?" Dad asked after a long stretch of silence. His question surprised me as I levelled my eyes on him.

"I don't know. Do you?"

"Of course I do. I was young, afraid of damaging my reputation. Why on earth do you think I've been putting all my energy into the McGregor case? What we had is in the past. It'll never been rekindled, but I'm trying to do right by Katherine by finally putting that monster away for good, even if it might be years too late."

"McGregor's the one who beat her?"

Dad nodded soberly. "He and his men. You were a wee girl at the time, and you'd just started expressing an interest in the police. It was ridiculous. Why any woman would put herself in harm's way like that still astounds me."

Even though what he said pissed me off, I could read between the lines. He'd never admit it out loud, but maybe he didn't like the idea of me becoming a policewoman because it frightened him. It was a little bit sad that he'd never be able to show weakness, admit his fears, even to his own daughter. He was too hard, too gruff, to ever be any kind of loving presence in my life, for us to ever have a relationship where we could share our feelings without worry of being judged. And on the matter of women joining the force, we were destined to forever disagree. Truthfully, it was a sorry state of affairs, because I'd known him my whole life, and that was long enough to know he'd never change, would never learn to admit he was wrong.

"I think you'll find, Dad, that men are made of flesh and bone just like women. They can be hurt, too. This has nothing to do with gender. Katherine was just unlucky, as I'm sure many male officers have been."

"You're not as strong. That's a genetic fact," Dad countered.

"We're not weak, either — far from it."

He stared at me, silent, and it felt like we'd come to something of an impasse. I'd hardly touched my tea, but Dad picked his up, downing the rest of it before rising from the table.

"I have to get back," he said, acting like we hadn't just been discussing something as monumentally important as we had. "If you can spare the time, it'd make your mother happy to see you visit this week."

With that he left, and I watched him go.

***

The following evening, I decided to pay a visit to the gym. What with everything that had been happening, I'd been falling behind on my workouts. Reya had a gig, so she couldn't come along, but I didn't mind. I needed some time alone to clear my head, my feet pounding hard on the treadmill as I pumped my legs fast. I was a hot, sweaty mess by the time I finished, and made my way to the showers, where I scrubbed my body clean.

My head was full of conflicting thoughts, the foremost being what was going to happen to Lee when my dad finally arrested McGregor. Would he get caught in the crossfire, just another piece of collateral damage? Or would he finally be free of the life he was embroiled in?

I so desperately wanted him to look me in the eye and promise he was going to clean up his act, get out of the game. But perhaps I was overestimating what I meant to him. Perhaps I'd allowed my feelings to grow too deep.

Piling my wet hair up into a messy bun, I quickly dressed in a T-shirt and some yoga pants before making my way out of the changing rooms to head home. I stopped in my tracks as soon as I stepped out and found Lee waiting for me. The gym was due to close in half an hour, so there weren't many people around. He stood leaning back against the wall, his arms folded across his chest as he eyed me.

"Hi," I said, wondering what he was doing here. After how we left things yesterday, I didn't think he'd want to see me again. I'd told him I didn't want to see him, but I knew the statement had fallen flat. I couldn't even convince myself it was true, never mind anyone else. His gaze travelled from my wet, messy hair to the scooped neckline of my T-shirt.

"Snap," said Lee, pushing off the wall and stepping toward me.

"Is everything all right?" I asked.

"Is it ever?" he asked back, expressionless.

"I'm sorry about yesterday." I eyed him meaningfully, my gaze flickering over his face. There was a tension in his features, and he seemed stressed.

"Nothing for you to be sorry about. We were both amped up, and everyone says shit they don't mean when they're angry." He paused, seeming tired, and ran a hand over his stubble. "Anyway, we both knew what we were getting into."

"But we got into it anyway," I finished.

He let out a quick breath. "Yeah, we did."

"Well, at least we were clever enough to end things before they got out of hand."

Lee's eyes sharpened, his lips forming a straight line, and I could tell that what I'd said pissed him off. All I got out of him was a flat, "Huh."

"So, I guess I'll be seeing you," I said, moving to walk by him. He stepped in my way, blocking my path, and kept coming forward, forcing me to retreat until my back hit the wall. Pressing his entire body into mine, he whispered, "You think it's going to be that easy, Karla?"

His question made me swallow as I brought my hands to his chest and pushed. He barely moved an inch. In fact, my pushing him only incited him to press into me harder. I could feel every inch of his torso, from his hard pecs and abs to the beat of his heart thumping wildly at his collarbone.

"Don't do this," I pleaded.

"I miss how you feel," he said, his voice deep and sensual.

My body grew soft against his, the tone he used making me melt. I needed to be stronger. "You should hate me."

"I know, but I can't. I don't think I ever could."

"Lee, you're making this harder than it needs to be," I said, my hands moving up from his chest to touch his neck. "It'll be easier if we don't see each other. Proximity is a problem for us, you know that."

He dipped his head, his mouth touching my earlobe. "I can't help it that you draw me in." His voice dropped to a whisper. "I want you back in my bed. I want to feel you shake for me."

I trembled, my throat catching as I responded, "It can't happen."

"It can. You just have to let it. I'll take care of everything else."

Suddenly, I realised I was letting him get to me just like I always did. I was letting him blur my vision and jumble up my thoughts with sex. His mouth fell from my earlobe as I drew back as far as I could.

"But don't you see, that's just the thing. You're not taking care of anything. You've gotten away with murder for so long that you've lost your fear. I know you steal. I know you work for a dangerous man, but you have to get out now." I paused to catch my breath and eyed him pointedly. "You have to get out before it's too late, and, believe me when I say this, it's going to be too late very soon, Lee."

His brow furrowed, and I hoped he got my message. I couldn't say it outright, but I could warn him in my own particular way.

"What are you saying?"

"The other morning I was silent. Well, now I'm not. You need to listen to me. Otherwise, I can't predict what might happen to you and your family. Do you understand?"

His eyes grew serious as his lips firmed, and a long moment of quiet passed before he nodded. "Yeah, I get you."

I exhaled deeply, knowing I'd done my bit. Now it was down to him to make things right. My dad was gunning for McGregor, and it was personal. He wasn't going to stop until he took down him and everyone who worked for him. I just hoped Lee pulled himself and his brothers out of the building before the bomb went off.

"I'm going home now," I said. "I have to work in the morning."

Lee allowed me to move away, but only because he was deep in thought. Reaching down, I took his hand in mine and gave it a soft squeeze before continuing on my way. It was a relief to know he'd taken my words to heart, and some of the tension inside me eased, knowing that Lee and his brothers might get a chance at a different kind of life.

The entire concept was flipped entirely on its ear the very next day when I arrived at the station to find the place packed to the rafters. Young men lined either side of the reception area, all sporting handcuffs. I had no idea what was going on, but one thing was clear: If the men hadn't been restrained, we would've had a riot on our hands. Hostility permeated the air like a real live thing.

It was only as my eyes travelled over those present that I saw Liam, Trevor, and Lee all standing by one wall. A constable began guiding Lee through the double doors that led to the interview rooms. Despite the fact that his face was all cut up, he wore a wide grin that was directed firmly at a dark-skinned guy on the other side of the room. Blood stained Lee's forehead, and there was a wound on his chin.

When I took a proper look at the man he was grinning at (who, by the way, was seething back at him), I recognised the neck tattoo. It was the same bloke who'd tried to intimidate me outside the grocery shop that one evening, the one I'd told Lee about. The blood in my veins turned to ice as an unsettling idea came upon me. This wasn't about that, was it?

"Real brave grinning at me like a smug fuck when I can't do nothing about it," said the neck tattoo. "Where'd you leave your balls, Cross?"

"Left them under your mum's bed. She's keepin' them warm for me," Lee quipped, and the neck tattoo dove for him right before two officers hurried to hold him back.

I stood in place watching it all unfold, and Lee's smile faltered only slightly when his eyes finally landed on me. He hadn't been expecting to see me there, that much was clear, perhaps because I'd told him last night that I had to work early. It was a lie to end our conversation. I wasn't due in until midday, which was why I was still on shift.

His jaw firmed as the constable continued to lead him from the room. I hurried over to Tony to ask what was going on.

"Seems to be some kind of gang rivalry. A woman called in to report the fighting going on outside her building. No weapons were involved, but a few of them are in a bad way. And get this, it was the Cross brothers who started the fight. The eldest one is being interviewed right now, and I'm about to question the other," Tony paused to glance down at the file he was holding. "Lee Cross. You wouldn't mind sitting in on it, would you? You've dealt with him before. Maybe he'll be more inclined to talk to a familiar face."

I felt about two inches tall when Tony looked at me with such sincerity and trust. He had no idea what a crappy excuse for a police officer I was, or just how deeply familiar Lee and I truly were.

"Sure," I replied stiffly. "Anything I can do to help."

Tony nodded and motioned for me to follow him to the interview room, which consisted of bare magnolia walls and a table with three chairs, one of which Lee was currently occupying. The constable who'd brought him there was standing by the door, while Tony and I took the seats across from Lee. I glanced at him, unable to prevent the pang of concern in my gut at seeing him beat up. My first instinct was to reach across the table and inspect his injuries, make sure he was okay. His cuffed hands were behind his back, and I desperately wanted to take them off, massage his wrists to ease the strain.

I tried to push those perplexing instincts aside and harden my resolve. Lee had instigated a dangerous gang fight. He deserved to be suffering. I hadn't even known he was part of a gang, or maybe Tony just presumed he was. After all, he was a boss, an under-boss, but a boss nonetheless, and he obviously had a lot of young men working for him, *stealing* for him.

I kept reminding myself of these facts, my expression sullen.

Lee's gaze fixed on me as the muscles in his jaw twitched.

"I've forgotten something. I'll be right back," said Tony, after rifling through the file he'd carried in. Once he was gone, I was alone at the table with Lee. The other constable still stood by the door, so I couldn't speak openly. We found ourselves in something of a staring contest. I didn't look away, nor did I let my expression falter. He needed to know I wasn't happy with any of this.

Lee smiled vaguely and leaned his body forward as much as he could, studying me as he cocked his head. "Why so blue, blue eyes?"

"I didn't give you permission to speak, so be quiet," I replied firmly, irritated by how his lips curved around the edges at my hot-tempered response, hating how it made my insides flutter.

"Such a pretty blue," he went on, goading me.

"I told you to shut it. That's your final warning."

"You know, I kinda like it when you boss me around, Constable."

Deciding he was enjoying himself far too much, I gave him the silent treatment, staring at the wall as we waited for Tony to return. It only took a minute, and his chair scraped against the floor as he pulled it back. Once he was seated, he cautioned Lee before starting the interview.

"So," Tony began, flipping through a new folder, "do you want to tell me what started all this, son?"

"My solicitor's on his way. I'm not talking to you until he gets here. End of."

"An eyewitness claims you were the instigator in the disturbance, says you walked right up to Carl Finley and attacked him, completely out of nowhere."

"Bit dramatic," said Lee.

"So tell me your version of events."

"You got a hearing problem? I said I've got nothing to say to you."

Tony raised his hands in the air. "That's fine by me. I'll just keep talking, then, shall I?"

Lee shrugged, his eyes flicking to me for a second and then back to Tony. I'd never felt more tense in my life. He could've outed us right then and there. He could've said anything, and there was nothing I could do to stop him.

"Our witness maintains you were shouting at Carl, saying he disrespected something that belonged to you. It sounds like maybe he had it coming, and you know, I've got to wonder what he disrespected. It must be something pretty special," Tony went on, and my entire body turned cold as my eyes rose to Lee's. He stared back at me, completely expressionless, but in that moment I knew. I knew he'd started the fight with the neck tattoo guy, or Carl Finley, because of what he did to me. It was unbelievable. Inexcusable. I dealt with aggressive individuals on a daily basis. I was used to it. And the fact of the matter was, Lee had no business starting fights over me. We weren't even together, and in spite of what he'd tricked me into saying during sex, I certainly didn't belong to him.

Lee levelled me with his gaze as he replied to Tony, "You have no idea."

My pores tightened, my tummy fluttering in response to the intensity in his words. The reaction pissed me off.

"You don't seem very remorseful for your actions," I put in, unable to keep quiet.

"I don't have any regrets, if that's what you're getting at."

I grabbed for Tony's folder, which contained details of those who'd been taken to hospital. "One of the men involved in the fight has a busted jaw, and another has a smashed kneecap. It'd take a fairly cold-hearted individual not to feel concern over such serious injuries."

"If Mugabe got his jaw broke, would you shed a tear?" Lee asked with derision.

"That's not the same thing."

"Oh, it's not? Do you have any idea the kind of disgusting shit Carl and his boys get up to? Gang rapes, violent attacks, muggings, intimidation, you name it. You heard about those drugs that've been going around? The ones that teenagers were overdosing on?" He paused to eye me pointedly. "He's threatened people at gunpoint. He's beaten people half to death, and he still gets to walk the streets like he's king of his own little empire. I think you'll find it's exactly the same thing."

"So, you started the fight as what, some kind of vigilante form of justice?" Tony put in cynically, and I suddenly remembered we weren't alone. I also felt awful, because Carl had threatened me and I'd let him away with it. If I'd arrested him that day, then maybe I could've saved a few of the people Lee had spoken about. The thought made me wither with guilt. I hated to admit it, but what he'd told me was true. The world wasn't all black and white, and I was starting to realise that a lot of my beliefs could be turned upside down when I took in another person's perspective.

"Did I say I started a fight?" Lee asked. "Because I'm fairly sure I didn't."

"All right, well, let's talk about the drugs, then. Can you give us any more details?" said Tony. "If you have information, we can work together to have him charged."

Lee shook his head as he let out a derisive chuckle. "Do I look like a fucking mug to you? Jesus Christ, pull the other one."

"You offered up the information. I was just curious to know more," Tony replied. He was being nice, playing good cop. Did that mean I was bad cop? No, I didn't think so, not with the amount of feelings that were swirling around inside me for the criminal on the other side of the table.

The radio of the officer standing by the door went off, calling him away on an errand. He told Tony he'd be back as quick as he could before leaving the room. With him gone, the place felt oddly smaller. I sensed movement under table as Lee stretched out his leg, his shoe knocking against mine.

Immediately withdrawing my foot, I narrowed my eyes at him and willed him not to do anything that might make Tony suspicious. I wanted to ask him if he'd started the fight only for me, or if he'd done it because of the other things Carl was guilty of. I wanted to tell him that I was sorry for ending things between us, but that it couldn't be helped. But most of all I wanted to take him in my arms and tell him violence wasn't ever a solution. I wanted to show him what the world could be like without it.

In reality, I'd never get to do any of that, because there would always be a divide. The thin blue line would always lie between us, with me on the side of order and him on the side of chaos.

"Have you seen a nurse for your injuries?" I asked, the tenderness in my voice unexpected. Tony shot me a curious look while Lee shook his head.

"My health doesn't factor very high on the list of priorities where the old bill are concerned, but thanks for asking."

"Well, how do you feel? Are you hurt anywhere we can't see?"

Lee's chin rose as his eyes twinkled mischievously. "Why don't you come a little closer and take a look, Constable?"

"Don't be cute." On the outside I sounded stern, while on the inside I was pleading with him to let me know he was okay. I remembered back to the time when Steve beat him up. He'd tried to hide his injuries from me then, too. I continued staring at him until his expression softened.

"I'm fine. Nothing a hot bath and a few beers won't fix."

His answer relieved me. Tony cleared his throat and addressed me formally. "Constable, can I speak with you outside for a moment?"

I glanced at him and nodded. "Sure." Rising from my seat, I frantically wondered if I'd done anything to give myself away. Had I shown too much affection when talking to Lee? I couldn't tell.

As soon as we were outside and the door was closed, Tony eyed me speculatively. "Are you feeling okay?"

I shrugged. "Yeah. No different from usual."

"You're acting strangely. Why all the questions in there? If I didn't know any better, I'd say there was something you're not telling me."

Every muscle in my body coiled tight, and I suddenly realised how transparent I was being. I never expressed concern over a suspect's health, not in the way I had with Lee. I also never lost my cool in interviews, or acted like I had a personal investment in the crime being investigated. Tony knew me well enough to know something was fishy.

"Well, now that I think of it, I am having a bit of an off day. I didn't get much sleep last night," I lied in an effort to explain my behaviour.

Tony let out a slow breath. "You're sure that's all it is?"

"Very sure."

"Right, well, it doesn't look like young Mr Cross is going to give us anything we can work with. Can you escort him to a holding cell until his solicitor gets here? I'm going to bring another of the men in for questioning."

"Of course, I'll do that right away," I said, turning to go back inside the interview room.

Sixteen

Lee looked up as soon as I entered, glancing behind me to see if I was alone. He seemed different now that Tony was gone, less cocky and more concerned. Even his voice was different when he spoke, softer.

"Everything all right?"

"Yes," I answered shortly. "Your interview is over. I'm bringing you to a holding cell until your legal advisor arrives."

"Hey," said Lee, his tone gentle as I motioned for him to get up from his seat. "I didn't expect you to be here."

"I have no idea what that's supposed to mean. Now move. We haven't got all day."

He stood, towering over me by a couple of inches, his eyes tracing my features. "What's up with you?"

I glared at him, incredulous, as I whisper-hissed, "Are you shitting me? You started this fight because of me, and now you expect me to act normal. This behaviour is inexcusable."

Lee bit his lip as though to keep from smiling at my attempt to scold him. "It is inexcusable — you're right. But it wasn't all for you. You know how I feel about drugs. Something had to be done." He paused and took a step closer until there was hardly any space between us. "And if it meant I got to teach him a lesson for so much as even thinking about laying his hands on you, then all the better." His voice was a low, husky murmur, and I felt my throat tighten with opposing emotions. I wanted to kiss him and slap him all at the same time.

"I don't know why you're acting so casual right now. If Carl decides to press charges, you could get six months for aggravated assault, more if it turns out that anybody was seriously injured," I told him.

Lee levelled his eyes on me. "Finley won't be pressing charges. That's not how we do things."

"Oh, it's a 'we,' is it? So you consider yourself the same sort of person as him? How reassuring."

"Not what I meant."

I shook my head and opened the door, gripping his upper arm to move him forward. "This conversation is over. Now start walking," I ordered him.

He stepped out into the corridor, and I heard loud voices up ahead.

"Fucking hell," Lee swore, looking to his right.

I stepped past him just in time to see Carl Finley head-butt one of the two constables who'd been trying to escort him to an interview room. Lee positioned his body in front of mine, as though to shield me from getting caught in the crossfire. My heart clenched momentarily at the protective move, but then the officers got the upper hand, restraining Carl to the floor. The one he'd head-butted kicked him hard in the lower abdomen, and Carl grunted in pain. Seeing that they had things under control, I began to guide Lee farther down the corridor.

He chuckled quietly as we passed by Carl, who twisted his head to look up at Lee, venom in his eyes. Lee glanced at the constable who'd kicked him, still laughing.

"That's bang out of order, mate."

"Shut it or you'll be next," the constable spat.

"Just try it," said Lee, baring his teeth.

The constable took a step forward, but I narrowed my gaze at him and intervened just in time.

"A little bit of professionalism wouldn't go amiss, Connors," I said sternly before continuing to guide Lee away.

"You're too good for this shit," Lee said once we were alone again, his statement surprising me. He walked ahead of me, so all I could see was his back. I still held his upper arm, whether to keep him from running off or to appease my need to touch him, I wasn't sure.

When I didn't respond, he kept talking. "I hate thinking of you being hurt, Karla, hate imagining you in all the dangerous situations you have to walk into every day."

His words stirred a pang of emotion in my gut, but I tried to bat it down and keep my voice steady as I whispered, "And you think that doesn't go both ways? I hate thinking of your life just as much as you hate thinking of mine."

Lee didn't breathe a word after that, and when I locked him into the cell, he stared at his hands, clearly deep in thought.

***

It was four days after seeing him at the station that I decided to visit Lee's garage. I drove over in my own car, hoping he'd be around. It was only when I arrived that I remembered they didn't open on weekends. Engaging the handbrake, I sat there for a moment, wondering what the hell I was doing.

The radio silence on his end worried me, and I desperately wanted to know if he was doing anything to remove himself from McGregor's inner circle. I knew the only way he was going to be able to do it peacefully was to buy himself out, but how much would that even cost?

I had no idea.

Finally deciding I was being an idiot for trying to see him, I determined to go home and quit wasting my time worrying over a man who wasn't even my partner. In the grand scale of things, very little had happened between us. We'd had sex a few times; that was it. I needed to give myself a good firm reality check.

It was evening, and the sky was just beginning to darken when I took one last look at the doors to Lee's garage. I furrowed my brow when I noticed something on the ground, and on closer inspection I realised it was actually *someone*.

Without thinking I got out of the car, hurrying over to help the crumpled body lying in a heap. He wore a peaked cap, but when I gently pushed it up with my fingers, I saw it was Liam. Half his face was bashed in, and blood stained his clothing. Feeling for a pulse, I let out a relieved breath to find he was alive and still breathing, albeit raggedly. It took me only a few minutes to look him over and determine his injuries. His body was badly bruised and he had several painful-looking cuts, but there were no bullets or fatal wounds as far as I could tell.

Pulling my phone from my pocket, I began dialling the number for emergency services when a hand suddenly shot out, plucking the phone from my grasp. Liam was awake.

"Don't," he croaked. "Just bring me home. Find Lee."

"You're hurt," I said. "You need an ambulance."

"No," he went on fervently. "No ambulance, *please*."

The fierce look in his eyes gave me pause, and entirely on instinct I ran to my car, opening the back door before returning to Liam and helping him to stand. It was a good thing I was strong, because anyone else might have had a hard time getting the muscular twenty-year-old into the back of their car. Once I had him situated, I slid into the front and started the engine, heading in the direction of Lee's house. Glancing through the overhead mirror I saw that Liam had passed out again.

I was already there, rushing to the front door and knocking frantically, when I wondered why I hadn't gone to the hospital, or called the station to make a report. It was a sobering thought, and not for the first time I questioned just how much of an influence my feelings for Lee were having on my actions.

Trevor answered the door, the smile instantly dropping from his face when he saw my panicked expression. Without saying a word, I grabbed his hand and yanked him outside, pulling him to my car and opening the back door. He swore profusely when he saw the state Liam was in, then ran back inside the house. Before I knew it, Stu and Lee were there, their entire forms twisting with rage when they saw their youngest brother. Sophie came out of the house, too, her hand going to her mouth in shock.

I watched silently as they worked together to get him inside. They all laid him carefully down on the couch, while Sophie ran upstairs to grab a first aid kit. Once Liam was settled, Lee came to me, his hands going to my face as he looked me directly in the eyes. There was a strain in his voice, his rage barely concealed. My breathing was still frantic, my heartbeat racing.

"Tell me what happened, Karla, and start from the beginning."

I quickly relayed how I'd gone to his garage to speak with him and found Liam on the ground. Trevor and Stu were mere feet away, listening to me as I spoke.

"This has Finley written all over it," Stu growled, his hands clenched tightly into fists.

Lee's fingers dropped from my face as he shot Stu a loaded glance. A hundred words were exchanged in the silence, and then all three brothers were on the move. I had no idea what was happening, but I followed Lee into the hallway, where he opened a storage closet, pulling out a baseball bat, a steel pole, and a hammer. He handed all three to Stu before running up the stairs.

I was in too much shock to react, staring at them as they gathered munitions with my mouth open. When Lee came back downstairs, he wore a black hoodie with the zipper pulled all the way to the top. Next he tied a bandana around his face, covering everything but his eyes before pulling up his hood.

"No," I said, my voice harsh. "No fucking way. You're not doing this."

Lee moved to step past me, but I grabbed his arm. He glared down at me, and I was startled by the fact that all I could see were his glacial blue eyes. "Stay out of it," he grunted, ripping his arm from my hold.

"Finley's got to pay," said Stu, like it was that simple. "You deal in justice, but so do we. We just have our own particular brand of punishment."

"Wait," I pleaded, my thoughts scrambling as a realisation hit me. "This couldn't have been Finley. Just listen to me for a second."

Lee turned, giving me his full attention, and I let out a long exhalation. "After your interview the other day, Tony's been like a bloodhound going after Carl. He found out where he was running his drugs from and searched the place. He and a good lot of his crew were arrested and have been held in custody ever since. It couldn't have been him."

Finally, the brothers were actually listening to me, and my pulse began to slow down.

Lee pulled the bandana from his face so that it rested around his neck. "You'd better not be lying to me, Karla."

"Hand to heart, it's the truth."

He looked to Stu, and again they had one of their silent communications.

"Couldn't have been Hartfield's lot. We sorted everything out with them weeks ago," said Stu.

Lee ran a hand over his stubble, his mind clearly racing. "This is completely fucked. Somebody beat Liam to send a message." Turning, he stormed into the living room, where Sophie was currently tending to Liam's injuries. We all followed, and Lee knelt on the floor, running a soft hand over his brother's hair.

"Liam, mate, can you hear me?"

At the sound of Lee's voice, Liam's eyes fluttered open.

"Who did this, bruv? Did you see?"

Liam stared at him, his attention landing on me for a second before returning to his brother. "Come 'ere," he wheezed, motioning for Lee to get closer. When he did, Liam whispered something in his ear and Lee's entire body went still, his every muscle coiling tight. Obviously, he hadn't wanted me to hear whatever it was he had to say.

When he stood, he gestured for Stu and Trevor to go into the kitchen. They both went and then Lee turned to me, taking my hand in his and pulling me out into the hallway. When he reached the front door, he drew my body close, embracing me in an unexpected hug.

"Thank you," he whispered into my hair. "I don't know what you came to see me for, but if you hadn't found Liam when you did, he could've been out there all night."

My hands fisted in his hoodie as I buried my face in his neck, inhaling his masculine scent. We stood there for a long time, holding each other, not exchanging a single word. I felt his gratitude in how tightly he held onto me, and I got the sense he had a lot of stuff churning around in his head. Drawing away a little to look up at him, I said, "I know there are things you're not telling me, but if you need help just say the word."

His expression turned tender as he ran a hand over my cheek. "If I asked you to go up those stairs right now and wait for me to come back, would you do it?" he asked, his eyes piercing.

"That wouldn't help either of us."

"Right now, it's the help I need."

I couldn't say no to him, not again, so I simply shook my head. Some of the tension returned to his body as his expression sobered. "You'd better leave, then."

"When I say I want to help, I mean it, Lee. Stop taking everyone's load onto your own shoulders."

"If you wanted to help, you'd go to my room, take off your clothes, and warm my bed," he growled, gripping my hair and tugging gently. The sensation gave me a small tingle between my legs. "You'd make everything I own smell like you, and you'd stop leaving me all the time."

"When I leave, it's not because I want to."

"Then stay," he murmured, dropping his mouth to mine and allowing our lips to meet in a brief, barely there kiss.

I stepped away from him, trying to communicate my turmoil in one tortured look.

"Nah, didn't think so," Lee said harshly.

I took a deep breath, turned on my heel, and walked out the door.

***

"Bad day?" Alexis asked when I came into her room, crawled into bed beside her, and rested my head on the rounded part of her belly, which was growing bigger by the day.

"Something like that," I answered tiredly. "Can I sleep in here with you tonight?"

"Sure. Want to talk about it?"

"Not really."

"Okay."

A quiet fell between us, and I could feel her stomach rising and falling as she breathed.

"Have you thought about what you're going to call the baby when it's born?" I asked, trying to think of something that made me happy rather than something that made me sad.

She let out a long sigh. "This is probably fucked up since he abandoned me, but if it's a boy, I don't think I can call him anything other than Oliver. Olivia if it's a girl, I guess."

"Those are both good names."

"Yeah," she said, her voice a whisper.

"Does your heart still hurt when you think of him?" I asked, unable to help it.

I heard her inhale in a quiet gasp, and she was silent for a long time before she responded. "Every day."

"My heart hurts when I think about Lee. Does that mean I love him like you love King?"

Another gasp escaped her, this time for an entirely different reason, as she looked down at me, her expression stunned. "Oh, Karla, I had no idea. I mean, I knew you two were doing things, but I didn't know it was like that."

"I don't want it to be."

"Neither did I."

I let out a small, joyless laugh. "What a pair we make."

Her answering laugh was just as joyless, the sound echoing my sentiments and agreeing wholeheartedly.

Two weeks passed. Two horrible, agonising weeks. Everything seemed to amplify my loneliness, like how the fabric of my uniform brushed coldly at my skin, no humanity in the touch, or how I'd lie in bed and get a phantom-like whisper of his scent. I knew it wasn't real, because I'd washed and changed my sheets several times since we'd last shared a bed. It was branded into my memory, though, and every time I was at work and smelled a man's cologne that reminded me of his, my gut twisted.

I was on the night shift with Tony, driving around town in the patrol car, when my phone buzzed with a text. Tony's attention was fixed on the road as I pulled it out, looking down to see Lee's name on the screen. All at once, a brick dropped to the pit of my stomach. He was making contact, but it was after eleven. I just hoped this wasn't some kind of booty call.

Lee: Its Stu. Ned u @ our boozer. Lee in bad wey.

My heart pounded as I read the misspelled text, questions swirling around in my head. Had he been in a fight? Had somebody beaten him like Liam had been beaten? Looking to Tony, I said, "Hey, I have a friend who's in a spot of trouble. You wouldn't mind taking a little detour with me, would you?"

"No problem, it's been a quiet night anyway."

A couple of minutes later, we were parked outside the pub. I gave my appearance a quick look in the mirror, taking my hat off and fixing my hair in the usual bun I wore to work.

"You want me to come in with you?" Tony asked.

"Nah, you take a break. Check in with the girls. I won't be long."

He nodded and I got out, my heart thrumming as I stepped inside the noisy pub. The place was busy for a Wednesday, but then I remembered there was a football match on earlier. They'd probably been watching it on the flat-screen TV that hung in the far corner of the bar. A couple of men eyed me aggressively, wondering what a police woman was doing in their local, but once I didn't bother them, they returned to their conversations and ignored me.

I walked through, scanning the faces of those around me, until I saw Stu having what appeared to be a heated argument with two other men.

"Put a leash on your brother, would ya? He's been on the sauce since midday."

"Oh, fuck off," someone shouted, and I turned to see Lee making a jerk-off motion with his hand, blind drunk and very clearly angling for a fight.

The man looked at Stu again. "I mean it — we don't want any trouble."

"He's been having a bad night. I'll make sure he behaves," said Stu, and the men seemed relatively appeased as they returned to their booth.

"Yeah, that's right, piss off back to where you came from," Lee slurred, and Stu scowled at him.

"You trying to start a war?" he hissed, disgruntled.

Lee let out a derisive laugh. "Like we're not already in one."

Finally getting my feet to move, I approached them, directing my question at Stu. "What's going on? What's wrong with him?"

"Snap," Lee said, blinking like he thought I wasn't real.

"He's drowning his sorrows, that's what, and trying to get us both killed," Stu answered. "You see that bloke over there? That's Ade Fowler. He just got out of prison for manslaughter. Killed the man who'd been having it off with his wife, and this dumb bugger," he says, gesturing to Lee, "rolls right on up and asks him how his Mrs is doing, big smarmy fucking look on his face." He paused, taking in my appearance properly. "Jesus, Karla, you could've at least gotten changed."

"I was working, and I thought it was an emergency."

Before he could respond, Lee was in front of me, his scent invading my senses as he grabbed my wrist and pulled my body to his. "I've missed you," he whispered, alcohol heavy on his breath. "Let's get out of here."

I tried to steady myself, placing my hand on his chest and pushing him back. "What are you doing to yourself? This isn't you," I said, my voice half angry, half sad.

"Yeah," he said, riled. "Well, this is what happens when I have to be without you." He paused for a second, his expression turning tortured. "Life is shit without you, Karla."

My eyes went to Stu, who was looking at me like it was all my fault his brother was acting like an alco. "Let me talk to him in private for a minute."

"By all means," said Stu, lifting his hands in the air.

"Come with me," I said, focusing back on Lee. Putting his arm over my shoulder, I led him from the crowded pub and into the ladies' toilets, which were thankfully empty. His face was in my hair, inhaling deeply. I tried to ignore the butterflies scattering around inside me at his touch. I'd missed him, too, desperately.

His hands went to my neck, his thumbs rubbing softly at my throat as a deep groan escaped him. I could feel that he was hard, his erection grinding into my hip.

Fingers fumbling at the collar of my shirt, he urged me, "Take this off."

I caught his hands to stop him. "No, Lee, look at me. What's going on with you?"

He lifted his head, his eyes a little bloodshot. "Everything's going to shit, and I can't sleep when you're not there. I need to feel your skin, just for a minute," he pleaded, and I swallowed tightly. His hands returned to my buttons, but this time I didn't stop him. I knew I was supposed to be the strong one, but I couldn't summon enough willpower. I wanted to be touched just as much as he wanted to touch me. His hands slid inside my shirt, gliding over my collarbones and caressing the rise of my breasts.

"So perfect," Lee groaned, and I breathed raggedly.

One hand sank into my hair, and he growled in frustration when he couldn't get it out of the bun. "Don't," I whispered. "I have to go back to work in a minute."

His face rose then as he looked me square in the eyes, and even though he was blind drunk, he still managed to look sexy and predatory. "Fuck work. I want to be inside you."

A second later his lips seized mine, his tongue invading my mouth as my entire body turned to mush. I needed this, needed him. He was still kissing me when his hands dropped from my hair and began fumbling at my belt. Before I knew it, his hand had disappeared inside my pants and his fingers were sliding along my folds, feeling how wet I was.

A deep, masculine noise rumbled up out of his chest, and his mouth went to my neck, kissing me feverishly below the ear. "Fuck, I love you," he swore, and I went utterly still. My pores tightened, and my hands pushed at him harshly.

"What? What did you just say?" I asked in panic.

"Shhh," Lee hushed me in a lazy voice. "No talking now."

I tried to get my heart to beat normally but it was no use. He'd just said he loved me, but he was drunker than I'd ever seen him, and he clearly wasn't thinking straight. He was horny and full of beer, and though they said that alcohol was truth serum, I wasn't quite sure that was the case in this instance.

People often mistook lust for love, and that was clearly what was happening with Lee. He wanted me, yes, but love? How could Lee love a woman who stood for everything he didn't?

He stroked at my clit, while two fingers dipped inside and I let my head fall back in pleasure. His mouth caught mine again, and I savoured how he devoured me, how he acted like I was the only thing in his entire world.

It was just as I was about to come that my conscience began to niggle at me. I was being a selfish bitch, letting Lee get me off when I knew full well I was going to have to leave him after. I'd walk right out of the pub and get back in the patrol car with Tony, go back to the job that meant nothing would ever be right between us.

"Lee," I breathed, grabbing his wrist and pulling his hand from my pants. "Stop."

"Why?" he asked, his chest heaving as he tried to catch his breath. "You were almost there. I could feel you swelling for me."

I blinked, bit harshly at my lip, and gathered all my courage. "Because it isn't right. You're drunk, and I'm taking advantage of you."

He laughed loudly, his face so handsome when he smiled. "You can't take advantage of someone who wants it."

I looked at the floor. "Yeah, well, there are lots of different ways to take advantage. Whatever way you want to look at it, I'm police. I'm in a position of power over you, and just being here is reckless behaviour on my part."

Lee leaned closer and tapped at my forehead. "You're thinking too much."

Now it was my turn to laugh. "No, actually, I'm not thinking at all. If I was, I wouldn't be here."

"Oh, for fuck's sake, not this shit again. Sometimes I feel like I just go around in circles with you."

"That's because we keep trying to ignore what's right in front of us," I argued.

At this he placed his hands on either side of my face, lifting my head so I was looking directly at him. "I'm ignoring nothing. I see what's right in front of me, and it's fucking perfect. You're perfect. Come back to me, Karla."

My eyes flickered between his, my mouth falling open as his terribly romantic statement washed over me. My heart pounded, my lungs filled with air, and all at once I wondered if I'd ever feel this way for any man ever again.

Before I could respond, the door to the ladies swung open, and I winced at the idea of being caught in a clinch by some random woman. It was only when I turned my head and saw Tony standing there that I wished that had been the case.

Seventeen

Tony's eyes flared wide as he took in the scene: me with the front of my shirt splayed open, my bra exposed, the fly of my trousers undone, Lee's hands cupping my face.

After just a second, his expression darkened, and he levelled me with a hard look. "Fix yourself up, Constable, and meet me outside. I'll be waiting in the car." With that he turned and left the bathroom, and I flew into a panic.

"Fuck, fuck, *fuck*!" I swore, backing away from Lee and right up into the opposite wall.

"Hey, it'll be okay," he tried to reassure me. "I'll go and talk to him."

"You won't do anything of the sort. This is my mess. I'll fix it. Just…just help me set my uniform back to rights."

Silently, he came forward, redoing my belt as I buttoned up my shirt and tried to straighten out my hair. Glancing in the mirror, I saw that my lips were red and swollen, my cheeks flushed. This was so, *so* bad. There was no way of convincing Tony that what he'd seen hadn't been what it looked like.

"I have to go," I told Lee, stepping away from him and heading toward the door.

"Wait," he said, grabbing my wrist.

I turned back, our gazes locking, and a sense of despair washed over me. All my recklessness had finally reached its climax. Either Tony was going to report me for seeing a man currently under police investigation, or he was going to keep my secret, and I had no idea which option was for the better.

"I'll come see you tomorrow," Lee promised.

"Yes, fine," I replied, flustered. "Right now I just need to go and deal with Tony."

With that I yanked my wrist from his hold and walked out of the ladies'. When I climbed into the car beside Tony, I found him staring straight ahead, his mouth a firm line. A moment of quiet passed before he spoke.

"How long's it been going on?"

Guilt and remorse roiled within me. We were supposed to be friends. Friends didn't deceive each other like I'd deceived Tony. "I never meant for any of this to happen. You have to believe me when I say that."

"How long, Karla?"

"Two months, maybe a little more. The first time I met him was six months ago, but nothing happened between us for a long while."

Tony shook his head and let out a slow breath. "You know what? I should've seen this coming. Looking back, all the signs were there. I just never expected this from you. You're supposed to be one of the good ones. Fuck knows there's so little of us left as it is."

"I am one of the good ones. My relationship with Lee is entirely personal. It's never had anything to do with my work."

Tony gave me his fatherly stare, the one that made me wither in place. "So you're telling me the time we searched his garage and came up empty, it had nothing to do with you?"

I turned to him, my expression agonised. "Okay, yes, but that was the only time, I promise. He was with me when you called and overheard the conversation. I never told him anything. It was just bad timing."

"Can you even hear yourself right now? You're having a relationship with a known felon. Christ, your own father is working on the case that will put him behind bars. You're one of my closest friends, Karla, so please listen to me when I say this. You need to get out now before everything implodes around you."

My voice was barely a whisper when I replied, "I've tried to get out. It's not that easy, especially when feelings are involved."

Now he looked concerned. "Do you love him?"

"No!" I exclaimed. "Of course not." A pause. "I don't know. I've never been in love."

He was quiet for a long minute, and I could tell that his temper was dying down a little as he contemplated things. His voice turned softer. "Look, I get it, believe me, I do. The bloke is charismatic, and, from speaking with him in the interview room, I get the sense he's out to set his own version of justice on the world. There's an appeal to that, and in a certain way I can respect it. But when it comes down to brass tacks, that boy lives in a different world from us, Karla, with an entirely different set of rules."

"I know that, but it's not been easy for him. He practically raised his brothers all by himself. That family had *nothing*. If either one of us were born into that, we'd be living by a different set of rules, too."

Tony stared at me sadly, his breath leaving in a heavy rush. "You do love him."

I focused on my lap. "Maybe."

He reached over and took my hand in his. "Listen, I have your best interests at heart. You're young. I look at you like I would one of my own daughters, so when I say this, it's with the utmost care. You need to step away and put this in the past. There'll be other men, ones who don't hold the ability to wreck your life, your career. You'll just have to go through the heartache before you can come out the other side."

I stared at the hand he was holding, completely deflated. Tony was talking sense, and I knew he'd never give me bad advice. He cared about me, and he was right. I had to be the strong woman I always claimed to be and stop seeing Lee for good.

"Are you going to report me to Jennings?" I whispered into the quiet of the car.

Tony let out a gruff breath. "If you promise to end it, then no. I'll forget this night ever happened."

"Thank you," I said, looking him in the eye, and I meant it. This was my final chance, and I had no intention of screwing it up.

***

The following day I was off work. It was late evening and starting to get dark, and I was on my way back from the corner shop, where I'd gone to pick up a few things. I was walking alongside a row of storage compartments, where some of the locals kept their cars and household tools. There were lots of them around London, because most people lived in flats and didn't have anywhere to keep extras like ladders and lawnmowers. I kept thinking I could hear feet pounding from above my head, but maybe I was imagining things. Why would anybody be running along the roofs?

Reaching the break between one row and the next, I looked up just in time to see Lee leap through the air, bridging the six-foot gap and making a perfect landing on the next row of compartments. For a second I stood there in awe. The sight was just so completely unexpected, and something about the way he moved niggled at my memory, like an odd sense of *déjà vu*.

"What are you doing up there?" I called, stopping in my tracks to peer up at him.

When he saw I'd spotted him, he stopped, shooting me a cheeky grin before backing up a few steps, then taking a run and jump to the ground. Whoa. He crouched when he landed, and I couldn't hide that I was impressed.

"I thought it was only Trevor and Liam who did…all that stuff." I motioned with my hands, pretending like I hadn't known.

Lee rose to standing, the grin still on his face as he dusted himself off. "Who d'ya think taught them?"

"Oh," I breathed, unsure what else to say. I wanted to ask him where he learned, if he ever got scared that he might fall and really hurt himself, but I didn't. Now wasn't the time. "What are you doing here?"

"Came to see you, like I said I would," he replied, stepping forward and taking my hand, his fingers intertwining effortlessly with mine. He was already tugging me forward, relieving me of my shopping bag before I could try to stop him.

"Let go, Lee."

He glanced at me over his shoulder. "Just give me half an hour, okay? Then I'll leave."

Knowing he wasn't going to take no for an answer, I allowed him to lead me inside the block of flats opposite mine. We climbed almost fifteen flights of stairs before we reached an emergency exit and Lee pushed it open, leading me onto the roof of the building. I pulled my hand from his, not too thrilled to be up so high. I didn't have a fear of heights, but there wasn't any proper sort of railing around the edge of the roof, which would make anyone a tad nervous.

Folding my arms across my chest, I shot him a wry look. "You're not going to try to push me to my death, are you?"

Lee smirked and came to pull me forward once more. I noticed somebody had left an old couch up here, and there were a bunch of cigarette butts on the ground alongside a few empty beer cans. Lee plopped down onto the couch, but I resisted when he tried to pull me down with him.

"I'm not sitting on that."

Without a word he stood, unzipped his jacket and laid it down for me, leaving him in only a grey long-sleeved T-shirt. Finally, I sat, inhaling his scent on the fabric almost against my own will.

"Well, this is romantic," I said, heavy on the sarcasm. We were both staring at the view beyond us. It was twilight, not quite day, not quite night, and there were rooftops and buildings as far as the eye could see. Smog hung thick in the sky, another day in the city drawing to a close.

"Glad you approve," Lee replied. "So, how'd the old guy take it last night?"

"Tony's forty. He's not old," I told him grumpily. Lee slid his arm around my shoulders, and I bristled at his touch.

"You took my jacket. The least you can do is let me snuggle close for warmth," he flirted, trying to charm me.

Letting out a long sigh, I finally explained, "He didn't take it well, but he's not going to report me." I paused, cocking my head and sliding my eyes to his. "On the condition that I stop seeing you."

Lee's expression gave nothing away. "I thought you already had."

"So did I. But you seem to keep turning up like a bad penny," I elbowed him in the side.

"Ouch," said Lee, putting his hand to his chest like he'd just been wounded. A quiet passed.

"Why did you drink so much yesterday? I've never seen you like that before."

His breath came out in a heavy whoosh. "A combination of reasons."

"Such as?"

Rubbing at his jaw, he answered, "It was the anniversary of Mum's death. It's always been a shit day, but it was shittier than usual this year." With his arm still around my shoulders, he picked up a strand of my hair and rubbed it between his fingers. "For one, I was missing you, and for two, I was dealing with the fallout from discovering who beat Liam."

I let out a quiet gasp. "Who was it?"

Lee looked away and into the distance. "My boss."

I gaped at him in disbelief. His boss was Tommy McGregor. Lee made a lot of money for the man, so why on earth would he do such a thing? As though he could read my thoughts, Lee continued, "He got an inkling I was fixing to get out, didn't like that, didn't like the money he'd lose if I left. So he decided to send a message, showed how he'd hurt my family if I ever fucked him over."

"Lee," I whispered, trying to absorb the fact that he was planning to go clean, wondering what his brothers thought of it all. "I know who you work for."

He exhaled. "I thought you might."

"So, he won't let you out of your…arrangement?"

"He wouldn't at first, but we spoke this morning, made a deal. He's gonna let me and all my brothers make a clean break."

"If?" I probed.

"If what?"

"There's got to be a catch."

"You don't need to worry about the catch, Karla. Just know that in a couple weeks' time, I'll be a free man."

I didn't like the sound of that, not at all. Nobody got out of working for a gangster like McGregor without losing something. You had to pay your way, and often money wasn't the only currency. I wanted to ask more questions, but I knew I wouldn't get anything out of him. Instead, I asked what my heart wanted to know.

"Are you doing this for me?"

"For you, and for my family. I never wanted this life for my brothers, but it was the only option in front of me at one time."

Allowing my body to settle into his, I asked gently, "Will you tell me about it? The life you've lived." I paused before adding humorously, "How you learned to jump through the air like Batman, etcetera."

Lee emitted a soft chuckle, his hand moving to my stomach and feeling up toward my chest. "You wearing a wire, Snap?"

"Oh, shut up, you know I'm not," I said, laughing when he tickled me.

His hand paused, his thumb brushing softly over my belly, as his smile turned contemplative. "The first time I met him was a couple months after Mum passed." Instinctively, I knew he was talking about McGregor. "I'd just nicked some old geezer's wallet, was halfway down the street when he came out from around a corner. I'd never seen anyone so flash — he had all these gold rings, designer suit, the works. Anyway, I thought I'd been caught, but then he started talking me up, telling me I thieved like a pro, said he had work for me if I wanted it."

"How old were you?"

"Fourteen. Sounds young, but I know people who started earlier. He asked me where I lived and then began coming around all the time. In the end, I didn't have a choice but to work for him. Stu got in on it, too, and before we knew it, we were turning over four or five cars a night. London's a big place, ripe for the picking. The money started to roll in, and it felt good. Being able to feed Liam, Trev, and Sophie, put clothes on their backs and send them to school gave me a high. I could give them something our parents never did.

"There were other perks, too. I could buy nice things, go places, have fun. In the end, supply wasn't meeting demand, so I had to recruit others. I couldn't hide what I did from Liam and Trev, and I told them point blank they didn't have to do what I do. They could go to college, get normal jobs, whatever they wanted. Stubbornness runs in the family, though, and they wanted to do their bit. Before I knew it, we were all fully embroiled in the life, no inclination of ever changing."

"And the Batman stuff?"

Lee laughed softly. "It's called parkour, you nerd. I suppose I picked it up sort of randomly. Saw a bunch of Spanish students doing it in Hyde Park when I was about fifteen and thought it looked cool as fuck. So I approached the one who seemed like he knew what he was doing the most and asked him to teach me."

"Clearly, he agreed."

"Clearly. His name was Alejandro," said Lee, camping it by putting an accent on the name. I giggled. "Good bloke.

I helped him with his conversational English, and he helped me learn how to drop twenty feet without breaking a leg."

"I'm sure that came in handy."

Lee nodded. "My brothers loved it, especially Trev. They all wanted to learn. Believe it or not, I never really set out to use it to my advantage. I just wanted to do something fun. I suppose the whole thing sort of...evolved."

"Is that why you pretend you can't do it?"

"Come again?"

"You're not like Trevor — you don't show off. I'm guessing it's for discretion. If you see a man hopping off a building to get away from the coppers, there are only so many people it could be." Almost as if my own words had led me to it, I realised why I'd had *déjà vu* watching Lee jump. It reminded me of the video Tony had shown me of the burglar robbing the cash-for-gold scammers.

"There's that," said Lee, drawing me from my thoughts. "Plus, Trevor's a flashy fucker. He can't help it, really." He paused to eye me curiously. "What's wrong? You look like you saw a ghost."

I shook my head. "It's nothing, I just...well, no, it's not nothing. Can I ask you something?"

"Might as well. This already feels like a *This Is Your Life* interview," Lee teased.

I mock-scowled at him. "I saw this surveillance footage of a robbery once. I think it might have been you."

Lee chuckled. "Was I wearing black and white stripes and carrying a sack with a dollar sign on?"

"No. You were wearing a balaclava, and climbed ten flights of a building before swinging down through the scaffolding."

A tension fell as his eyes shone in the dark, but he didn't say anything. Somehow, his silence was more confirmation than words.

"The people you stole from were scamming the elderly. You took their things back and anonymously handed them in to the police. Why?"

He didn't look at me when he spoke, his posture stiff, almost like he was embarrassed. "You know Mrs Spencer who lives on my road?"

"The old woman you saved dinner for, yes, I remember, Lee. That was really sweet, by the way."

He huffed awkwardly. "She's a widow. Been living in that house all her life. When we were kids, she used to get on to Mum about how badly mistreated we all were. She'd even give us food when she could afford it. Well, Mrs Spencer told me how she sent her old wedding ring and a few expensive pieces of jewellery off to those scammers, hoping for some money to do her house up. Obviously, she never saw a penny. I found out where the racket was being run from and put an end to it."

I stared at him, warmth suffusing my insides. "You're such a liar."

Lee frowned at me, confused. "Why would I lie?"

"You said you couldn't understand why I help people with no payback, but you do it, too. You did it for Mrs Spencer."

"I care about Mrs Spencer. She's my neighbour, and she was kind to me when I was just a kid. I could give a fuck about your average Joe Soap walking down the street."

I just smiled at him.

"I'm being serious, Karla. I'm no saint. Don't go building any fanciful ideas about me. I've robbed from people just like those scammers. I just don't rob from the vulnerable. I rob from the wealthy."

"High-end motor vehicles, I know."

"Yeah, well, not anymore."

"You really want to get out?" I asked, ever hopeful.

Lee emitted a weary sigh. "I can't stay on the second-last rung of the ladder forever, Karla. You either move up, or somebody else comes along and moves you out, and I don't want to move up. Liam's court date is a couple of weeks away, and if he gets sent down, I'll never forgive myself. Maybe it's too late, maybe it'll be all for nothing, but I at least have to try."

His words gave me confidence. Perhaps I didn't have to stop seeing him after all, not forever anyway. We could stay apart until everything settled down, and then we could see where this thing went between us.

Lee picked up my plastic bag and began rooting through it. Pulling out the milk, he asked, "You mind?"

I shook my head. "Not at all."

He opened the carton and took a long swig before wiping his mouth with the back of his hand. "I'm hung over as fuck, barely got a wink of sleep last night."

Right after he said it, I noticed the bags under his eyes. He looked tired. Reaching out, I placed a hand to his chest and rubbed. "You shouldn't drink so much."

Lee let his head fall back, savouring my touch. "Yeah, tell me about it."

Sometime between us arriving on the roof and now, the sky had darkened to night. It felt peaceful and quiet up there, civilisation far below us. Streetlights glittered in the sky, cars moving along on the roads in the distance.

"Lee," I said, my voice seeking as it broke though the silence.

"What is it, Snap?"

"What if something bad happens? What if even after you do everything he's asked of you, he still doesn't let you go?"

It was a while before he responded, like he was really thinking about it. "There are dishonourable thieves, and there are honourable ones. Despite everything you might have heard about my boss, he falls into the latter category. If he makes a promise, he'll stick by it, no matter what."

I stared at him, not sure if I believed that. If McGregor had honour, then he never would've had Jennings beaten, or Liam, for that matter. People like him liked to claim they had a code, but when it came down to it, it was dog eat dog. Or maybe Lee's version of honour was just a lot different from mine.

He looked at me, his eyes fierce. He seemed very sure of what he said. I just hoped his faith wasn't misplaced. I hoped his plan worked.

Because I wanted to believe that one day we'd look back on all this and wonder how our lives had ever been so tumultuous.

Eighteen

"I bet I can beat you to the ground," said Lee, his eyes flashing with devilry.

We'd been sitting on the roof for over two hours, talking about life, our past relationships, everything, really. I told him all about Gavin, and what a disloyal, narcissistic arsehole he'd been, and Lee told me all about his ex, Tammy, and how materialistic she was, only really with him so that he'd buy her stuff. What was left unsaid was how we both knew we were the opposites of our ex-partners. I wanted Lee for the core of who he was, and he would never cheat; it wasn't how he was wired. He was too loyal.

It felt like we'd been trapped together in a bubble neither one of us wanted to leave, subtly finding new ways to touch one another that weren't explicitly sexual, but still made my bones ache with need.

"What do you mean?"

"You take the stairs. Fuck, you can even take the lift, and I bet I'll make it to the ground before you."

His words gave me a little rush, my pulse starting to speed up. There was something about making bets with Lee that was always decidedly exciting.

"And if you win?"

He leaned close, his breath warm amid the cold night air. "I get to kiss you for the last time before everything changes."

His answer made me shiver. "And if I do?"

He smiled widely, and it only enhanced his handsome features. "*You* get to kiss *me* for the last time before everything changes."

I don't know why, but I laughed loudly, smiling back at him and holding out my hand. "It's a deal."

We shook, and Lee stood. I watched as he walked over to the edge of the building, and all of a sudden my panic set in as I realised what he planned to do. He was going to jump. He still faced me, his back to the edge, and I got up hurriedly, rushing toward him.

"Wait, no, I'm calling it off."

Lee took his final step backward, his foot meeting the last bit of concrete before there was nothing but air. He raised his hands, still smiling, "A bet's a bet, Karla."

Right after he said it he dropped, and I let out a startled yelp, my hand going to my mouth in fright. I ran the last few yards to the edge and looked down, shocked and exhilarated by what I saw.

The balconies of each apartment jutted out from the building, almost like steps on a ladder – if you were a giant. Lee leapt diagonally from one to the next, each balcony bringing him closer to the ground. I put my hand to my chest to feel how hard and fast my heart was beating, my fear lessening as excitement took over. His body moved with purpose, his rangy muscles perfectly aligned, his jumps measured to avoid injury. He was already halfway to the bottom when I realised what a head start I'd given him.

Even though we both got the same thing, no matter who won, my competitive streak set in and I hurried to the lift, no qualms about cheating. By the time I got to the ground floor, my breaths were coming out frantically as I ran from the carriage and outside.

Lee sat confidently on a bench facing the entrance, his arms folded and a cocky grin shaping his lips. I shook my head and laughed, hurrying toward him and stopping only a foot or two away.

"That was incredible. But I think you might be even crazier than Trevor," I breathed, my words all air.

Lee got up from the bench and closed the distance between us. He was covered in a thin layer of sweat after his exertion, and I savoured his warmth. I wore his jacket, having grown cold up on the roof after a while. He cupped his hands around my face and stared down at me.

"Crazy can be a little exciting, though, yeah?"

I laughed again, this time more breathily. "Yeah."

And then he kissed me, pressing his mouth to mine and coaxing my tongue to glide with his. I trembled under his assault, my chest on fire and my lungs too full. His kiss was piercing, too much and not enough, and through it I felt him communicate everything he felt inside. I gripped him tight, my fingertips pressing into the dips and lines of his shoulder blades, and tried my damnedest to communicate everything I felt right back.

***

"Mind if I sit?" I asked as I stood by the table Jennings was occupying in the break room. There were a few other officers milling about, but mostly the place was empty. She looked up from her newspaper and frowned, her mouth turning down grimly at the edges.

After a moment of consideration, she motioned for me to join her, and I took the seat on the other side of the table. My lunch consisted of a cheese and ham sandwich, an apple, and a carton of juice. Jennings proceeded to ignore me, reading her paper as I began to eat.

"Anything interesting?" I asked after a minute or two of quiet.

She let out an impatient sigh. "If this is about the application for sergeant, then you're wasting your time."

"Don't worry — I've long since given up trying to get on your good side, Katherine. And I'll keep applying for sergeant until you finally get sick of me and decide to give in. Simple as," I replied with confidence.

She glanced up from her paper. "Well, then, what do you want?"

"Is it so strange to imagine I might be here for the pleasure of your company?"

Jennings scoffed, and if I wasn't mistaken, something almost like a smile began to shape her lips. But that couldn't be right. Looking out the window, I didn't see any pigs flying.

"I find that terribly hard to believe," she said stiffly.

"Don't sell yourself so short. If you'd actually take that stick out of your arse and quit treating me like a particularly unpleasant fungal infection, you'd realise we actually have a lot in common."

Closing over her paper and giving me her full attention, Jennings folded her arms across her chest and levelled me with a cynical expression. "Now this I have to hear."

I held up all five fingers. "Well, for one, we're both tough bitches, and for two, we can handle working in a male-dominated environment without buckling under the pressure. Three, let me see, we both hate my dad. Four, we're funny."

Five, we both had love affairs that jeopardised our careers. I left the fifth finger standing.

"Funny?" Jennings asked with a huff of scepticism.

"The other day when Connors wanted to know if he had food in his teeth, you asked him if he cared so much about his appearance, then why was he walking around with a barnet like a crow's nest?"

"That falls more into the bitch category, if you ask me," said Jennings. "But he does have awful hair."

"And a bad attitude. You give put-downs where they're due. Well, except for with me, but I guess you have your reasons for those, which I'll allow," I told her cheekily. I was pushing my luck, but if I knew anything about this woman, it was that the only way to get on her good side was to stand my ground. If I tried licking her arse, she'd tell me exactly where to stick it. Sure, I was complimenting her, but with bite. In this instance, the bite was key.

"You're persistent," she said, eyeing me shrewdly.

"I have to be, with the likes of you."

At this she surprised both of us when she huffed a begrudging laugh. "You remind me a lot of your father in that way. And just to be clear, that's not a compliment."

"Don't worry, I know." I paused to lower my voice. "He does feel bad for what he did to you, though. Well, as bad as a man like my dad can feel about anything, which isn't much. Usually, his way is the right way, no ifs or buts." I paused to eye her seriously. "You do know he's been working so hard on the McGregor case so that he can finally get justice for you."

"Yes, well, it's all a bit too little, too late in that regard."

"Maybe, but we're all fallible. It's the ones who can't accept they've made a mistake who have problems."

Jennings stared at me for a long time, so long I began to grow self-conscious. "Do you know," she said, "none of the other constables have ever tried to join me for lunch."

"Well, I'm happy to break you in."

At this she let out another laugh, a real laugh. I looked out the window again. Yep, still pig-free. "Keep applying for sergeant, Sheehan. Who knows, maybe after ten or fifteen more attempts, you'll finally get what you want."

With that she stood and gathered her things, leaving me alone at the table. I picked up my sandwich and took a bite, and after a couple of chews, I started to smile.

***

"I'm telling you, the answer is 9 p.m.," I told Tony as we discussed the riddle he'd given me weeks ago, the one Stu had solved. It was one of those puzzles that even when you had the answer, it still took a while to get your head around.

"Nine p.m.," Tony repeated. "Nah, I'm still not seeing it."

"Just keep thinking, and it'll start to make sense."

His brow furrowed, and I grinned at how serious he looked when he concentrated. His thick black eyebrows were like two big caterpillars on his face. We'd just finished dealing with a homeless man who'd been causing a drunken disturbance on the tube, and were driving back to the station.

I heard the scratchy sound of the radio coming on right before a call from dispatch came through. My heart rate picked up when I heard the details of the report. The panic button had been pushed at a city centre bank, and all available units were being called in to investigate. Before the call had even cut off, I hit the sirens, put my foot down on the gas pedal, and hightailed it to the scene.

It was mid-morning, one of the quieter periods, and everything looked like normal when we arrived on the street where the bank was located. I scanned the area, noticing a few pedestrians strolling by and several parked cars. It was the black transit van that caught my attention, and just as I was pulling up to the kerb, the bank doors flew open. A number of men dressed in dark clothing emerged, their faces disguised beneath balaclavas.

I swore when I saw two of them were carrying Kalashnikovs, the others with weapons more discreetly hidden. They were also lugging a number of black gym bags. Tony was already on his radio, reporting what we were seeing. The men looked in our direction, the sirens drawing their attentions, then ran straight for the transit van, pulled open the back doors, and hopped inside.

Within seconds they were speeding away from the scene. Clearly, there'd been a driver waiting. Not even bothering to stop, I gave chase, calling out the van's licence plate number as the dispatch operator did a search.

"It was reported stolen two days ago," he told me, but I wasn't surprised. Stolen vehicles were business as usual for a bank job.

We were halfway to Canning Town when three other patrol cars joined in the chase behind us. They were unarmed units, just like us, which wasn't going to do much good once the thieves began to panic. The sentencing for armed robbery was seven years, more if they'd used their guns to harm anyone. If push came to shove, I had no doubt they'd open fire on us to get away. Suddenly, my palms felt clammy on the steering wheel, my adrenaline kicking in.

"Where's my ARV?" I asked dispatch.

"On its way. Just keep your distance and follow the van until they get there."

We were entering a rundown residential district, a jungle of tower blocks with half the windows boarded up. They weren't going to be able to lose us here, not in the van, anyway. The buildings were too close together, no space for them to speed up and make a break for it.

Almost as though confirming my thoughts, the van screeched to a halt about two hundred yards ahead of us and the men emerged. I had to stomp hard on the brakes to stop the patrol car before it collided with the van, and by the time we'd ground to a halt, the men were climbing the metal ladder that ran up the side of the nearest building.

With barely a second to think about it, both Tony and I got out of the car and ran after them. I was first to get on the ladder, and as I looked into the distance, I saw the ARV approaching. If we could just keep track of the thieves until the armed unit caught up with us, then maybe we had a chance of catching them.

I was probably six or seven rungs ahead of Tony, and the final thief had already disappeared over the roof of the building. By the time I reached the top, all four of them were on the other side. I got there just in time to see the first man jump and breach the gap between one building and the next, and all at once a niggling sense of dread fell over me.

I ran across the roof, my legs pumping on the flat concrete. I was too slow, though, and all of them bar one had already made the jump, headed for the next building. There was anywhere between fifteen and twenty towers all in the same vicinity, and with them able to jump from one to the other so easily, who knew where they'd end up.

For some reason, the final thief turned back just before making the jump, and I came face to face with a pair of blue eyes impossible not to recognise. Barely a second passed, but time stood still, the moment dragging out as my heart beat wildly in my chest.

No.

Memories flooded my vision. Trevor jumping a ten-foot wall the first time I'd caught him trying to steal a car.

Lee telling me he'd made a deal with McGregor to get out of their arrangement. And later, betting me he could make it to the ground from the top of a fifteen-storey building with nothing but his own two feet.

I blinked back to the present just in time to see him land on the roof of the next building before disappearing out of sight. Trying to gather some composure, I lifted my radio, spouting off details of what had happened, completely on autopilot. A minute later, Tony and several armed officers arrived. I told them how the men had escaped, and immediately a plan was put in place to search every building in the area. I kept busy, helping with the search and trying not to let my mind wander to the reality of what I'd seen.

Several hours later, after my shift had finished, I found myself sitting on a closed toilet seat in the ladies' bathroom back at the station, my face in my hands as I experienced a minor anxiety attack.

Thankfully, no employees or civilians at the bank had been harmed. The sight of the guns was enough to keep everyone from trying to be a hero. The search had been unsuccessful, though a forensics team was currently checking out the abandoned transit van. I didn't expect them to find anything. Lee was too clever for that.

He'd just robbed a bank. It wasn't so shocking when you considered the fact that he'd spent his entire life stealing cars, but then I thought of the amount he'd gotten away with.

Three million pounds in cash and bearer bonds.

It suddenly made sense that McGregor was willing to let Lee out of their arrangement. He was going to pay his way out, and good old-fashioned cash was the currency of choice. My entire body grew cold and clammy, and I felt sick to my stomach with the decision that was now weighing heavily on my shoulders.

Should I give an eyewitness account, saying I'd recognised Lee as one of the robbers? Or should I keep my mouth shut, let him pay his way out of a life of crime, and finally have some semblance of freedom?

I knew which option my heart desired, but could I live with myself if I allowed Lee away scot-free?

I wasn't sure how much time had passed when I finally left the cubicle. Staring at my face in the mirror, it was the first time in my life that I looked at my own reflection and barely recognised the woman who stood before me. In that moment, I knew I was never going to hand Lee in. Was it because I loved him? Was it because I knew deep down he was a good person and deserved a better life? Or was it because I was selfish and didn't want him to be taken away from me?

Right then it felt like a mixture of all three.

When I arrived home that night, it was late and Alexis was fast asleep, light snoring coming from her room. The flat was dark, and when I switched the lamp on, I got a fright to see Lee sitting on the couch.

Even though I knew it was him, I grew anxious. There was something about the tension in his shoulders that put me on edge. He wasn't here to whisper sweet nothings in my ear, that was for sure.

"How did you get in?" I asked into the dimly lit room.

"Alexis," he answered simply.

The last I'd spoken of Lee to my best friend, I'd been wondering if I was in love with him. She didn't know about Tony discovering our relationship, or about the bank job. As far as she was concerned, she was doing me a favour by letting Lee into our home.

Passing by the living area, I went and dropped my keys down on the kitchen counter, bracing my hands on the cold Formica and letting out an exhausted sigh. "Why did it have to be me? If I could rewind the clock and go back to this morning, I never would have gotten out of bed. I would've called in sick. Then I'd never have to know."

"You can't unsee what you saw," said Lee. "So, what are you gonna do about it?"

Turning abruptly, I scowled at him. "Is that the only reason you're here? You want to know if I'm going to turn you in?"

Lee's expression was sober. "I'm a survivor, Karla, first and foremost. If someone's fixing to feed me to the lions, I want to be prepared."

My hands clenched into fists, my mouth a firm line as I levelled him with all the animosity I had inside me. "And what if I say I'm going to do it? Will you hurt me? Will you threaten me to keep quiet?" I was glad I'd managed to withhold my tears and keep my voice steady, when all I wanted to do was cry.

Lee stood from the couch, his posture tense. "You think I have that in me?"

"I have no idea what you have in you, Lee. Not two days ago you told me you were getting out of the game. Today you robbed a bank. What do you want me to say?"

"I want you to at least give me the respect I deserve and believe that I'd never lay a hand on you. And if you were going to turn me in, then I think there should be enough loyalty between us by now for you to give me a heads-up. Let me get out of the country before you put me in the firing line."

"You'd do that?" I asked, disbelieving. "You'd leave London?"

"Yeah, and I'd take everyone I care about with me," he replied before a sad look passed over his features. "Well, almost everyone."

My heart hurt, my head swimming with emotions as I tried not to succumb to the tenderness in his voice. Several moments of quiet ensued, and I went to sit on the couch. Lee remained standing, his eyes glued to me like I was a wild animal who might bite at any moment.

"I'm presuming you gave all the money to McGregor."

Lee's voice was low. "Apparently, the price of freedom these days comes at a cool three million."

I flicked my gaze to his. "Do you have any idea what he's going to do with it?"

"Buy another villa in Spain for his mistress. Fuck if I know, Snap. All I care about is that he won't be bothering me or my family again. We can stay in London and go clean. It's a win-win."

"He could use it to do bad things, bring even more crime into the city."

"He's gonna do that anyway. Look, this isn't about him doing bad, it's about me doing good. You can sit there and spout all the moral philosophies you want. I still know it's all bullshit. Nice guys finish last, and I'd step over a thousand people if it meant the ones I cared about were safe, because I know every single one of those thousand would step over me, given half the chance."

What he said went against everything I believed in. I could name him a hundred times I'd put a stranger's safety before my own because it was my job. Still, I understood why he had such a cynical view of the world. His own parents had abandoned him when he was just a child, so too had his aunt. From a young age he'd learned that people were selfish, only out for themselves. It hardened him to believe everyone was like that. For Lee, true altruism didn't exist. Well, I was going to show him that it did.

"It's not true, you know," I said finally.

Lee looked back at me, clearly having been lost in his own thoughts. "What's not true?"

"That they'd all step over you. I wouldn't."

"Yeah, well, you're different."

"Not really. You just think that way because you're not looking in the right places. Good people exist, selfless people."

Taking a step forward, he closed the space between us and knelt down in front of me. When he spoke, his voice was a whisper. "Was I looking in the right place the day I met you?"

"Yes," I replied. "And I'm not turning you in."

Lee exhaled a heavy breath, all the tension going out of him. He bent his head to stare at the floor, like he couldn't bring himself to look at me.

"Why?" he asked, the quiet word laced with confusion. He was genuinely surprised, and I knew that up until this moment, he truly believed I was going to report him.

"Because in spite of everything, I can't help protecting you, the same way I would anyone else who needed it." As soon as the words were out, I knew they weren't entirely true, and though I was doing something good for Lee, I wasn't being selfless. In fact, saving him was probably the most selfish decision I'd ever make. I knew then that I cared more about him than I did my career, or the law, and it was downright terrifying. The thing was, sometimes when I looked at Lee I saw the boy he used to be, the one who had to grow up too fast. The fact that I couldn't be there to help him back then made me feel so powerless, but I could regain that power by helping him now.

He lifted his head. "So that's it? I could be anyone, and you'd still be making the same choice?"

"Your brothers need you," I answered, avoiding the question.

His expression sobered as he drew away, staring at me like he was trying to figure out my game. There was no game. I'd fallen for him, plain and simple, and I'd never be the same again.

"I won't forget this," he said, his voice steady. It wasn't full of gratitude or emotion, no tears of happiness were shed, but somehow I knew he meant it more this way.

For the rest of my life, Lee Cross would always believe that he owed me, when in reality he owed me nothing. Maybe someday he'd learn that real gifts were freely given, no need for payment in return.

Nineteen
POLICE REPORT

Case no: 78956012   **Date:** 25/02/2010
Reporting Officer: PC Tony Pollard   **Prepared by:** Arresting officer
Incident: Grand theft auto

Details of Event:
At 2:15 p.m. on 25/02, PC Karla Sheehan and I were informed via dispatch of a stolen vehicle en route to our location. Once spotted, we proceeded to chase down the vehicle. When arriving in an area of heavy traffic, the suspect, one Liam Cross, age 20, fled, and both myself and PC Sheehan pursued him on foot until he was caught and apprehended.

Actions Taken:
Initial caution was given. The suspect was arrested and transported to Bethnal Green Police Station for processing, where he remained in custody for several hours before a family member posted bail. A date has been set for a preliminary hearing at the Central Criminal Court.

Summary:
Liam Cross, age 20, resident of Hackney, East London, was arrested for Grand Theft Auto on February 25th, 2010. Based on his crime, he will face a preliminary court hearing on April 17th, 2010.

I stared at the short but succinct report Tony had made when he first arrested Liam, biting my lip and dreading the impending day in court. There was nothing I could do now to change what happened, and I'd have to take to the stand and detail the events for the judge, most likely in front of Lee and all his family. It wasn't going to be easy, but I didn't have another choice. I couldn't exactly call in sick.

It had been three weeks since I'd last seen Lee, and the investigation into the bank robbery had fallen flat. It'd been well-planned, and it was looking like Lee and his brothers were home free. For now. Whatever happened during Liam's case could throw the family into yet more turmoil.

The bank job hadn't been a victimless crime. The employees working that day and the customers present were surely dealing with all kinds of emotional trauma. Still, it was as victimless as you could get in this day and age. I mean, the bank's money *was* insured. I tried to reassure myself of this, that at least they hadn't hurt or killed anyone, but I still felt uneasy. And really, I wondered if it would even be possible for Lee to go straight. Would he go into work in the morning and feel bored? Would he miss the thrill?

Shouts sounded from the corridor leading to the locker rooms, and I stood to go and check out what the noise was about. When I rounded the corner, I found Tony and Steve in a standoff, DI Jennings with her arms crossed just a few feet away. She was eyeing Steve with nothing short of disdain as he argued with Tony.

"Nothing but a pair of bloody jobsworths, the both of you," Steve fumed, and Jennings raised her hand to pat her mouth, emitting a yawn like she was bored with his theatrics.

"You're been suspended indefinitely," said Tony. "You need to go home and calm down, maybe take some time to reflect on all these stunts you've been pulling."

"Please hand your badge and your weapons over to PC Pollard," said Jennings. "You're delaying my lunch, and I have a date with a tuna sandwich that's far more interesting than anything you've got left to say."

I almost laughed, but I reined it in. Tony held his hands out for Steve's things, and Steve reluctantly handed everything over. When he turned to leave and saw me watching, he shoved me purposefully in the shoulder, muttering something like "nosy bitch" under his breath.

"Jesus, what happened with him?" I asked, looking to Tony.

"PC Pollard discovered him taking cash from the evidence room," Jennings answered simply, before turning and, I'm assuming, going to have her date with that tuna sandwich. What she'd said didn't surprise me. Tony and I shared a loaded glance, mine laced with thanks. We'd discussed Steve and his underhanded schemes a few times over the last few weeks during our shifts, both of us eager to catch him doing something on camera so we could have him suspended. It looked like Tony had been a busy bee.

"Have I ever told you how awesome you are?" I said, grinning.

Tony smiled and casually shrugged. "All the time. Can't shut you up."

I laughed and went to give his hand a squeeze before going back out and returning to my desk. When I arrived home that evening, I found Alexis had cooked roast chicken and mashed potatoes for dinner. My stomach gurgled, reminding me I was hungry, as I went to change clothes and take a shower. The table was set by the time I came back out, and we both sat down to eat.

"Lee visited me today," said Alexis, and I almost choked on the food I'd just swallowed.

"He did? What did he want?"

"To see how I'm doing," she answered with no small amount of sarcasm. "I'm sure it was all just a front to check up on you."

I stared at my plate. "Yeah, well, I don't need checking up on."

"Liam's court date is this week, you know."

"I'm well aware of that, Lexie."

"You have to be there, don't you?"

I glanced at her, wondering what she was getting at. "You know I do."

She eyed me sympathetically and appeared torn over what to say. Dropping her fork onto the table, she rubbed at her belly.

"Is the baby kicking?"

She nodded her head. "Yeah, but it's not that. Lee told me something, and I don't want you walking in there with blinders on. It wouldn't be fair."

"Tell me, then."

She inhaled a quick breath. "He's having Liam's solicitor broker a deal. If he gives up the name of the person he was working for, they'll let him go free."

"But then Lee...." I gasped, unable to finish my sentence.

"Will do time," said Alexis, her brown eyes turning down at the ends sadly, our conversation falling into silence.

I barely slept that night, and the next day I seemed to have drawn the short straw, because everything that could possibly go wrong did. First off, a woman I arrested for shoplifting went crazy and attacked me at the station, resulting in me sporting an awful welt across one cheek. Secondly, the evidence I'd collected on a drug pusher from several weeks ago went missing, which meant he couldn't be prosecuted. I was willing to bet it was a last "fuck you" from Steve. And thirdly, just to add icing on the cake of a supremely shitty day, my car broke down.

It was dark, and I was on my way home after my shift. When I called the AA, they said it'd be one to two hours before a tow truck arrived, so I was stuck on the hard shoulder of a busy motorway with no other option but to wait it out.

Only about thirty minutes had passed when there was a steady knock on my driver's-side window. I thought with relief that the truck had gotten there early, but then glanced up to find Lee peering down at me through the glass.

Okay, so if my car breaking down was the icing on the cake, then Lee showing up was the magic sprinkles. I didn't open the door, only rolled down my window for him.

"Need help?" he asked. Damn, he looked good, his hair casually tousled. I noticed his eyes drifting over me, checking me out in the same way I was him.

Shaking my head, I answered, "No, thanks, I'm good. The AA will be here soon."

He didn't look like he believed me. "How long you been waiting?"

"Thirty minutes," I muttered, looking down at my phone.

Lee emitted a soft chuckle. "In that case, they're not getting here any time in the next century. Let me take a look," he urged me, holding up his hands and wriggling his fingers. "This is what I'm good at."

"It's fine. I'm happy to wait. I'm sure you have somewhere you need to be."

I wanted him to leave, not only because of the feelings his nearness provoked, but also because I was two seconds away from confronting him over his bullshit plan to go to prison instead of Liam.

He levelled me with a challenging stare, not breathing a word, but instead of arguing, he just walked around to the front of the car and proceeded to open the hood.

Oh, *no effing way.*

Getting out, I stomped toward him, pushing his hands back and slamming it down. Trying to ignore the spark I felt when our fingers touched, I scowled at him with all my might. "I said I don't need your help. Are you going deaf or something?"

Lee cocked his head, perplexed. "Why are you being so difficult?"

"I'm not being difficult. I'm just irritated by how you always think you know best," I huffed. Somewhere in the back of my mind, I knew I wasn't angry at him for being heavy-handed — I was angry at him because he was going to sacrifice himself for his brother, and refusing to let him fix my car was the only way of expressing how I felt right then.

Lee held firm when I tried to stand my ground, and before I could react, he gripped me by the waist, lifted me, and threw me over his shoulder. I wriggled in his hold, but seconds later he'd opened my car door and shoved me in the back. I hadn't even seen him swipe my keys, but by the time I tried to scramble forward, he'd locked all the doors.

My car was an old Nissan, so I could still open it from the inside. Lee saw me going for the lock and warned me, "If you get out, I'll kiss you."

He was such a little fucker.

I huffed a sigh and folded my arms, my annoyance written all over my face at his threat. Lee chuckled as he watched me, but then his expression sobered when he saw the welt on my face. His voice was muted since all the windows were closed, but I could just about hear him as he brought his fingers to his own cheek.

"What happened there?"

"A woman I arrested today did it. Absolute nutjob."

Lee frowned in concern, placing his hands on his hips before turning away. He returned to the front of the car, and I sat and waited while he fiddled around with the engine. A few minutes later he reappeared, sliding into the back seat next to me.

"Your HT leads need replacing. You should call AA and cancel. I'll hitch you up to the back of my car and drive you to the garage, replace them for you for free."

"Is this you paying me back the favour you owe me?" I asked.

Lee eyed me and smiled. "Nah, this is me trying to be more like you, helping the needy and all that."

I scoffed. "Sure."

Lifting his hand, he ran his fingers over my hurt cheek. "This looks bad."

"I've had worse."

"I hope you gave as good as you got."

"Oh, yeah, I kicked her arse right in the middle of the station while the other officers cheered me on."

Lee pursed his lips, still smiling. "Don't be a smart-arse." Picking my phone up from my lap, he shoved it into my hand and said, "Call them. Otherwise, you'll be sitting out here all night."

Giving in, I called and cancelled the tow truck. When I hung up we were both silent, and his plan to switch places with Liam burned heavily on my heart. I was upset and angry at him, but I couldn't let out everything I was feeling without coming across as hysterical. Still, I had to broach the subject. The court hearing was tomorrow. I needed to convince him to change his mind.

"Alexis told me what you're going to do for Liam," I said, my voice quiet.

Lee exhaled and stretched his legs out as much as he could in the small space. "I take it from the way you're looking at me now that you don't approve."

"Please don't do it, Lee," I begged, unable to hold back my desperation. A tear fell down my cheek, and he reached out to wipe it away.

"Don't cry," he murmured tenderly. "I've been breaking the law for years. It's only right that I finally serve my time."

I turned into him, burying my face in his neck as I whispered, "But I don't want you to go away."

"It won't be forever," he replied, stroking my hair as his lips pressed against my temple.

"I don't understand how you're just accepting this. Before you said it was going to be fine. You said your solicitor could get Liam off, no problem."

He sighed. "Yeah, well, when I stopped working for McGregor, I lost a lot of privileges. One of those included my legal representation. So now we don't have William Dunning on our side, and we also don't have a hope in hell's chance of getting Liam's charges dropped. I can't let my baby brother go to prison for something I got him into in the first place, Karla. It has to be me. You understand that, right?"

I looked into his eyes and knew I couldn't argue with him. If I ever had a sister, I'd do the exact same thing, no question. God, he'd been right all along. We were the same. Too stubborn and brave to know what was good for us, out on a mission to save everyone but ourselves.

"Yeah, I understand."

Soaking him in, I tried to comprehend the fact that in just a few short weeks he could go to prison. I wasn't going to see him for years, and that terrified me.

A surge of desperation clutched suddenly at my heart as I smashed my mouth to his, kissing him like my life depended on it. He was only twenty-five, so young and handsome and clever, and all his best years were going to be spent in a prison cell. The worst of it was that I knew he wouldn't come out the same man. He'd lose the spark that always shone so brightly in his eyes, would no longer be the flirty, carefree guy I was once met on a chilly London morning.

Lee's hands clutched my face, his tongue sinking deep into my mouth as a loud moan escaped me. My fingers slid beneath his shirt, tracing his hard abs. When he grabbed my thighs and pulled them around his waist, his erection was hard as steel against my core. It'd been so long since I'd gotten to touch him like this that my need was close to maddening.

Gasping, he broke our kiss, trailing his mouth down my neck and unbuttoning my blouse until my bra was exposed. He buried his face in my cleavage, a growl rumbling from deep in his chest, and the vibration made me tremble.

"Lee," I breathed right before a car went sailing by out on the road.

The horn honked as I heard a man shout saucily out the window, "Oi oi!"

Lee and I fell into awkward laughter after that, and I drew away, buttoning my top back up. "Do you, uh, have anything in your car we could use as a tow?"

His hand met my lower back. "Stay with me tonight, Karla."

I was helpless to refuse, and only nodded my head in response. Lee placed a quick kiss on my lips, then got out of the car and jogged to his, which was parked just a few yards behind mine. Minutes later, he had my car secured, and I climbed into his passenger seat. All throughout the journey he touched me, whether it was to tuck my hair behind my ear or to squeeze my knee, and every time he did, my stomach fluttered with anticipation.

He didn't bother going to the garage, but instead drove straight to his place, saying he'd have one of the boys come fix my car in the morning. I knew that tomorrow everything would change, but for tonight I just wanted to live in the moment.

Lee tugged me inside his hallway and immediately pressed his mouth to mine, his hands everywhere as we tried to find our way upstairs without stopping what we were doing. I giggled when we both simultaneously tripped and fell halfway up.

"Hush," Lee whispered, his lips finding mine again.

I loved how he kissed me; whether fast or slow, he always made it feel like it could be our last. I tried to push that thought aside when I realised how sad it made me. Somehow we managed to make it to his room, and proceeded to strip one another of all our clothing.

Completely naked, he laid me down on his bed, his handsome features serious in the dim light. "I hate everyone who gets to be near you when I'm not there. And

I hate it because I love my brothers more than anything, but you're the one I'll miss the most."

My heart ached at his proclamation, fear and sadness gripping me tight and not letting go. I placed my hands on his cheeks, my eyes flickering between his, struck speechless. Closing my eyes, I showed him with my body the things I couldn't tell him in words.

Flipping us, I climbed on top of him, bracing myself above his length and sinking down until he filled me completely. When I began to ride him, I lost all thought, totally consumed by sensation. Lee gripped my waist and held my eyes, never looking away once.

If this was the last time, I was going to make it count.

Lee reached down and found my clit with his thumb, rubbing intense circles with his practiced hands. His cock felt amazing, and it was only as I began to climb toward orgasm that I realised we hadn't used protection. He was inside me bare, but surprisingly, I didn't panic. I felt closer to him than I'd ever had, and if there was a single doubt in my mind that I loved him, it fell by the wayside.

I'd never loved before. Now I loved too much. And in the morning, I'd lose him.

There was a sweet sort of tragedy to it all.

When I came, I closed my eyes, dropped to his chest, and sank my face into the crook of his neck, whether for comfort or to hide my tears, I couldn't seem to tell.

"I'm sorry if I ever hurt you," I whispered into the dark room.

Lee was quiet for a long time before he whispered back, "Hurting with you is better than a painless life without you."

His words penetrated deep, and I held him tighter, wishing I didn't have to let go.

Twenty

Tony and I stood outside the Old Bailey, sipping on bad takeaway coffee and waiting out the last few minutes before we had to go inside. He knew just how difficult a day I had ahead of me, and he didn't try to fill the quiet with random small talk. He let me have my time to think and prepare.

I'd left Lee's bed early in the morning, my heart sore as I watched him sleep. My gaze traced the contours of his body, taking pictures to store in my memory. I was lost in thought when I felt Tony nudge me with his elbow, and looked up to see the Cross brothers arrive. They all wore suits, looking smart and professional. It was at odds with their usual laid-back, streetwise style.

My heart pounded when I locked eyes with Lee, flashbacks from the night before flooding my mind. I remembered how his lips tasted, how his hands roamed my skin, claiming everything they touched. It was a cold day, but I still felt too hot in my uniform. It was suffocating, and I suddenly found it hard to breathe.

Two men approached the brothers, their legal representation, I was assuming. Some words were exchanged, and then they all began to make their way toward the courthouse. The closer Lee got, the more my lungs constricted, and when he walked right past me without so much as a glance, I felt bereft.

"Come on, we better head inside, too," said Tony, his voice gentle.

Knocking back the last of my coffee, I followed him in, and we took our seats in the court room. There were a number of cases being heard that day, and when the judge came in, he looked harried and stressed. Why did judges always look like that? Like the last thing they had in the world was time, and you were being intolerably rude by presuming you warranted even a moment of it.

Several other cases were heard first, and I was glad because I wasn't ready for all eyes to be on me yet. Unfortunately, it all went by too quickly. Tony gave his account of what happened, and before I knew it, I was being called to the stand to give evidence. Every step felt like an eternity, and when I sat and cleared my throat, I couldn't see anyone else in the room but Lee, his expression stoic as he watched me from the public viewing stand.

I'd spoken in court countless times before, but today was different. Stammering nervously through my statement, I just wanted it to be over. When I was dismissed, I practically ran from the room, finding the ladies' and shutting myself inside. I seemed to be having quite a few bathroom panic attacks lately.

Trying to steady my shaking hands, I imagined they'd be calling Liam to the stand. He'd have his say, and then he'd be asked to give up the name of the person he worked for. He'd tell them it was Lee, and then everything would fall to pieces.

I was in there for at least twenty minutes when I heard voices shouting angrily from outside. Immediately, I hurried from the bathroom to see what was happening. Following the sound of the argument, I found all four brothers at the end of one corridor. Trevor held Lee back, who was fuming at Stu, a look in his eyes like he wanted to commit murder.

"How the fuck could you do this?!" Lee yelled, his face red with fury.

"I had to," said Stu, his expression resigned as he tried to reason with his brother. "There wasn't another way."

"Of course there was. We already decided. *Everything* had been decided!"

"You're wrong — none of us got a say. You made the decision for all of us, thinking you could just put your head on the chopping block like always. Well, this time I'm not letting you be the martyr."

"So you thought you'd be one instead? You're supposed to be my brother — you're not supposed to lie to me. You let me walk into that courtroom thinking Liam was going to give my name, knowing full well you'd convinced him to give yours instead."

Time stood still as my hand went to my mouth and I silently gasped. Stu had switched places with Lee. What the hell? The brothers stared each other down.

"Ever since we were kids you've taken the brunt of the shit we've had to go through, but I'm the eldest. It should've been me." Stu looked away, his shoulders turned inward with something close to shame. He ran his hands through his short hair before turning back. "Now it's my turn to make a sacrifice for this family, just like you've been doing your whole life."

Lee began shaking his head frantically, turmoil written all over his face. When he spoke, his voice was strained. "Nah, I'm not letting you do this."

"It's already been done," said Stu, stepping forward and placing his hands on Lee's shoulders. "You need to let it happen."

Lee growled, ripping Stu's hands off him and turning away.

"It's bullshit, and I'm not accepting it," he shouted before he began stomping down the hall in my direction.

I'd never seen him look so furious, like he was about to explode out of his own skin and transform into the Incredible Hulk. He stopped abruptly when he saw me, a million feelings mixing into one heartbreaking look. It was almost like I could read his thoughts, because in that moment, I knew he blamed me. I was the perfect scapegoat. I'd been the one behind the wheel that day, and I'd had a hand in Liam being here. I'd had a hand in all of this. I could almost *feel* the anger corrupting him, twisting and evolving into a raging bull just beneath the surface of his skin as he stared me down.

There was no reasoning with him now. I knew that, and I knew he said he could never hate me, but right then I thought he'd come close.

I didn't blame him, not one bit. Because it was right for him to hate me. Him hating me was the natural order of things, and he should've done since the moment he first laid eyes on me. This was good, I tried to reassure myself. Lee finally seeing the destruction us being together created was beneficial to everyone. I could handle this. Last night I'd said goodbye; I'd mentally prepared myself for the separation.

So why did it feel like my heart was breaking all over again? Inside the strings were snapping with a violent crack, indefinitely severed.

After locking me in his stare for what felt like forever, Lee didn't breathe a word, just stalked right by me and out the door. Somehow that was worse, his silence. I would have preferred him to shout something terrible, call me a bitch. That way, I could hate him in return, but I didn't.

And the terrifying thing was that I never would.

***

"Stu got seven years," Alexis told me a few weeks later as I drove her to the doctor's for one of her scheduled checkups. "With good behaviour he could be out in two."

"Who told you this?" I asked, my hands gripping the steering wheel too tight, instantly clammy with sweat.

"I bumped into the Trevor on the high street."

"Did he say how Lee's been holding up?" My heart pounded to think of him, knowing he'd have moved on from blaming me and started in on himself.

"He's angry, drinking too much, a nightmare to live with, according to Trevor," Alexis answered.

"I can imagine."

She glanced at me sideways. "He never tried to make contact with you, did he?"

"Not since the day in court," I answered, unable to disguise the sadness in my voice. A day later, I found my car keys in an envelope slotted through our letterbox. My car sat repaired and good as new outside the building, the final connection between us carefully cut. Sure, no contact was for the best, but it still stung that he never even tried to call, not once.

Alexis reached over and gave my arm a squeeze, empathy in her eyes. "When you grow up like those boys did, around people who'd knife you for so much as looking at them the wrong way, everything in life is either one extreme or the other. And they hold grudges, *serious* grudges. It's the only way they know how to operate."

"You think I don't know this? I deal with people like that every day."

"Then why are you acting so heartbroken? Deep down, you expected this. You know you did."

I heaved a breath. "Yeah, well, I have daddy issues. It's not surprising that I picked the wrong man to fall in love with," I joked flatly.

Her hand still rested on my arm, and she gave me another squeeze, her other hand going to her belly. "Why don't we make a pact to stop loving men who aren't good for us, and put all our love into the little one who'll be arriving soon?" Her smile was tender, and I practically squealed.

"You're having a boy?! When did you find this out?"

"The other week. I was going to keep it a secret, but you know me, can't keep my big mouth shut for love nor money."

I was so excited, I almost stopped the car. "So it's going to be an Oliver after all," I said, grinning widely, momentarily forgetting my worries. "I can't wait to meet him."

Alexis returned my grin. "Me neither."

***

Cheers sounded from inside the station, and I frowned curiously as I walked in to find a crowd of officers circling my dad, all congratulating him and patting him on the back. I stepped up to Keira, who was standing by the reception desk, and asked what was going on.

"Your old man just sent Tommy McGregor away for fifteen years. Got him up on racketeering and money-laundering charges."

"Seriously?" I asked, shocked.

I knew my dad was determined, but at the back of my mind, I'd almost thought McGregor would be his Chinese Democracy, his one unfinished piece of work. My eyes wandered across the station, where I saw Jennings standing in a doorway, arms folded. Her gaze was fixed on my dad, her expression revealing a begrudging sort of respect. I watched as my dad turned in her direction, caught her watching, and gave her a single nod of acknowledgment. She nodded back, then turned and left the room. It was like she'd silently accepted what he'd done for her without the need to exchange words. They'd never be friends, but the feud between them was finally over.

A strange relief hit me as I realised Lee could've been caught the same as McGregor if he hadn't gotten out when he did. And with the man behind bars, Lee and his family could relax, knowing he wasn't going to try to come into their lives again. Now I just worried for Stu, because truthfully, I wasn't sure he'd get out after just two years. Sure, of all the brothers, he was probably the most suited to prison. He was the biggest and least sensitive, and he was certainly tough. I couldn't see many men being brave enough to try to intimidate him. I just hoped he kept to himself and avoided unnecessary trouble.

***

Months went by, and I started to fall into a regular routine. The more time that passed, the less my heart hurt. My life was a series of work, studying for my sergeant's exam (yes, Jennings finally decided to approve my application!) and helping Alexis in the final stages of her pregnancy. We planned for either me or her dad to drive her to the hospital, depending on whoever was available.

I was on the late shift, just about to take a break, when I pulled out my phone to check if I had any missed calls. Glancing at the screen and seeing Lee's name caused everything inside of me to spiral out of control. Every painful feeling of heartache returned in an instant, just from looking at his name. Before I could delve too deeply into what that meant, my phone started ringing again.

With a shaking hand I answered it, lifting the phone to my ear, my voice scratchy. "Uh, hello?"

"Karla, thank fuck. Listen, you need to get yourself down the hospital. Alexis has gone into labour," he told me urgently.

All at once my heart did a somersault, half in panic, half in excitement. I hadn't been expecting this, because she wasn't due for at least another ten days. The baby was coming early. "What...uh, I mean, why are *you* calling?"

"She couldn't get through to you and her dad's at work. She called me to drive her to the hospital."

I was already on the move, mouthing the words "Alexis" and "Baby" at Tony, so he knew where I was going. He nodded and motioned for me to run. I knew he'd cover for me until I could get back.

"Okay, well, I'm on my way. I'll be there in a few minutes," I said, then heard someone moaning in the background, and it wasn't a moan of pleasure. "Are you in the delivery room?" I asked with a jolt.

Lee's voice held a hint of humour, but mostly he sounded stressed. "She won't let me leave until you get here, and I'd appreciate it if you hurried, because she's doing a good job of cutting off the blood supply to my hand right now."

I laughed, a high-pitched, airy sound, as I slid into a patrol car and put my foot on the gas. I even turned on the sirens, and Lee chuckled when he heard them. "Such a little rule-breaker."

I smirked at his comment and hung up the phone. I was on an adrenaline rush, not only because the baby was coming, but also because I hadn't spoken to Lee in months, and his voice alone had the ability to excite me.

When I arrived at the hospital, I rushed through the corridors, following the signs for the maternity ward. The place was like a maze, and it felt like it took forever for me to find the delivery room. Still in my full police uniform, I burst inside, all eyes turning to me as I stood there, breathless.

"I'm here," I announced dumbly, seeing Lee standing next to Alexis, who sure enough was gripping his hand like her life depended on it. Her face was red and sweaty, but it was etched with relief when she saw me, and she finally let go of Lee. He walked toward me, his eyes drinking me in like he hadn't seen me in years. Levelling his palms on my shoulders, he whispered, "Take care of her," and then he was gone.

I hurried to my best friend's side, lifted the hand Lee had just been holding, and began taking deep breaths right alongside her.

Twenty-One

Oliver was born at 6:12 a.m. He was ten days premature, had a tuft of blond hair, and weighed just under six and a half pounds. Both mother and baby were healthy and sleeping when I quietly left the room, feeling exhausted but happy. Finding the ladies', I splashed some water on my face, washed my hands, and did my best to fix my hair.

I planned to go home and take a shower, get some sleep, then collect some things to bring back for Alexis. When I stepped out and went to check on her one last time, I saw Lee sitting on a chair in the corridor. The empty space between us felt vast, though in reality it was nothing. I wanted to bridge the gap and run away all at the same time.

"You're still here," I said, standing before him.

He looked up, his eyes tired, and smiled. "I was waiting for you."

"Did you hear the news?"

Lee nodded. "Just spoke to one of the nurses. Healthy baby boy. I'm made up for her."

Not knowing why, I sat down beside him, staring at the wall in front of us like it held the answers to questions I hadn't asked yet. "It was so scary, being in there with her, not knowing how everything was going to turn out." I didn't voice the fact that it was also kind of sad, because I knew I'd never experience that for myself, would never get to hold my own baby in my arms. But I could hold hers, watch him grow up, and that was enough. It would have to be.

Lee shot me a look of compassion, like he sensed what I was thinking. He was one of the few people who knew I couldn't have children, and I remembered his words from months ago.

We're stronger in the places that we've been broken.

Our time together had broken parts of both of us, but were we stronger there now? Was there a patch of soil within us, with the capability of growing something new? I didn't know.

A silence fell between us, and I wasn't sure how to act around him. Since we hadn't seen each other in so long, there was a tension, like we were strangers again, but not. I watched as he laced his fingers together, staring at the work-roughened skin and trying not to succumb to the memory of how it used to feel when he touched me.

"How've you been?" he asked, breaking the quiet.

I slid my gaze to his. "Good. I've been keeping busy. Got my sergeant's exam coming up next week."

His eyebrows rose as he teased, "Sergeant, eh, moving up in the world, are we?"

"Something like that."

"Well, I think it's great. The more people like you they have in the police, the better."

I couldn't help but laugh. "What? Constables who use their sirens so they can skip traffic and get to the hospital in time for their best friend to give birth?"

Lee laughed softly. "Yeah, pretty much."

I smiled back at him, and the eye contact did something strange to my stomach. All at once I was aware of the shape of his lips and the way his hair had grown longer. He used to keep it clipped close to his skull, but now there was more length on top. His expression turned intense, and I cleared my throat to break the tension.

"So, what about you? What've you been up to?"

"Quite a bit, actually."

"Yeah?"

He paused, like he was hesitant to tell me. "Yeah, I'm, eh, I'm setting up a new business."

"Oh."

His eyes narrowed. "Not like that. A legitimate business. I'm opening a restaurant."

Gaping at him, I couldn't have been more surprised if he told me he was opening up his own beanbag emporium. "That's amazing news. What are you calling it?"

"Grub Hut. You should stop by sometime. We're not opening for another few weeks, but I'm there most days doing prep."

I nodded, smiling again. "I like the name. So you took Alexis' advice in the end. Remember she said you should open a restaurant? It makes sense. Your food is amazing."

"Well, I'm still learning. I've hired a team of experienced cooks to help run the kitchen, though, so I won't be on my own."

"What about the garage?"

"Sold it. It felt too strange staying there with everything that's happened. A fresh start is what we all needed."

I exhaled, and a foreign sensation came over me. After a moment, I realised what it was. He was going straight, and I was proud of him. Softening my voice, I asked, "How's Stu coping? Have you been to visit him?"

At this Lee's expression darkened. "He's coping, but it's hard inside, especially when you come in strong, with a reputation to uphold. It's…challenging, but he'll get there."

My stomach churned, reminding me of my guilt. I'd had a hand in Stu being behind bars, so I couldn't help feeling remorseful.

"Well, he's got a lot of people waiting for him on the outside. Just keep reminding him of that and it'll see him through."

"Yeah," said Lee. "I hope so." Turning his body slightly, his eyes wandered from the top of my head to my shoulders. I grew self-conscious, wondering why he was studying me so closely.

"You been seeing anyone?" he asked.

I shot him an incredulous look, trying not to smile. "Are you seriously going there?"

"Got a soft spot for ya, Snap. Always have." He winked, but there was a sadness behind his eyes. We both knew that what he'd felt for me was far more than just a soft spot.

I let out a sigh. "No, I haven't been seeing anyone. Like I said, I've been busy." I paused, not looking at him when I asked shyly, "Have you?"

I could practically feel him smiling, and when I chanced a glance, I noticed his chest puffing out as he rested his arm along the back of my chair. "No. There's no lucky lady in my life right now."

"Oh."

We shared a moment of eye contact, a fire in his gaze that made me swallow hard. His breath hit my ear when he broke the quiet. "I'm sorry for how I blanked you in court that day. It was a shitty move, but my head was all over the place."

"I know, and I don't blame you. You love your family, and a piece of it was torn apart. It's understandable that I was the last person you wanted to see."

"Still, I should've said something, should've tried to explain, but I felt so powerless. I thought I had it all figured out. I could throw myself under the bus and everyone else would be safe, no clue that Stu planned on beating me to it."

"I think he had to do it, though," I said. "He needed to be the one to take responsibility this time."

"Yeah, I get that now."

A quiet descended, and I smelled Lee's cologne. The scent provoked memories that I tried to push away.

"So, sergeant, eh?" he said, nudging me with his elbow. "Will you get to wear a new insignia?"

"RW 79, all the way," I answered, saluting him. "Plus, I'll get to boss all the constables around. It'll be ace."

"Oh, yeah, I can see it now, you shouting orders, all sexy in your uniform," Lee teased, plucking my tie between his fingers.

I rolled my eyes. "I swear, you must be the only bloke in the world who's got a thing for this uniform."

Lee's eyes sharpened as he continued to grin at me, and then he let my tie drop and stood. "Tell Alexis I said congrats. Oh, and I'll see you around, *Serg.*"

"Not sergeant yet," I called after him as he walked away.

He turned around long enough to reply, "You will be."

His faith in me stirred my emotions, and I slumped back into my seat, my lungs suddenly too full of air.

The following week, I found an envelope in my cubbyhole at the station. My heart leapt when I recognised the stamp. I'd sat my exam just the other day, and already the results were in. Becoming a sergeant was something I'd wanted for years, and I was nervous to open the letter. What if I'd failed? Sure, Jennings and I weren't mortal enemies anymore, but we weren't bosom buddies, either. I didn't want to have to face her smug look that was all, *I told you so.*

I almost gave myself a paper cut as I anxiously tore open the envelope, unfolded the letter, and let my eyes scan the contents. I'd passed! Without thinking, I emitted a highly unprofessional squeal of delight, fist pumping the air and grinning like a maniac. Excited, I first called Alexis, who was home from the hospital with Oliver. Next I called Reya, who insisted we meet for cocktails once my shift ended that evening.

I changed into some jeans and a silk blouse before I left the station, letting my hair out of its bun and running my fingers through the waves. Applying a small touch of makeup, I thought I looked good and headed to the bar where Reya had told me to meet her. When I arrived, I found her sitting at a table by the window, engrossed in her phone. There were two fresh margaritas in front of her, and I reached forward to take a sip just as she glanced up.

"Hey! Has anyone ever told you that you're silent like a ninja?" she asked, grinning.

"Oh, many times."

She rose from her seat and came around to hug me. "Well done! I'm so proud of you."

"Thanks," I said, and she went to sit back down, glancing at her phone again as she lifted her own margarita.

"Anything interesting?" I asked, arching a brow.

She waved away my intrigue. "Oh, no, it's just Trevor."

"Trevor as in Cross?" I gaped at her.

"Yeah, we text every once in a while. I gave him my number when we all went out together that night after my gig."

"Right," I replied. "So what do you two talk about?"

"This and that. He's got this harebrained idea to create a web series following him and a group of his friends who do parkour. You know, capturing their stunts and all that. He was originally going to ask me to be the presenter, but then he decided against it. Apparently, I have the 'look,' but I'm not outgoing enough," she scoffed.

"You're a singer, you perform on stage all the time. How is that not outgoing?"

"Yeah, but it's the whole 'not opening my eyes' thing that got him thinking I was too shy, which, by the way, I am. Anyhow, it's not like I would've said yes. Travelling around with a bunch of smelly boys barely out of their teens isn't exactly my dream job."

I glanced at her hands, noticing how she was fiddling with the cardboard coaster. It got me thinking that maybe she wasn't being entirely truthful.

"So there's nothing going on between you two, then?" I probed.

Reya blushed, which was a feat to achieve on her caramel complexion. "Nope, just texts. Oh, and he friended me on Facebook."

"Uh-huh."

"Don't 'uh-huh' me, Karla. There's nothing going on. He told me I'm not his type, and I'd well believe it. His profile is full of pictures of him with tiny blondes, and *I* am neither blonde nor tiny."

"Right, so you've been snooping through his profile," I continued, goading her.

"Yes, of course I have. I'm a student. I have lots of free time and I get bored. What else is there to do?"

"Plenty."

"Oh, shut up. You barely ever go online. You don't understand the temptation to snoop."

"Especially when there's a twinkly-eyed pretty boy in the mix."

Reya scowled. "That's it. I'm changing the subject. When do I get to come see Lexie's baby? I need some cuteness in my life."

"Whenever you like. I doubt she's gonna get the chance to leave the flat any time soon."

Reya smiled like she couldn't wait, and then a curious gleam lit her eyes. "So how was it with Lee? He drove Alexis to the hospital, right?"

"Who told you that?"

"Trevor," she answered, like it was obvious.

"That boy's got a big mouth. And it was fine, positively civilised, actually. We chatted for a bit. He told me he's opening a restaurant, asked me to stop by."

"I'm sure he did," said Reya. "He'll be all, *Oh, I just spilled marinara sauce all over my muscle-T, whatever shall I do?* Then he'll whip it off, flex his abs at you, and you'll be putty in his hands."

"And then we'll go at it right out in the open for all the world to see," I deadpanned.

"So you're saying there were no unresolved feelings, no longing glances or hot stares?"

"That's exactly what I'm saying."

"Liar!"

"Hey, if you want to talk about Lee, then we have to talk about Trevor. How's that sound?"

She pursed her lips, frowning. "You're no fun."

I shot her a pointed look. "Neither are you."

"That's not true. Talking about your love life is a lot more fun than talking about mine."

"Right, so there is something going on with you and Trev." I grinned.

"Oh, my God, shut up. Fine, let's talk about these cocktails, then, shall we? They're pretty amazing. I want to sample at least five different ones before the night is through."

Smiling wide, I lifted my hand to her for a high-five. "Sounds like a plan."

By the time I arrived home, I was more drunk than tipsy. It was barely ten o'clock, but we'd started drinking at six. When I got in, I kicked off my shoes, dropped my bag on the floor, and turned to find Alexis and Lee sitting in the living area, cups of tea placed in front of them on the coffee table. *Positively cosy*, my drunken brain mused.

"Looks like somebody was out celebrating," said Alexis with a smile. "Congratulations again, by the way."

I grinned at her in a way that revealed my drunkenness, and wobbled slightly on my feet as I went to the kitchen to find a glass of water. It was at the back of my mind to ask why Lee was there, but I thought he must have come to visit the baby and see how Alexis was doing. With my glass full, I hobbled my way over to them and plonked down on the couch next to Lee.

"Reya and I went for cocktails. I think I might have gone a little overboard," I said, trying not to slur my words. When I looked at Lee, I found him regarding me fondly, his arm resting along the back of the couch. I scrunched up my mouth and pointed a finger into his chest, half the water in my glass sloshing out onto my lap. "Did you know about Reya and Trevor?"

He shook his head. "What about them?"

"I dunno. I think they're having a thing."

"Sounds serious."

"Don't be cheeky," I warned, pointing at him again. A noise came from the baby monitor, and Alexis went to go check on Oliver. I might have been drunk, but I didn't fail to see the cynical, knowing look on her face as she glanced between the two of us.

"You should get to bed, Snap. Sleep off all that booze," Lee murmured.

"I have to drink this water first. Otherwise, I'll be hung over in the morning."

His laugh was soft. "I think that's gonna happen anyway, beautiful."

"Ugh, you're so...so...annoying," I said, and lifted the glass, downing the rest of its contents. Wiping my mouth with the back of my hand, I added, "And don't call me beautiful. You think I'll let you in my pants because I'm drunk, wellll, no way, José."

"Ah, you have me pegged. I'm a dirty opportunist." Lee sighed dramatically, unable to wipe the grin from his face. He thought I was funny. Getting up from the couch, I stumbled slightly, but he caught me in time to prevent my fall.

"Easy," he murmured, his hands clasping my elbows.

Looking up at him from beneath my lashes, I swallowed tightly and stepped out of his hold. Turning, I managed to make it to my bedroom, where I unceremoniously bumped into my wardrobe.

"Ow," I whined, clutching my knee.

Lee stood just a few feet shy of my doorway. "Are you all right?"

"I'm fine," I answered, and then proceeded to face-plant onto my mattress. Fully clothed; I had no intention of going to the effort of undressing. I could sleep like this.

Lee entered my room. "You sure you don't need some help?"

"Nope, I'm good," I said, waving a hand in the air.

"You're just going to sleep in your clothes?" he asked.

"Pretty much."

"Karla, let me help you."

Annoyed, I flipped over onto my back and levelled him with a hostile glare. "I said, I'm fine."

Lee sighed and went back out into the living room, not bothering to shut my door. I closed my eyes and tried to go to sleep, but the waist of my jeans began to bite into my skin, and I felt uncomfortably sweaty in my silk blouse. Only a minute or two had passed when I called out sheepishly, "Lee?"

The smile in his voice was unmistakable. "What is it, Snap?"

"Maybe I could use some help." No way were these skinnies coming off on their own. Chuckling, he returned to my room and stood at the foot of my bed, grinning down at me.

"You're adorable when you're drunk."

I scoffed. "Sure."

"Let's get these off you, then," he said, resting a knee on the mattress and bending forward to undo my fly. With effort he pulled them down my legs, finally getting them off. I was already unbuttoning my blouse when I realised he'd gone quiet, and looked up to find him standing over me, heat in his eyes as they traced my bare legs.

"You good from here?" he asked, swallowing tightly.

I couldn't answer, because his stare was creating a burning need between my thighs. My throat was thick when I finally said, "Yeah, I'm good."

He had turned to leave when I added, "Wait, can you help me with the duvet before you go?"

I shouldn't have said it. I could easily deal with a bloody duvet by myself. The truth was that I didn't want him to leave. Not yet. Nodding, he didn't say a word as he returned, slid an arm around my waist, and lifted me up while pulling the duvet out from under me. Exhaling heavily, I stared at his thick lashes, then at his lips, before finally resting my gaze on his.

Acting purely on instinct, I seized his mouth, moving my lips and coaxing his to open. He groaned as I kissed him, his entire body still and tense. My skin heated, my body responding to the contact as I arched my hips and felt the stirrings of an erection in his pants.

"You're drunk," he said as he broke away briefly, like he was trying to reason with himself.

"Mm-hmm," I murmured indistinctly, pulling him back as I slid my tongue into his mouth and wrapped my arms around his neck. Lee hissed when I ground myself off his dick, seeking friction. For a second he kissed me hungrily, drinking me in and tasting me. Then a moment later he was gone, rising off the bed and running his hands through his hair.

"Fuck," he swore. "You can't test me like that, Karla. I'm not strong enough," he said gruffly.

I lay there, staring up at him, breathless. "I'm sorry."

Lee frowned and shook his head. "Don't be sorry. I just don't want to take advantage...."

"It's okay, I know. You're a good person, Lee," I told him, not sure if that was drunk Karla talking, or sober Karla.

The way his eyes raked my half-naked body gave me chills. "The thoughts I'm having right now are far from good. Tell me to leave."

"Leave?"

"Okay, I'm going," he said, still staring at me, or my chest, to be more exact. "Yep, definitely leaving now."

Turning, he walked out of my room, this time closing the door behind him. I pulled the blanket up around me, savouring the warmth but wishing it was another kind. In the end the alcohol in my system won, and I passed out cold.

Twenty-Two

I woke up to the sound of Reya's voice, and, sure enough, when I walked into the kitchen, she was sitting across from Alexis, holding Oliver in her arms and cooing at him like an annoying grandmother. Or maybe I just found it annoying because my head was spinning.

"How are you not dying right now?" I asked, opening the fridge and pulling out a carton of orange juice.

Reya shrugged. "I don't really get hangovers."

"Just you wait," said Alexis, pointing to me. "A few years, and you'll be as bad as this one."

"Yeah, no offence," I added, "but I kind of hate you right now. I'm going to take a shower."

When I came back out, clean and dressed, I found breakfast waiting for me. Apparently, Reya felt guilty for her lack of a hangover and decided to cook me bacon to make up for it. She was such a gem. Sitting down at the table, I dug into my food. Her phone went off with a text, and she hurried to check it. I was willing to bet I knew who it was.

"Trevor?" I asked between bites.

She nodded sheepishly and put her phone back down. "He wants to hang out today."

"Really? You should go."

She shook her head. "It's more of a group hangout. He and a few of his buddies are practicing for some free-running competition. He wanted to know if I was interested in coming to watch."

"That sounds exciting. I could think of worse ways to spend a Saturday."

"So why don't you come with me?" she put in eagerly. "It'll be fun, and I'll buy you ice cream."

There was something about the innocent look in her eyes that I couldn't say no to. "Sure, I'll come. Got nothing else planned anyway."

"You're the best," she said, reaching across the table to squeeze my hand.

A half hour later we were on the Tube, heading toward Hyde Park. Trevor texted Reya, telling her to meet him at the Albert monument. When we got there, we found him, Liam and a bunch of their friends leaping up and down ten steps at a time, like they were running drills. There were also lots of people hanging about watching; not surprisingly, they were mostly female. That wasn't what caught my attention most, though, because sitting off to the side and shouting encouragement was Lee.

I grabbed Reya's arm, my voice tight as I said, "You never told me he'd be here."

She shrugged out of my hold, smiling at me like butter wouldn't melt. "Trev never mentioned it."

I knew she was lying when I caught the both of them sharing a secret little smile as Trevor waved to her from the steps. They were trying to play Cupid, I could tell. Deciding not to let it get to me, I continued walking toward Lee.

"Hey," I said tentatively, and sat down next to him on the steps. "So what are you, their coach or something?"

He looked up at me, eyes moving down my body before settling on my face. "Or something. How's the head?"

"Thumping. I'm sorry about, uh, last night," I said, fiddling awkwardly with the zipper of my jacket.

Unfortunately, I remembered every second of my embarrassing attempt to kiss him and his subsequent rejection. I wished I could scrub the humiliating behaviour from my brain, but they hadn't created a pill for selective memory loss yet.

I knew from the set of his mouth that he was trying not to smile. "Nothing to be sorry about." Leaning forward, he nodded to Reya.

"Good to see you again."

"You, too," she replied shyly. My friend tended to get quiet around good-looking men, which explained her behaviour with Lee. What it didn't explain was her friendship with his brother. Then again, when Trevor decided he was going to be friends with someone, they didn't really get a say in the matter. I'd learned that firsthand.

"So what are they all practicing for?" I asked in an effort to make conversation.

Lee rubbed a hand over his jaw, where an attractive bit of stubble was growing. "Big competition up in Brighton next week. The winning team gets a round trip to Thailand to climb the Doi Inthanon Mountain."

"And that's their idea of a good time?" I said. "I'd rather stay on the beach."

Lee chuckled. "That's you and me both."

I noticed Trevor and the rest of them stopping to take a break, and he ran over to us, plopping down next to Reya. Waggling his brow at her, he teased, "I know I'm delectably sweaty right now, but do try to resist." He leaned closer, but she pushed him away.

"Eww, get off. You need to take a shower."

"I'll just go hop in the pond, shall I?" he joked, lifting the end of his T-shirt to reveal an inch of toned stomach.

Reya laughed tightly. "I dare you."

"And I'll second that dare," I added, goading him. "Crack on."

Trevor scowled at us both playfully. "It's a good thing I'm immune to peer pressure. There's probably typhoid in that water."

"And cholera," said Lee. "So don't even think about it. I'm not taking you to the hospital."

"You just don't want to clean up after I get the shits." Trevor grinned, trying to gross him out. Lee stared at him, expressionless, which was kind of funny.

"Can we leave bowel movements out of the conversation, please?" I grimaced.

"You don't know what he's like," said Lee, still eyeing his brother. "He's off his nut. Can't back away from a challenge."

Trevor scoffed. "Jumping into a pond is no challenge. Now, if you'd asked me to climb atop old Albert, strip off all my clothes, and jump to the ground while crying out the lyrics to 'Dancing Queen,' I might have to take you up on it."

Reya stared at the monument. "You'd break your neck."

He leaned closer to her. "Is that a dare?"

Her eyes flared with worry. "No! Absolutely not."

"Too bad. Could've been fun."

"I think there might be something wrong with you," I said, my brow furrowing.

Lee smirked and shook his head. "Nah, he's just flirting with your friend."

"Hey, now, bruv, don't be tellin' porkies. Reya here's a good buddy of mine," said Trevor, throwing his arm around her shoulders. Reya looked away for a second, and I thought she might be feeling awkward. It was clear that she fancied him, so maybe she was embarrassed that her crush was unrequited.

Lee eyeballed his brother, his *pull the other one* expression pure comedy gold.

Reya caught my attention, a pleading look in her eyes. "Do you want to go get ice cream now? I spotted a stand on our way into the park."

"I'll go," Lee said. "You stay where you are, love."

Reya frowned, annoyed that he'd thwarted her escape plan, and settled back onto the grass beside Trevor. I was about to lie back and enjoy the unseasonably sunny weather when I felt Lee nudge me with the toe of his shoe. "Come help," he said, eyeing me pointedly.

"Oh, sure," I replied, and got up to follow him. I waited until we were a good enough distance away to whisper, "They're trying to set us up."

Lee smiled. "I know. You like how I turned it back around on them?"

"I do. You're an evil mastermind."

"Just giving them a taste of their own medicine. See how they like it. By the way, I never got to congratulate you properly last night, what with you being shitfaced drunk and all."

"I do believe that's the technical term for it, yes."

He laughed. "Well, I heard you passed your exam, so, well done." Reaching out, he gave my hand a small squeeze. My skin tingled where he touched me. It wasn't long before his hand was on me again, this time when we reached the ice cream stand. He placed his flattened-out palm to the base of my spine, standing beside me as I scanned the choices. His warmth spread through me, both soothing and disconcerting.

Slipping his other hand inside his jeans, he pulled out a small business card and handed it to me. Glancing down, I saw it was for his restaurant.

"Address is on there," he said. "You should come see the place."

"You already invited me, remember? At the hospital."

"Just wanted to make sure you knew the invitation was still open," he replied, eyeing me intensely. I swallowed back the lump in my throat that always seemed to come when I was around him these days.

"I'll come next week on my day off."

"Good." I saw his Adam's apple bob in his throat. Was he feeling this just as much as I was?

After we got the ice creams, the walk back to the monument was quiet. I thought I could feel him looking at me out of the corner of my eye, but I couldn't be certain.

"So, are you both coming out with us tonight?" Trevor asked as we ate.

"What's tonight?"

He nudged Lee with his elbow. "It's this one's birthday bash. He's being an old curmudgeon and won't let us throw him a party, so we're just going for a few drinks at the local boozer."

I gaped at Lee. "It's your birthday? Why didn't you say?"

He lifted a careless shoulder. "Not really big into birthdays, Snap." There was something sad in his expression, and I wondered if he didn't like celebrating because of when he was a kid. I didn't imagine birthdays were very fun for him back then.

Since I was sitting next to him, I reached out and gave him one of those consolation prize half-hugs, wishing I could give him a full one. "Happy birthday," I said, my voice quiet.

He turned his head, his mouth only centimetres from mine. "Thanks."

Time stood still, and I couldn't look away from his lips. I watched him inhale sharply, his nostrils flaring as his hand came up and wiped a spot of ice cream away from the corner of my mouth. Bringing it to his own, he licked it away, and I felt all of my insides clench tight.

In the end, Trevor broke the moment by announcing loudly, "Oh, my God, just kiss her. This is getting downright inappropriate for my youthful gaze."

Reya laughed quietly next to him, and I looked away, trying to control my blush. Right then I wanted to kick him, annoyed that a cocky little twenty-three-year-old could embarrass me like that. Thankfully, there was a distraction when a group of girls barely out of their teens approached, smiling demurely and giggling as they eyed the aforementioned cocky little shit.

"Hi, Trevor." One of them finger-waved.

Reya began fixedly studying the crumpled ice cream napkin she held as Trevor flashed them a charming smile. "Ladies."

"We were watching you earlier. It's amazing the stuff you guys can do."

"Oh, yeah?" Trevor preened.

Reya quietly stood and announced, "I just remembered I have to go collect my laundry. I'll see you all later." With that she turned and walked away, an urgency in her gait.

I glanced at Lee. "I'd better go after her."

He nodded. "Go. Will I see you tonight?"

"Sure, we'll stop by around eight or nine."

His eyes warmed. "Okay, see you then."

***

When I caught up to Reya, she still wouldn't admit that she had feelings for Trevor, and swore out and out that she really did have laundry to pick up. In the end I left her to it, with a promise to meet up later for Lee's birthday drinks. My stomach was all a-flutter at the thought of seeing him again, but it felt different now. There was no anxious sense of foreboding, no feeling like I was doing something wrong. All I felt was excitement that I was going to see a man I found attractive and had some deep unresolved feelings for.

So, you know, the usual.

Look, at least he wasn't thieving anymore, nor was he on my dad's watch list. Although Lee and his brothers were being monitored by Dad's team originally, he knew he didn't have anything on them. Plus, he seemed satisfied enough that Stu was doing time, the person he'd always thought was the ringleader.

That was the problem with my dad. He was so wrapped up in his own alpha maleness that he couldn't see another alpha when he was staring him right in the face. And sometimes, the big dog wasn't necessarily the largest.

Feeling the need to get Lee a birthday gift, I stopped by a bookstore on my way home and picked up a Cordon Bleu cookery book that I knew he'd like. I smiled to myself, remembering the time I'd teased him for baking lemon cakes like a little old granny. In truth, the idea of him with his shirt sleeves rolled up, tattoos all on display, and wearing an apron was kinda sexy. Or maybe I was just a weirdo.

I spent the rest of the day helping Alexis with Oliver, then went to get ready. Settling on a pair of black skinny jeans, boots, and a white shirt, I thought I looked good without making too much effort. I tied my hair up in a stylish ponytail before heading out. Reya met me on the Tube, since she lived two stops away, and when we got to the pub, the place was busy. I spotted Lee, Trevor, Liam, and two other blokes sitting at a big table, drinking pints.

"Hey, everyone," I said in greeting, and Lee immediately stood to place a kiss on my cheek. His gaze travelled over me as I shrugged off my jacket, and then he whispered in my ear, "You look hot as fuck."

I shivered at his words, wondering if he only said it because he was drinking, but the alcohol on his breath wasn't heavy. I sat down, and Trevor proceeded to quiz Reya on where she'd run off to earlier. He'd been so busy flirting with his gaggle of groupies that he hadn't even noticed her leave, which just said it all. I thought maybe my friend was better off with him staying oblivious. Sure, Lee was a handful, but I imagined it'd take ten women to keep up with Trevor's hyperactive personality.

Reya needed someone kind, someone safe. Not an adrenaline junkie who jumped off buildings and climbed mountains just for kicks. Sure, Lee was…okay, you get the point. Of all the brothers, Trevor was the wildcard. Speaking of brothers, Liam was eyeing me cautiously from the other side of the table. I understood why he was sceptical, especially with Stu's current incarceration. But I wasn't there for any reason other than the fact that I was drawn to Lee.

We'd been out of each other's lives for three months. I'd thought I was over him, insomuch as you could ever get over a lost love. But the second I walked into that delivery room and saw him there, standing by my best friend's side as she went through one of the most difficult and important experiences of her life, I knew I wasn't over him. Not by a long shot. All my feelings had come rolling back, but with a renewed sense of warmth. I didn't have to worry about my career or my reputation. He was just a man now. Just an ordinary man. Anything could happen. The idea caused my every pore to draw tight with anticipation.

I wanted to say something to Liam, but I knew that if he was ever going to accept me, it was going to take time. I'd have to get him to warm up to me little by little. For now, I simply nodded my head at him in lieu of a hello. He nodded back. This was good. I'd half expected him to flip me off.

"Oh, I brought you a present," I said, turning to Lee. My knee knocked into his, and I was far more aware of the simple touch than I should have been. Pulling the gift-wrapped book from my handbag, I passed it to him. Lee stared at the gift, a grin tugging at one corner of his mouth.

"Aw, Snap, ya shouldn't have," he said, leaning forward and giving me yet another peck on the cheek. This time it was dangerously close to my mouth, and I inhaled a sharp breath. A second later, Lee's attention was on the book as he pulled it from the wrapping. The smile took over his entire face then, and his eyes lit up as he looked at me. "This is great, thanks."

"All right, it's time for tequila shots," said Trevor, returning from the bar. I'd been so wrapped up in Lee that I hadn't even noticed him leave the table. He slammed a bottle of Patrón down, alongside some salt and limes. Then he went to grab a bunch of shot glasses from the barman before returning.

"Nah, man, that stuff makes me puke," said Liam, shaking his head.

"Lightweight," Trevor jeered, then turned to Reya, flashing a devilish grin. "How about you, Queenie?"

She blushed at him using her stage name, her eyes downcast as she nodded. "Sure."

Trevor glanced at me. "And you, Constable?"

"Hey, it's sergeant now," said Lee, and Trevor looked at me, wide-eyed.

"No shit? You made sergeant? In that case, you definitely have to do a shot. All sergeants are notorious tequila fiends," he said, making no sense whatsoever, but that was Trevor for you.

"Okay, I'll do one," I said, feeling Lee's attention next to me. "But only one."

Trevor began lining the shots up in front of us. When Reya passed me the salt, I licked a line between my thumb and forefinger, poured it on, and picked up a slice of lime. Before I could react, Lee grabbed my hand and levelled me with a hot look. A moment passed, and then he bent his head to lick off the salt, his tongue hot and wet on my skin. My tummy fluttered wildly as I tried to steady my breathing, especially when he glanced up at me, eyes dark with mischief. I watched, transfixed, as he knocked back his shot, then bit down on the lime. It was probably one of the sexiest things I'd ever seen.

"Your turn," he said, voice husky as he held his hand out to me.

"Oh," I breathed, heart pounding loud in my ears.

After a second of hesitation, I brought my mouth to his skin and licked. This close, all I could smell was him, his salty taste on my lips. To my horror, I found myself lingering, and a rumble only I could hear rose from his chest. I drew away quickly, downing the shot and biting into the lime.

Expecting to turn around and find everyone watching our borderline pornographic exchange, I was relieved to see they were ignoring us completely. That was mostly because Trevor was on his third shot, and the boys were egging him on to do more.

There was music in the pub and a small dance floor, a few women and men busting sloppy, drunken moves. Lee's breath hit my skin right before he whispered, "Come dance with me."

He didn't give me time to respond, only grabbed my hand and pulled me up with him. I followed, my head foggy with either arousal or tequila, I couldn't seem to tell. My eyes traced the muscular lines of his broad shoulders, shoulders made for hard work and fucking, and I began to imagine where this night would lead.

Some cheesy eighties rock ballad played through the speakers as Lee spun us around, pulled me close, and slid his arms around my waist. I stared up at him, his bright blue eyes arresting. The way he moved was purposeful, every brush of his body against mine designed to seduce.

"Lee," I said, unsure whether he could hear me over the music, "why did you leave last night?"

I knew by the set of his mouth that he didn't like my question, but he answered it anyway. "I didn't want to, if that's what you're asking."

What he said was a relief, because although he was showing all the signs that he wanted me, there'd always be that lingering doubt in the back of my mind, questioning whether or not he still harboured blame.

"So…." I ventured. "You just didn't want to take advantage while I was drunk?"

"Yeah, I want to do things right this time."

"This time?"

He nodded, a predatory gleam in his eyes. "If you think I'm here for friendship, Karla, you're shit out of luck." The growl in his voice did wonderful things to my insides. "I want you back in my bed, for good."

"Oh," I breathed, uncertain as to what to say.

"But it won't be like last time. I refuse to sneak around or keep things secret. I won't have you letting go of my hand because you're ashamed to be seen with me. That shit is over. I want you to be proud to be by my side. I want you to want everyone to know you're mine. But most of all, I want to be worthy of you."

"You were always worthy. Circumstances just weren't…optimal."

He shook his head, still swaying our bodies gently to the music. "Nah. You said something to me once that rang true. You said I'd gotten away with murder for so long that I wasn't afraid of being caught anymore, and you were right. When you're in as deep as I was, you get numb, but you also start justifying your actions. You begin to believe you're doing good, that it's either you or them. You convince yourself that the law's wrong. That's where my head was at when I first met you, and little by little you broke down the walls of bullshit I'd built up. You showed me all the lies I'd been telling myself until I finally woke up and believed you."

I stared at him, taken aback by his admission. Because the truth was that he'd shown me so much, too. The law wasn't perfect. There would always be Steves around to screw people over and take advantage of the power that came with the job. There would always be corruption and unfairness. And it was those like Lee and his family who bore the brunt of that, because he'd shown me that people's actions are a result of their circumstances, and sometimes breaking the law is the only choice.

I thought on all this as I lowered my head to rest on his shoulder.

"What I'm trying to say is, I want to date you, Karla Sheehan," he said, a smile in his voice.

I laughed softly and nuzzled my nose into his skin. "Like an old-fashioned courting?"

He breathed deeply and drew me closer, his mouth at my temple. "Maybe not so old-fashioned. I'm not sure I can keep my hands to myself for that long."

"I'm not sure I'd want you to," I whispered, and felt him shudder when my breath hit his earlobe. "But there's just one more thing."

"Oh, yeah, what's that?"

"When do you plan on announcing your intentions to my father?"

As soon as the question was out, we both burst into laughter. It went without saying that my dad was never going to accept Lee. It was a good thing I'd never been one to wait around for parental approval.

"How about this, if I promise you never have to meet my old man, then you have to promise I never have to meet yours?"

Eyeing him in amusement, I took his hand and we shook on it. "It's a deal."

Twenty-Three

Lee was working out some kinks in his menu. This was exactly how he phrased it when he called and asked me on our first official date. *Come over to the restaurant*, he said. *Let me cook for you, and you can tell me what you like and what you don't like.* It didn't take too much convincing for me to say yes, especially since he made all that sound decidedly sexual. But now I was nervous. I had no idea what to wear, and had changed my outfit several times.

The previous night we'd said goodbye without so much as a kiss, with Trevor drunk from too many tequila shots, and Lee and Liam helping him into a taxi. Needless to say, I was all amped up, excited and nervous for what would happen when I got to the restaurant. Would there be workers around, or would we be alone?

In the end I chose a dark purple skater skirt, boots, and an old Metallica T-shirt. It harkened back to my teenage grunge years, but it looked sexy and casual at the same time, so I forced myself not to try for another outfit change.

When I arrived at the Grub Hut, the sign above the premises was done in stylish carved metal. Peering in the window, I saw there was still work being completed on the interior, but I imagined it was going to look great when it was finished. I texted Lee to let him know I was outside, and a minute later he appeared from out the back, the end of his black T-shirt covered with flour and his hair tousled.

Opening the door, he welcomed me with a warm smile and pulled me into a hug. "Hey," he murmured, placing a kiss on my temple.

"Hi," I replied, stepping inside. "The place looks great. I love the sign."

Lee grinned at my compliment and took my hand, leading me out back to the kitchen. The place was brand new, all stainless steel, with a long metal work top in the centre of the room. My mouth watered as I took in all the ingredients. There were bowls laid out with all manner of foods: chopped tomatoes and onions, avocados, coriander, quartered lemons, chilies, fresh tortillas, and a whole host of spices. It became clear that he was planning on making some kind of Mexican dish.

"Those shots last night gave me inspiration," he said with a wink, and I got a little tingle along the back of my neck as I remembered his tongue on my skin. Lee's eyes darkened, like he was remembering, too, and then he came over and took my jacket.

"Nobody else around?" I asked, trying to sound casual.

He shook his head and smirked. "We're all alone."

Trying to act like his flirting wasn't affecting me, I hitched myself up onto the counter opposite his workspace and folded my arms. Looking around, I knew it must have cost a pretty penny to do the place up, not to mention the rents in London weren't cheap. Though I didn't suspect he'd used dirty money to fund the new business. Selling the garage would've left him with more than enough to start over.

"So how's everything been going? You had any old acquaintances sniffing around?"

"No, and if they're smart, they'll steer clear. A couple of the boys who used to work for me wanted to go clean, too, so I gave them jobs here. If anyone comes trying for a protection racket, they'll be shown where the door is."

"That's good. Do you expect they will?"

Lee shook his head. "Spent years building up a certain reputation, Karla. If anyone tries messing with this place or me, they'll have to be dumb as fuck."

I let out a breath and braced my hands on the edge of the counter. "Well, I'm glad to hear it, but if you ever have any problems, let me know. So, what are you making?"

He motioned to the ingredients. "Isn't it obvious? Tacos."

"I love tacos."

He smirked. "Me, too."

I rolled my eyes, but couldn't help smiling. Lee went to wash his hands and then returned, throwing some minced beef into the pan and mixing in a few spices. I found it strangely relaxing to watch him cook, and my stomach was rumbling by the time he was finished. He set three tacos on a plate for me and pulled up a stool.

"Okay, so each one has a different spice mix in the beef. Tell me which one you like best."

I grinned, enjoying myself. "The second one is best. I like the smokiness," I told him after I'd tasted all three.

"Yeah?" Lee asked, his eyes lighting up with interest. "What about number three? I tried a pinch of cardamom just for shits and giggles."

"It's good, but not as good as the second."

He stood before me, his arms folded. "Okay, I'll take your word for it. Now we move onto my béarnaise sauce recipe. I'll make mini-steaks to go with it." He tried to take my plate, but I pushed his hands away.

"Hey! I'm not finished yet."

Lee chuckled and raised his hands in surrender. "No need to bite my head off. I just thought you might get full."

"Ha! I'm a cop. I'm never full."

"This is true. I should see about frying you up some donuts."

I narrowed my gaze, still chewing. "Don't be a dick."

"You want my dick? Whoa, ease up there, serg. I'm not a piece of meat." His cheeky wink held pure mischief as he bent to pull a pot out of the cupboard.

I scowled playfully at his comment, slightly annoyed by how easily he could get to me, and honestly, feeling a little turned on now that he'd switched up the conversation. I watched as he began melting butter in a saucepan and adding shallots. Already the smell was heavenly, and he hadn't even put in the other ingredients yet. When he got some melted butter on his thumb, he stuck it in his mouth to suck it off, and without even realising it, I was clenching my thighs at the visual. When the steam made him too hot, he lifted his T-shirt to wipe the sweat from his brow, exposing his abs. I swear, if anyone ever decided to make a cookery show about Lee, they'd get top ratings.

I put down my empty plate and took a sip of water. Yes, because I was thirsty, but also because I was too warm.

"The sauce looks great," I told him, and he glanced up.

"Yeah? You should come over again tomorrow. I'm makin' a Ruby Murray."

"Oh, my God, you're such a Cockney sometimes." I mock-cringed.

Lee grinned impishly. "You don't like it?"

"Danny Dyer doesn't really do it for me."

"You lie. All the ladies love a bit of the Danny. They want him to take them down the rub-a-dub and dip his Hampton Wick in their Morris Minors."

I almost wheezed, I laughed so hard. "That's truly awful. Please don't ever talk dirty to me in Cockney again. It'll put me off sex for life."

Lee was laughing too, his face handsome as he raised his hands. "Okay, understood. We wouldn't want to put you off sex."

"And why's that?" I asked, suddenly feeling flirtatious.

"Because you get the orgasm version of hangry. If I don't make you come, you're in a right mood."

"Shut up! That's not true."

"Happened a few times, Snap," he asserted teasingly.

"Oh, you're a little liar." My expression showed my annoyance, and he looked pleased as punch that he was riling me. Clearly, that had been his intention all along.

After we ate the mini steaks, and I told Lee which version of his béarnaise recipe I preferred, he grabbed two beers from the fridge and brought me upstairs where there was a rooftop terrace. It was only a two-story building, so you couldn't exactly see for miles, but it was still nice. The weather was mild, and the sky was starting to darken.

Lee popped open the bottles, handed one to me, and took a long swig of his own. We sat side by side on folding chairs, our feet propped up on an old wooden bench.

"I like it here," I said, breaking the quiet.

"Yeah? I'm gonna get some of those funky coloured lights and hang them over the fencing, set up a few outdoor heaters and get some deck furniture. Make a nice little outdoor dining area."

"Sounds like you've put a lot of thought into it."

"If you're gonna do something, might as well do it right," said Lee, tipping his bottle to mine.

"I'll drink to that."

We sat in quiet for a few minutes, letting the nighttime city noises wash over us. Lee had pulled his chair up close to mine, so our shoulders were only inches apart.

My hair was up in a ponytail and my old T-shirt hung lazily off one shoulder. I was vaguely aware of a feathery sensation before realising it was Lee's lips brushing just below my hairline. Letting out a low sigh, I tilted my head farther to the side to grant him more access.

"You know I love you, right?" he whispered, shocking me out of my reverie. My heart pounded, and I momentarily lost the ability to breathe. He'd told me he loved me once, while drunk beyond belief, but this was different. This time I knew it was true. Emotion clogged my throat, blocking my voice, and I felt wetness prick at my eyes.

"I know," I finally managed to whisper.

"I understand if you can't say it back yet. I just wanted to tell you how I feel."

Involuntarily my mouth dropped open as I stared him. How could he ever think I didn't feel just as strongly for him as he did for me?

"Lee," I said, my voice scratchy, "I know I never admitted it, but I started falling for you a long time ago. It was impossible not to."

I saw him hesitate, his face stoic as he watched me. I knew what he was waiting for. He needed me to say the words. After a moment that felt like forever, I managed to muster the courage.

"I love you, too," I said, and he reached over to caress my cheek.

"Yeah?" he asked, his eyes searching mine like I might change my mind between one second and the next.

"Yeah," I whispered.

In quick succession, he took both our bottles and set them down on the bench. Then he was back, his mouth devouring my neck, kissing and nipping in a way that sent tremors throughout my entire body. How was it that a few carefully placed kisses could reduce me to a quivering, breathless pile of need?

Lee tugged me over to sit on his lap, dragging my mouth to his and kissing me with a relaxed, confident sort of urgency. The spot between my legs ached to be touched while his erection dug into my hip. Before I knew it, I was straddling him, and he'd pulled the tie from my hair, letting the strands fall around my shoulders.

I was delirious with arousal, needing his mouth everywhere at once. Lee shoved my calf-length skirt up around my waist, his hands finding my underwear and hastily pushing the fabric to one side. When he slid a finger down my folds, he broke our kiss, leaned back, and stared up at me.

"You're fucking beautiful," he said, his voice fierce.

I let out a weak moan, my breaths quickening.

"I'm going to watch you come," Lee went on. "I bet it'll be fast."

He wasn't wrong. I'd been without sex for months, and being around him for the last few days had me wired. I was in woeful need of a release. Lee pushed two fingers inside me, and I savoured the feeling of fullness while he began rubbing my clit with his thumb. Enjoying the pressure, I closed my eyes, and his other hand slid beneath my T-shirt, pulling down the cup of my bra and palming my breast. He moulded it with his hand, then plucked my beaded nipple, causing me to shudder, ever closer to orgasm. His thumb flicked lazily back and forth. I opened my eyes just as I was about to come, locked gazes with Lee, and shook as pleasure overtook me.

"So fucking beautiful," he repeated, devouring me with his stare.

Once my orgasm faded, I snuggled close to him, breathing in his scent. His hand was still on my breast, and he absentmindedly massaged it as we sat there in the afterglow.

I was disappointed when he gently moved me, helping us both to stand, and said, "I should get you home."

I wanted to pout and complain like a child, wanted to beg him to take me right there on the roof, but I had to maintain some measure of decorum. So instead I nodded and followed him back down to the kitchen, where I'd left my jacket and handbag.

I was standing by the counter, gathering my things, when I felt his heat at my back.

"Ah, fuck taking it slow," said Lee, his hands at my waist. I gasped when he pushed my skirt up again, this time pulling my underwear off and stuffing it in his pocket. All of a sudden I was reminded of our first time, in the dark of the crowded nightclub, absorbing one another like it was our last night on earth. We'd been so desperate for each other back then, had spent so long in a dance, playing a game without any set rules or guidelines.

Lee's hand clutched my neck, his mouth at my ear as he asked, "Do you want me?"

"Yes," I whimpered.

His hold on me wasn't gentle, and I savoured the hint of pain. With his other hand, he undid his belt and shoved down his jeans. When I felt his warm cock brush my arse, I arched my spine, seeking. His breath stuttered out of him, like he was having a hard time keeping it together.

"So perfect," he growled right before he gave me a light slap on the bottom.

"I need you. Now," I breathed, my voice airy and light.

His hands roamed up my back, removing my bra and letting it drop unceremoniously to the floor. Everywhere he touched me, I shivered. When he cupped my bottom with both hands, his thumb slipping into the crease and smoothing over a forbidden place, I shuddered, my eyes fluttering closed.

His cock brushed my entrance teasingly, hands gripping me now as he pushed inside in one hard stroke. When he was embedded deep in me he stilled, his mouth on my nape, planting wet little kisses that got me going even more.

We were both still standing, the sensation more intense that way. Lee's hips began to move, hammering in and out quickly as he unleashed his need for me. One hand came up to mould my breast, the other spread out flat on my stomach, holding me in place. I arched my spine, letting him in as deep as he could go.

"Come back to mine tonight," he breathed harshly.

"Yes," I said, my voice high as it mixed with my moans.

He bit down on my shoulder. "Maybe we'll stop by yours first, pick up those handcuffs."

A quick, unexpected laugh escaped me.

"I can't wait to put my mouth on your pussy," Lee continued in a growl. "God, you're clenching me so tight right now."

Man, when he didn't go all Cockney, he was *really* good at dirty talk. His voice filled my ears, telling me all the naughty things he planned on doing to me. I was so wet right then, his cock pounding me hard. I lost the ability to think and fell into the sensation. Lee's mouth went to my neck, sucking my skin as his movements sped up even more. He was going to leave a mark, but I couldn't even summon the urge to care. I was sure my uniform would cover it at work.

When he came, it was with a sharp, gravelly expletive, his teeth grazing me as his hips slowed and his warmth filled me. I sighed as my walls tightened around him and he pulled my body tight to his.

"Love ya, Karla, always will," he said as he finally caught his breath.

"Love you, too," I replied, turning my face and capturing his lips in a slow, tender kiss.

***

Here's what you need to know: We did go back for the handcuffs, *and* it was incredible. I was going to order a pair of furry ones online, because real cuffs hurt like a mother…especially when you couldn't help straining against them.

Aside from prying ourselves apart when we had to work, Lee and I were inseparable over the following week or two. When the day finally came for the opening of his restaurant, I made sure I had the night off to attend. Lee was putting on a big shindig, with free food and drinks to celebrate the grand opening.

I wore a figure-hugging black dress with heels, and styled my hair in loose waves. Alexis even had her parents babysit Oliver for the night so she could come. My BFF never turned down free food, even if she had to drag herself away from her adorable newborn for a few hours. This was her first night out since giving birth, and I was glad she was getting the chance to let her hair down.

Reya came, too, looking stunning in a dark blue dress that hugged her curvy form. She'd slotted herself right back into Trevor's friend zone, but there was no reasoning with her. Trevor had an energetic sort of charm that could become addictive, especially for an introvert like Reya. She got to live vicariously through his extrovert behaviour. In any case, he and his group of traceurs had won their competition and were headed off to Thailand for a month of sightseeing and mountain climbing. Since the two of them had been spending so much time together, I wondered how she'd handle his absence.

Lee had been at the restaurant all day, preparing for the party, so I hadn't seen him since the night before. Arriving with my two friends, I saw him standing by the service window, a row of plates lined up before him as he okayed the dishes. He looked busy so I left him to it, accepting a glass of white wine from the waiter carrying around a tray.

A little while later I excused myself to use the bathroom, and bumped into Liam on my way back out. He was sitting on the staircase, nursing a glass of whiskey. His eyes grew wary when he saw me, knocking back the last of his drink and slamming down the glass.

"Not feeling the crowds?" I asked, hovering close by.

"Big parties aren't really my thing," he said, and I took that as an invitation to sit down.

"Yeah, mine neither."

I felt him looking at me curiously as we fell into a silence.

"Lee seems happy these days," said Liam after a time.

"I like to hope he is."

Turning his body, his voice and face were serious as he said, "Can I ask you a question?"

"Of course."

"Do you think I'd make a good copper?"

He couldn't have surprised me more if he'd asked if he'd make a good micro-pig farmer. My brow furrowed as I hurried to reply, "Oh, well, sure, I think you could be a good anything if you put your mind to it, Liam."

He turned away again, his gaze levelled on his hands. "That's a pat answer, Karla. Give it to me straight. I want your honest opinion."

"Is this something you've been thinking about?" I asked. I was still trying to get my head around the fact that Liam was considering joining the police. I wasn't an easy person to surprise, but this certainly took the biscuit.

"I wouldn't be asking if it wasn't," he said, his voice low and uncertain. It made me wonder if he felt insecure about opening up to me.

"Liam, I think you'd make a fantastic policeman, and that's the God's honest truth. But you've got a record. You could find it difficult getting your application accepted."

"Yeah, that's what I thought," he said glumly.

I studied him, my eyes tracing his handsome profile and short brown hair. Liam was the Cross brother I'd spent the least time with. But looking at him now, I was beginning to think he was the most self-serious, even though he was the youngest. I thought maybe he pushed himself harder to prove his worth to his older siblings.

Nudging his shoulder with mine, I said, "I could help you, you know. Put a good word in. It can't hurt matters. And if it doesn't work, there's always the army."

Liam shook his head. "Nah, the army's not for me."

"So why the police?"

He lifted a brow. "Honestly? It's got a lot to do with all the stuff we used to be involved in." He paused and sighed. "I just feel like stealing's the only thing I've ever really been good at. It's the thing I know best, but I can't do it anymore. So I thought maybe I could switch it around, use all the stuff I know about thieving and be the prevention instead of the cause." He glanced at me. "It's stupid, I know."

I grasped his shoulder. "It's not stupid, not at all. I actually think it's very noble. Half the people I work with got into policing because it's a government job with a steady paycheck, and those are the good ones. You don't even want me to get started on the bad."

Liam seemed hopeful, and a little embarrassed at my compliment. "So you think I've got a chance?"

"I do. And I'll do everything I can to help."

A few minutes later, I crept up on Lee in the kitchen as he stood typing out a message on his phone. I slid my arms around his waist and squeezed tight.

"Hey," I murmured. "Everything going okay?"

He let out a breath and twisted in my arms. "Yeah, we've run out of beer, though. I was just texting the supplier, seeing if he can get another delivery in before closing."

I nodded. "Fingers crossed he can. Hey, I was just talking to Liam."

Lee's brow furrowed. "What did he say? He's been a moody little sod the past few weeks. I don't know what's going on with him."

"He told me he's been thinking about joining the police," I said, my words coming out in an excited rush.

Lee shot me an arch look. "Is this a wind-up?"

"Believe me, I was just as surprised as you are. But no, it's not a wind-up. I think he's been considering this for a while."

Lee still seemed sceptical, but he gave me a small smile anyway, his hands lowering to cup my arse as he whispered, "Maybe having you around's been a good influence."

I pressed a kiss to his lips before drawing away. After all, there were half a dozen staff milling about, and PDAs weren't my thing. I lifted a cracker spread with cream cheese smoked salmon off a tray and shoved it in my mouth. Lee gave me a playful smack on the bottom and told me to stop picking at his finger foods. Just as I rubbed away the sting, threatening to get him back, Liam walked into the kitchen.

"Well, well, well, aren't you full of surprises," Lee announced loudly at the sight of his younger brother. "Thinking of joining the coppers. Our dear old granddad would be turning in his grave. You know mum's old man was a black marketer back in the day."

Liam shot me an exasperated look. "You didn't have to run right off and tell him."

"What?" I said, already shoving another cracker into my mouth. "I was excited."

He sighed and turned to Lee. "And why the fuck would I give a shit about some old geezer I've never met?"

"Because you're making a change, cleaning up the Cross name," Lee replied, slipping his arm around my waist and preventing me from eating any more of his finger foods. "Hey, who'd have thought the coppers'd be the new family business?"

I grinned and stuck out my tongue. "You should be thanking me for the improvement. And I'm not family yet."

Lee barked a laugh. "*Yet* being the operative word. I'll have a ring on that finger before the year is out."

I gaped at him but couldn't help the smile that spread from ear to ear. "Shut up."

"Make me," he purred, capturing my lips in another kiss.

Liam groaned and left the kitchen, not wanting to witness any more of our smug coupledom.

***

Lee stood across the street from the police station, his arms folded as he leaned against his parked car, waiting for me. I got a warm fuzzy feeling in my tummy as I walked across to him and he pulled me into a hug, pressing a kiss to my temple. It was nice having a boyfriend to pick me up after a long day on the job.

"Hey," he said, pressing his face into my hair and inhaling deeply.

"Ugh, please don't smell me right now. I had to chase down a mugger earlier, and I stink."

"You smell amazing," he countered huskily. "And you're a sergeant now. Let the others do the grunt work...."

"Ah, but you've gone straight. I have to find my excitement somewhere."

Lee chuckled and ran a thumb across my lower lip. "I'll give you excitement, you cheeky little minx."

His laughter died when his attention snagged on something just behind us. I sensed my dad's presence before I even turned around, my skin prickling when he said my name. "Karla."

I stepped out of Lee's arms and turned to face him, his frown and thick, narrowed eyebrows signalling his disapproval. I didn't necessarily need to be doing anything bad; he just disapproved of me in general.

"Dad," I said firmly as I stood up straight.

He was studying Lee, his face stern with concentration as he tried to figure out how he knew him. Lee and my dad had had a small few run-ins over the years, plus Dad had pictures of him from the McGregor investigation. Still, Lee's hair had grown out and he wore a trim, fitted shirt, a suit jacket, and slacks. He dressed like that on days when he was in business mode, so he didn't look the way Dad was used to seeing him. I swear, it was crazy the things a suit could do to blind people. Though in this case Lee was a retired wolf in sheep's clothing. Dad's attention came back to me as he cleared his throat.

"I heard you passed your sergeant's exam," he said.

He wouldn't be giving me any "congratulations" or "well done" hugs. God forbid he show some actual emotion. However, the fact that he'd approached me at all was out of character. Dad was the kind of man who waited for you to come to him; otherwise, he'd lose his sense of importance.

"I did."

"At least now you won't be in the trenches," he said cynically.

And there it was. I knew he couldn't keep up the good behaviour for very long.

A silence fell, and Lee slid his fingers into mine as a show of support. I didn't really hate my dad, but I knew I didn't love him, either. I felt a strange sort of disconnection, and it was kind of sad, but that's how it would always be between us.

Dad's attention returned to Lee. "I supposed this is your young man."

"Very pleased to meet you, Superintendent Sheehan." Lee smiled widely and reached forward to shake his hand. I could tell he was getting a real kick out of this.

"Likewise," said Dad. "Karla, it'd please your mother greatly if the two of you came for dinner this Sunday."

"Oh, sure," I said, trying not to simultaneously stutter and choke on my own restrained laughter. "We'll try our best to make it." The fact that he didn't recognise Lee was too hilarious for words. If Dad knew who he was really inviting over for dinner, he'd probably turn around and vomit all over his shiny brown leather shoes.

"Good. I'll let her know," he said before tipping his hat to us and turning to walk away. Before he could complete the turn, he twisted back, eyes on Lee. "I'm sorry, I didn't quite catch your name."

"The name's Lee. Lee Cross," my boyfriend replied, and as soon as the words left his mouth, my dad's eyes practically popped from their sockets.

"Well," I blurted. "We're in a bit of a hurry, so we'd better go."

Tugging on Lee's hand, I ushered him over to the car. We were already pulling away from the kerb when Dad finally came to his senses, his jaw firming and his expression darkening as he watched us drive away.

"I'm sorry, but that was priceless," said Lee, laughter bubbling out of him.

"My poor dad," I chuckled. "I don't think I've ever seen him look both furious and confused at the same time."

"Serves him right, the old prick. Couldn't even muster up a single congratulations for you. See the difference between him and me? I lift you up, he pushes you down. You don't need that shit in your life."

God, I adored him. "No, you're absolutely right. I don't."

Lee shot me a tender smile and focused back on the road.

"Hey, by the way, 007," I said, poking him in the arm. "Don't think I'm letting you away with that cheesy line. I'm telling everyone how you introduced yourself. And I mean *everyone*."

Lee gripped my thigh and gave it a firm squeeze, his other hand still on the steering wheel. "Do it, and I'll withhold oral sex for a month."

I mock-gasped. "You wouldn't!"

"I most certainly would."

"Fine. I'll keep your James Bond secret. Wouldn't want to tarnish your rep, now, would I?" I mocked him before continuing, "Anyway, I'm willing to bet the invitation to dinner at my parents will soon be rescinded."

"Yep."

"You could at least pretend to act disappointed."

"Nope."

I laughed. Seriously, there was no way I could love the man sitting beside me any more than I already did. Placing my hand over his, I rested my head on his shoulder and exhaled. I was happy in the moment but also looking forward to the future.

And it felt good.

Later that evening, I stood on the edge of a seven-foot wall in an old industrial estate near the docks. Lee was beside me, holding my hand. The other week I'd asked him to teach me the basics of free-running, and he'd thought I was joking. I wasn't. Just because I was a sergeant didn't mean my days of chasing down thieves were over, and who else better to teach me than one of the best?

"Loosen up," said Lee. "When we fall and hurt ourselves, it's because our bodies go rigid when we panic. You ever see a cat break a leg? No, because they're all loose and springy. Pretend you're a cat."

I resisted the urge to meow. "Okay, I'm a cat."

"Just so you know, the first time I tried a jump like this, I sprained my ankle."

"I can deal with a sprained ankle."

"Liam broke a leg once. And Stu nearly shattered his knee when he didn't warm up properly."

"Are you trying to freak me out? Because if you are, it's working."

Lee's fingers squeezed mine. "I just want you to be aware that this won't be easy. You're gonna have bruises and sprains. Shit, you'll ache in places you never knew existed before."

I firmed my mouth and narrowed my gaze. "You're trying to put me off."

"I don't want you to get hurt," he replied simply, affection bright in his eyes.

I leaned over to kiss his cheek, my voice turning unexpectedly soft. "Everything good hurts first. If we hadn't soldiered on, we wouldn't be here right now."

His expression shone with love, but he stayed silent, smiling at me tenderly before finally whispering, "No, we wouldn't. You ready?"

"Yes." No.

"Just relax. I won't let go of your hand."

Staring at the ground, I leapt at the same time Lee did, the air whooshing past my ears as my heart pounded in an exhilarating rush. Our feet landed simultaneously, and I crouched low like he'd instructed me to do. And, like he promised, he didn't let go of my hand.

Epilogue
2 years later. HM Prison Belmarsh, London.
Lee

Hands on the steering wheel. Gear stick in neutral. Heart lodged firmly in my fucking throat.

I've been waiting at her good Majesty's prison for the last half an hour. Any minute now my brother will walk out those gates and finally be a free man. After serving two years of a seven-year sentence that should've had my name on it, he's finally going to walk. I'm not angry. Not anymore. But I'm not grateful, either. Life's too short to go around acting like you owe people. Stu did for me what I would've done for him. It was simple. We were brothers.

We still are, but recently it hasn't felt like it.

For the last three months, he's refused to take my visits. I haven't had a single phone call, letter, or smoke signal, and I'm beginning to get worried. Fuck it, that's a lie. I was worried long before now, but I have it on good authority that Stu's alive and in perfect health, so why the hell has he cut off communication?

I sit up straighter when I see the gates open and two screws step out. They usher forward three blokes, and I immediately recognise Stu as one of them. He walks straight, head down, wearing a hoodie and jeans.

I smack my hand down on the horn to get his attention and he looks up, recognising my motor. I see him mutter something to himself, a few effs and jeffs, I'm willing to bet, before turning his wheels in my direction. Liam and Trevor are at the house, helping Sophie and Karla set up the welcome-home party. By the looks of it, they're going to have a fuck of a time getting Stu in the party mood.

He opens the door and slides into the passenger seat. "Didn't ask you to come," are the first words out of the moody bastard's mouth. If I had less restraint, I'd give him a kick in the balls.

"Wasn't going to let you get the bus, now, was I?" I say, starting up the engine.

We drive in silence for a couple of minutes, Stu staring out the window, big horror head on him.

"Well, I must say, Stuart, you're a veritable ray of fucking sunshine today."

All he does is turn his head, level me with an expression that has "piss off" written all over it, and resumes looking out the window.

"So you're not going to explain why I've gotten nothing but radio silence off you for months?"

He tilts his head to me, all snotty. "Wasn't feeling chatty."

"I thought they put you in the hole. Found out from Jimmy Kelly's cousin that you're walking around fit as a fiddle."

"Jimmy Kelly's cousin can go fuck himself."

That does it. I slam my foot down on the brakes and pull the car off to the side of the road. He's putting up a front, I can just tell. Snapping free my seatbelt, I turn to him, placing a steady hand on his shoulder. He flinches at my touch, and let me tell you, seeing your six-foot-two, brick-shithouse brother flinch away from a friendly touch would do a number on anyone.

"This is me, Stu. There's nobody else here. No bullshit, so stop blocking me out." I keep my voice measured, not letting my temper get the better of me.

All of a sudden, Stu slumps in his seat. His breathing goes funny, and he closes his eyes. I stare at him, not knowing what to do. It seems like he's ignoring me again, but then I see the wetness on his cheeks and I realise he's crying.

"Ah, fuck," I swear quietly, emotion biting at my gut as I pull him into a hug.

He heaves in my arms, all two hundred and some pounds of him, and I notice he's become a lot bulkier during his time away. The pain he's been dealing with rolls out like a riptide now that he has a safe place to expel it. It's a bullshit social standard that men aren't supposed to cry anyway. Fuck, I'd cried like a baby into a bottle of Jack when I thought I'd lost Karla, and I'm man enough to admit it. I know Stu had a rough time of it when he first got sent away, trying to avoid fights and stupid political mind games. A bloke like me can disappear into a crowd, become wallpaper, but not Stu. He stands out.

"*Fuuuuck*," he curses, gripping my shirt as he pulls back and runs his hands down his face. "I'm sorry."

"Not necessary."

"It is. You don't need me coming out with a chip on my shoulder. And I missed your wedding."

I laugh softly. Missing my and Karla's wedding is the last thing I expected him to feel bad about. "It's not like they were going to let you take a day trip."

"Yeah, but, I could've, I dunno, Skyped myself in or something. I always thought I'd be your best man."

"Me, too. Trevor did an okay job."

"Little prick stole my thunder."

I chuckle and grip his hand in mine. "You didn't miss nothing fancy, that's not mine and Snap's style, but it was the best day. I wish you could've been there."

He perks up, sliding his eyes to mine. "Yeah?"

Sitting back in my seat, I describe the day, knowing it'd be good for him to picture something other than a six-by-eight cell and high walls. "Yeah. Alexis was her bridesmaid. You would've appreciated the low neckline."

Stu groans. "Don't fucking torture me. It's been two years, bruv."

I frown. "I know. My bad."

"Not your fault. What else?"

"Karla had her hair up in this thing, looked like a bloody Danish pastry. I don't know how birds do that shit. It's like it's purposefully designed to make you want to pull it and make a mess. Obviously, her old man didn't show. Her mum made a brief appearance, though. Karla seemed real happy about that. We had Liam give her away. Trevor, the greedy little git, wanted to play father of the bride *and* best man, but I wasn't having it."

Stu laughs.

"And during the afters he tried getting off with Larry Murphy's wife. The bloke nearly de-bollocked him. Trust Trev to pull a stunt like that, but fuck it, a wedding's not a wedding without a bit of colour."

"True."

A quiet falls between us, and I cast him a look. "Are we good?"

Stu nods before letting out a long exhalation. "Yeah, we're good."

"Great, because Soph's throwing you a welcome-home party, so you're going to have to plaster a smile on that ugly mug for the next few hours."

Stu chuckles loudly. "You're jealous of this mug and we both know it." A pause as he side-eyes me. "She hasn't invited a bunch of people, has she?"

I shake my head. "Nah, just the family today, bruv. I'm making you a slap-up meal, by the way. Been planning it for weeks. It's gonna blow your socks off, make you forget about all that prison slop you've been eating."

Stu groans. "I never thought I'd miss fruit, but Christ, I swear I'd get a stiffy if I saw an apple right now."

"All round and ripe for the picking," I say with a grin. "Sexy little bitches."

Stu barks a laugh, and it makes me feel ten feet tall to see him smile, even if it is only for a minute. I pull a pack of ciggies from my pocket, light one up, and hand it to him before lighting another for myself. We sit in quiet as we smoke, staring at the road ahead. When we're done, we throw our butts out the window and I start the car up again.

"Wait," says Stu, putting his hand on mine. I turn to him. "Can I drive?" he asks.

"Go for it," I reply, and we get out to switch seats.

All the way home I watch him, little by little seeing the tension seep out of him the farther we get away from the prison. Still, he seems different, more stoic and thoughtful somehow. I mean, being put away would change anyone, no matter how strong they are going in. I wonder what it's like to be all caged up like that, stuck looking at the same dumbfuck faces every day. That fate was almost mine, and I'm resolved to do everything in my power to make life better for my brother from here on out.

By the time we arrive at the house, Stu almost looks like his old self again. We step in the front door and everyone's waiting in the kitchen, shouting "welcome home" and blowing on party whistles. Stu shakes his head, but I know he's secretly loving it.

Karla steps up and gives him a hug, and he seems to sink into the touch. It doesn't make me jealous, far from it.

He hasn't smelled a women in over two years, so I understand that he can't help absorbing her softness. She smiles when she catches my eye, letting go of Stu and moving across the room to greet me.

I love her punch-to-the-gut beautiful smiles, love her bright blue eyes and sexy red hair. I love her body, love how everything about her seems like it was made for me. But most of all I want that for my brother. After everything he's been through, I want him to find a woman who grabs his heart by the balls and shows him what it feels like to truly love someone.

"You look gorgeous," I tell her, laying a quick kiss on her mouth while my hand slips down to cup her arse.

"Oh, but you're prettier," she teases me, giving my lip a saucy little bite. For a second I consider dragging her upstairs for a quickie, but then I remind myself that today isn't about me and my horndog needs. Today is about Stu.

Letting go of my perfect, tough, kickass police sergeant wife, I head to the fridge and pull out the ingredients I prepared earlier. I'm cooking Stu an Angus steak with all the trimmings.

"Fuck yes," he says when he sees what I'm making, clapping me round the shoulder and knocking back a slug of the beer Sophie handed him the moment he stepped through the door.

Karla goes to sit at the table, in between Liam and Trev. She smiles at them both as she pulls Billie up onto her lap. The kid's been living with us full time ever since Karla helped Sophie foster her. She affectionately pushes a strand of her hair behind her ear and asks Liam how he's getting on at the police academy, then questions Trev on his latest adrenaline-junkie endeavour.

Stu sits on the other side of the table, beside Sophie, content to listen to the conversation flow around him. It's like a strike to the chest, seeing Karla surrounded by all my family. They're her family now. And she doesn't even realise it, but she's become like a mother to all of them, looking out for their welfare, giving them help when it's needed.

I'd always done it alone, but now I have someone to hold my hand and shoulder some of the burden. She'll never have my kids. I know that and I hate it, but it doesn't take away even an ounce of the love I have for her. In fact, it only makes me love her more. Because she's made my brothers her sons, Sophie her daughter, and bettered all our lives in the process.

The world isn't blue, isn't lonely any more, and though I was supposed to be the thief, she was the one who stole my heart.

End.

Look out for the next books in the *Hearts* series, releasing in 2016; Trevor & Reya's story, *Hearts on Air*, and Stu's story, *Thief of Hearts*. Read on for the blurb.

Seduce the teacher.

Meet the cousin.

Make a deal.

Steal the painting.

Andrea Anderson has no clue of the thoughts churning around in the dark and dangerous ex-con's head as he enters her classroom. In fact, she's momentarily lost for words. Not in her entire teaching career has she had a student who looked quite like Stuart Cross.

A widow at just twenty-eight, love is something Andie hasn't considered a part of her life for a very long time. However, when lingering touches turn to whispered words and hot, searching stares, she begins to wonder if maybe she should take a leap of faith.

But Stu is in her class for a reason, and it has nothing to do with love. He's there to burrow his way into her life and repay a debt, otherwise his family will suffer. Andie is the first person to show him true kindness since he left prison, and though he doesn't want to mislead her, he doesn't have another choice.

Before long, Stu can't tell whether or not he's acting anymore, and his feelings for Andie could throw all of his carefully crafted plans into complete and utter disarray.

Check out more books in L.H. Cosway's *HEARTS* series!

Praise for *Six of Hearts* (Jay & Matilda's story)

"This book was sexy. Man was it hot! Cosway writes sexual tension so that it practically sizzles off the page." - A. Meredith Walters, New York Times & USA Today Bestselling Author.

"There is a way that certain authors write that just grips me by the throat because I can see the world, I can smell the sounds, I can hear the voices, and I can feel their hearts." - Marie Hall, New York Times & USA Today Bestselling Author.

"I loved the twist at the end. I loved how sexy it was. (DAMN IT WAS SEXY!!)" - Penny Reid, Author of Neanderthal Seeks Human.

"Six of Hearts is a book that will absorb you with its electric and all-consuming atmosphere." - Lucia, Reading is my Breathing.

"There is so much "swoonage" in these pages that romance readers will want to hold this book close and not let go." - Katie, Babbling About Books.

Praise for *Hearts of Fire* (Jack & Lille's story)

"This story holds so much intensity and it's just blazing hot. It created an inferno of emotions inside me." - Patrycja, Smokin' Hot Book Blog.

"I think this is my very favorite LH Cosway romance to date. Absolutely gorgeous." - Angela, Fiction Vixen.

*"Okay we just fell in love. Complete and utter beautiful book love. You know the kind of love where you just don't want a book

to finish. You try and make it last; you want the world to pause as you read and you want the story to go on and on because you're not ready to let it go." - Jenny & Gitte, Totally Booked.

"Babies! I want to have babies with his book. Ladies, you will drool over Jack, want to run away to the circus and play with matches and hot wax. Definitely going in my top 10 favorite books of 2015." - Katie, Babbling About Books and More!

Praise for *King of Hearts* (Alexis & King's story)

"Addictive. Consuming. Witty. Heartbreaking. Brilliant--King of Hearts is one of my favourite reads of 2015!" - Samantha Young, New York Times, USA Today and Wall Street Journal bestselling author.

"I was looking for a superb read, and somehow I stumbled across an epic one." - Natasha is a Book Junkie.

"5+++++++ Breathtaking stars! Outstanding. Incredible. Epic. Overwhelmingly romantic and poignant. There's book love and in this case there's BOOK LOVE." - Jenny & Gitte, Totally Booked.

"The writing was stunningly beautiful, and the emotions that this story brought out of me has definitely placed this book on my top 10 favourite shelf of 2015." - Arabella, I Love Book Love.

About the author

L.H. Cosway has a BA in English Literature and Greek and Roman Civilisation and an MA in Postcolonial Literature. She lives in Dublin city. Her inspiration to write comes from music. Her favourite things in life include writing stories, vintage clothing, dark cabaret music, food, musical comedy, and of course, books.

She thinks that imperfect people are the most interesting kind. They tell the best stories.

Find L.H. Cosway online!

www.facebook.com/lhcosway
www.twitter.com/lhcosway
www.instagram.com/l.h.cosway
www.lhcoswayauthor.com

Books by L.H. Cosway

Contemporary Romance
Painted Faces
Killer Queen
The Nature of Cruelty
Still Life with Strings
Six of Hearts
Hearts of Fire
King of Hearts
The Hooker & the Hermit

Urban Fantasy
Tegan's Blood (The Ultimate Power Series #1)
Tegan's Return (The Ultimate Power Series #2)
Tegan's Magic (The Ultimate Power Series #3)
Tegan's Power (The Ultimate Power Series #4)

Thank you for reading *Hearts of Blue*. Please consider supporting an indie author and leaving a review <3

Made in the USA
Middletown, DE
08 February 2017